AN UNCOMMON
BLUE

Colorblind Book I

5th Anniversary Edition

By

RC HANCOCK

CONTENTS

*to Emi, who contributed more to this edition
than any other single person*

"Let your light so shine before men."

-THE CRÉATEUR

GUIDE DE PRONONCIATION

Académie   (ah-kah-DEM-ee)
André   (ON-dree)
Arnaud   (ah-NO)
Aro   (EYE-roo)
Baptiste   (bah-TEEST)
Benoit   (ben-WAH)
Boudreaux (boo-DROW as 'tow')
bonsoir   (bone-SWAH)
Capitaine   (CAP-ee-ten)
chanmé   (SHOWN-me)
Christelle   (crees-TELL)
Claude   (CLOH-duh)
Commissaire   (coo-me-SEHR)
conseil   (cone-SAY)
Créateur   (cray-uh-TOOR)
cuivre/s   (QUEEV)
D'issoir   (DE-swah)
DeLaney   (DO-la-nay)
Dominateur   (duh-me-nah-TUH)
Drea   (DREY-ah)
DuPont   (DO-pahn)
Ereaut   (ERGH)
Faringoule   (FAH-ring-gool)
flic   (FLEEK)
Gaspard   (gas-POWL)
Gouroux   (goo-ROO)
Gravois   (gav-WAH)
Hameau Vert   (AH-mo VER)
Haut   (OO)
imbécile   (ahm-bee-SEEL)
Jade   (ZSHAHD)
Juenes   (ZSHEN)
LaCroix   (LA-QUAH)
Lefebvre   (loo-FEHV-ruh)
Livius   (lih-vee-OHNG)
Loisible   (loo-eh-ZEE-bluh)
Loup   (LEEOO)
Mallory   (mah-low-REE)

Marcoux   (mah-COO)
Marin   (MER-ohng)
Mélangé   (mel-AHNJ)
Meuglé   (MUG-lee)
Molyneux   (moh-lee-NUH)
mon frère   (moh-FRER)
monsieur   (muh-SYOOR)
Nazaire   (nah-ZEHRL)
Nicolas   (nee-co-LAH)
Ocheanum   (oh-chay-AH-noom)
Orie   (uh-REE)
Philippe   (fill-EEP)
Pont en Pierre   (pohn-pee-AIR)
Raplapla   (rah-PLAH-plah)
Ro   (ROO)
Rouge   (ROOZSH)
Rue Principale   (ROO prin-see-PAL)
Sébastien   (seh-bass-TYAH)
sentier   (SAHN-tee)
Sergent   (ser-ZSHO)
Talbot   (TAL-boh)
Taudis   (toh-DEE)
Télesphore   (tel-ees-FOR)
Terry   (teh-REE)
Tremper   (TLAHM-pee)
Véronique   (ver-oh-NEEK)
Ville Bleu   (VEE BLUH)
Wedel   (WE-dl as 'needle')
Zacharie   (zeh-sheh-REE)

CHAPTER ONE

TRADITION

T here are three unspoken rules in high school rugby.

1. Your team members are family.
2. You support your family.
3. This support must be shown periodically with an affectionate slap on the backside.

After two years as a starting forward, I had somewhat learned to tolerate this.

But first thing in the morning? In the middle of the sidewalk? Marin was lucky I didn't break his nose.

"Hello," I said. "Good morning, *Ta erlich*. These are all acceptable greetings. Notice none of them require you to put your hands on me."

Marin massaged the spot where I'd punched him. "Take it easy, *mon frère.* I've got to use these pecs today."

I fished in my backpack for a rubber band, then pulled my hair into a ponytail. I needed to have another talk with Granny about cutting it. Who cared if shaggy was trending? I wanted my peripheral vision back.

Marin stretched the neck of his shirt, raised his light hand to his chin and peered down. The blue light from his palm made his coffee-colored skin look almost purple.

"Didn't mean to punch you that hard," I said. "But you did

scare the serum out of me."

Marin released his shirt. "Since when are you jumpy before a match? Or is it exams you're worried about?"

"I'm not worried."

"You're jumpy."

"I'm taut." I took a protein bar from my bag and offered it to Marin.

He shook his head.

I tore into it and squinted over the tops of the trees. Good weather for rugby. The white sky looked like a blank sheet of paper.

"Did you notice my fire is different?"

I glanced at the large raised bubble of skin covering his palm. "Can't tell. Is it brighter? You get a serum transfusion or something?"

He grinned. "I may have reacted yesterday."

"Seriously? With whom? Do your parents know? Your mom is going to—"

"They know."

I waited, but Marin didn't offer any details. "That's what, six? Anyone in *Ville Bleu* you haven't reacted with? I thought your mom taught you to keep your hands to yourself."

"She tried."

I started walking again. "You sure you weren't secretly raised across the river?"

Marin walked backward in front of me. "You know, that rumor that Reds spend all day holding hands and hugging is false. A Green kid told me he caught one and had to let it go. Kept trying to bite him."

"Ladies and gentlemen, the friendliest Blue on the island! He reacts with whomever asks and even chats with grass-palms."

"They clean our house. Am I supposed to pretend they aren't there?"

"Hi, Bruno!"

I glanced to the winterdark side of the street where two

blue lights shone in the shadow of the Crystal Cathedral. Although I couldn't make out faces, I lifted my own fire in greeting.

Marin fell into step beside me. "Who's that?"

"Who are they," I corrected him. "Middle school girls, I think. But notice they didn't need to slap my body to say hello?"

"You and your glutes."

A dog yapped from behind a blue picket fence. I tossed over a piece of my breakfast. "One of these days, you're gonna get too friendly with a Green and end up at *L'académie Mélangé.*"

"Being a mixed freak wouldn't be too bad. I've heard their trees are easier to climb than ours. And I saw a coffee-skin Yellow once. She was freaky hot."

It was hard to stay mad at Marin Faringoule. His chipped front tooth made him look years younger than sixteen. The time he'd spent bulking up had earned him a place on the front line of the scrum, but it didn't do much for that baby face. As soon as he got facial hair, the girls would be all over him. I was actually looking forward to it. Then he'd see it wasn't as great as he imagined.

Marin cocked his head. "You hear that whistle?"

We glanced beyond the cathedral to the Blue Gardens. Through the towering oaks and manicured bushes, I caught a glimpse of powder blue uniforms. "*Ulfig?*" I said. "I thought they were coming after lunch."

"Boat must have landed early. Wonder why they aren't at the stadium."

We crossed the cobblestone street and slowed our walk. A group of Blue families I didn't recognize sat near the pond feeding the swans while others watched the players stretch. A toddler with an alloy glove waddled toward the water. I took a couple quick steps down the grassy slope, but the boy's mother had already scooped him up and shouted something at a nearby Blue man.

"What did she say?" Marin asked.

I returned to the sidewalk, feeling a little silly for my moment of panic. "I don't speak Ulfish."

"*Ta erlich?*"

I sighed. "Besides a few phrases Granny taught me."

"You should go down there," Marin said. "Find out if they're passers or kickers. Get dirt on the forwards."

"I'm sure they'll offer their team secrets to anyone who asks."

"You can do a Figgy accent. Pretend you came from the homeland to watch the match."

"I won't pretend to be someone I'm not to get an advantage," I said. "Anyway, we're going to be late for first period."

"Of course, St. Nazaire never lied in his life."

I stopped and faced him. "You're confusing lying with cheating."

"So you do lie?"

"Occasionally. Last week I told my mom I liked her dye job."

"But never cheat?"

"Can we go?"

"So, you passing your Algebra final despite not knowing the difference between variables and coefficients? What do you call that?"

"I did my best. I guess it was good enough for Monsieur D'issoir."

"And the fact that Télesphore City would lose the match without you today had nothing to do with it."

"No."

Marin slid a hand over his smooth scalp. "For someone who wants to be a brain surgeon, you sure are dense."

"Fire surgeon. Are you saying D'issoir upped my grade so I could play?"

"And because he's afraid of what your parents would say if you failed. Don't deny it."

"I won't deny you'd lose without me," I said. "But I think

you're jealous I test better than you. I pulled a Y on the Creature Science final."

"Yeah, and I copied off you until you marked that invertebrates were part of the primate family."

I suppressed the urge to punch him again. "Is there a point to all this or are you just draining my fluid?"

The Figs applauded. I turned, glad for the interruption. The idea that the faculty babied me was humiliating. Although numbers and facts often got jumbled in my head, I was good with words. I had thought my communication skills made up for my other academic failings. Apparently it was the size of my neck.

The Ulfish families had left the pond and now sat facing a middle-aged blonde with a whistle around her neck.

The players formed a line, shoulder to shoulder. The Ulfish spectators went quiet.

"Must be some sort of team ritual," Marin said.

The female held out her fire to a skinny boy in uniform.

What in the black rainbow? They brought a first-year over with them?

Marin's eyes went wide. "It's a Figgy initiation. The entire team has to react with the new player."

"You are so full of—"

A flash of white light illuminated the gardens like a silent bolt of lightning.

I blinked. The boy released hands with the woman and moved to the first of his teammates in line.

"*Crêpes*," I whispered. I couldn't look away. Why were all the parents smiling? I felt like I'd walked in on someone using the toilet.

Another flash. The boy stepped sideways and clasped light hands with the next youth in powder blue shorts and jersey.

"I think it's *chanmé*," Marin said with a dreamy smile. "Can you imagine how much closer we'd be as a team if we all —"

"Increased our fire age by fifteen? Maybe you don't care about your future, but I'm not going to dilute my shade just for fun. The Classification Committee looks at the fire evals as much as test scores."

The flashes came faster now. I couldn't imagine what was going through that kid's head. Years ago, I'd reacted with my parents and Granny. A third-age fire was plenty high enough for me.

"So dramatic," Marin said. "They're all Blue. It's not like his shade will change much."

I stared at Marin. "How are we best friends?"

"Very carefully."

A motorized scooter rumbled past us and squeaked to a stop. Two brown-clad royal soldiers dismounted and strode down the grass toward the crowd.

"Time to go," Marin said.

"You scared of pokers?"

Marin grabbed my backpack and pulled me summerlight toward the school. "I've seen them use those shock gloves. It's the opposite of *chanmé*."

"You went to a poker graduation?" I asked. "I thought that was family only."

Marin released my backpack. "Remember when Drea and I reacted on the swings in first grade?"

I smiled. "That's when your parents bought the locking alloy glove."

"What you don't know is Drea's dad convinced Dom Gravois that I painted her."

My throat seemed to close up. "That son of a Violet. Didn't Drea tell him? Everyone on the playground would've known if you had forced her."

"It doesn't matter. Monsieur DeLaney and I are on good terms now. But my punishment was a four thousand quivre fine and a ticket to the poker graduation."

"Was it as bad as they say?"

Marin stared at the cobblestones. "They popped a Red for

crossing the river and painting a Green baby."

I felt slightly queasy. "Good. He deserved what he got."

"She," Marin said. "It was a five-year-old girl."

I opened my mouth but couldn't make my voice work. My little brother had also been five when he died.

"Glad we're Blue," Marin chanted softly. "Aren't you? A million things to say and do. If you're Blue."

I forced a smile. Mom used to sing that to me and Ro. She stopped after...

"Let's go meet the newbies," I said in an overly-peppy voice. "We can both pretend to be Figs."

"I thought you didn't want to be late for class."

"Homeroom started five minutes ago. At this point, it would be better to skip it. Besides, if the grasspalms give you any trouble, I'll use my rugby moves on them."

Marin started down the street toward the stadium. "Well, I've got Axelle first period," he said. "And she's not the type to coddle the talent."

"See you at lunch." I lifted my fire in an approximation of a farewell, but my eyes were still on the Figs. Most of them were now on their feet. The new recruit had stopped reacting a few fires from the end of the line.

Yeah, it was disgusting, but if it was a cultural thing—Dad told me that in Tjarda they once used baby teeth as currency but switched to coin and paper when the child population got out of hand.

No one knew that eighteen of my own teeth sat in an old serum pouch in the back of my sock drawer. Just in case they made a comeback. People would think that was disgusting too. I should probably get rid of those before I went to medical school.

The coach seemed to be explaining something in Téle, but the men in brown canvas answered with shouts and menacing jabs of their index finger.

How embarrassing. Royal Soldiers or not, they had no right to speak to their betters like that. Didn't Télesphore pride itself on tradition? Did shade mean nothing anymore?

I dropped my backpack into a bush and strode down the hill. "Hey, frogspawn!"

In tandem, the pokers' heads swiveled toward me. One had coffee skin and a dark bushy beard, the other was a bald crême-skin with a perfectly trimmed goatee. The bald one held up a glowing green hand and glared at me. His lonely orange eyebrows seemed out of place on his milky scalp. "You better show some respect," he said. "We take our orders from the *Haut Commissaire* of Télesphore Island. He wouldn't be too happy with this public bespectacle."

The man was clearly a moron.

"This 'bespectacle' would have been over by now, if you had kept your lights to yourself." I tacked on a particularly offensive Ulfish word for the crowd's benefit. I was pretty sure it meant horse dentist. Granny only said it when she was furious.

The poker's eyes bulged and his light hand went to the bulky watch attached to his brown glove. It's a wonder they didn't put those gloves on their light hands to hide their shade. I'd wear gloves all day if my fire looked like that.

"Black off," the bald man said. "We aren't talking at you."

"Clearly," I said. "Why talk when you can wave your zappy finger and scare the foreigners? You going to paralyze several dozen citizens of a country that's three times bigger than Télesphore? Yeah, the Commissaire will be really pleased with that."

A young Blue with dark braids smiled at me. I winked at her and stepped toward the pokers. "How about you climb back on your dung buggy and go find some river trash to bother?"

The poker with the full beard pulled at his companion's elbow, but the bald one continued to stare needles at me.

"Or stick around," I said, "and we'll see how well your electric gloves work in the lake. But I promise you'll be cleaning pools and mowing lawns by the end of the week."

"...not make a scene..." Bush Beard said quietly to his companion. "...really want to take on the whole crowd of..."

Orange Goatee pulled his arm away and shot a glare toward me. It wasn't a petulant I'm-upset-with-you glare. It was more of an I'd-like-to-rip-your-fingernails-off-with-pliers kind of glare. Finally, the pokers returned to their scooter, spoke into their radio for a moment, then disappeared down the winding streets of Ville Bleu.

"If you ask me, they shouldn't even be on this side of *Rue Principale*," I said.

I expected cheers. I'd even braced myself for shoulder pats. Instead the Figs kissed the back of their light hands, their blue fires trained toward me.

Uh... Was that another custom? I briefly raised my light hand halfway to my lips and hoped they didn't expect me to go down the reaction line.

"We thank the *Créateur* who sent you," the coach said in Téle with hardly any accent. "I hope you will not have later probleming with the police."

I shrugged. "Those were Royal Soldiers. The police have a different uniform." I pantomimed a cap. "The cops stick to the *Hameau Vert* side. Actually, they're an even bigger joke than the pokers."

The woman cocked her head as if not sure she heard correctly. "We have heard tell that your country is fond of public executions."

"Just criminals," I said. "And that only happens at soldier graduations. Other than that, we're pretty nice."

"In all cases, we thank the *Créateur* for you."

I cleared my throat. I'd forgotten Ulfig was a theocracy. Everything they said and did dripped with religions significance. "I thank Him too?"

One man raised his eyebrows and smiled. Several other Blues nodded. I took a few steps away from a wizened old lady who kept kissing the back of her hand at me.

The rugby line reformed and the newest player finished

reacting with his teammates. This time, however, the crowd remained standing as if to shield the scene from any heathen Télesphorians who might object.

I found myself wedged between the pond and a trio of barely-teen girls.

"What is the name of your body?" asked the girl who'd smiled at me earlier.

I took a small step toward the muddy water. "Bruno."

"And your shine hand? What name?"

One of the girls pushed her as if she'd asked something indecent.

"Um..." Did they name their fires in Ulfig? "I call it Bruno too. Pretty much all of my body parts go by Bruno. Kind of a package deal."

The girls giggled.

A polite applause erupted as the rugby players lifted the new teammate onto their shoulders. Good to see they were feeling comfortable again. Although they did lower him after only a few seconds, and I noticed more than one anxious glance at the surrounding houses.

"I'd better get to class," I said, inching along the shoreline. "Finals today." I motioned toward the bush where I'd left my backpack. "Just need to grab..."

I trailed off as a glass sedan pulled up, and a man stepped out.

"Ooh, pretty car. Who is that body called?"

I felt cold on my ankles and realized I had stepped backward into the mud.

"That body," I said in a voice slightly higher than normal, "is called the Haut Commissaire of Télesphore."

CHAPTER TWO

PAINTED

I'd never seen the Commissaire in person. From the newspaper sketches, he'd always seemed old and boring, but the clean-shaven man who slid out of the back seat positively exuded regal authority. He had long white hair, perfect posture and wore a pale blue suit the exact shade of his fire.

Where was his contingent of gloved soldiers? Did he not fear the Figgy masses?

A bushy-bearded man sat in the driver's seat, but I was pretty sure it wasn't the poker I'd seen earlier. Maybe it was a bodyguard planning to jump out with the magic scepter when things got ugly.

I took the opportunity to step out of the mud. Apart from that, I wasn't sure whether I should approach the Commissaire and try to explain things, or quietly slip away and run for campus. Considering that my backpack was hidden in a bush only a few feet from the glass car, quietly slipping away wasn't a valid option.

The players continued to practice, although now it was as if they were all moving in slow motion. When the Commissaire began shouting at them in Ulfish, everyone froze.

The coach raised her fire, approached the Commissaire and answered in her language. Their conversation grew quiet.

"That body is like as the king?" one of the girls asked. "Télesphore is a monarchy, not?"

"No one's sure what we are anymore." I scraped my shoes on the grass as best I could and subtly moved through the crowd toward the coach. I had no intention of drawing attention to myself unless strictly necessary. This situation, however, was likely going to require some damage control.

But then again, the Commissaire didn't seem angry. It was several Figs that were shooting me dirty looks, like I'd done something wrong. What was I missing here?

"What was that old man shouting at first?" I asked the dark-haired girl who was following in my wake.

"He said, 'which body of you said you would drown my soldiers?' But his speaking of the sacred language is not as skill as he thinks."

"I didn't threaten to drown them," I said in a louder voice. "I just said I'd toss them in the pond."

The girl held her fingers to her lips. "The Rugby Leader stood in your place of guilt."

No wonder the other Figs were glaring at me. I was going to get their coach deported before the biggest game of the season.

Harrassing the Green pokers was one thing, but now that the Commissaire had gotten involved I realized how reckless I had been. What would the man do if he found out it had been one of his own citizens who defied his authority? At the very least, I probably wouldn't be playing in the match. My parents would certainly be charged an enormous fine. But I couldn't let the woman be punished for me. Could I somehow take credit for the "crime" without revealing who I was? I wouldn't have to lie exactly...

After a brief whispered vocabulary lesson with the dark-haired girl, I raised my fire and called out, "*Eskorp sa wein. Tumich.*" It was me. Sorry.

None of the Figs burst out laughing, so maybe I'd said it right.

The coach shook her head slightly, but the Commissaire seemed pleased to have someone else to speak with. He raised his fire toward me and said something in Ulfish.

"Come here and tell me what happened," the girl translated under her breath.

Ah, black.

Maybe I could pretend to be an imbecile. I pushed through the crowd and bowed obsequiously in front of the Commissaire. "*Tumich.*"

I chanced a look up, and the old man smiled at me. He had really white teeth. He seemed to be waiting for something, but when I only repeated my apology word-for-word, he said, "*Nant asasu eskorp?*"

Remarkably, I understood him.

"*Eskorp nant asa* Br... Brandt. Karl Brandt."

What a *Mélangé*. I'd been so excited to be able to reply I'd almost told him my real name.

"Brandt?" The Commissaire seemed surprised. Or suspicious? Was Brandt not Ulfish? It was the last name of Granny Jade's father, so it had to be.

I nodded.

He said a few more things in Ulfish, which I pretended to agree with, then he finally returned to his car. The door shut with a hollow ring, and the transparent vehicle drove off.

I turned to find several dozen people staring at me. I was about to verify what the Commissaire and I had been talking about for the last ten minutes when the skinny new recruit kissed his light hand at me and then extended it. Did he want me to kiss it too?

It wasn't until I saw his teammates nodding that I realized what this meant. The boy wanted to react with me.

The dark-haired girl smiled. The coach had tears in her eyes.

"Tumich," I said.

Then I grabbed my backpack from the bush and sprinted all the way to Blue Campus.

I got through the rest of the morning without angering any more government officials. Although in fourth period, Madame Loisible scowled at me for tracking mud onto the carpet. I grimaced in apology as she handed me a pair of pencils.

"Exam is on your desk. Pencils eared until lights out."

I slid one behind each ear and took my seat.

Once everybody was at their desks with their palms down, Madame Loisible darkened the room. I opened the test and read the first question by the light of my fire.

(1) According to Télesphorian legend, how did the first man and woman populate the world?

(z) One at a time, through natural reproductive means

(y) Teaching wolves to walk upright and speak

(x) Bringing stones to life by touching them

(w) Planting their severed fingers in the soil to grow children

My grimace became a grin. Grandpa Zacharie had told me at least a hundred times how the ancient couple had wandered the planet, touching rocks and turning them into people. I clumsily wrote an 'x' with my dark hand. One thing I wouldn't miss about Blue Campus was taking exams with no artificial light. Even if it made it harder for us to see our neighbors' answers, trying to write while using my hand as a lamp was awkward as blank.

I completed the first several pages before I noticed a folded piece of paper at the corner of my desk. After checking to make sure the teacher wasn't watching, I unfolded the note.

I wagered my college fund on the match today.
I know you'll shine, Bruno!
-Orie

I glanced at the blonde seated next to me, her nose nearly touching the test. She'd hardly spoken to me all semester. Why tell me about her bet? And why gamble so much on a single game? Defeating the Figs wouldn't be a problem, but still.

Did this mean Orie was interested in me? She wasn't bad looking. She wore her bangs a little low, which made her look like she was constantly peeking out from under a bed, but she did have graceful limbs. Her father was a doctor, so Dad would approve of the match, however I had hoped to convince my parents to let me do my courting on the mainland. I still had a year before the betrothal paperwork was due.

"Ten minutes," said Madame Loisible from the back of the room.

Ah! No time for daydreaming. I thrust the note into my pocket and turned the page of my exam.

```
(11) Which of these things did King Johannes not do?
         (z) rediscover Télesphore Island
         (y) start a petition to rename the world
         (x) invent the Téle language
         (w) reform Naissance observance
         (v) Johannes did all these things
```

Before I could pick one of the choices, another, smaller

note appeared on my desk. Instead of the neat, centered script, the paper contained four lines of clumsy print.

Is Psycho Eyes offering you answers?
Because she has a Y average.
If you actually want to PASS the test,
here are the first three pages:
1X, 2Z, 3Z, 4V, 5Y, 6Z, 7W, 8X, 9Y, 10W, 11V, 12Y, 13Y

I recognized the handwriting. Emma Raplapla had written me several such notes in the last week alone and her parents had submitted paperwork to mine for the previous four years. Thankfully, Monsieur Raplapla was in real estate. Mom found that distasteful.

This was the first time Emma had tried to give me answers, though. What was she thinking? I moved to brush the paper onto the floor but noticed Madame Loisible, light in pocket, walking down the aisle toward us. If the note was found—even if it was nowhere near me—Emma would automatically fail the final. I popped the paper into my mouth and chewed.

I managed a painful swallow as the teacher passed. She narrowed her eyes at my shoes but continued down the row. I picked up my pencil. The clock on the wall said I'd already wasted two of my last ten minutes.

"Nazaire!"

I smelled Marin before I saw him. When I noticed who was

walking down the hallway at his side, I understood the cloud of cologne.

"Hey, Mare-Bear. Saved you a place at lunch." I forced my backpack into my locker and spun the dial. "Hey, Drea."

Drea nodded. Even with spiky orange hair, she was stunning. Before last summer, she'd often been mistaken for a boy. But that all ended when puberty hit. With both fists.

"Sorry about lunch," Marin said with an eyebrow waggle. "We ate off campus."

I cocked my head. "Papers involved?"

Marin's grin became a blinding exposition of bicuspids. "Didn't want to say anything until I was sure, but I guess Monsieur DeLaney signed the courting prelims this morning."

"That's brilliant!" Despite my genuine enthusiasm, something writhed in the pit of my stomach. Irritation? It couldn't be jealousy. While Drea was now the most attractive young Blue on the island, I was one of the only Blue mecs that hadn't injured himself trying to impress her.

"She's a way good kisser."

"I'd rather not think about that. Or your sloppy grammar."

"But it's great, right?"

"It's really great. Seriously."

And I meant it. Marin had gotten lucky. I was happy for him. And sad. My best friend had paired before me. It made me feel suddenly adrift as if Marin had jumped ship and left me with no oars. It would be years before they married, but his time and focus would be severely limited.

"How'd you do in calculometrics?" Drea asked me. "That section on polyhedral-derivatives made me want to empty my bubble."

I winced. That phrase always brought to mind Ro's tiny light hand, swollen with infection. Dad drained it every few hours to keep it from rupturing.

"Uh, Drea," Marin said in a low voice. "Bruno's still in Basic Rithmatique."

Drea's pleasant expression didn't change. "Do you hear something, Bruno? So strange when random mecs interrupt other people's conversations."

Marin sighed. "Oh yeah. And she's not talking to me."

I smiled at Drea. "But you'll walk him to class?"

"Keeps the other boys away. Besides, he's walking *me* to class."

"She also thinks I smell good," Marin added.

"Strange," Drea said. "I keep hearing things."

I couldn't tell if she was genuinely angry or being silly. Either way, it was making me extremely uncomfortable. I decided to distract her for Marin's benefit. "Did you smash your religion final?"

Her expression darkened. "Missed it by two blackened points. Choked on the question about invoking harborage."

"You mean the twenty-ninth dictum?" I asked. "About limiting royal jurisdiction and granting sanctuary rights on church-owned property?"

For a moment, Drea just stared at me.

"Don't you remember? Axelle talked about it in Political Science."

"Amazing," Drea said. "And I'm the one with a High Priestess for a sister."

Drea stalked off and joined a line of students entering Madame Axelle's classroom. Marin pantomimed slamming his head repeatedly into my locker.

"She's not happy with the pairing?" I asked.

"Still getting used to 'Drea Faringoule', but otherwise, she's thrilled. Said she always wanted coffee-crême babies."

I cocked my head. "So, somehow in the first few hours of your relationship you managed to drain her fluid."

"Apparently I failed to notice the soldiers ogling her."

"Pokers? The ones we saw at the park?"

Marin shook his head. "When we were coming back onto campus we ran into a couple of different ones. I think I was supposed to defend her honor by shouting profanities at them."

"I wonder what they're doing here."

"Probably headed to the stadium to keep an eye on the Figs," Marin said. "Speaking of which, I think one of them is looking for you."

"One of the pokers?"

"Figs. Some fat kid with an A-glove is wandering between buildings asking people if their last name is Nazaire."

"You sure he was asking for me? I've got Axelle this period. How old was he? Was he lost?" The only one I'd seen wearing an alloy glove was the toddler.

"Calm down, *mon frère*. Go take your final. I'm sure he'll be around after class." He opened my locker and pilfered a protein bar from my backpack. "Hey, what happened at the gardens after I left?"

I shrugged. Even though the hallway was nearly empty, this was not a conversation I wanted to have in public. If word got out that I had made a fool of the Commissaire, my parents would pair me with Widow Meuglé to keep me in line. It was a threat Mom often made when we butted heads. Whether she'd actually marry me to a forty-year-old woman was debatable.

"I'm done for the day," Marin said. "Probably go home for a nap before the match."

I nodded. "Congrats again. Drea's *chanmé*."

"She is, isn't she?" He sauntered to the exit wearing a wide grin.

I scratched at the edge of my fire. Something Marin had said bothered me. Why would the Ulfish boy be asking for Nazaire when I'd introduced myself as Karl Brandt? Had the Figs figured out my real name? If so, it couldn't be much more difficult for the Commissaire to identify me. Since the opening match against Deatherage last year, I'd become something of a celebrity in town.

I groaned. It was probably nothing, but I'd never be able to concentrate on my finals until I knew what this was about. Anyway, it wouldn't hurt to be a couple of minutes late for class—political science was one of my best subjects.

Instead of empty sidewalks I found several pokers jogging between buildings. Probably a bomb threat or an incendiary event. Typically, the police organized volunteers to work the hoses, but maybe the pokers dealt with combustions at schools.

I didn't see any smoke.

The pokers weren't looking for me. They couldn't be.

I made a quick circuit around the Lit Building, trying to act like I had every right to be out of class. The soldiers ignored me for the most part. Apparently they weren't searching for a brown-haired, crême-skin boy with a large build.

"Nazeer?"

The voice came from near the History Building. At first I saw only perfectly trimmed foliage in vibrant contrast to the circular white walls.

I stepped onto the grass. "Who said that?"

No one answered. I approached the bushes and spotted a pair of dirty sneakers.

"I'm Bruno Nazaire. You looking for me?"

A roundish child crawled out of the bushes. "Um, yes."

He couldn't have been more than ten years old, and he wore an alloy glove so clean it looked fresh from the box. In contrast, the rest of him seemed rather shabby.

"Is everything okay?" I asked. "Are you here to watch the match? Where are your parents?"

The boy wrinkled his face. With his curly blond hair and chubby cheeks, he looked like he'd misplaced his harp and wings. "No."

No what? "Listen, I don't have a lot of time, so..."

The kid stared past me and began rocking slightly. Either he had to go to the fan, or I was making him nervous.

"Can I please have your autograph?"

What in the rainbow? I surveyed the grounds. Where were the pokers when you needed them? This kid didn't sound Ulfish, and he clearly didn't belong here.

I glanced at the Political Science Building. It would probably take Madame Axelle a couple of minutes to settle everyone down and hand out the tests.

I swallowed my impatience and forced a smile. "What's your name?"

"Jean-Baht..." He trailed off and flinched, like he'd said something he wasn't supposed to.

"Well, Jean Baht, did you really sneak in here to get my signature?"

"It's Jean-Baptiste." He then proceeded to spell his name including the hyphen and "silent P".

I resisted the urge to grab him by the shoulders. "Nice to meet you, Baptiste. Why don't you go hang out at the stadium, and I'll sign whatever you want before the match?"

Baptiste took a deep breath and launched into what seemed like a well-rehearsed speech about how he watched all the TC rugby games and wanted to be a lock when he got older.

"Okay," I said, "I guess I can do a quick signature."

He fished a pen and candy wrapper out of his pocket. A strange choice of stationary, but I managed to scrawl a brief note on the waxy paper.

I'd already handed Baptiste his pen and was preparing to sprint to class when I noticed his expression. He looked ready to cry. "You okay?"

He hesitated. "I turned thirteen today and my mom says I've got to react with my older sister."

The kid was thirteen? What was he doing wearing an alloy glove? He seemed old enough to keep his hands to himself. Four-year-olds were the ones who tried to touch their light to everything they saw.

"Let's talk about it after the game, okay?"

I took two long strides toward my classroom and heard a sob behind me.

Son of a Violet.

Don't turn around. Keep walking.

I glanced back. The sight of the boy's tear-streaked face

stirred a memory of a tree-house sleepover. Ro woke me half-way through the night—said he was scared and wanted to go inside. But I was too tired to carry him down from the tree-house. I fell asleep to his quiet sobs and in the morning, found him huddled in the corner, clutching one of my shoes like a teddy-bear.

It currently topped the list of worst-things-I've-ever-done.

I crouched in front of Baptiste. "Blueberry, it's normal to be scared your first time. It doesn't hurt, though."

"But I don't know what to do with my fire."

Huh? Was this kid just dimmer than most? "Haven't you seen a reaction? You hold hands for a minute with your palms touching, and it happens automatically."

Baptiste wiped at his face and held out his light hand. "Can you show me?"

It was a strange request, but since he was wearing the alloy glove, I figured it wouldn't hurt to run him through the motions. Anything to end this conversation. I glanced toward the Political Science Building.

"Fine, but then I've seriously got to run, okay?"

He nodded.

I grabbed his glove with my light hand and pressed my palm into his. It felt weird touching fires with a stranger, even if he did remind me of Ro. "See? Just like Greens do sometimes when they meet. Of course they use their dark hands. Since you and your sister are both Blue, your shades won't even change very muAAAHHH!"

My hand felt like it had swollen to several times its normal size. My arm jerked back reflexively, but my fingers were frozen in place. It was as if all my joints had fused together and would be forever entwined with Baptiste's hand. My fire flared, sending a tingling sensation up my arm.

In seconds, it was over and I wrenched my hand free.

"What the black was that?" My body was so full of adrenaline, I could have picked the kid up and thrown him halfway across campus. "Did you just paint me?" But the glove. It should have—

Didn't matter. The kid had forced a reaction and now he stood grimacing as if waiting for me to knock his teeth out.

"Why did you do that?" I screamed. I held my hand out, fingers splayed. My impulse was to scrub it with soap and water, but I knew that would be useless.

A single poker appeared from behind a building and jogged toward me.

I held my fire aloft and stumbled to meet him. "He painted me!"

Had the boy done it on purpose? Why would he want to react so badly with another Blue? Unless... all my internal organs seemed to vanish. I'd never actually seen his shade. If he wasn't Blue, that would mean I'd become a—no, he had to be Blue. He couldn't have gotten in otherwise.

"Who painted you?" the poker asked. It was the bald one I'd met at Blue Gardens, his bright orange goatee starkly contrasted against his brown clothing.

"That boy!"

I spun to find only an empty stretch of grass.

CHAPTER THREE

DEAD GRASS

There was only one place Baptiste could have gone—behind the Political Science Building. I sprinted across the grounds and shouted for the poker to follow. I would catch that kid. I would make him sorry he ever stepped onto Blue Campus.

But on the other side of the building, I found only the chain-link fence that separated our school from L'académie Mélangé. And the Green side of town.

No. Please no.

The poker staggered to my side, breathing like an asthmatic. "Having a ... little joke?"

"The kid has to be here somewhere. No way he got over that razor wire."

And even if he had, an open park area lay on the other side of the fence—no place to hide. Those short legs wouldn't have carried the kid that far in a few seconds. But then where was he?

The poker walked to the fence and picked up a section that had been cut free.

No. No. No.

The poker unhitched his radio from his belt. "I'll call Hameau Vert patrol and—"

"Wait." I pointed at an old landscaping shed against the back of the Political Science Building. The wooden door of the shack hung open.

The poker nodded. We strode toward the shed, and I noticed a large, high window in the building behind it. Was that

Madame Axelle's window? Although the glass only reflected the trees and fence behind us, I remembered that her classroom faced the mixed-freak school. On the other side of the glass, my classmates were collecting the final points needed to ensure promising futures.

I tried not to speculate about my own. There was still a chance Baptiste hadn't come from Hameau Vert. The chainlink could've been cut ages ago. Maybe the kid really was Blue and actually wanted advice from his hero. The faulty alloy glove might have been an honest mistake.

Except...

If the kid had come to all my games he wouldn't need to ask random people whether their name was Nazaire—while mispronouncing it. He'd probably read about me in the paper and decided to use my name as a pretext to be in Ville Bleu. I was a fool not to have seen it earlier. An arrogant, idiotic blackhead.

The poker gestured with his chin and smiled. Under a workbench, just visible in the dark interior, was a leg.

Finding him brought no relief—only dread. Now I had to take off Baptiste's glove and face the consequences of my recklessness. It almost didn't matter what shade he was if it wasn't Blue.

The poker pushed a button on his oversized watch, and a green light appeared on the face. He wiggled his gloved fingers, like Dad did before surgery.

I tried to follow the poker through the door, but my legs locked up. Outside, I was Bruno Nazaire, starting forward and future medical professional. As soon as I stepped inside and saw the shade I had mixed with, that life would be over. Not even a wide neck could save what stupidity had destroyed in thirty seconds.

The poker crouched inside the doorway. I expected him to pull the bench away from the wall, but instead he extended his gloved index finger and touched Baptiste on the calf.

The boy yelped like an injured dog and hit the underside

of the bench. He scrambled to get out of reach, but the poker moved faster. With his light hand, he grabbed Baptiste's ankle, yanked him out from under the bench, and dropped him onto the grass.

My chest grew tight. I steadied myself against the shed and forced a deep breath.

The poker ripped off Baptiste's glove.

The ground seemed to disappear beneath my feet. The rest of the world receded into the horizon until all that remained was the boy's unnatural light.

He was a Mélangé.

Although the deep blue of his fire was only slightly tinged with green, it was enough. That small amount of contamination was all it took to exclude the boy from Ville Bleu—to keep him on the other side of the fence. In a few hours that tiny amount of green would be enough to keep me out too.

I punched the shed. The weathered siding splintered. Stupid worthless shack. It should have been torn down years ago. It didn't belong here.

But I did. I was a Blue—no matter what my hand looked like. Couldn't they see that? Would they still make me move to Hameau Vert? Surely Dad would be able to do something. Talk to somebody. The Doms had to have some sort of provision for paint victims.

I swore. Who was I kidding? The Dominateur didn't make exceptions. I stared at my perfect fire. I knew it was too early, but in my mind I could almost see sickly green tendrils spiraling inward to pollute my life force. There was nothing I could do to stop it. Cutting it off seemed somehow less horrible than watching it change.

The poker threw the glove at Baptiste's head. "You're off sides, little freak."

Baptiste looked down at his dirt-streaked clothes, clamped his hands over his ears, and began rolling on the grass.

The poker raised an orange eyebrow at me.

What was the kid doing? I felt like shouting at him to get

up. Did he not care what he had taken from me? My future, my family, my career. What did Mélangé even do for a living? Deliver mail? The thought of going out in public with a mixed fire brought another flash of humiliation quickly followed by fury.

"Why are you here?" the poker shouted.

A useless question. It was obvious why Baptiste had risked crossing the shade border. A reaction with a Blue would take away some of his green. Make him better. But no matter how many perfect Blues he reacted with, that green would always be there, however faint, standing between him and pure society.

He had upped his status slightly by crippling mine.

Before I could pick up the kid and shove him against the wall, the poker stepped on his forearm. Baptiste stopped rolling and attempted to free himself.

"You want me to believe this butterball overpowered a muscle-head three times bigger than him?" He emphasized 'three times bigger.' My exact words when I humiliated him in front of the Figs.

"Get over yourself. This is serious. The kid tricked me. He must have removed the alloy plate in his glove. I'll have proof soon enough." I closed my fingers over my fire.

He smiled and released Baptiste's arm. "How about that. A smart-mouth Blue out-thunk by a mixed freak."

"You find this funny?"

"What's funny is you saying you'd throw me in a pond. Now I get to throw you across the street."

"Touch me, and you'll be working in the tin mines."

"So sure of yourself. For a few more hours anyway."

The reality finally hit me and the feeling went out of my legs. I fell back against the shed, hands pressed to my forehead. There was no point in going back for the test. I could get a perfect score and the Classifications Committee wouldn't care.

The poker kicked Baptiste. "On your feet, chub-chub."

I checked my fire. Still blue. Should I run home before it

changed? How was I going to explain this to my parents? Could they somehow hide my shade?

Baptiste curled into a ball. The poker kicked him harder. "You Mélangé too stupid to understand Téle? Stand. Up."

Baptiste whimpered with each boot to the stomach.

I winced. "You're going to break his ribs." Not that he didn't deserve it.

"He'll be dead within the week," the poker said with another kick.

"They're not going to execute a kid." At least not a Blue Mélangé. The girl Marin saw had been Red.

The poker sneered. "You bluebirds live in your own little world, don't you? They probably would have popped him for sneaking in here. Turning you into a freak just sealed the deal." He lowered his boot again, this time on Baptiste's teal fire. "I'm tempted to do it now and say he got out of control."

The man was a crêpe bag. But I resisted the urge to put him in his place. What was the point? He was right about the boy's fate. You didn't destroy the life of a Blue without serious repercussions. Maybe it would be better for Baptiste if the punishment happened quickly. He wouldn't have to endure the spite of the *beau monde* community. Or wait in a cell for the next poker graduation. Did he even understand what was happening?

In a sudden movement, Baptiste twisted and kicked the back of the poker's knee. Clumsy, but also unexpected. The poker stumbled sideways, and Baptiste began a frantic crawl toward the fence.

The poker recovered quickly and adjusted something on his watch. Before Baptiste had gone five feet, the poker caught him and touched the back of his neck. This time there was no yelp, only a small snapping sound. Baptiste went limp.

Bile rose in my throat. I got to my feet. "You didn't—"

"Still alive." The poker displayed his watch face as if the yellow light was supposed to mean something to me. "Help me carry him to a scooter."

Still alive. The wave of relief surprise me. Why did I care so much if the boy lived? He may as well have murdered the old Bruno Nazaire. He'd brought this on himself.

The poker grabbed Baptiste's wrists. "Get his feet before he wakes up."

I reached for the boy's legs but stopped. Unconscious, Baptiste looked impossibly young. Where were his parents? Did he have siblings? Maybe an older brother who was supposed to protect him but failed miserably?

I straightened my back. Ro was gone. But maybe I could save this boy.

"What's the problem?" the poker asked, still holding Baptiste by the arms.

"I... lied about him painting me."

The poker dropped Baptiste and sighed. "Here we go."

"He's actually my friend's little brother. He's not right in the head. I reacted with him because I felt sorry for him. Then I sorta freaked out."

The poker scoffed. "You *beau monde* are something else. Happy to have us pop faceless convicts every six months, but when it's someone you know, you've got to play the hero. Throw your blue around until we kiss your light and pardon whoever you want."

"Whomever," I said automatically, then cringed.

"Unbelievable."

"Would it cost you anything to let him go? Do you get a bonus for every helpless kid you sign up for execution?"

The poker made a face of exaggerated concern. "I have an idea, bluebird. Why don't I take care of the fat little painter, and you can go say goodbye to all your snobby little friends."

I held out my fire. The pure blue was a lie. Soon my palm would reflect my prospects for the future. On the up side, a little more green wouldn't make much difference. Which gave me a unique bargaining chip. "How about this?" I said. "You take some of my blue and forget you ever saw the kid."

The poker's orange eyebrows rose. He opened his mouth,

then closed it.

"What's to think about? Discounts, priority service." I swallowed. I couldn't believe I was doing this. But it was the only way to keep Baptiste alive. "Instant respect. You can say you were born Blue and gang-painted. The Green ladies will fall over themselves to buy you a drink."

The poker's eyes refocused and his scowl reappeared.

Whoops. By mentioning Greens, I had reminded him his status would be relative. A blue-green shade would impress only the lower colors. Those that truly mattered would see him for the freak he was. Just as they would me in a few hours.

"A royal soldier earns his respect," the poker said. "One way or another."

I straightened my arm, and turned my fire upward until the poker's eyes shone with twin sparks of deep blue. I'd never appreciated how beautiful my light was. "Last chance," I said. "I've heard that in Dita, anyone with blue is treated like a celebrity. Even Mélangé."

"Keep your fancy shade," the poker said with sudden venom. "You think I'll give you the chance to say I painted you?"

"Okay then." I lowered my light and took up a position directly over Baptiste's body. "Now your options are: leave or fight me for him."

The poker looked me over, his eyes lingering on my arms. He gave me a stiff smile and reached for his radio.

"Calling for help was not on the list. But I guess if you can't handle an unarmed sixteen-year-old..."

It was a half-hatched scheme. Even if I beat this grasspalm into the ground, there was no way he'd let me walk off with Baptiste over my shoulder. He'd just call for someone else to chase me. But rugby trained me to look for weaknesses and exploit them. The man had the look of someone who'd rather get punched in the face than be called a coward.

"Let's put it this way," I said. "If you call your soldier buddies for help, I'll make sure they know you played it safe. I'm sure they'll be impressed."

His scowl deepened.

Baptiste stirred. I stepped away from him and drew the poker's attention toward the building. If I kept the man distracted long enough, maybe Baptiste could sneak back through the fence. "Your colleagues will be glad to know you don't take any chances when dealing with dangerous students. I mean, you can't be more than ten years older than me. It's no wonder—"

The poker struck.

I knocked the glove away and drove my shoulder into his stomach. He went over like a rotten log and landed on his back. With his light hand pinned beneath him, I had no trouble getting control of his gloved hand. I forced his index finger out and brought it within a few inches of his cheek.

"We finished?"

He growled.

I took that as a yes and allowed him to lower his hand, though I still kept a tight grip on it. Despite my exhaustion, I grinned. I'd bested a trained soldier. "No one needs to know about this. Just let the kid—"

The poker kicked off the ground and arched his back. For a horrifying second, I thought he would flip me over, but I landed on top of him again and pinned his zappy-glove to the grass.

Should've been worried about his head.

I heard the crack before I felt it. Pain exploded in my jaw, and the world went blurry. When my vision cleared, I was on my back. A figure loomed over me, shadowy against the blinding white of the sky. Even more than my face, my wrists screamed in agony. Was he kneeling on them? With both arms pinned down, I squinted and tried to focus on the poker's face.

"Whatever you want," I managed to get out. It was difficult to breathe with his full weight on my chest. "My parents. Have money."

"Good point. They'll try to pay your way out of this. Not

to mention eat up whatever lies you tell them. Excuse me—whomever lies."

I could handle being called a snob. I could even take the physical abuse. But that grammar...

"This is unit nineteen," the poker said into his radio. "Winterdark side of Blue Campus, near the shade barrier. Just got assaulted by a Blue male, late teens. Tried to calm him, but he grew more violent."

Late teens. What a blackhead.

The radio crackled. "Copy that, nineteen. Four and twenty-six are on their way. What's the status of the assailant?"

The poker smiled at me. But it wasn't a smile of humor or even pity. It was a smile of satisfaction. "To protect myself and the students, I had to use lethal force."

I forgot about trying to breathe.

"Copy, nineteen. Help is en route. Leave the body where it is."

Body. The two syllables felt like stab wounds. One through each lung.

The poker pushed a button on his watch and the light went from yellow to red. "Too bad," he said. "I was looking forward to your shademates' expressions when they saw the new you."

I made one last pathetic attempt to free my arms, but without oxygen, my muscles refused to work. Couldn't anyone inside see what was going on? Although the window was fairly high up, we were positioned directly in front of it. By now, one of my classmates should have gotten up to sharpen a pencil or something. Surely they weren't all distracted by a silly test.

No faces appeared at the window. No muffled shouts from inside. Just birds. Maybe it was best this way. I wouldn't have to go home and show Dad my palm. I would die Blue.

The brown glove seemed to move in slow motion toward my face. The index finger grew closer until the metallic dot at the tip looked impossibly large. Somewhere beneath my suffocating panic, a part of me watched with detached fascination. I could almost hear my father's voice explaining the process of death.

Once the silver contact point touches skin, it will completely empty the watch battery of its stored power. The current will super-heat the victim's serum, converting it almost instantly from liquid to gas. The pressure will rupture the membrane surrounding the fire with an audible pop. In the unlikely event that the electricity surge does not burn away the stamen, the victim will have approximately eight to nine minutes before lack of fuel causes luminogenic arrest. Much more often, the distinct odor of charred soft tissue indicates irreparable damage to the fire organ. The time of death should be recorded at respiratory and cardiac arrest, not the cessation of luminogenesis, as the exposed stamen may continue to glow faintly for several minutes postmortem.

A dull clunk stirred me from my oxygen-deprived stupor.

The poker swore.

Another clunk. Why was I still alive?

The glove disappeared, followed by the weight on my chest. I could breathe! Feeling worked its way back into my limbs. I rolled onto my side and saw the cause of the delay. A chubby boy with a shovel backed away from the advancing poker. Why hadn't the kid run? Instead he'd trapped himself against the building.

I had to get up. Baptiste needed help. The poker's watch was still set to kill. But my body felt like it was moving through tar. It took incredible willpower just to keep my eyes open. I breathed deeply and wiggled my fingers. The blood rushed into my light hand. My palm tingled as my fire struggled to keep up with the fresh wave of oxygen.

Stand. Up. Bruno.

I could almost hear Coach Fontaine's voice shouting, "Is that all you've got, Baby Blue?"

I rolled to my knees and threw myself at the poker's legs,

dropping him to the grass. Baptiste yelped, and the shovel clattered at his feet.

I tightened my arms around the poker's ankles. "Get to the fence!"

A foot pulled free and kicked me in the shoulder. It felt as if my arm had been torn from the socket. The boot came down again on my arm and I let go. The poker crawled toward Baptiste at startling speed. The boy didn't bother to run. He knew it was over.

There was one way to end this fight for good. The watch had to be destroyed. My fire pulsed with energy. It had finally caught up with my labored breathing. Heat bloomed in my palm and flowed up my arm. I picked up the shovel.

Baptiste closed his eyes. The poker rose up on his knees to free his hands.

I stood, my weariness gone. The poker reached for Baptiste. I raised the shovel and brought it down, aiming for the man's watch.

Like something out of a nightmare, the poker twisted his torso and caught the head of the shovel with both hands. For a split second he smiled. Then his grip shifted, and the tip of his index finger brushed metal.

A pop echoed off the building, like a single firecracker. At first I thought it had come from inside. Then the smell of burnt flesh made my stomach turn.

The shovel fell to the grass, and the poker stared with wide eyes. Not at the shovel, or even at me. His eyes were locked on the bloody crater that used to be his life force.

The world fell silent. My body still thrummed with energy. How had that happened? "I didn't..."

The man made a gurgling sound, twisted on his knees, and grabbed my foot. I pulled free, and he landed face first onto the ground.

Then he went still.

CHAPTER FOUR

LIAR

I mages flashed through my mind, each one like a blow to the chest.

A window with blue pinstripes. A circle of doctors. Sightless eyes. A tiny outstretched arm. Brilliant artificial light illuminating the oozing hole in Ro's hand.

For a second, Baptiste and I looked at each other. Then I flung my arm at the fence. "Go!"

"I'm sorry. It was Aro. He told me what to say. I didn't know—"

"Ro? What about Ro?"

"No, Aro. He said—"

"It doesn't matter. More are coming. Go now!"

"He tricked me into—"

"You've probably got ten seconds to get through the fence or you'll be popped. You. Not this 'I-Rue' person. Move!"

Baptiste hopped like he'd been stung, then began a sort of jogging waddle toward the fence.

The Créateur help that child.

At some point I'd find him again. Then he would explain why he ruined my life. But we both had to survive first. I glanced at the body of the bald man, and my stomach twisted. I stifled thoughts of Ro. I needed to figure this out. Should I explain to the other pokers what had happened? They'd never believe it was an accident.

And I wouldn't tell them the poker painted me even if it might protect Baptiste. They wouldn't buy it anyway. The bald poker already told them I'd assaulted him. If they would

41

execute a Mélangé for painting a Blue, they'd certainly execute me for killing a royal soldier.

Negotiation was out. Time to do what I did best.

I took off around the far side of the building at a speed that would've impressed Coach Fontaine. Once out of view of the windows, I pasted myself against the smooth white wall and peeked around the front—just in time to see two pokers disappear around the opposite side.

I hoped Baptiste was faster than he looked.

Sidewalks now empty, I realized I had no idea where to run. My instincts told me to get as far away from the scene of the crime as possible, but I didn't want to draw attention to myself by sprinting out the front gates.

The dead poker hadn't given anyone my description, but being seen outside in the immediate area would certainly make me a suspect. My best bet was to get into a building without being seen. We had less than an hour until school let out.

I forced myself to step out into the open and walk casually toward the entrance. Out of the corner of my eye, I saw a poker emerge from the Lit Building a hundred yards away.

I suppressed the urge to dive for the double doors. Urgent, but not panicked. I pretended to check my watch, then opened the door. Just a student late for class. I stepped into cool air. The door closed behind me. Through the small window, I watched, waiting for the poker to change course and follow me inside. Instead, he joined another poker headed toward the fence.

Once they were out of sight, I began to breathe again. Should I go to class? No, that would only draw attenntion to myself. Everyone would wonder where I'd been. Best to hide in the fan until the final bell. I walked quickly. The empty hallway seemed absurdly normal after everything I'd been through, the familiar cerulean carpet, almost comforting.

Until I remembered. In a few hours I wouldn't be welcome here. I felt a rush of fury toward Baptiste. I would find him again. He would tell me everything. If this I-Rue person was really responsible I'd make him pay.

The fanroom door opened, and Director Boudreaux stepped out, wiping his hands on his pants. "Nazaire? Everything okay?"

I realized my face had been twisted with thoughts of my shattered future. "Just stressed about finals." Crêpes. Should have said I was sick.

The Director looked at his watch. "Madame Axelle doesn't usually allow fan breaks during exams. Why are you in the hall?"

Lie. Lie.

I swallowed. There had been too much deception today already. Each new lie felt like another weight around my neck. I couldn't do this. This wasn't me. I had to tell him the truth.

I met the Director's eyes. To my surprise, he was smiling.

"Tell you what," he said. "If you promise to pound Ulfig this afternoon, I won't write you up for trying to ditch."

I stared at him. I'd completely forgotten about the match.

He winked. "I may have placed a small wager on TC."

"I... will do my best, 'sieur."

He escorted me to Madame Axelle's door, pushed me through, and stuck his head into the darkened room.

"Don't mark Nazaire tardy," the Director said loudly, causing the bluebirds to panic and fly around their cages. "He was lending me a fire with something."

From her desk, the large, bejeweled woman raised perfect eyebrows.

I nodded. Another lie. The weight on my shoulders increased, pulling me deeper into the mud. How long before I couldn't move? Before I couldn't breathe? I'd have to lie again when my green appeared. At least school would be over by then.

I dreaded telling my parents, but they'd know what to do, how to spin this. We were the third wealthiest family on the island. That had to count for something.

Boudreaux left. I approached Madame Axelle who handed me two pencils and an exam packet. Twenty minutes ago, I'd been excited for this test. It meant less than nothing now. The best-case scenario was that I'd survive long enough to lose everything I'd ever worked for.

On the walk to my seat, I couldn't help glancing out the window. Half a dozen pokers stood close together, their eyes on the ground. From my angle, I couldn't see the body. No sign of Baptiste. I really hoped he'd gotten away.

I managed to make it across the room without anyone accusing me of murder. Although as I took my seat, Drea did give me a questioning look.

I pretended not to notice, eared one pencil, and flipped over the first page of the test.

ESSAY 1: Compare and contrast
monarchical and meritocratic forms of
government. Show how the transition
impacted Télesphorian schools, and
whether the changes were initiated
by the Dom of Education, the
Dominateur as a whole, or the newly
appointed Haut Commissaire.

The words may as well have been written in blood-scratch. The room seemed unbearably hot. My mind formed questions faster than I could process, and none of them had to do with kings or education.

Was I finally safe? Could anyone prove I was outside during the poker's death? Had I really murdered him? No, it was an accident. Wasn't it? My chances to disappear would improve drastically once I changed shade. The pokers were looking for a Blue, not a Blue-Green Mélangé.

What would I even do in Hameau Vert? Maybe I should leave Télesphore altogether. Could I get past the wall checkpoints before I turned?

"Ten minutes left," Madame Axelle called. "I want to have

everything cleaned up before the evaluation officer arrives."

Evaluations? I leaned back in my seat and carefully glanced behind me. "Not Thursday?"

Drea twisted an earring, eyes still glued to the test. "Inspector wants to take the boat back with the Figs."

"Who's talking?" Madame Axelle boomed from her desk.

I leaned forward and pretended to write while my mind raced in completely new circles.

The last evaluation before classifications was the most important. Next to fifth-year test scores, blue category was the biggest factor in determining career placement. The Nazaire family line carried some of the best blue in the world. If I could get evaluated before the reaction completed, the Classifications Committee would most likely sort me as an Electric Mind, which would allow me to apply for a medical apprenticeship. I'd have to show up as a Mélangé to the ceremony, but I could wear a cast to hide my fire. Forwards break bones every so often.

For the first time since Baptiste grabbed my hand, I felt a genuine flash of hope. Maybe I wasn't as blacked as I thought. After classifications Dad could help me hide my shade. Surgeons did wear gloves, after all.

Madame Axelle got up from the desk and began her rounds. I wiped my forehead on my sleeve. Whatever my plan, I wasn't going to get a medical apprenticeship if I failed my last final.

I had ten minutes to save my future.

I reread the first question and scribbled out a short but accurate list of how things changed in the interim between the king's death and the Commissaire's appointment. Granny always said Télesphore was still officially a monarchy. I couldn't resist adding that Commissaire Livius was a temporary placeholder. Maybe I'd get extra credit. I wanted to include the entire King's Requirement, but I knew it would probably just drain Axelle's fluid. She hated when I debated the usefulness of the Commissaire. And anyway, I had several more pages of test to complete.

I held my pencil between two fingers and trained my fire on the second question.

ESSAY 2: Explain the process used
to elect a member of the Dominateur
Council. List the criteria to
determine whether a Blue is old enough
to vote and the Green occupations
eligible for a quarter vote.

So easy.

But in my hurry to single-handedly maneuver the pencil into writing position, it flew from my hand, bounced off my desk and disappeared into the darkness enshrouding the floor.

Stupid lights-out policy. It was a wonder students didn't puncture themselves.

I pulled the back-up pencil from my ear and pressed it to the page.

The lead snapped off.

Son of a blackened Violet.

I leaned over and trained my light on the carpet. Where had that first pencil landed?

I shifted my foot. A cold sweat broke out down my back and arms. There on the white leather of my sneaker, was a bloody handprint.

I instinctively closed my fingers around my fire and pulled my feet under the chair. Thoughts of finishing the test and trying to fool everyone at classifications evaporated. As soon as the artificial light came on, it was over. I may as well have carried the bloody shovel in with me.

"Five minutes," came Axelle's disembodied voice.

How had Boudreaux not noticed? Could I run to the fan and pretend to be sick? Axelle would probably send some-one to check on me. Maybe I could lose the shoes completely —drop them in the trash on the way out? No, someone was bound to notice. I spit on my dark hand and pretended to scratch my foot. My palm came back red. I spit again and wiped my hand on my shorts. Was Axelle watching? Surely one of my classmates had noticed me acting strangely. I didn't usually try to polish my shoes in class.

I pressed my fire into my chest and squinted into the darkness. Axelle stood near the bluebird cages, eyes sweeping the room. In the front row, Benoit stared lazily at the ceiling. Everyone else still seemed engrossed in the final.

A flashing blue light caught my eye—at the side of the room near the window. Orie Talbot stared toward the front of the room while her fingers tapped a quick pattern on her fire.

Thumb to third finger, then index, then she made a fist. A space. She was sending a message in firespeak. I found myself momentarily distracted. If she were caught giving answers, she'd fail and end up working in the post office for the rest of her life.

Even though I hadn't used the code since elementary school, I recognized most of the signs. I didn't want to waste the last few minutes of the test, but from Orie's frantic signing, her message was important.

I used my fingernail to expose a bit of lead on the broken pencil. Then, in the margin of the test, I scribbled down the letters I was sure of.

_I_E BRUNO I _A_ U OU_ _I_E BRUNO

It was intended for me.

First two fingertips covering the fire was either 'D' or 'S', definitely 'S'. And that meant 'D' was thumb to third finger. Index and little finger down was 'T'. No, 'W'—'T' was a three-quarter covering. I watched the circuit again and filled in the blanks.

BRUNO I SAW U OUTSIDE

The heat of my body seemed to drain into the floor, leaving me numb with cold. How much did she see? Baptiste? The shovel? Why had she not said something to the teacher? Maybe she had. Maybe law enforcement was on their way to collect me.

But then why the secret message? Was she expecting something in exchange for not turning me in? Even if she didn't know about the dead poker, she'd find out soon enough. I either needed to swear her to silence or make a run for it now. If I ran straight through the front entrance, across town, and to the summerlight gate, I might beat the pokers on their scooters.

I was debating how difficult it would be to get onto a ship without being seen when Orie glanced back at me. We stared at each other for a moment, then I clumsily signed: NO TELL I PAY U. I had nearly four thousand cuivres saved up for my medical apprenticeship. I would need most of it to start over on the mainland, but I could probably offer her a thousand. That would buy her a nice boat, or a week-long vacation on the Isles of Evor.

Orie abruptly faced forward and trained her fire on her test. Madame Axelle strolled between us. I pretended to write while I rubbed the bottom of my muddy shoe onto the one the poker grabbed. The red stain wouldn't be so easy to erase, but at least now it might look less like a hand.

Orie rested her cheek on her knuckles, light out. Her fingers moved more subtly this time, but I could still make out most of the letters—which I scribbled down.

U R SAFE
DID U Kill HI

Artificial light flooded the room. "Pencils on the floor."

I jerked so violently I nearly fell out of my chair. A cry of discontent rose from the students, followed by a clatter of wood on carpet. I dropped my pencil.

Drea chuckled behind me. "Little tense?"

"Bruno?" Madame Axelle called from the front of the room. "Why don't you read to us Mademoiselle Talbot's message."

It took a second for her words to sink in. I looked at Orie's profile. She seemed paler than usual.

"Message, Madame?" Guilt dripped from my voice.

Axelle raised her light hand and spelled N-O-W in firespeak. "I wouldn't have thought you capable of cheating. But I saw you scribbling her code in the margin of your exam. Let's have a look why don't we?"

The expressions of my classmates ranged from surprised to smug. I glanced at the scrawl on the side of my packet.

BRUNO I SAW U OUTSIDE
U R SAFE
DID U Kill HI

It was incriminating. And plenty legible. Black my tidy handwriting. Then on the lower corner of the page, I noticed a smear of red.

What! How? My breath escaped in a huff and, along with it, my last shred of hope. Clearly the Créateur was determined to see me pay for my crime. Why else would a bloodstain miraculously appear on my test?

I stood, packet in hand. At least this finally felt right.

"I don't think he copied it down correctly," Orie said. She pulled a sapphire-encrusted billfold out of her backpack and extracted a folded piece of paper, worn smooth by age or use. "I have the original here."

I hesitated, unsure if I should continue to Axelle's desk or sit down.

Orie walked the paper to the front and then returned to her seat. Her eyes didn't once leave the carpet. Axelle opened the note.

I remained standing, sure she would ask for my packet the moment I moved back toward the chair.

"Bruno."

I almost responded before I realized Axelle was reading.

"Hair like chocolate. Eyes like the sea. His strong arms, a blanket I would wrap around me." Madame Axelle looked up. "That's quite good, Orie."

Drea made a gagging sound. Several students laughed. Orie's face looked like newborn rivertrash. I realized that rather than her bangs, it was her green eyes that made her look peculiar. They were so large they seemed to swallow the rest of her face.

"Oh, and there's a dedication on the other side."

Orie grimaced at me. I couldn't tell if it was supposed to be an apology, or if she was regretted coming to my rescue.

"Dear, Monsieur Nazaire." Axelle raised an eyebrow. "Bit formal for a love letter."

Orie lowered her head onto the desk and placed both hands on her head, as if trying to hide.

"Nice job, Talbot," Drea said from behind me. "You finally found the nerve to tell him. But who would want their chocolate to taste hair-like?"

More laughter. Orie shot Drea a nasty look.

"Quiet," Axelle said. "I'll read the last few lines, then we need to prepare the room for evaluations."

I slowly sat and tucked my bloody shoe under my chair. Could I somehow destroy the top page of my test while Axelle was distracted? Was this a sign from the Créateur that I was supposed to keep fighting? Keep running? Why was Orie humiliating herself for me? Granted it was better than her failing the final for cheating. Was that what she was worried about?

"I wrote this for you in third grade," Axelle continued reading. "If Drea told you about my locker, she's lying. I only drew *one* portrait of you, and it's because you're such a good friend. Unless you want to be more."

That did it. The class lost complete control.

I ripped the top page from my packet, wadded it, and shoved it down the front of my pants. Not extremely comfortable, but at least if Axelle had me turn out my pockets...

The laughter cut off.

Into the classroom strode three smiling pokers.

CHAPTER FIVE

BAD HAIR DAY

I t was over. They'd found me. Why did I think I'd be safe twenty feet from the body?

Madame Axelle glanced at the door and wrinkled her nose. "What do you think you're doing in here?"

The tallest of the pokers bowed in apology and his smile grew stiff. "Excuse us, Madame, but there was an incident outside your window. We thought one of you might have seen something."

The knot in my chest loosened a little. The pokers' smiles were obsequious, not triumphant. They weren't here for me. No one had seen me outside. Except Orie, who I was fairly certain meant to keep my secret.

Would that change when she realized the poker had died?

"What kind of incident?" Madame Axelle asked.

The poker looked at his companions, then spoke in a soft voice, "A royal soldier was killed."

Most of the class jumped out of their seats and ran to the window. I figured it would be wise to blend in. I stood and glanced at my foot. The clumsy attempt to disguise the handprint had been surprisingly effective. Spots of red still glared up at me, but in general it looked like I'd stepped in some unusually colorful mud. I gave the shoe another quick polish with my other foot, then stepped toward the window —and Orie, who still sat in her chair, staring straight ahead as if frozen. Was that fear or surprise? I would've given half my serum to see inside her head at that moment.

On my way past her I laid my light on her shoulder. She

flinched but didn't look at me. I hoped the touch conveyed everything I couldn't say—*Thank you. I'm sorry to put you through this. Please don't tell.*

"His fire exploded!" Benoit said from the window.

I made a half-hearted attempt to see over the heads of my classmates. I saw trees. And the fence. That was enough.

"Holy black," Drea said, her face to the glass. "Holy blank, I mean," she added after the teacher squeezed in next to her.

"Créateur save us," Axelle whispered. "Who did this?"

After a several seconds, the awkwardness of touching overpowered morbid curiosity, and the students disentangled themselves. I stumbled back to my desk but didn't sit. My fire ached with heat. It used to hurt like that before important matches. My mind was calling for energy, for speed, while my body remained still. The power had no outlet and thrummed in my hand like a silent scream.

At any minute someone would say, "Hey, Bruno, weren't you late to class?" That is if Orie didn't say something first. From her furrowed eyebrows and twisted lips, she was either having stomach cramps or wrestling with a serious moral dilemma. If I didn't know better, I would've sworn she had killed the man.

"We believe it was a student," the tall poker said. "Could we have a few minutes to speak with each of your pupils individually?"

Madame Axelle glanced at the clock. "We'll have to inform the evaluation officer. He should've been here by now."

The poker nodded. "He's likely stuck at the front gate. Le Sergent Whisnant won't let anyone in or out until we find the killer."

Madame Axelle pressed a hand into her bosom. "In your seats, Blues."

As I sat, I noticed a thin streak of brownish-red on my desk.

Where had that come from? Nothing a little spit couldn't handle. I crouched over and surreptitiously brought my dark hand under my mouth.

And froze.

My palm was covered with dried blood.

That's right, I'd already tried the spit shine once. Bad idea. No wonder I was seeing streaks everywhere. I rubbed the smudge off the desk my with my thumb, dusted the blood residue off my blue shorts—as much as possible—then thrust my dark hand into my pocket.

No visible red. Orie was going to come through. I was fine.

"You okay, Nazaire?" Drea asked on the way back to her seat.

Clearly my expression wasn't the neutral mask I was going for. My insides were so twisted with fear and guilt, it was a wonder I hadn't burst into tears. I nodded and shrugged as if I saw dead bodies every day.

We passed up our exams while Benoit gathered the pencils from the floor. The pokers split up, produced notepads, and began questioning the students on the first row. One of the pokers looked in my direction. Had someone told him I was late for class?

I turned around in my chair to avoid eye contact.

"What is going on with you?" Drea said in a quiet voice. "You look like you swallowed your toothbrush."

I opened my mouth to tell her the truth but realized it wasn't a good idea. Too many people knew already. Orie wasn't dealing well with the strain. I wasn't going to put Drea in the same position of having to risk herself to protect me.

"I failed the test." It felt like the truest thing I'd said all day.

"This is about Orie, isn't it?" Drea said. "I heard she put a quarter of a million quivres on TC. That kind of pressure would affect any—"

"Yes," I said, a little too eagerly. Her mention of the match had given me an idea. "I forgot my cleats at home. How would you feel about distracting the Axe while I sneak out of here?"

"Didn't they just say Whisnant isn't letting anyone out?"

"I'll bribe him or something. Anyway he's probably got money on the game too. Please, help me? I think I also left my bubble glove. You don't want me to spring a serum leak, do you?"

Drea narrowed her eyes. "Aren't you always getting on Marin for forgetting his equipment?"

"Yes, I'm a self-righteous half-light. But if I'm late for the match, Fontaine will disembowel me."

"If I help you, Marin and I have unrestricted gloating rights for your natural life."

Did she have to put it quite like that? I nodded.

Drea stood. The pokers stopped their interviews and watched her. For a breathless moment, I thought she might proclaim me the murderer. Instead she strode over to the bluebird cages, fiddled with the latch, then called, "Why are these locked?"

Axelle asked the question everyone in the room was thinking. "Drea, what in the blank rainbow are you doing?"

For a moment, Drea seemed ready to admit defeat, then her eyes fell on Orie, who was still cowering at her desk.

"Talbot!" she shouted, startling even the pokers. "I told you not to lock those blackened bird cages!" Drea strode across the room, opened Orie's backpack, and dumped everything out onto the floor.

Axelle stood. "*Mademoiselle!*"

Orie had either fallen asleep or was determined to ignore Drea's theatrics, because her head was still buried under her hands.

This clearly irritated Drea because she grabbed Orie's ponytail and pulled her head up. She opened her mouth, but before she could spout any more nonsense about the bird cages, Orie backhanded her across the mouth.

"Girls!" Axelle called as she pushed past the pokers.

Drea shot me a what-are-you-waiting-for look, then removed Orie from her desk with some sort of flying headlock.

Suddenly I remembered why I'd never gotten around to

asking Drea out.

Still, you can't argue with results. Students scrambled out of their seats to watch. Axelle practically knocked kids over in her effort to reach the kicking, clawing brawl on the carpet. I moved to the far side of the room as if horrified by the unladylike display of bloodlust. When I was sure everyone in the room was completely focused on the fight, I slipped behind the pokers and into the hallway.

My first stop was the fanroom where I washed my hands and scrubbed at my cold-blooded-killer shoe. Unfortunately, removing the mud actually accentuated the red stain, which was still vaguely hand-shaped. I once again considered dumping my sneakers in the garbage and going out in my socks but figured that would draw more attention than a faded smudge.

Back in the hall, I made straight for the exit. My original plan to hide out in the fan no longer felt wise. If the pokers noticed me missing from the classroom, it would likely be the first place they'd check. And above all, the idea of getting cornered again terrified me. Even at the risk of being seen, I had to get out in the open where I'd at least have space to run. Worst-case scenario, I could run to the hole in the fence, make my way to the coast, and find a ship headed for the mainland.

When I stepped out onto the sidewalk, it was all I could do to not start my sprint toward the fence. Campus was crawling with men in brown fatigues. The Commissaire had sent reinforcements. I'd never seen so many pokers in one place. The trick would be to act innocent. They had no proof of anything.

I'd barely taken three steps when a short, coffee-skin poker rounded on me. I resisted the urge to run. Innocent people didn't run.

"I'm sorry, 'sieur, but you can't be out here right now."

"I..." All I could think about was the red stain on my shoe. Why was I such a bad liar? "I came out to find my cleats." Idiot! That would only draw attention to my feet. I turned around. "I just remembered they're in my locker." Why hadn't I thought to put them on? I was acting like a Mélangé. Was the green affecting my mind already?

"The school is on lockdown and anyone outside, we're to bring in for questioning."

No. They were not going to trap me again. Time to act Blue.

"For what? I've got a match in an hour."

The poker reached for my arm with his light hand, but I pulled away. "Black off, grasspalm." I started walking. Once I made it through the back fence, I'd lose him in the trees.

"Come in dispatch, oh-six."

"Go ahead, oh-six," the radio crackled.

I picked up my pace. The poker followed.

"Agitated Blue male on the sidewalk near the Athletics Building. Possibly a student. Fits description of late teens. Resisted questioning."

The campus went strangely silent. No wind, no birds. Just the sound of several dozen heads turning toward the Athletics Complex.

Should have stayed in the fan.

Pokers emerged from buildings, others strolled up along the grass. All of them headed straight for me. No way I'd make it to the shade border.

Out of the corner of my eye, I saw one begin to jog.

That did it. I switched directions, turning right into the poker behind me. With a quick shove, I sent him stumbling toward the bushes and I ran for the gym entrance. Once inside, I released the latch that kept the doors unlocked. Hopefully them having to find a key would buy me time to get out the back entrance.

The quickest route was through the basketball court. Unfortunately, it was in use. At least the players were running in the right direction. I joined the sprint toward the far basket and then caught sight of Coach Fontaine lugging the equipment bag out of the locker room. He was headed out the back entrance.

"Where is everybody?" Coach said when he saw me. He

motioned for me to help with the bag. "My assistants were supposed to…" He trailed off when he saw me rummaging through the equipment. "What are you looking for?"

"Just making sure it's all here." I fished out a scrum cap, put it on, and tucked my hair up inside.

Coach gave me a strange look. "Bit excited about the match?"

I nodded and pulled a jersey over my white t-shirt. "Let's get down there."

We had only carried the bag a few steps out the back entrance when a pair of pokers huffed to a stop next to us.

Coach dropped his end of the bag. "What's all this?"

"Murderer on the loose," one of the pokers said. He didn't look much older than I was. The older poker glared at the first one and said, "We don't have all the information. Apparently a royal soldier was attacked by a teenage Blue. 'Sieur, we're gonna have to ask you both to stay where you are."

"You sure it was one of ours?" Coach asked.

The poker cocked his head.

Coach gestured toward the stadium. "Ulfig Prep has been on campus since lunch. I wouldn't put it past them to cause a little trouble."

The pokers looked at each other.

"That's where we're headed." Coach picked up the bag again. "I can introduce you to their coach. Nice lady."

The older poker hesitated, then spoke in a low voice to the younger one. "This could be your chance to prove Whisnant wrong."

"What do I do?"

"Go talk to the Fig coach. See if any of his players left the stadium. I'll stay and watch the door." He handed him a radio. "Any leads at all, call it out on channel two. And don't let the others try to steal the credit. You will make it as a soldier."

We set off for the stadium, the poker trailing behind us. It took all my willpower to keep from glancing down at my shoe. "How long have you been wearing the brown?" I asked in an effort to distract myself.

"A year." He held his radio in front of him like a snake.

I needed to distract him. Put him at ease. "How much does one of those gloves cost?"

He swallowed.

"Bet you have to go through a lot of training, huh?"

The poker glanced at me. "They shock us."

"Really?"

"On the lowest setting. So we know what it feels like." He was loosening up.

"What's your name?"

"Gabe. You?"

I faltered for a moment. Faintaine was listening, so I couldn't very well lie. Would it be suspicious if I didn't answer? I supposed it wasn't a big deal if the poker knew my name. But just in case...

"My best friend calls me Bru-Baby."

Gabe smiled.

Coach Fontaine rolled his eyes, then stumbled. He would've fallen if Gabe hadn't reacted quickly and caught his elbow. Far from being grateful, Coach recoiled and dropped the bag. Gabe looked to me as if waiting for me to explain what had just happened.

"We'll get it, Coach," I said. "Go on ahead and tell them we're coming."

Coach glared at Gabe, clearly relieved to put some distance between himself and the handsy Green.

We picked up the bag. Once Coach was out of earshot, I asked, "So who'd you have to pop at your graduation?"

"Some Red drug dealer."

We passed through a copse of maples and the massive stadium loomed before us. It was the most expensive high school facility on Port. But since Télesphore had a history of producing world-class athletes, the Education Board looked the other way.

"I would kill to play rugby here," Gabe said.

"Can't your school use the pitch?" I asked, knowing the answer.

"We only have individual sports. Table tennis, wrestling. I guess team sports aren't..." he trailed off. A jersey had fallen from the bag, and he stooped to grab it. Next to my foot.

I fell to my knees and dropped the bag. "Let's take a break. Is it true Greens all have to take landscaping courses?"

Before he could answer, his radio crackled to life.

"Attention all points. Squad leaders are holding students in classes a few more minutes. We need all other fires combing the grounds for a newly-identified person of interest. Blue male, crème-skin, approximately sixteen, large build, shoulder-length brown hair, white t-shirt with blue lettering on the front. Last seen entering the Athletic Building. Report any sightings immediately."

The radio went silent. I tensed, ready to sprint.

"Landscaping is optional," Gabe said, still walking. "It's culinary arts that's required."

"Oh." I almost looked down at my chest before I remembered the jersey was hiding the blue Rugby Regional Champs banner on my shirt. I tucked a stray lock of hair under my cap, then picked up the bag of equipment. It seemed heavier somehow.

When we entered the stadium, the poker stared up at the triple-tiered seating levels. "Looks way bigger when it's empty."

Télesphore's official religion was Neocatholicism, but rugby was a close second. It was no wonder they spent several million cuivres to build their place of worship. Although we still had an hour before the match, a few hundred diehard fans dotted the stands.

Coach Fontaine approached, taking care to give the poker a wide berth. Was he scared of the electric glove or the green fire?

"That blonde is the Figgy coach," he said. "She speaks Téle and says she'll answer any questions you have. Now quit prancing around with the equipment." Coach Fontaine grabbed the enormous bag from us and threw it over his shoulder.

Gabe and I exchanged a glance. For a moment, he was almost like any other *mec* my age. If he'd been born into a Blue family, might we have been friends?

"I better help him," I said. "He'll probably give himself a hernia."

"Nice to meet you, Bru-Baby." The poker started to extend his arm, then seemed to think better of it. Had he wanted to clasp my hand? It was such a strange practice, intentionally touching a complete stranger. What if you accidentally touched light palms instead of dark? Still, I was going to be part-Green soon. The reminder filled me with despair, but I knew it would be easier to blend in if I learned the culture.

I offered my dark hand. "You too, Gabe. Good luck finding whomever you're looking for."

After an exceptionally awkward handclasp, the poker set off toward the far end of the field where the Figs ran drills. I followed Coach Fontaine to help him set up the equipment table.

"Wonder what all that nonsense is about," Coach said as he unpacked the first-aid kit.

I made a noncommittal grunt.

He pulled a pair of underwear out of the bag, sniffed them, then threw them in a nearby trash bin. "Biggest game of the year, do they care?"

I couldn't tell if he was talking about the pokers or his players.

"Soldiers are holding the students in class," I said carefully. "In fact, I'm surprised the soldiers let all these people—"

That's when I noticed the open gate.

Blue Stadium sat at the edge of campus, and the main entrance opened directly onto Rue Principale. It was a straight shot to freedom.

Coach began talking game plans, but I wasn't listening. I couldn't tear my eyes from that section of the street. Had the pokers forgotten to lock down this end of campus?

"I'm gonna fill the bottles." I grabbed the crate of water containers and casually walked toward the fountain. Did I just say *gonna*? The stress was affecting my ability to string words together. I glanced back. Coach was wrestling shoulder pads out of the equipment bag. I passed the fountain.

In my peripheral vision—thank you, scrum cap—I saw Gabe step away from the Ulfish coach and move toward the eyefall entrance. What was he...

Two more pokers had arrived from upper campus.

Walk slowly. Don't draw attention. The open gate somehow got farther away with each step I took. The stench of grass threatened to suffocate me.

Any minute, Coach would ask where I was going. The pokers would noticed the open gate. They would see the approximately sixteen, large-build male walking directly toward the only exit. My hand grew hot.

Each new moment of silence felt like a gift from the Créateur. When I was ten yards from freedom, a group of medical apprentices sauntered through the street entrance, still wearing their scrubs and stethoscopes. I set down the crate and knelt as if tying my shoe. One of them made a joke about what Green waiters would do for a tip.

Would the students recognize me? I used to love running into the doctors-in-training at the hospital. Now they were just another reminder of the life I would never get back. I pretended to count the water bottles as they passed.

The laughter faded. Go.

Back on my feet and walking faster now. I'd forgotten the crate. Five yards. Three more steps and the grass turned to gravel. No one moved to block my exit. I could see individual cobblestones in the street.

"Bruno!"

My head snapped up, and I peered back across the field. There, in the center of the lower section with a Blue woman I didn't recognize, sat my grandmother.

She waved her fire. "Up here. Where are you running off

to?"

I hesitated. As much as I wanted to tell her everything, now was definitely not the time. She'd make a big scene and attract the attention of the three pokers at the other end of the stadium. This was my only chance to get out.

I glanced around as if I couldn't tell who'd called me, then resumed my slow-motion dash for safety.

"Bruno André Nazaire! Get up here—I have someone I want you to meet!"

Okay, so she was going to make a scene anyway. And now that everyone in the stadium was looking at me, it probably wouldn't be a good idea to waltz out the main gate in my rugby gear. Especially since she'd kindly shouted my identity to all of Télesphore.

I waved to let Granny know she could stop screaming and started toward her.

Maybe I could casually mention there had been an emergency and ask her to leave quietly with me. Less conspicuous than leaving alone. Out of the corner of my eye, I saw the trio of brown uniforms approach Coach Fontaine on the pitch.

I climbed the stairs and braced myself for a list of inconvenient questions. Instead Granny Jade beamed at me. It was impossible for me to think of her as old. When most people entered their seventies, they started a sliding plummet toward disorientation and frantic vanity. But Granny had only gotten sharper and classier. Her minimal make-up and wavy chin-length silver hair made her seem approachable, almost casual. But each word and gesture betrayed her royal blood.

"Bruno, this is Madame Blanc. She is on the Education Board."

I showed my fire and tried not to glance back toward the pokers. "Good afternoon."

"It is a pleasure, Bruno." The white-haired woman seemed about fifty, but it was impossible to tell because of her sloppy facelift.

Granny winked at me. "We met at the jewelers and got

talking about scholarships." She raised her eyebrows at the last word.

Madame Blanc patted at her hair. "Technically, I'm not in charge of sports scholarships, but I often make suggestions to those who are. Your grandmother said you'd like to go to Tjarda for your apprenticeship."

I nodded, trying to think of an excuse to leave. Who knows how much longer I had before my shade changed? "Actually, I'm not feeling—"

"Oh!" Granny said. She pulled a bubble glove out of the pocket of her business suit. "Found this on your dresser. Safety first."

It was my old one, but right now it was exactly what I needed. A way to hide my soon-to-be hideous fire. I pulled the glove on backward so the vinyl showed the back of my light hand instead of my glowing palm.

"I think it goes the other way," Madam Blanc said with a confused expression.

"The padding hurts my fire," I said. "Getting over an infection."

Granny narrowed her eyes but didn't say anything about my lie.

"The whole point," Madam Blanc said, "is to cushion your —"

"Why are you wearing that ridiculous headgear?" Granny said, her tone a little too bright. Before I could stop her, she pulled off my scrum cap. The rubber band broke, sending my hair cascading around my shoulders. "Didn't I tell you, Angélique? He's always bugging me to let him cut it, but it's much too pretty."

Thankfully Madame Blanc wasn't paying attention. "What are those soldiers doing on the playing field?"

I took the scrum cap from Granny, pulled it back on, and tried to tuck my hair up into it.

"Don't be silly, Bruno. Long hair suits you."

"Granny, I think I ate something—"

"You there!" yelled Madame Blanc, suddenly on her feet. "Come here!"

I flinched. One of the pokers bounded up the steps toward us.

"Why are you fraternizing with the Blue players? You should be at your posts. When Whisnant hears about this—"

"All royal soldiers are to aid in the search, Madame. Sergent Whisnant's orders."

"What search?" Madame Blanc pulled the poker down a few steps and their conversation grew quieter.

I crouched in front of Granny. "There's not much time. I need—"

"Shh, I'm trying to hear what he's saying."

"He's saying a Blue student killed a poker, and the entire royal army is hunting for him."

Granny shot me a sideways look. "And how do you know all this?"

For a moment, I stared at her turquoise bracelet, unable to speak. Granny lifted my head and looked into my face. Her eyes were red, but her expression was hard as granite. "What happened?"

"An accident," I whispered. "To save a Blue-Green boy. He painted me, and they were going to kill him if I didn't—"

"He what?" Granny grabbed my hand and examined it.

"In a couple of hours, I'll be Mélangé."

Granny put a shaky hand to her mouth.

"I'll figure this out, Gran. I just need to get out of here. Tell everyone I went home sick, I'll try to meet you—"

Madame Blanc stomped back up the steps. "I've never seen such incompetence."

I feigned interest in the bleachers behind me.

"What is it?" Granny asked. She sounded surprisingly composed considering she'd just been told her only grandchild was wanted for murder.

"Oh, they tried to lock down the school while they searched for some troublemaker. I don't care what the boy did, they can't keep the entire Blue student body against their will. Can you imagine the calls I'd get from parents?"

I felt an urge to kiss the woman on her collagen-filled lips.

"Honestly, Jade—they have a description of the student. I told them to set up at the exits and watch for him. It's not fire surgery."

My affectionate impulse faded. I looked toward the street. The three pokers had already taken up positions in front of the gate. Could I get past them?

"By the Créateur's light," Madam Blanc said, "what's wrong, blueberry?"

With a start, I realized she was talking to me. "I... "

"Girl trouble," Granny said. "But once he wins this match"—she gave me a pointed look—"the ladies will be all over you again and things will be back to normal." She emphasized "normal".

Was she telling me to act like nothing happened?

"Go get warmed up," Granny said. "And make sure the game doesn't drag on. I've got a hair appointment."

Hair appointment? Mom always cut Granny's hair, and she was in Deatherage with Dad. Obviously Granny was hoping I'd win before my shade changed.

My legs felt like lead as I started down the steps. Granny was probably right—leaving now would be too obvious. I'd be the only one moving that direction.

I still had my cap and jersey disguise. At this point acting normal was probably my best course of action.

And for Bruno Nazaire, normal meant playing rugby.

By the time our entire team made it down from campus, the stadium had filled and I could no longer see Granny. Hopefully she'd gone to call Dad.

"Nazaire! You injured?"

I dropped the alcohol wipe on the grass. "No, 'sieur."

"Then quit daydreaming and boot up!"

I shoved the first aid kit under the equipment table. My shoe looked better, but a red stain would be the least of my worries if I was the only mec on the field without cleats.

The loud speaker crackled to life, and the Dom of Diplomacy welcomed the visiting team. I stood.

Earlier I'd made the mistake of asking the first forward to grab my backpack from the lockers. Roy scoffed at my request, then realized I was wearing his best scrum cap and tried to rip it off. Luckily I won the scuffle, and he went to find another cap. The rest of the team seemed to buy the story that I was having a bad hair day and needed to keep my head covered. When they asked about the backward bubble glove I changed the subject. Marin's absence provided a perfect distraction. No one had seen him since before the lockdown. Fontaine was chewing rocks.

Immediately after Dom Bush's welcome came a scratchy recording of the Ulfish national anthem. The Figs scrambled to form a line on the pitch, obviously annoyed at the short warning. Their equipment still lay scattered near the perimeter wall.

An extra pair of cleats poked out of someone's duffel bag. My chest tightened. It wouldn't be stealing. I was giving someone an opportunity to save a life.

While the Ulfish players pointed fires toward their flag, I jogged over and knelt by the duffel as if it were my own. I grabbed the cleats. Before I could make my retreat, a thought occurred to me. This was also a chance to get rid of some evidence.

"WHERE'S NAZAIRE?" Coach screamed.

Crêpes. I yanked off my sneakers, shoved them deep into the bag, and ran.

"Why are you prancing around in your socks like a Mélangé?" Coach yelled when he saw me. "Get those boots on and get in line!"

Mélangé? I glanced at my inverted bubble glove to make sure my light wasn't showing. Was I still blue underneath? How long since Baptiste had painted me? It felt like a week.

During the Hymn to Télesphore, I discovered the cleats were two sizes too small. Still, I managed to cram them on in a semi-dignified manner, earning only a brief glare from Coach. As the anthem ended, Marin appeared, hair tousled, and took his position for the kick off. The whistle blew, and thirty teenage boys began to make use of their testosterone.

I tried to get my head in the game. I really did. But whether it was the pain in my feet or the pokers that seemed to be multiplying on the sidelines, I was definitely not playing my best. When one of the Ulfish players rolled an ankle twenty minutes into the game, I was ready for a break. I already had my cleats off and was trying to rub feeling into my toes when Marin approached with a water bottle.

"What's the problem, Nazaire?"

"Foot cramps."

"I meant with your game."

I mumbled something incoherent.

"Bru-ster, you gotta step it up. Coach is fixing to take you out. And Principal Boudreaux has been screaming about tardy detentions?"

I glanced at the street exit. The guards had gone from three to six and they'd pulled Sergent Whisnant's brown patrol car into the gate, limiting the foot traffic to single file. They must know I was here somewhere. They were tightening their net. How had they figured it out? Had Orie finally cracked? Or maybe Axelle noticed I was missing and told the pokers.

The ref blew his whistle, indicating the injured player had been replaced and Ulfig Prep was ready for the scrum. I crammed my feet back into the tiny cleats and followed Marin to take my place on the front line.

"My shoe is wearing you."

It was the Ulfish scrum-half who had spoken. He stood to the side, waiting to toss the ball into the opening between teams. Was it the same kid who had tried to react with me in the Gardens? I tucked the hair up out of my eyes as if I hadn't heard him.

"Is thanks gift then," he said. "Keep you."

I grimaced then nodded. "Tumich. Forgot mine."

Next to me, Marin cocked his head. "You stole that kid's boots? What is going on with you today?"

"Head in the game, Nazaire!" Coach called from the sidelines. I looked toward him and froze.

A short, coffee-skin Green stood next to Coach Fontaine. It was the poker I'd shoved off the sidewalk. He said something to Coach, then pointed directly at me.

The strength left my legs, and I grabbed Marin's arm for support.

"You okay? Why you suddenly scared of the... " Marin trailed off as comprehension dawned on his face. "You're the reason they're watching the exits."

I swallowed.

"Bru. Tell me what really happened at the gardens this morning."

I shook my head, but before I could explain about the murder, another face appeared and startled me.

"You take punishment with helping us," the skinny scrum-half said. "We can talk them for you."

"It's too late," I said. "Should have run when I had the chance."

"Go now," Marin said. "I'll take off my shirt and do cartwheels or something."

I managed a sad smile. I would miss Marin most of all. I wiped my eyes with my forearm before anyone could see. "Let's just play until they stop us."

"Crouch," the ref called.

I bent over and locked shoulders with my teammates, forming a wall of backs. Marin whispered something. I realized he was still talking to the Ulfish scrum-half. And one of their forwards? In fact, the entire Ulfish scrum seemed abuzz with chatter.

"Hold," the ref called.

We reached out and touched the forwards of Ulfig Prep. The Fig in front of me grinned. But not in an I'm-gonna-cream-you sort of way. His smile seemed almost comradely.

"Listen up, TC," Marin said. "Our boy has gotten himself in trouble."

"What, he react with a Dom's daughter?"

"This is serious, Roy," Marin said. "The Figs have a plan to bust Bruno out of here."

"The Figs?!" someone said from our back row.

A couple of the Ulfish players laughed.

"Just follow my lead," Marin said. "This isn't about the score anymore. It's about protecting one of our own."

I shook my head. "It's not worth the risk, if you—"

"Don't worry, Nazaire," Roy said. "We got your back."

"Wait, what's going on?" someone called from the back row.

This was a mistake. They didn't understand what they were getting into.

"Engage!"

Bodies slammed into each other. Cleats tore at the grass. The scrum-half tossed the ball directly to Marin. Instead of breaking apart, the scrum opened on one side and stretched into a single oblong wall of players, still attached at the shoulders but now all facing the same direction.

Toward the street.

Marin held the ball aloft like a banner and screamed, "Charge!"

CHAPTER SIX

HALF NAKED

Marin wasn't the rugby captain. He wasn't even a very good forward. But he made up for it with what Coach called psychotic tenacity. That's probably what made him so easy to follow. We all knew that even if the Fig's half-baked break out plan was destined for failure, it would at least be spectacular.

So we followed him.

The cheering faded until only the announcer's voice remained, and even he was having trouble making sense of the traveling scrummage. A referee watched us pass, whistle halfway to his mouth as if trying to figure out which team to penalize.

Coach Fontaine's reaction was slightly less docile. "What in the black rainbow are you doing?" he screamed from the sidelines. "This isn't synchronized swimming!"

On both sides, Figs and Télesphorians whooped and laughed as they ran. There was something oddly fulfilling about breaking the rules together. Maybe that's why the Feu Noir had grown so quickly in the Red slums.

The whistles finally sounded as we ran out of bounds. Spectators on the sidelines scrambled to move equipment and chairs. The scrum began to separate. The person next to me was being pulled darkways. This wasn't going to work.

"Trash can ahead," Marin called. "Move lightward. Forwards get ready to block."

Block what? We were headed directly for the brown vehicle. It didn't matter how fast we ran, we weren't going to move that car. Several yards in front of the vehicle, a handful of pokers stood gawking as if they hadn't yet realized what was going on.

One of the Figs shouted something in Ulfish.

Marin slowed a bit, allowing the group to reform and the blockers to get in front, then the entire team put on a burst of speed toward the exit. Guttural war cries erupted around me, and I found myself screaming along with them. It felt like winning the world cup. No, it felt like stealing the world cup and getting away with it.

"Brace for impact!" Marin yelled. Each of us tightened his hold on the person next to us and lowered our head. At that moment, I felt invincible.

This is what it meant to be Blue.

A few of the pokers shouted orders. Some fiddled with their watches, but there was no time. The wall of thirty sprinting teenagers smashed through them like a wrecking ball.

The stands roared to life. For nearly a decade, Ville Bleu had endured Whisnant's Green peacekeepers. Whether feared, hated, or even supported by the people, something about seeing them bowled over by a bunch of boys seemed to inspire a rush of Blue pride.

Now only the car blocked the path through the gate. Were we all going to squeeze through single file? The wall of boys slowed. Before I could ask what the plan was, Marin dashed in front of the group, jumped onto the hood of the car, and vaulted over the top.

Most of the team seemed as confused as I was, but still we cheered when Marin landed on the sidewalk and took off down Main Street, the ball tucked under his arm.

The kid was perfect for Drea. They were both slightly insane but in the best way possible.

One poker scrambled over the car in pursuit. A dozen others clambered to their scooters or piled into the vehicle. Once the gate was unblocked and most of the pokers had set off after Marin, the players and spectators spilled out onto the street to watch the chase.

Only then did I realize what Marin had done. I was outside and no one was paying any attention to me. Hopefully he wouldn't get into too much trouble. He hadn't technically done anything wrong, but I had a feeling Sergent Whisnant wouldn't appreciate his sense of humor.

I took off my jersey and cap and pushed them at Roy. "Can you take care of these?"

He grinned. "You were right about the bad hair day."

I did a quick scan for pokers. Only a couple had stayed, and they seemed busy dealing with the crowd. Panicked foreigners trying to get an explanation, angry parents wanting to know what the Dominateur had against high school rugby.

Roy took the equipment and gave me a slap on the rear. "Get lost, brother."

With my heart thumping out of my chest, I went for a little stroll down the street—in the opposite direction Marin had gone.

No one stopped me. No one said, "Hey, there goes a Blue male with long brown hair and blue lettering on his shirt!"

All the same, as soon as I was out of sight of the crowd, I took a couple random turns and found a phone booth to hide in. I sat on the floor and ripped off my bubble glove.

Thank the Créateur. For the time being, I was still Blue.

Alone at last, I doubled over and let the emotion of the last few hours pour out of me. After a few minutes of hyperventilating into my fire, my stream of panicked thoughts slowed and I was able to introduce a few of the more rational kind.

Safe. I was safe. And for the moment—free—but it wouldn't be long before they discovered Marin wasn't the one they wanted. Where could I go? Not home. Even if Axelle hadn't told the pokers my name, Coach probably would have. The location of Chateau Nazaire wasn't exactly a secret.

The safest bet would be to get out of the area—the farther

the better. But first, I was going to have to do something about that physical description.

As much as I hated it, I'd have to leave the glove. Outside the stadium, a backward bubble glove would be even more suspicious. Besides, I had to avoid anything that associated me with rugby. But there was still the problem of my long hair and blue lettering.

I removed the shirt and ripped off both sleeves. One I tore into a single long strip, which I used to tie my hair back at the nape of my neck. The other I kept whole and slipped over my hair like a wide headband, taking care to hide my ponytail up inside. I rolled up the shirt and tucked half into the back of my shorts. As an afterthought I unscrewed the studs from my cleats.

This would work. People jogged the streets all the time. Without my shirt and hair to give me away, I'd blend right in.

I stood. A pair of senior citizens stumbled to a stop outside the booth. The man switched places with his female companion as if to shield her from my partial nudity. I smiled, picked up the receiver, and held it to my ear, as if it were perfectly normal to talk on the phone half-naked.

After the couple crossed to the other side of the street, I emerged from the booth and set off at a jog for Rue Principale. Even without the studs, the cleats still made a lot of noise, but I found if I rolled my foot it sounded less like I was tap dancing.

Once back on Principale, I ran along the Ville Bleu side, occasionally glancing down at my fire to make sure it hadn't changed. I welcomed the warm rays of the celestial eye on my shoulders and back. The sweatier I became, the more natural I'd look. People who saw me would think, "That mec must have been jogging for hours," instead of, "What's that kid running from?"

In front of a nail salon, a group of Blue women stopped their conversation as I passed. Four sets of eyes followed me, their faces expressionless.

My mouth went dry. Did they recognize me? Had the

pokers already circulated a suspect drawing?

I was preparing to dart down a side street when I heard laughter and caught the tail end of a comment about husband trade-ins. It was safe to say they didn't know I was in high school. That was comforting in a disturbing sort of way.

Although I hadn't changed shade yet, I crossed to the Green side of the street. A Blue running in Hameau Vert was easier to overlook than a Mélangé running on the Blue side.

I'd only gone a block when a Green female police officer pulled behind me on a bicycle. Whatever sense of security I'd gained from putting a sleeve on my head vanished.

Officers reported to the Police Chief rather than Whisnant and were usually out of the loop when it came to royal business. But if Whisnant was desperate to track me down, he might have recruited them in the search. Did that mean the Dominateur was joining in the hunt as well? Had they informed the Commissaire? Would Livius know I was the same boy whom he spoke to in the gardens? No, that was impossible. And I wasn't going to give him the opportunity to figure it out.

I picked up the pace and turned down a random street. The policewoman followed. "Hey you, stop!" she called.

I turned another corner and sprinted. I couldn't outrun a bike for long, but if I got to Green Park, maybe I could lose her in the vegetation.

I fell into rugby mode and began taking corners on impulse. The streets on this side were narrower and much more twisty than in Ville Bleu—perfect for losing a pursuer.

Also for getting lost.

With each new turn, I grew more confused, and the squeaking of the bike chain grew louder. My feet were numb from lack of circulation, and my lungs felt like I'd inhaled sand. I slowed to get my bearings. The park should be close. One more turn ought to do it. I forced my legs to pump faster and skidded around the corner.

Son of a Violet. Dead end.

The officer screeched to a stop behind me and dismounted. I turned to face her. She was small. I could get past her as long as she didn't pull her weapon. Compared to the soldier's gloves, the police tranq guns were a bit of a joke, but they did have the range advantage.

Who was I kidding? Even weaponless, she could probably take me down. At this point, it was all I could do to keep from falling over.

She took a few steps toward me. "Blank, you're fast."

I stared at her, taking in ragged breaths. Was she proud of herself for cornering the Blue Campus murderer?

She held up a white shirt. "You dropped this a couple blocks back. I tried to get your attention, but…"

I waited. No way she'd been chasing me to give me back my shirt. It made no sense. She must have known who I was. This was a ruse to throw me off. Or a distraction while she waited for back up.

She held the shirt out to me.

I took it. "Thanks. I guess I was in my own little world."

"I'm Officer DuPont, by the way." She pushed her stringy, brown hair back from her face. She was probably in her early twenties with a wide nose and acne-scarred cheeks.

"Benoit," I said. "I'd better go. Gotta keep my heart rate up."

"What are you doing on this side, Benoit?"

"I didn't realize I wasn't allowed—"

"Oh, no, you're fine. It's just that a Blue in Hameau Vert is about as common as a Red swim team." She gave me an awkward grin.

Either she was an incredible actress or she had no idea who I was. Why in the rainbow would anybody chase someone across town to return a ripped shirt?

Then I noticed her eyes drift to my chest. I was glad my face was already hot from running. If this lady had any idea how old I was…

It took all my willpower not to fold my arms in front of

me.

"I wanted to run through Green Park," I said, taking a step back. "Guess I got a little lost."

Officer DuPont, or Sheri, as she insisted I call her, turned out to be the extra-helpful sort. Not only did she tell me twice how to get to Green Park, she then proceeded to escort me in case I got lost again.

The walk was torture. In addition to the three hundred personal questions I had to invent answers to, each step felt like bolts were being screwed into my feet. I did my best to walk normally and not draw attention to the fact that I had gone jogging in rugby cleats. Details like that tend to stick in people's heads.

Once Sheri finished the family questions—making sure to verify I was single—she moved on to my occupation. I told her I worked at the hospital. She asked a lot of detailed questions which I was able to answer thanks to Dad constantly breaking patient confidentiality.

When we arrived at Green Park, Sheri wished me luck, paused just long enough to be awkward, and hopped back on her bike.

The first thing I did was take off my shoes and get the blood recirculating in my feet. Then I put my shirt on inside-out. Remarkably, I was still Blue. Until it changed, I'd look out of place. I needed somewhere to hide.

Although the vegetation in Green Park seemed sparse and unkempt compared to Blue Gardens, it also felt homier. Maybe because the pines reminded me of decorating the tree for Naissance. Or maybe because the park was clearly designed for kids—lots of slides and things to climb on. In the gardens, the main activities were chess and Firearchy.

After a brief internal debate, I dropped the cleats in a trash barrel. I'd probably regret the decision later, but for now, all I felt was relief at never having to pry them on again.

I stood there, thinking. The eye was already halfway behind Tremper Mountain. Soon darkness would make it harder for people to recognize me. I wished my shorts were a little thicker so my light didn't shine through the pocket. I decided to ditch the socks as well. Kids went barefoot all the time. Nobody wore just their socks to the park.

I walked to an unused play structure and hid in the tube slide. It wasn't exactly comfortable being wedged sideways, but at least with my fire pressed against my stomach, I'd be completely invisible.

It worked perfectly—until a toddler decided she wanted to go down the slide. The girl appeared at the circular opening and shone her Green light in my eyes. From the expression on her face, she knew there was a problem but hadn't yet worked out how to fix it.

"Go play somewhere else, okay? This slide is broken."

The girl began to cry.

A face appeared at the bottom of the slide. An adult face.

"What are you doing in there?" the woman said. "What did you do to my daughter?"

"Nothing." I took the slide to the bottom, feeling like a complete idiot.

The Green woman had already collected the girl and watched me as if waiting for an attack.

My fire hand ached from pressing it into my stomach. "I'm sorry, I was just looking for a place to be alone."

"Right. Hiding in a toddler playground Show me your

fire."

"It's okay, I'm leaving."

"Show me your fire!" she screamed.

I yanked the hand from my stomach.

It had happened.

For nearly three hours, I'd expected this. I had imagined what it would look like a hundred times. I'd almost convinced myself that everything was going to work out. But seeing my teal fire was something I never could have prepared for. It was the difference between knowing I was going for surgery and watching the doctor open me up.

The woman backed away with her daughter. "Please don't report me for yelling. I thought you'd snuck across the river."

Somewhere in the distance, an animal began a high-pitched howl. My scalp tingled, and I started to lose feeling in my lips.

The woman said something else, then wandered off with her baby.

The park grew quiet—except for that distant keening. I realized I was still staring at the light on the end of my arm, trying to figure out how someone else's fire had gotten there. I sat in the sand, head between my knees. I pocketed my fire. Then took it out. No reason to hide it now. I belonged here.

My dizziness grew worse, so I rolled onto my back. But another glance at my fire brought on a sudden wave of nausea. I had to focus on something else. I took a deep breath. This close to Taudis Rouge, I could smell the river. An image of Dad's face swam into view. His eyes reflecting blue-green light, his lips twisted in disgust. I heaved.

Stop thinking. Listen. Focus.

The repeated howls sounded like a dog. At times it almost seemed to evolve into language. What was making that noise? The more I listened the more it sounded human.

"Ayroo." A pause. "Ayroooo!"

Sounded almost like they were saying Ro.

It was the thought of my dead baby brother that pulled me out of my stupor. I was still alive. Get a grip. Green or not, it was time to get off the ground.

I pushed myself to a kneeling position, then slowly stood up. The sky had faded from white to gray—only minutes until dark. Best time of day to go unnoticed. Half-light, Granny called it. When the dying light made it hard to pick out faces, but it wasn't yet dark enough for fires to stand out.

Despite Whisnant's many resources, he hadn't found me. The best part was that the pokers wouldn't be looking for me on the Green side. They didn't know anything about Baptiste or my shade change. No one did. Well, unless there really was someone who had orchestrated the whole painting thing.

What had Baptiste called him? Eye something or other?

"Aye, aye, aye, aye. Roo, roo, roo, roo. Ayroooooooooo-ooo!"

Would that person just shut up?!

"Ayro, Ayro, Ay—"

"Shut up!" a second, deeper voice shouted.

Thank you!

I needed to find a payphone to call Granny. There should be some public phones along one of the main streets. I didn't have any coins, but she'd accept the charges. I started toward downtown Hameau Vert.

"Finally!" the wolf child cried out. "The arcade is probably closed!"

It sounded like a screechy little girl. It would serve her right if someone reported her for disturbing the peace.

"I said shut your mouth," yelled the second voice. "You want the whole—"

"Why'd you bring Baptiste?"

I froze mid-step.

CHAPTER SEVEN

POISONOUS

I n four words the obscenely annoying girl became my new favorite person. Forget finding a phone. If her Baptiste was my Baptiste, I was finally about to get some important questions answered.

I jogged in the general direction of the shouted conversation. Predictably, the voices fell silent as soon as I tried to follow them. At least I didn't have to worry about looking suspicious in bare feet. The park was deserted. Did Hameau Vert really have twice the population of Ville Bleu? I hadn't seen a single fire since the playground-lady. Maybe the quiet rules also came with a curfew.

At the edge of the park, the pines parted to reveal a weathered stone arch. I'd seen Pont en Pierre plenty of times from my roof, but up close, the bridge didn't seem quite real—for one thing, it looked jarringly out of place next to the run-down buildings across the river. As if someone had snatched the enormous structure from the grounds of a Shandezian castle and plopped it unceremoniously between the the two poorest sections of Télesphore. At the highest point of the arch glowed a single Orange fire. My stomach flipped. Such an unnatural shade.

At the foot of the bridge on the Green side, two small figures stood under the golden light of an emergency beacon. I immediately recognized the squat form of Baptiste. The other was a boy, maybe three or four years younger than myself. Since I was close enough to hear them, I sat on a nearby bench and pretended to tie my shoe-less foot.

"Go home, Jeannette," the older boy said. "I need the bridge."

The Orange light moved. "You said—"

"Now." The boy picked up the emergency phone. "Or I'll report you off sides without an escort."

"So Baptiste is your new friend?" asked the Orange wolf-child.

He put the receiver to his ear. "Hello? I need police at Pont en Pierre."

"Fine!" The orange light bobbed, then disappeared down the Red side. But she didn't go quietly. I caught several words I'd seen written on fanroom stalls, and a few I didn't even recognize.

The girl must have been older than I'd thought—maybe eight or nine. I almost felt sorry for her. But even stronger than my twinge of sympathy was an underlying sense of vertigo when I watched her. Was it because of her shade? I'd often seen Mélangé through the barrier fence. The exotic colors at the Académie had always seemed interesting and even funny. But it was different seeing one up close, hearing her speak—made it harder to think of her as a novelty.

The little mec hung up the phone without a word of explanation to the police. He'd probably held down the switch-hook so it never connected. The two boys started up the side of the bridge, and I noticed Baptiste's fire. A little bluer than I remembered. My blue. My light hand grew hot, and I breathed through the rush of anger. Calm down. Baptiste had been manipulated, and unless I was way off, the Créateur had miraculously led me to the one responsible.

The older kid pushed Baptiste forward, and I caught a glimpse of his light. Deep turquoise. What in the rainbow? Not only was it the brightest fire I'd ever seen, the shade was an even mix of blue and green. A Green would have to react with a half-dozen Blues to get that shade. A serial painter?

Why would he need the bridge so badly he'd risk creating a scene? Was he looking for a secluded place to paint Baptiste?

Despite receiving the occasional push, Baptiste didn't seem like a prisoner. He'd had several opportunities to make a run for it.

Were they going into Taudis Rouge for some reason?

No. Even Mélangé weren't that stupid.

The only other explanation was that the Turquoise needed to have an important conversation and didn't want to take the slightest chance of being overheard. Which was exactly why I had to get up there. Before I accused strangers of staging elaborate schemes to ruin my life, I needed evidence.

I stood as if finally done tying my shoe and walked slowly upriver. Just an evening stroll toward the bridge.

Following the boys up the bridge wouldn't work. The bright light of the beacon would announce my coming well before I could get close enough to hear much. I could sprint and take the chance they wouldn't notice me, but if I lost the gamble, it could mean losing my proof and any chance of fixing this mess. After all, it was this Turquoise that was ultimately responsible for the poker's death. Once I knew the details, Dad would at least have something to work with. He could pull some strings, call in some favors, and make sure the Turquoise took the heat.

Actually, maybe my first priority should be to find a payphone. Granny would have contacted my parents by now. It had been hours since she last saw me. All of them would be fit to spring a leak.

But the coincidence of hearing Baptiste's name shouted across Hameau Vert wouldn't happen twice. This was clearly a path ordained by the Créateur. I had to follow it through, which meant I'd have to swim across the river, come up the Red side.

Enough musing. If I didn't get up there quickly their secret conversation would be over.

Before I could lose my nerve, I pocketed my fire and waded into the water.

Holy crêpes that was cold.

Was this a good idea?

Yes. Man up. One-handed breaststroke would be difficult but not impossible. I steeled myself to leap into the rapids but paused. On the far side, a faint orange glow illuminated a tangle of tall weeds. The girl was doing a little surveillance of her own. If I splashed out of the river and tried to climb the bridge, she'd notice me for sure. I couldn't take the chance that she'd alert the boys. That left only one route to the top of the bridge.

Straight up.

To be fair, I hadn't eaten anything since lunch, and my brain had gone a bit soft. It also didn't help that I'd wanted to climb the cobblestone supports from the moment I'd first seen the bridge through my bedroom window. Lastly, the Créateur of Heaven and Port was obviously on my side, so scaling a fifty-foot vertical pillar seemed perfectly logical.

Light still pocketed, I crept under the muddy underside of the bridge. It smelled slightly rancid like decomposing vegetation. I'd planned to climb the upriver side of the pillar to avoid being seen by the Orange, but my light would still draw attention from the surrounding homes—especially if it was moving steadily up the side of a national landmark.

I pulled off my shirt and secured it around my light. A little bulky, but I still had use of my fingers. More importantly, my fire was totally concealed.

I sprinted toward the water and leaped for the first concrete base.

Although I made it—barely—I was grateful for the lack of witnesses. I dabbed at my now bloody shin with my wrapped hand, then stood and touched the pillar.

The cobblestones provided decent handholds. I climbed. The increased heat of my fire filled my limbs with energy and washed away the pain of my scraped leg. The jagged crevices bit into the soft flesh of my toes, but I was grateful for the extra traction of bare feet. Around the halfway mark, my light hand began to ache. The pain in my fingers and toes became harder to ignore. Still, I continued upward. After a few more yards my fire went tingly. My hand began to cool and reality set in. I suddenly felt like I was doing pushups on a greased tightrope.

What remained of my sympathy for the Orange girl evaporated. Now the only sentiment running through my head—besides ouch—was a steady hatred for Mélangé in general. I'd known three so far. The one that painted me, the one who put him up to it, and the one who didn't go home when she was told so I could take the blackened bridge like a normal person.

"...be such a Violet," came a voice. The Turquoise mec?

I listened but couldn't make out much over the rushing water. A little higher. I could do this. Pain now is power tomorrow. The phrase seemed just as ridiculous when Coach said it during practice. But it was either keep climbing or fall.

Step. Step. Hand.

Still ten feet from the top. I glanced down. Fifty feet seemed a lot higher when looking from this direction. Would I hit water or concrete?

"Aro, you promised!" came Baptiste's voice. "R and S volumes contain a lot of important information."

"If you want the truth, I threw your books in the garbage the first day I took them. I thought you'd be smart enough to check the bin before you left school—guess not."

Their voices were so clear, I was worried they'd hear my gasping for breath. All I had to do was hold on long enough to find out what they were talking about, then launch myself far enough from the pillar to avoid a messy landing.

"How about it?" came Aro's voice. "I swear I'll leave you alone forever."

"Why do you want me to do it so badly?" Baptiste had great grammar for someone his age.

"I told you," Aro said. "It's like a final test. To prove you're brave enough to be the boss of yourself. Otherwise, I'll have to keep being your boss."

"I don't swim well."

"You're also fat and stupid. I'm surprised your parents

haven't dropped you off the bridge already."

My stomach tightened. Whatever I'd been expecting, it wasn't this. I ignored the urge to leap over the railing and throttle the kid. If I twitched a muscle, I would lose my hold on the pillar. As it was, I probably only had a few more seconds. Why weren't they talking about me? Had Baptiste lied about Aro's involvement?

"My mom left when I was little," Baptiste said.

"Big surprise. Bet fifty cuivres she took one look at you and bolted."

"Will you really leave me alone if I jump?"

"Only if you don't come up again. What do you have to lose? All your friends? Don't make me laugh."

Baptiste's sob twisted my chest into a knot, and I nearly lost my footing.

"They're going to kill you anyway when they find you. It's because of you that the poker's dead. They'll probably cut off your body parts one by one and feed them to the Commissaire's dogs."

FINALLY!

"But it's not my fault. You didn't tell me about the glove. I only did what you said."

"You think they'll care that someone told you to do it? You crossed the boundary. You painted a Blue and helped kill a Poker. That's all that matters."

"I'm not going to jump."

"Your choice. But I'll steal the rest of your encyclopedias. I'll burn every last one of them. I'll tell everyone that you peek under the boys' stalls when they're -"

"You promised you would stop telling lies about me if I shook hands with that older boy."

"How do I know you really did it?"

"Look at my fire!"

"You could've reacted with anybody."

"It was him! His name was Brutus Nazeer."

Brutus? I saved his life and he couldn't remember my

name?

"What did he look like?"

Baptiste went quiet for a moment. "He was really big with long hair."

I slipped a few inches. The pain in my hands jumped from agonizing to excruciating.

"Was he full of himself?"

"He seemed nice to me. I wish you would've told me the glove was broken. Did you take out the alloy plate?"

Things were making more sense now. Baptiste was probably the only one who knew Aro was responsible. No more Baptiste meant Aro's secret was safe.

Except now I knew his secret too.

I smiled.

Then all my muscles gave out at once. I kicked at the pillar and threw myself backward into space.

I had planned to shout something enigmatic and inspirational as I fell. Something that would let Baptiste know he wasn't alone, and at the same time give Aro nightmares for the rest of his life.

Hopefully my high-pitched scream of terror had the desired effect.

CHAPTER EIGHT

A WARM WELCOME

Weightlessness enveloped me like a plastic bag. The deafening rush of air seemed to tighten around me, suffocating my scream.

Then I hit.

For a split-second I thought I'd landed on cement, then the world went soft and cold around me. What followed was a wet blur. I'm pretty sure I drowned at least once. Somehow I ended up tangled in the reeds on the shore, coughing up my innards.

When my burning lungs finally stopped trying to expel water, I collapsed into the mud.

"He'll be fine," came a distant female voice. "If your father..."

I managed to lift a hand. "Help," I croaked. But the voice faded, leaving only the babble of water, and the occasional amorous frog.

Had I passed out? How had I made it to shore? Pieces of memory bubbled to the surface but refused to coalesce. Cold darkness. Stars. An arm tight around my neck. A blinding green light—that became yellow? Clearly I had drunk too much river water. And clearly this river was not meant for swimming. Especially not with a shirt wrapped around my hand.

Something rustled in the reeds.

I raised my head.

"Don't move," came a low voice.

A figure stood above me on the embankment. Definitely not the woman I'd heard earlier.

I tried to raise my hands in surrender.

"I said freeze," the voice came again. "I have a gun aimed at your back, and it is not loaded with tranq darts."

I managed to remain semi-motionless. "Please," was all I could get out. My throat felt like it had been ripped apart and stitched back together with dental floss.

"Show me your light," the man said.

Kind of impossible without moving. "Can't."

A brilliant green light appeared. "When are you fools going to learn to stay on your own side?"

He thought I was Red. While this was preferable to him recognizing me as the Blue Campus Murderer, I also couldn't let him think I'd snuck across to paint babies.

"It's knotted." I indicated my wrapped fire.

He sized me up for a moment, then crouched and tugged at the shirt. His firelight revealed another set of footprints in the mud. So there had been someone else. The mysterious Green lifeguard and her Yellow friend. Had they pulled me out? Why run off?

The shirt came free, and my nauseatingly blue-green light illuminated the Green's features. He was middle-aged, had a blond unibrow, thin lips, and a chin the size of Mount Tremper. I could tell from his eyes that he hadn't expected a Blue Mélangé. His forehead wrinkles told me he was either in his mid-forties or did a lot more scowling than smiling.

He holstered his gun, grabbed under my arms, and lifted me to my feet. "What's your name, boy?" I realized he was wearing a really nice suit. For some reason, it made me more comfortable.

I wobbled but found I could stand on my own. "Thank you. I had better head home."

"Name. And while you're at it, tell me what you're doing on royal property. Are you the fool that's been opening the dog pens?"

Royal property? No way the water carried me all the way to the Estate. I lifted my light. Sure enough, the retractable bridge loomed above us, a thin metallic tower draped with cables and razor wire. Beyond that, I could see the distinctive flame-shaped roofline of the newest building in Télesphore: the Commissaire's home.

Ah, black.

"Let's you and me go inside and have a talk," the man said. He gestured toward a boxy two-story building at the top of the embankment.

"You and I," I said before I could stop myself.

He backhanded me across the face.

The boxy building turned out to be the Green Barracks, the only royal building in Hameau Vert. The man in the navy blue suit who had bloodied my lip and was now blowing hot tobacco smoke in my face, was clearly one of the Commissaire's personal bodyguards.

I expected him to immediately realize who I was, but as the minutes dragged on, and he was still talking about dog fences and Red gangs, I began to relax. Well, as much as I could while being interrogated with my shirt off.

Maybe I was getting better at lying. At least the guilt no longer crippled me. I'd finally decided that although honesty was an important guideline to live by, rules could be bent during war. And until the Télesphorian government stopped trying to kill me for defending a mentally-disabled kid, we were most certainly enemies.

It probably helped that I had something else to talk about. I told him as much as I dared about the boys I'd noticed on the bridge before I fell into the water. Maybe the Créateur had led me to the one person in Hameau Vert who could help Baptiste. Then when Aro was in custody, I'd make sure he took the fall for the painting and the accidental death.

"I can take you there," I said.

"You're not going anywhere until you tell me your real name."

We sat at a metal table in a common room that seemed to take up the entire first floor of the barracks. We were the only lights in the room. Were all the other guards asleep upstairs?

"What's wrong with Jacque Pierrot?"

"You think I can't tell when a name's made up?"

He had to be bluffing. How would I act if it actually was my name, and he refused to believe me? Probably impatient and anxious to change the subject.

"Well, detective, your instincts have failed you this time. Call me whatever you want, just help that kid. He could be drowning as we speak."

"Not my job."

A phone startled me. The guard ignored it. "What's your middle name?"

"Andres." Not like he could identify me from that. Hopefully the automatic answer helped my credibility.

The phone stopped ringing, then immediately started again.

"If you're an innocent bystander, why hide your fire?" Still he made no move to get the phone. Was this some sort of psychological trick to make me crazy? It was working.

"To get close enough to hear without being seen. If you're not feeling especially heroic, at least let me go so I can help the boy. That Aro kid is psychotic. He's probably already convinced him to jump."

The cigarette fell to the table. "Aro? What shade?"

"Turquoise. Does it matter? From what I overheard, he's

obviously been up to something illegal, and he's forcing Baptiste to—"

The guard stood and pointed four meaty fingers at my face. "Let me tell you a secret. I don't actually care what your name is. If it was up to me, every single Mélangé would be working the tin mines. It's lucky black for you, I'm not in charge."

The phone fell blessedly silent.

I resisted the urge to explain shade economics to him. With the amount of Blue I carried, I could unclog toilets and still make twice as much as he did. So why was he treating me like a Red? Surely he knew where Blue-Mélangé fell on the superiority scale. Way ahead of Greenborns, that's for sure.

In fact, if I really had been innocent, I probably wouldn't have humored him even this far. Maybe I should walk out. He hadn't tied me up or anything. And there was no evidence of a crime.

Although if I tried to walk out, nothing would prevent him from shooting me and sending my lightless body down the falls. Yeah, maybe a safer bet would be to stroke his ego.

"'Sieur, I've been kind of a blankhead. I really do appreciate you helping me out of the river. I'm sure you—"

The door opened.

Two young Greens entered wearing dark blue suits. "Capitaine?" One of them said. "Where is Eloi?"

Great. For the last ten minutes, I'd been arguing with the captain of the royal guard.

"I'd like to know that myself," the captain said. "I found a prowler in the area he was supposed to have secure."

A half-drowned prowler. What an idiot. But I smiled as if the captain were making a joke. Maybe I could escape while the guards distracted him. Behind me, a large winterdark-facing window looked out over the river. Unfortunately, it was barred.

"Sergent Whisnant is trying to reach you," the taller guard said. "The soldiers finally caught the boy. They're holding him at the police station."

My head jerked back toward the entryway. They'd caught Baptiste? How had the pokers known about him? Maybe Aro had given up trying to make him jump and turned him in. It would be Baptiste's word against Aro's and, between the two of them, I knew which one would be more convincing.

The captain moved toward the door. "Gouroux, inform the Commissaire. He asked to be awoken as soon as there was news. Mallette, stay here. If Eloi returns, handcuff him to the door until I return from the station."

The tall guard—apparently named Mallette—nodded and glanced at me. "Will Bruno be waiting with me?" he said.

The captain spun. I thought he had forgotten something, but then it sunk in.

Mallette had called me Bruno.

"You know this Mélangé?" the captain asked. Gouroux paused in the doorway to listen.

"Bruno Nazaire. He's one of TC's starting forwards," Mallette said. "My dad maintains the stadium. I caught a few games." Mallette gave me a questioning look. I couldn't tell if it was because I wasn't wearing my shirt or because he wondered how I'd become a mixed freak. Or maybe he was just confused by the panicked look on my face.

The captain cocked his head. "Now why would Monsieur Nazaire not want anyone to know he was a rugby star?"

Gouroux shrugged as if the question had been directed at him, then stepped into line next to the Captain. He seemed to have forgotten about his message to the Commissaire.

Before I could invent an excuse for my situation, three things happened in quick succession. The captain's eyebrows raised in comprehension, the phone rang, and the back window shattered. A smooth riverstone slid to a stop at the captain's feet.

"Gouroux," the captain said, "Hold him." Then he ran out the entrance, shouting something about accomplices.

Gouroux strode toward me. I stood, trying to decide

whether I should feint or bowl him over, and if Malette would have time to draw his weapon. I settled on a double feint and prepared to spring at Gouroux.

He stopped and picked up the phone.

"Sergent Whisnant?" he said. "Yes, Le Capitaine Sébastien is here. He asked me to hold you on the phone until he got back."

I hesitated a moment, then turned toward the shattered window. A patchwork reflection smiled back at me. This Gouroux character was either an amazing soldier or someone's nephew. He certainly hadn't become a Royal Guard on brain power.

Now the question was whether I could slip out before the captain got back.

"See anything?" Malette had joined me at the window.

I shook my head. "Should we go help him?"

"Nah, Cap likes to fly solo."

Of course he does. "I should probably go find, Ellie."

"Eloi?"

"Yeah, I call him Ellie sometimes. I'm pretty sure I know where he is. Don't want him to get in any more trouble than he's already in."

I made to step past Malette, but he grabbed my arm.

"What was Sébastien grilling you about? Does he still need to talk to you?"

I resisted the urge to elbow him in the face and run. "I jumped into the river to try and save someone. Tell Le Capitaine he's already got my report, and if he has any other questions, I'll be back in ten minutes. I should really go find Eloi." I pulled my arm free.

"Can I get a quick signature before you go? Probably won't be here when you get back."

I swallowed. The last time someone had asked for my autograph, it had not gone well, but at least this mec had gotten my name right. Malette had a pen, but when he started opening drawers to find paper, I pulled the soggy, blood-stained shirt from my pocket.

"How about my old rugby shirt?"

"You sure?"

No. Beside my large build and long hair, it was the only thing linking Bruno Nazaire to the death of the poker. But if my suspicions about the Captain were right, he had already figured out who I was running from. Getting out of here before he came back was worth any risk. We didn't have time to look for a clean sheet of paper.

I unrolled the shirt on the table. "Just give it a week before you show anybody, okay? My Mélangé status is not common knowledge. My parents will need to figure out what they're gonna tell the neighbors."

Malette handed me the pen. I signed the shirt, smiled, and started for the door.

"Thanks," he called out. "Tell Eloi to hurry. I've never seen his dad this angry."

His dad? I waved in acknowledgment. The Captain was about to get a whole lot angrier when he found his prowler missing and Gouroux chatting on the phone. I nodded at the guard as I passed, but he took no notice of me. He was busy explaining to Sergent Whisnant about the broken window and assuring him the Captain would be on the line shortly.

Ten feet from the door. Nothing stood between me and the cover of darkness.

Five feet.

I pushed the door open and stepped through. I'd half expected the Captain to be there, waiting to pounce. Only an empty parking lot greeted me.

At my back, the door clicked closed. Without waiting to catch my breath, I sprinted toward the police station.

If Aro had been telling his lies about Baptiste, I was the one who could set the record straight. I had the information I needed now. Between me and Baptiste, we could make sure Aro took the fall for his painting scheme. And maybe I'd finally get some answers as to why he'd picked my life to ruin.

CHAPTER NINE

ARRESTED

Thanks to mumbled directions from a Green leaning out his window with a cigar, I finally made it to the gray cinder-block police station. Clearly the builders were more concerned with functionality than style. Or maybe the creepy half-finished warehouse atmosphere was meant to intimidate criminals.

I couldn't decide if it was working. Although I didn't feel particularly worried about entering, my hands shook as I tried—unsuccessfully—to fasten the top three buttons of my newly-procured silk blouse. I debated going back to the clothesline and grabbing something less dainty, but visions of Baptiste being tortured for information kept me striding toward the main entrance.

A female in brown fatigues exited the station, mounted a scooter, and sped off. Whether she'd noticed me or not, she hadn't made eye contact. I stopped wrestling with my stolen lady-shirt, took a breath, and went inside.

A single hanging bulb illuminated the narrow entryway. The cinder block motif had also been applied to the interior with great effect. I was definitely feeling that intimidation now. A rusty bell sat next to a thick plastic window with a hole in the center. I hit the bell. It sounded like a silverware collision. I knocked on the plastic.

"Hello?"

The only other door read LAW ENFORSEMENT ONLY. Possibly the most aggravating door I'd ever come across. Not only was it spelled wrong, it was securely locked. A feeling of claustrophobia welled up in me. I spun and pushed into the crash bar of the exit. The cool air had never felt more inviting. It had already become synonymous with freedom in my mind. Was I risking mine again for no reason? What if Sergent Whisnant didn't believe me? What if Baptiste was too scared to tell the truth? My decision-making of late had been questionable at best. I should have at least contacted my family first and figured out a plan. My eyes fell on a payphone across the street.

"In or out. You're drafting up the place."

The voice startled me so badly, I almost bolted. A hunched woman sat at the window. Long, white hair flowed down from her oversized police cap. Her wrinkled eyes regarded me with curiosity. Her name tag identified her as Officer Juenes. She looked about three hundred years old.

My panic faded. It shouldn't be too hard to get some information out of this sweet, old lady. I could even give her a semi-anonymous tip that the kid they captured was innocent and the real criminal was Baptiste's friend, Aro.

I let the door close.

"What brings you in, young man?"

"Bonsoir," I said. "Did Sergent Whisnant come in here dragging a chubby little blond boy?"

"No."

"Um... are you sure?"

"You mean am I blind and deaf? Again, no."

"I don't care!" a deep voice shouted from a few rooms away. "He can call me when he finds the time. I have my own issues to deal with."

"Who was that?" I asked.

"Sergent Whisnant."

Was he still on the phone with Gouroux? "You said he wasn't here."

Juenes tweaked an eyebrow. "I'm the one with a hearing impairment?"

"Look, I just need to know what Sergent Whisnant is doing here, and if he has a boy with him."

"Worth more than my job to discuss royal business with strangers off the street."

"Can you give the sergent a message for me, then? I have information on the incident at Blue Campus earlier."

Her eyes widened a fraction. "Asking a lot of questions for summin who already knows so much."

"You going to take the message or not?" I caught a whiff of something hot and cheesy. My stomach tried to claw its way up my esophagus. How long had it been since I'd eaten?

Juenes brought her dark hand up and around in a slow-motion wave. Her hand got lower, and lower, then disappeared. It took me a second to realize she was reaching for something under the counter.

"Fine, I'm leaving!" I said.

My back was to the door when she lifted a piece of paper from a drawer.

"Change your mind, here's the form to make a report."

"Oh." I casually stepped back to the window and took the form.

She handed me a pen, and I scribbled down an abridged account of what had happened with Baptiste and what I'd heard on the bridge. I emphasized that the heavyset blond kid was innocent as was the Blue rugby player who had been painted and forced into defending himself and the boy. I didn't include names except Aro's and, while I described him in as much detail as possible, I kept the other descriptions vague.

Meanwhile Juenes had left and returned with her dinner. Thankfully I was almost done with the report. The smell of her food hijacked my brain. It took me several minutes just to write the last couple sentences. Finally, I slid the form back under the plastic window.

She finished chewing, then wiped her mouth. "Didn't fill out the name and address section."

"I can't make it anonymous?"

She shook her head. "I'd get reported for submitting an incomplete report."

I took the form, filled out the name section, and slid it back.

She glanced at it. "Have notarized identification, Monsieur Pierrot?"

"Let me guess. You need transcription of my ID card and a sketch of my profile in order to submit a report."

"Not normally." She finished her dinner, wiped her fork clean, then dropped the container in the trash. She moved like an arthritic tortoise.

"Not normally?"

"Don't believe your name is Jacque. Hate to be reported for submitting a fraudulent report."

"Is there anyone else I can talk to?"

"Shouldn't have trouble finding conversation, handsome boy like yourself. Might could use a haircut. Still, best wait until morning. Curfew's on, eyefall to O-six-hundred." She pushed the now wrinkled paper under the window at me.

Maybe it was the grain of rice spreading grease on the form or the deafening wails of my angry stomach, but I felt my control slip. "You call yourself a police officer? The only one you're protecting and serving is yourself."

The woman's eyes grew small and cold. "Who you really protecting, 'Sieur Pierrot? Don't tell me it's the fat boy. Already missed your chance to help him."

Missed my chance?

"Has he already been executed? Is that the real reason you won't accept my report?"

Juenes rolled her eyes. "If you had proof, and if I thought it might actually change something, I would risk my job and my life to see that le sergent knew about it."

I blinked, momentarily stunned. All she wanted was proof? "My name is Bruno Nazaire. My ID is in my backpack on Blue Campus, but if you call the guard Malette at the barracks, he will confirm my identity."

"You're not understanding me."

"How about having the real killer in custody? Would that

'change' enough to merit your cooperation? I—" My voice faltered. Was I really about to give myself up just so Baptiste could be free? My common sense screamed against it, but a deeper part of me stepped forward and nodded. My life was already in shambles. I was the only one who could save Baptiste now.

"I'm the proof," I lifted my fire. "Aro blackmailed a kid with a mental disability into painting me."

"Why would he do that?"

"I have no idea, but I intend to find out."

Juenes sniffed and peered at me from under wispy white eyebrows. "What does that have to do with the murdered soldier?"

"His death was an accident," I said. "But I did fight the soldier. He wanted to kill Ba—the boy."

For a long moment, Officer Juenes scrutinized me. Finally she shook her head. "You're expendable. Maybe if you were Blue..."

"My shade has nothing to do with the truth," I said. "The law is the law."

"Worthy sentiment," she said, matching my tone. "One I happen to agree with. But I think you'll find we are in the minority."

"Are you saying Sergent Whisnant won't believe me?"

"Like to know how I've survived forty-seven years on the force?"

"Must be your moral courage."

Juenes glared at me. "I tell people what they want to hear, then do what I want behind their backs."

I opened my mouth to say something cutting but found I was completely speechless. Whether it was her bluntness or the sincerity in which she admitted to being a sociopath, I didn't even know how to respond. Finally I shook my head. "You think you've been telling me what I wanted to hear, then?"

"No. This is me doing what I want behind le sergent's

back."

This woman really was crazy. I should just ask her for change to use the payphone and call my parents to deal with the situation.

"So, you admit that le sergent would want to see my report."

"Most definitely. He'd probably believe it too."

The miracle wasn't that the woman had remained on the force forty-seven years, it was that she hadn't driven away all the other officers. "Then why—"

"You see the female soldier storm out of here earlier?"

I blinked at the sudden change of subject, then nodded.

"She was the one who finally caught the boy."

"So he *is* here!"

"She was also just let go."

"What?"

The old woman bowed her head and gave me a sideways glance, as if what she said next was strictly off the record. "She's no longer a soldier. Someone else wanted credit. She became a liability."

I scoffed. "If that were the case, she could just go to the papers."

"Which newspaper do you think would print slanderous accusations about the commander of the Armée Royale?"

"Word would still get out."

"She might tell a few people she can trust. But it would only put them in danger."

I stepped closer to the window. "Are you saying Sergent Whisnant is corrupt and would get rid of people who tried to expose him?"

Juenes laughed. "The Royal Army is doing the job it was created for—and that was never to protect the people."

A chill ran up my back. The woman was a traitor to the crown. But then did the crown even exist anymore?

"I could take you back to see Whisnant this very moment," Juenes continued. "I could tell him exactly what you told me. He'd probably take the report, pretend not to believe you, then send you home."

I opened my mouth, but she cut me off.

"Except you wouldn't get home. A Red fisherman would find you washed up on the beach. What would law enforcement gain for seeing justice done? They'd get to look like fools while a young, attractive rebel became the hero. The beau monde would be outraged at the Dominateur. Or at least pretend to be. People would lose their jobs. It might even put the credibility of the whole system in question. Especially if the public found out the wrong person had been caught and tortured."

"Tortured?"

"If it's any consolation, Aro and I would probably end up dead. The Conseil de Dominateur doesn't make mistakes and it doesn't leave witnesses. Where do you think I learned my philosophy? The Dominateur are the masters of telling people one thing and doing another."

I folded the police report in two, then again. A week ago, I would've said the old woman belonged in a padded room. Blank, I'd been thinking it a few minutes ago, but suddenly she was making sense to me. It helped that she'd dropped the green-collar way of talking, which had clearly been part of her harmless-old-lady act. She actually reminded me a lot of Granny Jade. Opinionated, blunt, and smarter than she looked. But why did she trust me?

"You're not worried I'm going to tell le sergent everything you just told me?"

Juenes watched me for a moment. "If you do, then I've misjudged you. You seemed like someone I'd like on our side."

"Our side?" Was she trying to recruit me to her underground rebel organization?

She smirked. "The side with—how did you put it—moral courage?"

"So, it's morally courageous to let an innocent boy be executed?"

"Conscience is only a liability if you assume it's universal."

"Huh?" Were we really having a philosophical discussion about moral courage while Baptiste was being tortured for information? How long had I been arguing with this woman? I realized with a stab of panic that Captain Sébastien could show up at any time.

"Play their game. Wait for your opportunity. Then make sure it's worth it."

What did that even mean? At least Granny Jade made sense once in a while. I slid the folded form into the pocket of my flower shirt. "You don't happen to have a phone I could—"

Something behind me creaked. Cold air hit the back of my neck and legs. Someone screamed.

I spun to find a poker standing in the doorway—or rather, crouching. He seemed to be lifting something from the ground, a child in stained clothes with long black hair. The poker, who didn't seem much older than me, slung her over his shoulder. He straightened and the child's arm swung forward, casting an orange glow on the bare concrete floor.

Orange? Was it the girl who had been shouting at Aro?

Juenes made a noise somewhere between a laugh and a grunt. "Another soldier with a prisoner. Don't know why you all bothered to build a barracks."

Another? I knew she'd been lying. Baptiste was definitely in there.

The poker hesitated. I realized it was the young Green I'd walked to the stadium with—Dane or something? Would he recognize me? Would that help things, or had he already figured out that I had duped him?

He looked at his oversized zapper watch, then at the girl. Jeannette? I was fairly certain it was Aro's friend.

"Don't got funds to be putting up every river-jumper," Juenes said. "Take her back afore the Feu Noir sets in on us."

"Buzz me through, old hag," the poker said, the uncertainty gone from his expression. "I'm here to see Le Sergent

Whisnant, not listen to you cackle."

I blinked. Was this the same kid who had seemed terrified of his own radio? Had his awkwardness at the stadium all been an act? Or maybe this was the act. Maybe his poker mentor was building his confidence by training him to treat everyone like rivertrash.

Juenes' eyes glittered—and not in a sparkly fairy-princess way. "Going in there right now is probably not the best—"

"Do your job, witch."

"As you say, 'Sieur."

The door clicked. Without looking in my direction, the poker pulled open the Law Enforcement Only door and carried Jeannette inside.

I grinned at Juenes.

"Don't you dare," she said.

I slid the form from my pocket and caught the door before it closed.

CHAPTER TEN

FIRECIDE

A sweet, rancid smell permeated the inside of the police station, like sewage and maple syrup. The hallway appeared only slightly wider than the entryway, but at least it was better lit. If the poker noticed the reflection of my light when I entered, he didn't turn. Even so, I pocketed my fire.

On my dark, Juenes glared at me through another window. She was clearly trying to get off her chair in a hurry. So far she'd managed to brace herself between the counter and a file cabinet to slowly lower herself to the floor. Next to the window, a door had been labeled RECEPTION with permanent marker. Juenes was ancient, but I didn't want to take a chance on her sabotaging my rescue attempt.

I waited until the poker had turned a corner, then slid a heavy metal trash can in front of the RECEPTION door. It would probably only buy me a few minutes, but that might be enough to hand the sergent my report and tell him what I knew of Aro's extracurricular activities. Only if Whisnant refused to believe me, would I reveal my part in the poker's death. Maybe I could even get the young poker on my side. Another spike of dread reminded me my parents wouldn't approve of me risking my life for Baptiste again. But then, they weren't here to give me an alternative.

The door hit the trash can. Juenes mumbled something like, "Serum-draining toothpaste junkies." A wrinkled hand appeared, feeling around for what was blocking the door.

"Sorry," I said. "I'll try to be quick." I thought about asking her directions to the interrogation room but didn't push my luck. Instead I padded quietly down the hallway, my folded form clutched tightly in my dark hand.

The concrete felt gritty under my bare feet. Microclouds of dust rose into the air with each step. Since I seemed to be alone again, I unpocketed my fire and examined the floor. Bits of rock? No, cinderblock. I noticed the gouge marks in the unfinished walls. Did the officers walk through the hallway swinging their nightsticks? And who was in charge of cleaning this place? I coughed as I passed a pair of cockroaches sharing a stained bandage.

How could Juenes work in these conditions? I'd need to sanitize my feet when I got out of here. Or rather, if.

I passed several doors, a few shelves containing random tagged objects—evidence?—and even a water cooler repurposed as a planter. The solitary dried yellow stalk seemed to encapsulate the station's commitment to incompetence.

A man's voice came from up the hall. I approached and found a door ajar. Someone laughed inside. The door read JANITORIAL OFFICE in the most professional lettering I'd seen so far. It was even spelled correctly. I ran a hand through my hair, tried in vain to coerce another button into place on my shirt, then pushed open the door.

"Confound it. I thought I had enough for that green. You're halfway to beating me again."

"Hardly. The blues swim to the surface for you, while I draw nothing but red. I'm starting to suspect you know the texture somehow."

The room wasn't lit by artificial light. Illumination came from three green fires, the unconscious Orange—now on the floor—and a box covered with tiny glowing spots of color. It took a moment to process what I was seeing. Two Green men sat on folding chairs, huddled over the most ornate light box I'd ever seen. One had long, dark hair and wore a half-unbuttoned police uniform. The other's dark poker fatigues looked like they'd been ironed and starched just before I walked in.

Even sitting, he was easily the tallest man I'd ever seen. He had thick, black eyebrows and a silver handlebar mustache. This had to be Sergent Whisnant. The young poker stood at attention against the wall, apparently the only one to notice my entrance. He cleared his throat.

"I asked you to wait, soldier," Whisnant said, without looking up from his game. "One more sound, and you'll spend the night in a cell."

The young poker looked to the long-haired officer, who chuckled and placed a tiny glass orb on an empty slot in the box. The light from inside the box immediately lit the marble a brilliant green. "Now we're putting up your troops, Balthis? Will we get royal funding for waste disposal and police supervision?"

"Louis, I'll even pay to launder the bedding. A small price to be free of simpering ladder-climbers for a single evening. No reflection on you, of course."

The officer waved him off. "When the boy's in uniform, he's your problem. You can beat him for all I care. Although I've found it doesn't work long-term."

Where was Baptiste? Had Juenes told me the truth about him not being here? Or had I come too late? I certainly wasn't going to proclaim my guilt and ask to be taken away if Baptiste had already been dealt with. The thought made me dizzy.

"Father, if you'll just—"

"In my presence," Whisnant said, apparently forgetting his previous threat, "you will address Chief Collins by his title. And only when ordered to speak."

This slob was Chief of Police? That explained a lot about the state of the station. Baptiste was probably stuck in a cell somewhere. I'd need to think of an excuse to try to get him freed. I lifted my fire.

The chief glanced at me. His eyes narrowed a little, but he didn't seem inclined to interrupt his game.

"I spoke to Dom Gravois last week," the sergent said. "He informed me that you requested royal funds to deal with the

Red problem."

The chief's expression darkened. "He expects us to keep two hundred thousand people in line with eighty-five officers. For years I've been telling Gravois to execute the Red inmates and send the rest to the mainland."

"So dramatic," Whisnant said as he dropped a brown marble into his bag. "That's the point of an army. We step in when needed. And anyway, it's more like seventeen thousand under your jurisdiction. I take care of Snobville, remember?"

"A thousand soldiers for thirteen square miles?!"

"Those numbers are the only thing keeping Estoria on their side of the Ocheanum."

They grew quiet again and turned their focus to the game. I debated who I should address or what I should say. Charging blindly into the police station seemed a lot stupider now that I stood three feet from the man hunting me. I'd prepared myself for an argument, or even a fight—but hadn't expected to be completely ignored. Should I back out of the room and search the cells for Baptiste?

"You still owe a green if you want to buy the Mélangé," the chief said. Then he added with a sly grin. "Until the Sports and Betting Board officially changes the rules, blue-Mélangé are worth more than the green orbs."

"It will happen. As soon as Dom Marcoux retires, the proposition will pass."

On the floor, Jeannette stirred, and the young poker squinted through the darkness at me. Did he recognize me? Would he still be so friendly now that I was a fellow citizen of Hameau Vert? Maybe he was the key to getting Baptiste freed. Could I get him out into the hall somehow? Maybe he knew where his father kept the keys to the cells.

"To make history as the man who banned multicolored marbles." The chief laughed loudly, and Jeannette's eyes popped open.

The young poker noticed as well. He quickly touched his watch, then extended his index finger toward her.

"Wait," I said, automatically.

Sergent Whisnant, jumped in his seat, then glared at me. "What is this, Cirque du Freak? This is a restricted area."

The young poker swallowed. "That's why I was trying to get your—"

"What part of 'keep quiet' don't you understand, Cauliflower?"

Jeannette was now fully awake and blinking as if trying to focus her eyes.

"It's Collins, 'Sieur," the young poker said, an edge to his tone. "And I'll happily leave as soon as you tell me what to do with this Red Mélangé I caught in town."

Whisnant glanced at the chief and raised his black eyebrows. "Maybe he has a little of his father after all."

"Well, while you figure that out," the police chief said with a yawn. "I'll check on the prisoner." He stood and picked his way across the room toward a door marked CLEANING SUPPLIES.

"Baptiste needs help," came a small voice.

Everyone looked at the muddy little girl on the floor. To my surprise, Jeannette was looking directly at me. She must have recognized my shade from the bridge. What did she think I was doing, if not helping Baptiste?

"All right then, Collins," Whisnant said with a sigh. "Drop the freak down the mine shaft, and go get some sleep. We'll need our troops looking fresh tomorrow. I have a feeling there's going to be an awards ceremony."

Collins and I shared a look. Was Whisnant serious about dropping the girl down a mine shaft? Didn't the law require a trial and witnesses?

Whisnant glared at me again. "If you have an issue, you can take it up with the receptionist." Then to himself, he added, "Old woman probably asleep at the desk again."

The chief opened the door to the closet.

All thought drained from my mind, leaving a cold slab of shock.

Upside down in the closet hung my best friend.

How did—? What were they doing do him? An extension cord secured Marin's ankles to the top of a metal shelf directly above the mop sink which was half full of pink water.

Pink? Then I saw his eye—nearly swollen shut. A dark line of blood ran down his face and dripped the few inches to the water. The chief pulled the gag from Marin's mouth so it hung like a sweatband around his hairless scalp. Marin's good eye swept the room, landed on me, then grew wide.

My fire felt like it had spontaneously combusted. The heat actually hurt my hand. I opened my mouth, but everything I wanted to say and scream became compacted and lodged in my throat.

Collins seemed to remember he'd been dismissed. He grabbed the kicking girl by both wrists and pulled her toward the exit.

The chief turned on a faucet. Water ran from a hose into the plugged mop sink. Marin wore only his rugby shorts and a single knee-length sock. The water level rose until it reached the top of his smooth head.

"Ready to tell us the whole story?" the chief asked. "Or are you enjoying this game?"

Collins looked back once and received a vicious kick to the shin. He finally shocked Jeannette into unconsciousness. He sighed and dragged her into the hallway.

I nearly screamed at him to leave her alone, but my eyes involuntarily returned to Marin. The water level rose past his eyes and he began jerking his head back and forth to splash water out of the sink. The water would soon reach his nose.

"Leave me alone!" Marin screamed, his good eye still locked on mine. "Leave me!" Was he talking to me?

The phone rang.

The sergent stood, as if to answer it, then turned and faced me. "Still here, blueberry grasswipe? I know you think your shade gives you an all-access pass to wherever-the-black-you-want, but unless you're aching to end up like this soldier killer, I suggest—"

The phone rang again. Despite my thumping heart, I knew exactly what I had to do. I rolled my eyes, stepped to the desk, and answered it. From the moment of the first ring, everything had fallen into place in my mind—the sergent's positive response to Collin's defiance, the realization that my confession would never rescue Marin or even Jeannette, the knowledge that the only person who might have any influence on these two men was the captain of the royal guard.

"*Bonsoir,* Capitaine," I said into the phone. The sergent stared at me, his eyebrows in knots.

"Uh, *bonsoir,*" came a voice that was definitely not the captain. "Is le sergent available?" I almost answered him before I caught myself. I had to make Whisnant and Chief Collins think I was receiving important instructions from the captain.

"I haven't had a chance," I said into the phone. I had unconsciously adopted the voice my mom uses when she fights with my dad. "The Blue is still tied up by his feet," I continued in an impatient growl. "They caught your spy and have decided to dump her down into the mines."

"Uh..." came the voice on the phone, which I was pretty sure belonged to that nice guard Malette to whom I'd just donated my shirt. "Can you give le sergent a message?" he said quickly as if worried I'd interrupt him again. "Sebas—the captain of the guard just left the barracks to go to the police station. He should be up there in a few minutes."

I winced and pulled the phone away from my ear as if the captain were screaming profanities.

"I know," I nearly shouted back into it. "Would you like to speak with le sergent?" Pause. Malette had fallen silent and was probably wondering if he'd dialed the right number.

"Okay," I said, the phone again at my ear. "I'll take care of it."

I hung up and surveyed the room. Whisnant was actually watching me, as if waiting for the captain's orders. In another situation, I might have smiled or even laughed. But the image of Jeannette's body crumpling to the floor and the sound of Marin's frantic splashing had kept my fury as hot as my hand. Still, I forced my voice into an almost whisper, lacing each syllable with absolute authority.

"The Orange belongs to Sébastien. Get her back."

Whisnant swallowed, then barked a laugh. "Le Capitaine, working with mixed freaks? I'd sooner believe he's engaged to a Red."

I faltered. This wasn't working. I was considering picking up a chair and trying to fight my way to Marin, but then I noticed Whisnant's smile twitch. He wasn't as confident as he pretended. He was testing me.

I picked up the phone and pressed a few random numbers. I thought I might have to pretend to speak with the Captain again, but Whisnant held up his fire. "Fine, fine, fine." He moved to the door and stuck his head out. "Collins, get back here with the frea—with the girl!"

He startled when Officer Juenes appeared in the doorway. She opened her mouth to say something, but I cut her off.

"Juenes, I'm glad you're here." I slammed the handset down on the hook. "Le Capitaine wants the boy moved immediately. His father is a lawyer and he's on the way to the station. Sébastien thinks the chief and le sergent should both stay to meet the lawyer. Obviously you're to deny any involvement with the boy."

"What?" came the chief's voice from the closet. "Let me talk to him." The water was still running.

This was taking too long. The captain would arrive any minute. "Get him down!" I shouted. "There is no time for discussion. Leave his hands bound—the Commissaire wants him hidden in the Estate before the public gets wind of this."

For a moment, everyone stared. The phone rang. I picked up the headset and receiver together and threw them against the wall.

I thought for sure I had gone too far—but it seemed bullying was the language bullies understood best. The shattering of plastic and metal finally jolted the men into action. While they cut Marin down, I moved to the doorway.

"Thank you for your help," I said to Juenes, willing her not to blow my cover. She watched me with calculating eyes. Behind her, Collins approached, brow furrowed.

"Officer Juenes, will you help this soldier take the Orange across the river? Try not to be seen. Le Capitaine doesn't want the whole island to know he employs Red informants."

Juenes glanced into the room. The chief and Whisnant turned Marin right-side-up and wiped his face with a soggy jersey.

Juenes shook her head. "I don't buy it."

Great blackened crêpes, was she serious?

"Then get back to your box and stay out of the way."

She seemed to prefer this suggestion, and after casting a dirty look at me, she began the long shuffle down the hall.

Whisnant appeared beside me. "You won't moving very fast with him." He pulled Marin forward and, for the first time, I appreciated the full effect of his mangled face. He'd been badly beaten. Was that during the interrogation or on the street? Marin swayed a little and watched my face as if trying to focus on it.

I looked down at the unconscious girl lying in the hallway. I had to take them both. I didn't trust either of them to Collins. At least I'd finally get to make use of the energy explosion in my hand. I leaned into Marin's stomach, grabbed him behind the knees, and lifted him onto my shoulder. I gestured to my lightward shoulder. "Give me the girl."

Collins cast a doubtful glance at me but picked up Jeannette and slung her over the other side.

"Now get the door. His father could be here any minute." I pointed at the light box. "Wash down the supplies closet and hide your game. Convince the mec you're still looking for his boy. Say nothing of the murdered poker." Soldier. I should have said soldier.

Rage flared to life in Whisnant's eyes. "How dare you speak of—"

"Get ahold of yourself, Sergent," I said. "That's the term the Blues will use, so focus on the task at hand."

I took a long, steady breath and felt the strength from my hand move up my arm and into my chest. With each step toward the door, my legs felt sturdier.

Collins held both doors for me, his eyes wide as I passed with my load.

"Best get home," I said under my breath. "You're not going to want to be around when the Captain arrives."

"You're the mec from the stadium," Collins said. "How did—"

"Long story, mon frère. Trust me—make yourself scarce." I took a few steps down the dark sidewalk, then paused. "Nice work in there with Whisnant."

I resumed my plodding in what I hoped was the general direction of the river. Marin squirmed and tried to say something, but I shushed him. The sound of Collin's jogging footsteps grew softer. Then louder. With a start, I realized the sound was now coming from up ahead. Someone was running toward me. No way to outrun anyone. We'd have to hide.

I made a sharp turn behind an apartment building and collapsed into a dark alley—and several metal trash cans. The sound of tin on concrete shattered the silence. Marin groaned, but I took his fire, along with my own and Jeannette's, and shoved them through the dark plastic of full garbage bag until the alley was once again completely dark.

Although Marin was still not at a hundred percent, he seemed to grasp what was going on. He quieted his panting and didn't pull his hand from the pungent assortment of rotting food and containers.

A man appeared for a moment, running along the sidewalk I'd just vacated. The illumination of his green fire was enough for me to make out a chin the size of Mt. Tremper. The Captain's light disappeared again as he continued past the narrow alley where we lay.

After a few moments of silence, I carefully extracted my hand from the bag. Jeannette stirred. About time. The burst of energy from my fire had run out, and I knew there was no way I could continue carrying them.

Marin pulled his fire free and coughed. "Can't breath. What is that smell?"

I laughed softly. "Pretty sure it's you, Mare-bear."

He lifted his fire and trained it on me. "Bruno, what are you wearing?"

I was trying to think of an appropriate quip when Jeannette's hand gripped my wrist.

"Brutus Nazeer? It was Aro's fault."

"I know. Do you know where Baptiste is?"

She nodded, her eyes suddenly full of tears. "Under the bridge. He used a ruler on his light."

Used a ruler? To measure? Then it hit me. Jeannette was crying because she thought Baptiste was going to die.

He had used the sharp edge of a ruler to puncture his fire.

CHAPTER ELEVEN

HOMECOMING GREEN

W e found Baptiste lightless. He lay on his side, arm extended. The skin of his fire dome, instead of being translucent and slightly raised like a blister, was flat, jagged at the edges, and leaking a clear fluid. His backpack lay next to him in the mud, his pencil box open, supplies scattered everywhere. I picked up the filthy ruler and could tell without bringing my nose to it that it was covered with serum.

My head swam. I took Baptiste's limp hand in mine. At that moment, the little boy on the ground became Ro. The devastating pain of losing my baby brother slammed into me full force, as if the anguish had never left, only hidden itself, waiting to be set free.

Marin swore softly, then glanced at me as if he didn't understand my tears. "Did you know him?"

As I closed the impossibly little fingers around his palm, his fire flickered.

Marin saw it too. "He still alive?"

While Marin listened for breathing, I tilted Baptiste's hand, allowing the small amount of serum left in his fire to wash over his stamen. His blue-green light flared to life, and Baptiste took a shuddering breath. Everything my father had taught me about fireleaks came flooding back. Wrap the hand loosely. Keep it moist. Get to a hospital for a serum pouch.

"Baptiste, can you hear me?" I asked.

His eyes remained closed.

"He needs a pouch," I said.

Marin stepped out from under the bridge and peered at the dark trees. "I'll find someone. Hameau has to have a clinic."

"No time. Blue Hospital is only a couple blocks from Rue Principale."

"That'll take you at least fifteen minutes to walk," Marin said. "The kid isn't exactly tiny."

"I carried you." But I knew Marin was right. My fire still hadn't recovered from carrying him and Jeannette half a block. And anyway Baptiste didn't have fifteen minutes.

Jeanette, who until this point had watched in silence, took off toward the park.

"You need to get back across the river!" I called to her. What was she doing?

Marin gingerly touched his swollen eye. "We're gonna have pokers, police, and royal bodyguards after us soon. Maybe we should find a place to hide."

"We need to stabilize him." I took off his shoes, peeled the socks off and handed them to Marin. "Can you wet these?"

When he came back with the river-soaked socks, I carefully cushioned his damaged fire with one, then pulled the other over his entire light hand. A barely visible glow penetrated the sock layer. The filthy river water would probably cause problems later—but better infected than dark.

"If you can hear me, buddy, keep burning serum."

He groaned and tried to turn over.

I picked Baptiste up and slung him over my shoulder. Or tried. The first attempt ended with me headfirst in the mud. With Marin's help, I finally balanced Baptiste on my back and secured his arms in front of me.

"Got him?"

I nodded, but my mind was screaming no. I didn't think it was possible, but he actually felt heavier than Marin.

"We should carry him together," Marin said.

I shook my head. "You have to get home before Whisnant figures out your name. It shouldn't take him long since your dad is the only coffee-skin lawyer in Ville Bleu."

"You sure you'll be okay?"

I took a couple hunched steps, careful to keep Baptiste's weight centered. "Have your mom call my Grandma. See if my parents are coming back and what they want me to do."

Marin nodded but continued to watch me with a dubious expression.

I was going to do this. I readjusted Baptiste higher on my back. "Ready, little mec? Let's get you some help."

Without looking at Marin, I began a slow jog up the embankment.

And fell on my face.

Thankfully, that's when Jeannette showed up with a jogging stroller. I didn't ask where she had gotten it. Baptiste was much too big for it at first, but I found if I buckled him in upside down, his legs hung over the top rather than dragging under the wheels.

As soon as he was situated, I maneuvered the stroller onto the street, then sprinted for Rue Principale. Although I hoped Jeannette and Marin would make it home safely, they were on their own. Despite the knowledge that Baptiste wasn't actually my dead brother, saving him had somehow become my number one priority.

Which is why I barely considered the risks of going back to my old neighborhood. Yes, people were more likely to recognize me, and unless they had some sort of official business, the lower shades weren't supposed to cross the street, but whatever the punishment, it couldn't be worse than luminogenic arrest.

By the time I'd made it to Ville Bleu, I was thinking fondly of those tiny cleats. Walking in a park was one thing, but pavement and concrete were not kind to sprinting bare feet. Even more than the lacerations, it was the bruising I knew I'd be feeling in the morning. Luckily there was plenty to distract me from the pain—mostly trying to keep Baptiste from flopping out onto the sidewalk.

Once we got across the shade barrier, we began to draw stares. A group of punk middle-schoolers noticed me as they came out of the theater. They laughed at the awkward cargo and yelled at me to get on my side but apparently didn't care enough to look for a poker.

Finally, I crested a hill and looked down on Blue Hospital. I knew that cluster of white buildings as well as I knew Blue Campus. People would recognize me as soon as I walked in the door. Most of the doctors had known me since I was little. Hopefully they'd help Baptiste without asking a lot of questions.

By this point, I was fairly certain the Captain and Whisnant would've figured out my name and why I was trying to evade law enforcement. As soon as Baptiste got in for treatment, I'd need to disappear again.

The automatic doors opened and I pushed the stroller through. A security guard with a long, pointed beard gestured at Baptiste.

"He Blue?"

I didn't recognize the guard. Had he recently been hired? I'd never made an effort to get to know the Greens around the hospital.

I unbuckled Baptiste from the stroller and turned him right-side up. A bluish flicker shone through the sock. "Nearly. But he punctured his fire and I—"

"The Green Medical Center is across town."

"He's not going to make it. Look, my dad's head fire surgeon and I—"

"I don't care if your dad is the Legendary White King, the hospital insurance doesn't cover non-Blue patients. Those are the rules. Get out of here before I call the soldiers to help you back to your side."

"Can you just bring out a serum pouch? Please. He'll die otherwise."

The guard stared at me a moment. "Stay right there."

"Thank you."

A Green cleaning lady scowled at me and took out her mop. I realized she was cleaning my bloody footprints off the tile. The asphalt had been harder on my feet that I realized.

"Sorry about that."

The woman's expression softened. "You two better clear out of here. That guard went to call the police."

"No, he's getting us a serum pouch."

She gave me a whatever-you-say look.

I glanced down the hall. The guard was talking into a phone.

That blackened piece of—

"Bruno?"

I never thought the sound of my own name could startle me so badly.

Orie stood in the middle of the entryway. A short blond woman had her by the elbow in an effort to get her outside.

"Get in the car," the woman said.

Orie slapped her hand away. "I told you not to touch me, Claudette."

The guard hung up the phone and started toward us. I glanced at his hands—definitely not holding any medical equipment.

Orie's eyes traveled to my teal fire and then to Baptiste. "What happened? Who is this kid? By the way, silk looks really good on you."

I doubted Orie had been the one to rat me out to the pokers, but I certainly didn't have time to chat. If the hospital wasn't going to help, I'd have to take Baptiste to my house. For years, Granny's mortal fear of doctors inspired her to squirrel away medical supplies. She had enough to run a small clinic by this point.

I picked up Baptiste. I could barely see his light through the sock.

"Don't follow me." But when I tried to position him back

in the stroller, my foot slipped on the blood and I fell hard onto one knee. Baptiste rolled onto the floor, and the wet sock went dark.

I ripped it off his hand. The one inside fell away, slightly singed with spots of red. Baptiste's fire organ glowed faintly like the tip of an extinguished wick. From the blood on the sock, I knew his stamen had failed. It had been working too hard to keep the reaction going, and the microscopic capillaries were starting to burst. Blood had mixed with what little fuel he had left, polluting it to the point of uselessness.

He needed fresh serum.

"I need something sharp," I called out. "A needle, or a pin, quickly."

Orie grabbed at the lapel of Claudette's business suit and yanked. Claudette gasped like she'd been shot. Orie presented me with a silver dragon-shaped brooch inlaid with diamonds.

"It has a pin."

I unfastened the clasp and slid the needle into the meaty part of my palm.

"No!" Orie cried.

Claudette tucked her Blue fire under her armpit and waved her dark hand, as if I might come at her next.

"It's okay," I said. I hadn't punctured my fire but instead made a *sentier* as I'd seen my father do. The shallow puncture wouldn't bleed but would allow controlled access to the serum supply without increasing the risk of infection or pressure failure.

Orie grimaced as I pushed the pin in deeper. Not into the muscle but along the surface of my palm. I finally reached the fire chamber and a painful vacuum sensation bloomed in my palm. The body regulated serum pressure to within a few pascals, so I wasn't sure what kind of effect this would have on my luminatory system.

I pulled the needle back out and a few drops of serum seeped through the tiny tunnel of skin onto the heel of my hand. I held it over Baptiste and applied pressure to my palm.

A wave of dizziness hit me. I blinked it away and continued to press gently on the dome of my fire. Four or five drops of serum landed on Baptiste's wound and sizzled. His light flickered, then grew brighter. I pushed out a few more drops and then slid the sock back over Baptiste's hand. As long as I didn't elevate my fire, gravity would keep my serum in place until he needed another few drops.

The guard grabbed the stroller and shoved it out the front entrance. It rolled, hit the curb, and toppled sideways into the street. He expanded a metal baton and, before I could stand or even protest, he slammed it across my back.

I fell forward, unable to draw breath.

"Stop!" Orie shouted.

The guard cleared his throat, obviously surprised by her outburst. "I didn't mean to startle you, 'selle. Someone will be here to remove these Mélangé shortly."

Orie glared at the guard. "Put that away, *imbécile.* We've got room in our car. We can drop them off at Rue Principale."

Claudette folded her arms. "Absolutely not."

As if she hadn't heard, Orie bent to grab Baptiste's arm. I took the other side, and together we half-carried, half-dragged him outside.

"I said no," Claudette growled.

"Then I'll call a cab," Orie said. "And you'll have to explain to Father why I had to puncture my fire to keep the boy alive while we waited."

"Don't be absurd. Get in the car. Alone."

"Bruno," Orie said. "Can I see that pin for a moment?"

"Why do you have to be so dramatic?" Claudette shouted. "I'll take your little charity projects if you'll just grow up."

The three of us fit easily into the back seat of the baby blue convertible. Claudette turned out to be Orie's stepmother, and I got the idea they weren't exactly close.

"You missed the turn!" Orie said. "Maybe if you stopped trying to put the top down."

"It smells like serum in here," Claudette said.

"You really want people seeing you chauffeuring Mélangé?" Orie said. She immediately cast an apologetic glance toward me.

I smiled to let her know I understood. She was worried about people recognizing me.

"Turn around," Orie said. "It's Rue Chêne. Second to last house on the left."

"I said I would take them," Claudette said with a stiff smile. "I didn't say where. I don't know when you started hanging out with freaks, but this stops now. The police will sort this out at the station. And your father will hear about it."

Orie's expression darkened. "That's fine. Father will also hear about Victor."

Claudette turned her head so quickly she should've snapped her neck. "I have no idea what you're—"

"And Eduardo, and that greasy Olish dentist. That is unless you want to leave father and the police out of it. Oh, and just so you know, if this boy dies before we get him help, I'll tell daddy what you spend your 'salon' money on."

The tires squealed as Claudette made a sharp U-turn and gunned the engine.

I steadied Baptiste's fire and carefully slid the sock off his hand. The stamen continued to flicker like a candle, but the occasional drops of serum seemed to be keeping him stable. It looked like he was going to make it.

"Will you be okay once you get to your house?" Orie asked in a whisper.

"I think so. Glad you happened to be at the hospital."

Orie held up a splinted finger on her dark hand. "You can thank Drea."

"Sorry. She was trying to help me sneak out. The girl doesn't do anything halfway. Of course, you helped too." I grimaced as I remembered Orie backhanding Drea across the face.

"So she knows?"

"I'm not sure what she's figured out, but I told her I was in a rush to get my cleats."

Orie nodded. After a brief pause, she whispered, "I wanted to ask you... what do you look for in a companion match?"

"What?" I'd been expecting a question about my newly acquired Mélangé status or motivation for this afternoon's grisly murder—not my taste in girls.

"I mean, everyone has a type." She stared out the window, her face suddenly bright pink. "I like athletic mecs with dark hair." She swallowed. "About your length."

She couldn't honesty be interested in me anymore. Had she missed the green in my fire?

"So...," she said, eyes still glued to the passing houses. "What are you and your parents looking for?"

I cradled Baptiste's hand. I really didn't want to have this conversation right now, but Orie had been willing to jeopardize her own safety and family relations for me. I could at least humor her.

"What do you think of Drea?" she asked before I could answer.

"She's nice, I guess. Kind of... spontaneous." Spontaneous was a synonym for insane, wasn't it?

"So you like spontaneous girls?"

Why were we talking about Drea? "Uh, sure. Not that I really have a chance with any of them now since I'm Blue-Green. You know Drea and Marin's parents signed papers, right?"

Orie's face indicated she hadn't been aware of Drea's betrothal and wasn't exactly heartbroken by the news.

Claudette turned onto my street and slowed.

Before Orie could ask about the other girls in our grade or explain she was into Mélangé rugby players, I asked, "Did the Axe notice I'd left early?"

"I was scared she would," Orie said. "Or that the soldiers would see your shoe."

Crêpes. If Orie had noticed from the other side of the room...

Orie put her dark hand on my forearm. "But if anyone noticed, they didn't say anything." She looked down at her hand, then removed it. In any other situation, I would've felt exceptionally awkward, but at the moment, my focus was entirely on keeping Baptiste—and myself—alive.

So if Orie and Axelle hadn't ratted me out, how had the pokers figured out I was on the team? Had the young poker suspected I was the murderer after all? Collins hadn't acted strangely toward me at the station. Well, he had but not as if he thought I was the city's most wanted fugitive.

I rolled up the sock and pressed a few more drops of serum onto Baptiste's exposed fire organ.

"I think you've given him enough," Orie said.

"I'll be fine." But even as I said it, the bubble of my fire sagged a little. Had I lost too much? I had attributed my increasing dizziness to the acrid smell of serum. But my limbs were starting to feel like I was moving through water. We both needed pouches quickly.

Orie tapped Claudette's headrest. "It's the three-story on

the left. Park under the big tree."

The car slowed. The towering oaks gave way to immaculate grounds and the only home I'd ever known. There were only a few larger on the island. As usual, Granny had every light in the house on—a habit she picked up after Grandpa died.

Claudette shifted into park and blinked up at the structure. "What are you going to do here? Actually, never mind. I don't want to know."

Orie smiled at me expectantly. Instead of relief, the large glowing windows and turreted roof filled me with gut-wrenching pain. Chateau de Nazaire had always meant happiness and safety. Not now. It no longer belonged to me. With a jolt, I realized those walls held my best memories of Ro. How could I let them take him away again?

Baptiste groaned and stirred slightly.

Ro wasn't the one who needed me right now. I had to get Baptiste inside.

I propped him up so I could open the door, but Orie stopped me.

"Not that side. They're watching the car."

I squinted into the darkness. Two pokers stood on opposite sides of the house, fires covered, all but hidden in the foliage—waiting for someone.

So it was official. They knew who I was and what I had done. Whether they'd found out from Sébastien or someone else, it didn't matter. Even if I managed to convince Orie and Claudette to drop me off in the woods, Baptiste would die. If I stayed, the Dominateur would most likely execute us both. Juenes knew the whole story. So did Aro. By this point, the Commissaire himself probably knew of Baptiste's involvement. They wouldn't care that it had been an accident. They wouldn't care that I'd been trying to save the life of a Mélangé.

"I'll distract them," Orie said.

"Huh?"

"I can't imagine they'd have more than two watching

your house. If I draw their attention to the front, is there a back door you can get him in?"

"The cellar storm-doors are next to those bushes."

"Perfect."

Claudette tapped the steering wheel.

Orie reached for her door handle. At that moment, the image of Marin hanging by his ankles flashed in my mind.

"Wait," I said. "Just a simple distraction. Don't do anything crazy."

Orie flashed me a nervous grin. "I thought you liked crazy." Then she slipped out onto the empty street.

I gave Baptiste another two drops of serum. Still burning. Barely. A wave of lightheadedness blurred the edge of my vision. I leaned my head against the cool window and took a deep breath. Orie stood at my front door, repeatedly pressing the doorbell.

This wasn't going to work. The pokers hadn't moved.

Orie knocked, then shouted. What was she doing?

The door opened and Granny appeared, her gray hair gathered in a silk night scarf. Orie spoke softly, a little too close to Granny's face. Was she swaying on her feet?

Claudette swore, and I followed her gaze to a third lightless poker on the other side of the street. He was walking through our neighbor's yard as if it were his own, his eyes locked on our car.

Granny and Orie continued to stand there, talking. How was this a distraction? Granny looked toward the car and said something. Orie nodded, steadied herself against a pillar, then collapsed sideways into the flowerbed.

Granny seemed genuinely surprised and dropped to her knees next to her. Then Granny cast another quick glance at the car. Or at the poker still moving toward it.

"I need help!" Granny screamed. "I can't find a pulse!"

I'd never heard her raise her voice before. Was she talking to the poker across the street?

At that moment, I realized Orie's fire had gone out.

I couldn't help the cry that escaped me. Her light hand was clearly visible, but the light had vanished. She was dead. But how?

Claudette, however, didn't seem concerned. Had she somehow poisoned her stepdaughter?

Just as I was about to grab Claudette by the shoulder and demand to know what she'd done, Orie's light reappeared. A little dimmer than it had been but still burning. Did that mean she was still alive? What in the rainbow had just happened?

"Help me lift her," Granny shouted. "We need to get her inside." The door opened wider, and two Greens appeared in the doorway. The porch light illuminated their features as they stepped outside. My internal organs jumped into my throat.

The Chief of Police and Sergent Whisnant had been waiting inside for me.

At the appearance of the men, the two soldiers hiding in the trees jogged toward the entrance, removing shutter gloves as they ran. To my great relief, the poker on the other side of the street abandoned his course toward the car and headed for the porch.

Even with all the attention focused on the front door, I didn't think I'd be able to slip out with Baptiste and not be noticed. I gave him a single drop more, ignoring the blurring of my vision and Claudette's grumbled objection at the smell.

Should I take Baptiste somewhere else? I didn't see how I'd be able to get him help here—especially since two out of three heads of law enforcement were hanging out with Gran. But I couldn't abandon my own grandmother, either. She'd given no sign that they'd been rough with her, or even inconvenienced her, but she'd always been a great actor. If those two idiots laid a hand on Granny, they would regret it for the rest of their lives.

One of the pokers crouched to lift Orie, then recoiled. I could see Orie moving erratically on the ground. She seemed completely out of it. I really hoped it was an act. The three pokers lifted Orie and carried her into the house. The police chief and Sergent Whisnant followed. Granny entered last. Before she shut the door, she looked directly at the car and motioned toward the side of the house.

She still wanted me to come inside? Maybe she had a plan.

I got out of the car and pulled Baptiste onto my back by his arms. Blank, he seemed twice as heavy as he had earlier. There was no way I could hide my fire and still hold him in place. Hopefully there weren't any more pokers hiding in the underbrush.

At the last minute, I remembered my signed confession still in the pocket of my stolen shirt. Wouldn't want to be caught with that on me—now that I understood how the law worked on the island. There was still a slight chance that they might not know exactly how Baptiste was involved. I slid the folded form into the pocket behind Claudette's seat.

"Thanks for the ride."

"Stay away from us."

Nice lady. I guess I didn't blame her for hating me. I'd put both her and Orie in incredible danger.

I shut the door and carried Baptiste a few steps from the sidewalk to my yard. I was thinking how nice the damp grass felt on my lacerated feet when I suddenly found myself on my stomach.

Had I fallen? I must have passed out. Claudette's car was gone. How long had I been laying in my front yard? Baptiste lay beside me, flickering fire still barely visible through the sock. It couldn't have been very long if Baptiste was still alive.

My head felt full of rocks. I'd definitely lost too much serum.

The front door opened. Light spilled out onto the yard. I turned my head, but a pillar blocked my view of the porch. Whoever it was need only step onto the walkway, and Baptiste and I would be in full view.

I pressed my light into the grass as a male voice spoke. One of the pokers. Why couldn't I have made it a dozen more feet? I whispered a prayer into the grass. Surely the Créateur wouldn't guide me this far only to have me fail. I thought I heard Granny's voice, but I couldn't make out the words. There were no shouts of alarm. The door closed. Silence.

Had they gone back inside? I tried to get up onto my knees, but my limbs felt like they belonged to someone else. My light hand was strangely weightless. No longer caring if people were watching, I lifted my fire. A line of serum ran from the puncture hole I'd made. From wrist to elbow, my arm was slick with oily fuel. The dome of my palm resembled a deflated beach ball. As I watched, the residual serum shifted away from my stamen and my light flickered.

Pain like I'd never experienced shot up my arm and seemed to spread throughout my body.

Créateur help me.

I was dying.

Somewhere in the distance, a creak of metal signaled the opening of the storm-doors. It meant as much to me as the chirping crickets. The only thing my foggy mind could comprehend was that I hadn't saved my brother.

CHAPTER TWELVE

FIRST AIDE

I remembered voices. Falling. Pain. Was I dead? I couldn't breathe. A snow lizard sat on my chest, chewing on my hand. Flesh became ice. Thoughts collapsed. My brain shrank and slid down the back of my throat.

Then heat.

The fiery warmth traveled up my arm and into my chest. It filled my lungs with life and pulled my mind back into position. My first thought was an ungrammatical request for air.

My eyes and mouth opened together, and the world flooded back.

Drea grinned and pushed the hair back from my forehead. "Thought you were blacked," she whispered. "You should really keep pointy things away from your fire."

"Baptiste," I croaked. The words felt as if they'd sprouted nails on the way up.

"Doing better than you. Stop moving your hand."

The ground pressed cold against my back. I felt the serum pouch cinched tightly around my wrist. The viscous texture of the artificial serum sent perpetual shivers up my neck. But with each moment that passed, the pain in my hand lessened, and my body felt more 'right.' My feet had been cleaned and bandaged. Baptiste lay a few feet away, snoring softly—also wearing one of Granny's serum pouches. Bless that woman and her iatrophobia.

The cellar smelled of dusty boxes and damp wood. The artificials were off, and Drea's red hair looked purple by the light of her fire. What was she doing in my basement?

Another blue light appeared, and Marin's face joined Drea's.

"You were amazing," Marin said in a soft voice.

I managed a weak smile, and was about to say something about how my best happened to be good enough this time, when Marin took Drea's face in his hands and kissed her. Apparently he'd been talking to his girlfriend.

I pretended to drift off again, glad it was probably too dark for them to see my face which was certainly bright red.

The affection only lasted a moment, but watching it made me feel like I needed a good scrubbing.

"You should have seen her," Marin said, to me this time, presumably. "The pouch wasn't working so she ripped your fire open with her teeth."

It took me a moment to realize he was serious. "Oh. Guess it worked. Thanks." I tried not to imagine Drea's face on my fire. It felt disloyal to Marin somehow—even if he didn't seem bothered by it. I was glad I'd been asleep for that particular procedure.

I pretended to be interested in the directions printed on the side of the dark blue serum pouch.

-Break and completely remove inner seal.

-Gently cup fingers around esca and insert entire hand into pouch.

-Tighten drawstring. DO NOT cut off circulation.

-After 6 hours (minimum), if esca is not improved, reinsert hand and seek medical attention.

I smiled. The directions made me think of Grandpa Zacharie. He had always referred to the fire organ by its scientific name—used to drive Mom crazy. "That word is disgusting!" Sometimes Dad and I would join in.

My smile faded. It felt like a century ago. Losing Grandpa and Ro had been hard enough. I wouldn't let the sergent take the rest of them from me.

The thought of Whisnant brought with it the image of Orie, prone and lightless at my front door. "What about Orie. Is she still alive?"

"Why wouldn't she be?" Marin asked.

"I saw her light go out. Her hand was there, and the light was on, then it wasn't. She fell, then it came back on."

Drea looked at me like I'd just tried to correct her calculometrics homework. "Pretty sure that didn't happen. You were probably delirious from serum loss."

"Anyway, we saw her leave a while back," Marin said with an apologetic smile. He pointed at a small window at grass level.

"How did she fit through that?"

"No, she left through the front door—we *saw* her through the window."

"Oh... So, Drea—you just happened to be hanging out in my basement?"

Drea raised an eyebrow. "Really? You show up half-dead, green in your fire, wearing women's clothes, and I'm the one who has to explain myself?"

"She's got a point," Marin said.

I pushed myself into a sitting position and tried to block out the throbbing in my hand. "I told you in Green Town, Mare —the less my friends know the better. I don't want to involve you in this."

"Bru-Baby," Marin said in a flat voice, "I've already been tortured for information I didn't have. The polite thing would be to give me something to divulge for next time."

I knew he was trying to keep the conversation light, but I could hear the edge of hysteria in his voice as he mentioned the interrogation.

"Baptiste painted me, but it wasn't his fault."

Drea and Marin exchanged looks.

"A kid named Aro blackmailed him. A poker was going to kill Baptiste, so I fought him."

"You fought Baptiste?" Marin asked.

"Yes, I beat up a kid with a mental disability."

Marin's brow twisted.

Drea rolled her eyes. "Bruno killed the soldier who was going to kill Baptiste who'd been sent by Aro, to paint Bruno."

"Bruno killed someone?!"

Drea frantically shushed him.

Clunky footsteps moved across the ceiling. Pretty sure Granny didn't own a pair of military boots.

For a breathless moment, the three of us watched the door at the top of the stairs. Another set of footsteps made the wooden floorboards creak. Marin silently padded to a nearby desk and picked up something metallic.

Another moment passed. The door didn't open. Maybe they hadn't heard.

Finally, Marin blew his non-existent bangs out of his face and grinned.

Drea's posture relaxed. "So glad we have you, mon amour," she whispered. "I wouldn't have thought to grab the stapler."

I stifled a laugh.

Marin squinted at the object in his hand. "I thought it was a cork-screwy thing. Who keeps a stapler in their wine cellar?" He set it back on the desk.

"Careful," Drea hissed. "It could be loaded."

"Stop," I mouthed to Drea. I would've whispered it, but my vocal chords were clamped down tightly on my throat to keep my laughter silent.

The door at the top of the stairs burst open.

Before any of us could scream, run, or pick up the stapler, a duffle bag bounced down the stairs. Granny stood silhouetted against the kitchen's artificial light. She hesitated a moment, put a hand to her chest, then closed the door without a sound. Was she trying to give us a message? Or had her gesture been relief at seeing me alive?

Drea opened the duffel bag. It contained several ham and cheese sandwiches, scissors, a scrap of paper with writing, and a mayonnaise-scented suit. Marin looked at the note, shook his head, and held it out to me. "I don't think she meant to include this."

I didn't take it. I had a sandwich in each hand and was trying to fit both in my mouth at the same time.

"Bruno, the Créateur gave you teeth," Drea said. "Choose to chew."

I ignored her advice. My stomach supported this decision. After a couple arduous swallows, I was able to de-sandwich one hand.

I took the note. It was in Granny's loopy handwriting.

TO-DO LIST
Call Christelle ✓
Plan Fri dinner for Andre ✓
Haircut
Out at 11. Stormy
Take suit to HV
Award "Outta Sight" certificates
Call Orie soon
Write favorite grandchild love letter ✓

"I'm pretty sure this is for me," I said through a mouthful of food. "But I can't tell what it all means. Why didn't she just speak plain Téle?"

"It's probably code in case the crêpe bags got a look at it." Drea snatched the note and examined it. "She already called your mom—that's checked off. And it seems your dad, if not both your parents, will be here by Friday night."

Marin chewed on his lower lip. "So, what's he supposed to do for two days?"

I eyed the dark pants and jacket laid out on the ground. A

baby blue shirt and navy tie had also been stuffed into the bag. "Deliver my dad's suit to Hameau Vert for some reason?"

"Your grandmother sadly misjudged your deduction skills," Drea said with a smirk. "She expects you to wear the suit and find a place to lie low in Green Town."

Marin grinned. "You could totally pass for an adult. Well, maybe a college student."

"But where am I going to sleep?"

Drea glanced at Baptiste. "Maybe tubby will put you up."

"Don't call him that," I said.

"It's not like he can hear me."

"Just don't." I picked up the suit pants and made a twirling gesture to Drea. She made a pouty face and turned to face the stairs. While Marin helped me—one-handed dressing proved a virtual impossibility—Drea studied the to-do list.

"It's ten-fifteen," she said. "Your grandma wants you to leave in forty-five minutes, the way you came—out the storm doors. I'm assuming she'll create another distraction."

"So, how did you two end up in my basement?"

Drea returned the note. "Everyone was out looking for my missing boyfriend. I happened to spot him crossing Rue Principale. Well, staggering across it like he was high on serum. He kept trying to go home even after I told him his parents wanted him to find a place to hide."

"He finally agreed to come to my house—with some persuasion," Drea said with a sly glance at Marin. "But he insisted we stop by and give your grandma an update. Thankfully she invited us in—otherwise we would've been standing on the porch when the blackheads showed up."

Marin adjusted my tie. "Turned out to be a great place to keep out of the way. In fact, maybe we should hang out down here and plan our next move. Drea could take Baptiste home."

"To be honest, that sounds a lot better than running around Hameau Vert," I said. "But Granny's not stupid. I'm sure she's thought about this. If I ignored her advice and she got caught trying to hide me... We'd better stick with her plan."

"Put on a suit and stay out of sight?" Marin said as he slid one of Dad's shiny leather shoes onto my foot. "That's not a plan. And why wait for your dad? What's he going to do in three days that we can't do now?"

I adjusted the shoe to lessen the pressure on my bandaged foot. "I guess he'll talk to Whisnant and try to come to an arrangement."

Drea and Marin didn't comment. They knew what kind of an arrangement I meant. A Blue's last line of defense was cold hard cash.

Marin seemed to grow tired of crouching and sat on the floor to tie my shoe. It was a bit awkward but also nice in a way. It felt like something a brother would do. He cocked his head and lifted my foot. "That's a lot of heel for a man."

I smiled. "My dad's on the short side. He said two inches earns him twice the respect."

"Still don't see the point of all this," Drea said. "I'm sure if you just explained to Sergent Whisnant that it was an accident, they wouldn't hold you responsible. I mean, it's common sense."

Marin met my gaze briefly before starting on the other shoe, but I caught the flash of panic. We had both experienced how Télesphorian law enforcement worked. Honor and common sense were not in their mission statement.

Marin finished my shoe before he spoke. "It's about control."

Drea glanced over her shoulder, saw I was mostly clothed, and came to help with my buttons. "Are we talking about controlling the crime rate?" she said with surprisingly little sarcasm. She seemed to sense Marin was navigating some dangerous emotion terrain. "Or controlling punk teenagers?"

"Humans. Télesphorians," Marin said. "The officials control the lower shades with ugly threats. They control the beau monde with attractive lies."

I had never heard Marin wax philosophical. I certainly hadn't expected his argument to make sense. "You're saying that instead of trying to do the right thing, they're trying to make the things they do look right."

Main shrugged. "If enough of the Blues believed law enforcement was in the wrong, the Conseil del Dominateur would have to take notice. Whereas if a Red tried to complain, pokers would just zap him for being offsides."

"That's why Whisnant wants us dead," I said with a sudden realization. "Not justice for the poker's family—but because we're probably the first people in fifty years to defy his authority."

"We might give the rest of them ideas."

"When your parents get back," Drea said, "send them directly to the Cathedral to request an audience with the Doms."

Marin shook his head. "They'll side with Whisnant."

"You don't know that," Drea said. She tilted my head and began hacking away at my hair.

I grimaced. Not from vanity, but because Drea handled the scissors like an amateur gardener at a speed-hedging competition. After several terrifying minutes, she grunted in satisfaction. She looked to Marin for approval.

He glanced at my now hair-covered suit and nodded. "Would've been better if you did it in your underwear."

Drea slapped him. After a second, she said, "Oh, you meant Bruno. Sorry."

Marin gave me a what-have-I-got-myself-into look, but it softened almost immediately into an at-least-life-won't-be-boring grin.

Drea, now with slightly rosier cheeks, brushed at my suit and pulled a pair of shadow glasses from her pocket. "Stole these from my dad to watch the match."

I put them on. "Well?"

"Those two inches do make a difference. As long as you don't smile you could pass for twenty."

"I can't smile?"

"Adults pride themselves on keeping their emotions invisible. Basically the boreder you look, the older you'll seem."

I winced a bit but managed not to say anything about her reckless suffix improvisation.

"And I know boreder is not a word," Drea said. "I see your eye twitching."

I feigned confused surprise and ran a hand through my short hair. I liked it. I felt like a new person. We might actually pull this off.

"Papa! Papa!"

I fell to the floor and clamped my free hand over Baptiste's mouth. "You're safe. But you have to be quiet, okay?"

He flapped his arm to free his hand from the pouch.

"No. It's helping you get better. Calm down, buddy. That's it."

Several pairs of boots clomped overhead. Drea swore and pulled Marin into the corner behind a shelf. I didn't have time to move before the door opened, letting in a shaft of blinding illumination from the kitchen.

"No, it came from down here," came the police chief's voice. "And it weren't no cat."

The light didn't hit us directly, but I kept motionless anyway. We were close enough to the far wall that I could only see his boots. It was a mark of how terrified I must've been that I barely noticed his double negative. And the misplaced subjunctive.

Okay, it was impossible for me not to notice, but it only heightened my anxiety. I knew this was the end. Now the only question was how I could avoid getting everyone else in trouble.

The boots began to descend the stairs.

"Don't come down!" Drea shouted abruptly. "I'm not dressed."

"Who is that?" the chief called. "Cover yourself, I'm coming down."

"Give me a second to get my shirt on, perv!" Drea waved me toward the storm-doors.

I took my hand from Baptiste's mouth and pulled him to

his feet. I put a finger to my lips and then pointed toward the door. Our walk to the cement steps wasn't exactly silent, but at least the chief had stopped descending.

Drea stuffed my old clothes and used bandages into the duffel, along with the note, then threw the bag at Marin. "Go!" she mouthed. Then over her own tank top, she pulled on the silk blouse I had stolen. She fastened a couple buttons, then stepped into the light. "What do you want?" she said in an irritated voice.

I eased one of the metal doors upward with a loud creak.

Drea abruptly shouted and kicked the serum pouch packaging under the desk. "I'm so sick of having my workout interrupted." Then she shouted again, loud and obnoxious.

As her tantrum escalated, Marin pocketed his fire and we slipped outside, quietly closing the door behind us.

In full view of a poker.

My heart pirouetted in my chest until I realized we were in the shadows, the poker had bright landscaping lights shining at him and was already striding across the lawn toward the front door—toward the shouts of unhinged feminine fury still coming from inside.

Thank the Créateur he hadn't followed her shouting to the side of the house.

We stumbled through bushes and shrubs until we crossed into the neighbor's property—then we split up. Marin took off his shirt and began jogging toward Drea's house. Baptiste and I speed-walked for the shade barrier.

"If anyone stops us, I'm your big brother, okay?"

"Where are we going?" Baptiste asked.

"Listen, this is important. We both injured our fires climbing trees and my Blue friend brought us to his house to be pouched. Can you remember that?"

"I think I'd be more likely to retain a cover story if I was sure I wasn't being kidnapped."

I blinked. Was this the same kid who'd been rolling around on the ground earlier?

"Where are we going?" he repeated.

"You're going home," I said. "As soon as you tell me where that is."

"You're not going to tell my dad about what I did, are you?"

I didn't answer. A Blue light bobbed toward us. "Walk normally."

"How else would I walk?"

A man passed us with a large dog on a leash. I waved with my dark hand. The man's brow furrowed, and he looked like he was about to ask me something when the dog began sniffing my suit.

"Down, Gracie."

The dog ignored the man and grew more intent on examining every inch of my lower half.

"I have a cat," I said with a laugh. A mayonnaise flavored cat.

The Blue finally managed to pull the dog off amid apologies and embarrassed chuckles. Baptiste and I both let out relieved sighs as the man disappeared around a corner.

We'd gone two more blocks when Baptiste saw a moth, slapped his hands over his ears, and took off at a sprinting waddle.

"Hey," I called after him. "It's just a bug. It's not going to hurt you." But it was nice to have him moving a little faster. I jogged after him until he tired, then we resumed our previous pace toward his side of town.

It was only after we'd crossed Rue Principale that I remembered the pokers would be looking for me in Hameau Vert as well. In fact, Sébastien and Whisnant could probably identify my Mélangé shade from a mile away.

More reason to take Granny's advice and stay out of sight.

We arrived at Baptiste's red-bricked apartment building around two in the morning. Partly because we both needed frequent breaks as our fires healed, but mostly because "everything looks different at night" as Baptiste put it after the third dead end. At least my feet were clean and comfortable inside Dad's dress shoes. And the long walk gave me time to slowly tease information out of Baptiste.

The more I spoke with him, the more I realized his disability had less to do with his intelligence and more to do with social skills. He clearly didn't want to talk about Aro at first and sometimes he seemed to not even hear my questions. Little by little, a picture emerged.

A few years ago, Aro had appeared at the Académie without explanation. According to Baptiste, "origin stories" were traded among the students like marbles. That kid was painted as a baby. This one fell in love with a Blue.

Aro refused to say how he'd become Mélangé, but he did make sure everyone knew his grandfather was on the Conseil de Dominateur. Other times he said his grandfather worked with the Dominateur. He used this dubious connection as leverage whenever possible to get his way.

Baptiste was a special case. Aro took particular pleasure in tormenting and humiliating him. On the day Aro stole two of Baptiste's encyclopedias and saw the look of horrified desperation, he knew he could make Baptiste do whatever he wanted.

Those encyclopedias had started it all.

Once we got to that point, Baptiste seemed to find his stride and quickly divulged the rest of the details.

In the end, it was a small miracle we hadn't run into any law enforcement on our stroll. I'd been so engrossed in Baptiste's account, I probably would've walked right into them.

"Are you going to be okay?" I asked Baptiste at the door to his building.

Baptiste pointed at the only illuminated window. "Papa's home. Probably quite worried. You're not coming up?"

I still had a dozen questions for Baptiste, like why he didn't just tell an adult about being bullied, what was the reason for all the rolling around in the grass on Blue Campus, and whether his punctured fire had been Aro's doing or his own. But I was beyond exhausted. I had no desire to explain everything to Baptiste's parents, and even less to put them in danger.

"I'll find a place to lie low, catch a nap. Do people use this elevator a lot?"

"Probably not in the middle of the night."

"Sounds like I found myself a bed."

Despite my bone-aching fatigue, I couldn't relax in the stuffy elevator. My mind insisted on reprocessing everything that had happened that day. Soon I began to feel claustrophobic in the enclosed space, so I went for a circular walk in the lobby.

But the entrance had too many wide windows, so I explored the stairwell and found the door to the roof unlocked. The view was worth climbing seven flights of stairs.

From my upstairs window in Ville Bleu, the city had always seemed like a series of hills receding into the horizon, losing detail and color with each rise. But this higher, central angle brought every boundary, every cross-section, into sharp relief. It was like rooms of a house each with its own style. The tidy brick buildings of Hameau Vert could have been designed by the father of the house, emphasizing utility and efficiency. With Ville Bleu, the mother had created something flawlessly beautiful. The squalor of Taudis Rogue could only be the child's room—a smelly, filthy, disaster that needed not so much a deep cleaning as a complete renovation.

The glittering river seemed an entity of its own, a star-encrusted serpent winding its way downhill to the Royal Estate. The tail stretched from high on the mountainside, cutting through the thick carpet of trees. The most impressive landmark in the vista was also the ugliest. At thirty feet tall with an additional six underground to prevent tunneling, the razorwire-topped concrete barrier protected Télesphore City from outside attacks.

Well, maybe at one time it was meant to protect Télesphorians. But now it felt like two pale hands encircling a throat.

In the shadow of the wall, not too far from my old house, the Crystal Cathedral shone like a multifaceted beacon. It was the most beautiful building in Ville Bleu but not the largest. That honor went to the stadium. The pitch of that enormous building had been my second home for the last three years. The place where I learned to put goals above comfort, to turn my pain into power, as Coach would say. Now, thanks to Aro, the only time I'd be allowed inside was to be classified. Except I'd surely be arrested before they got around to awarding me a career.

In my mind, I went over Baptiste's account again, still unable to comprehend how one boy could be so cruel to another —and a fellow shademate at that. Stealing those encyclopedias seemed like a childish prank compared to what had followed.

For several weeks after taking the books, Aro had used Baptiste to make money. The Mélangé students played Firearchy before school or during lunch. Baptiste would sit next to Aro at an outside table, pretending to do schoolwork. When Aro drew a marble he didn't want, he'd casually drop it onto the grass. Occasionally he'd knock Baptiste's book or pencil off the table. That was Baptiste's cue to pick up the discarded spheres and keep them in his pocket. If the other player suspected cheating—accusations doubled after Aro instituted the betting of lunch money—Aro would pour his glass spheres onto the table and have Baptiste count them.

Apparently Baptist was a savant with numbers and, simply by glancing at the pile, could count them and say how many of which colors were missing. Naturally Baptiste was forced to lie, and if the other student—who'd typically just lost a week's worth of lunch money—wanted to count them himself, Baptiste would make sure the marbles in his pocket ended up on the table without anyone noticing.

Baptiste said he'd quickly become proficient at his part. Every day, Aro promised to return the encyclopedias, but the next day there was always an excuse and another student to fleece.

This morning had been different. Aro had arrived late to school. During lunch, instead of setting up the Firearchy box, he pulled Baptiste into the fanroom and gave him a pair of wire cutters and an alloy glove. Aro explained he'd just placed a bet on the upcoming Rugby Championship, wagering all the money he'd rifted so far from his classmates. He had picked the 'dog' to win.

Baptiste didn't follow pre-collegiate rugby so he assumed TC was the "dog team". Why would Aro bet on foreigners?

In order to ensure that Aro made a lot of money—and returned Baptiste's books—all Baptiste had to do was cut the barrier fence, sneak onto Blue Campus, and ask for a student named Nazeer. If he could convince Nazeer to shake light hands with him through the alloy glove, Baptiste would complete the mission and earn back his belongings.

Less than two hours later, my future imploded.

Aro had destroyed my life to make a quick profit. Knowing the why didn't make the reality of my situation any easier to stomach. Neither did the realization that if I hadn't been the most celebrated TC player for the last two years, my athletic and academic career would still be intact.

Eventually I grew cold and made my way down to the elevator, where I folded my suit jacket into a pillow-shaped mass and went to sleep.

Not my best idea, sleeping in an elevator. Not only was it too cramped for me to stretch out properly, the late-night janitors don't lug their carpet shampooers up the stairs. After being woken up twice by startled screams, I lay down under the stairwell.

In my dreams, I was drowning. Nobody cared. No one tried to help—except one woman. She pulled me from the water with eight compelling words.

"I'm sorry, 'sieur, but you can't sleep here."

I sat up—right into a pipe jutting from the underside of the stairs. Morning eyelight reflected off a pair of shiny black shoes. I rubbed my forehead. "What's the problem?" It came out sharper than I intended, but I'd never been pleasant in the morning. Especially before breakfast.

"Manager called us. Thought you might be a barrier jumper."

I recognized the voice now: the female officer who'd chased me down to return my shirt. This was not good. She was definitely going to have a lot of questions.

Or maybe she wouldn't recognize me. Yesterday I'd been a shirtless Blue with hair nearly to my shoulders.

"Can't be a comfortable place to sleep," she said.

I faced the wall and put on Drea's dark glasses. "I'm not Red, if that's what you're worried about."

"There a particular reason you're hiding under here?"

Lost my key? Forgot my apartment number? "My mom locked me out. Came home too late, I guess."

"You still live with your parents? So you're not classified."

Whoops. I should have said wife.

I crawled out from under the stairs. The officer's name tag said DuPont—and unless the green had eaten away at my memory, her first name was Sheri.

Officer DuPont frowned at my serum pouch but otherwise showed no signs of recognition. "Must've been some party. How old are you?"

Party? Did she honestly think I'd get high by drinking my own serum? I suppressed a shiver. I needed to end this conversation quickly before she realized I was the mec she'd seen sprinting away from Ville Bleu. If I acted like a serum sucker, maybe she wouldn't make the connection.

"I'll be seventeen in Janvier," I said in a lethargic voice. "Wait... yeah seventeen." I casually extracted my hand from the serum pouch. It looked horrible. I could actually see where Drea had bit me—but the pouch had done its job. The wound was scabbed over, and my dome seemed much less droopy.

DuPont's eyes widened slightly, whether because of my mixed shade or the obvious teeth marks, I couldn't tell. Her face, however, quickly resumed a disinterested expression. I almost laughed. Drea had been right about adults' lack of emotion.

"Let's get you home," she said. "Maybe your mother and me can come up with some safer methods of discipline."

I decided correcting her grammar wouldn't fit the persona of brain-dead serum addict. But I was certainly not going with her upstairs. I could imagine the awkward questions after I showed up at Baptiste's door with a police officer. I needed to get out of the building before she insisted.

"Actually, I'm glad you woke me up," I said as I pulled on

my suit coat and grinned like a fool. "Supposed to be at school early. I'll just head on down there now."

"In a suit?"

"I've got a presentation. That's why I'm going early."

I hoped she didn't think too hard about why I'd gone out with my friends in my presentation clothes.

"Do you normally party in your presentation clothes?"

Crêpes.

"You weren't worried you'd spill something on it?" She raised her eyebrows.

"I uh, like to look nice sometimes. I mean, the girls like it. My girlfriend. She likes it. It's awfully bright outside, what time did you say it was? I should probably get to school."

Sheri sighed. "I'll walk you, then. I know an old man who sits at his window looking for curfew breakers to report."

"Does he smoke a cigar?"

She laughed. "You know him then."

"He gave me directions to the pol... I've seen him around."

My second stroll with Sheri was slightly less awkward than the first. Although I was still terrified of being identified, at least I didn't have to make up details on the spot. Sheri was much less flirty this time. For the most part, this was a relief. But in an unexpected and totally ridiculous way, I also found it distressing. Bruno Nazaire had never not been flirted with. Yes, the attention had always bothered me before. But clearly some part of me needed that validation.

I secretly hoped her obvious lack of interest was because she knew how young I was or because I'd mentioned my girl-friend, and not because Drea had somehow messed up my hair. For years I'd harassed Granny to let me get it cut, but maybe I should've listened to her. What if it was the only thing girls liked about me?

I felt a desperate urge to flirt with Sheri, see if I could get a reaction but knew that was wrong on so many levels. I did pretend to stumble and grab her arm, though. And I may have mentioned that her uniform had a nice floral scent. Okay, I couldn't help myself.

She steadied me, then pulled away without so much as a smile.

It was worse than I imagined. I was hideous. First thing I would do upon arrival to the mainland—grow my hair out again.

In the ten minutes it took to walk to L'académie Mélangé, my ego had been reduced to a fraction of its former glory. When I realized the parking lot was empty, however, I forgot about my hair—mostly—and began to consider my options.

I could run for it. She'd probably follow. I was tired of lying. Sheri seemed like a nice enough person. Maybe if I explained who I was and how I was innocent, she'd actually help me.

I should've tried earlier, when I was a long-haired, shirtless Blue.

Now I was a serum-sucking, hack-haired Mélangé in a baggy suit. My descent into obscurity was happening much faster than I expected. If I survived until tomorrow, I'd probably be running around the Taudis in my underwear eating out of trash cans.

"Looks like you're a little early," Sheri said. "Well, it's six now, so at least no one will report you."

"Oh. Right."

Sheri tilted her head as if trying to get a glimpse behind my glasses. "You wouldn't happen to have a Blue older brother named—"

"Oh, there he is!"

I pointed to a man that had just pulled into the parking lot on a large tricycle.

"Thanks so much for your help, Sheri," I said in the voice of a twelve-year-old with a hangover.

I took off toward the parking lot before she could ask again about older brothers who might go running shirtless. I'd planned to alter my course as soon as Sheri turned her back, but every time I looked behind me, she stood there watching with a disturbing intensity.

Maybe she was starting to like my short hair.

Tricycle man noticed me. I had no choice but to wave and approach him as if we were old friends.

He would've looked like a mechanic except that his full body jumpsuit was electric orange with yellow and red stripes. I'd seen illustrations of Estorian jesters, but he was missing the hat with bells. Maybe he was a janitor with histrionic personality disorder.

"Good morning," I said.

"Glorious, isn't it?"

Holy crêpes, she was a woman. She squinted and cocked her head. "Are you from the..."

I nodded. Prematurely it seemed, because she stopped talking and I had no idea what I'd just agreed to.

"Nice surprise. They told me my request for an aide had been denied."

"They, uh... reconsidered on account of the great work you've been doing here."

She narrowed her eyes, which was quite a feat considering she'd already been squinting. "The Board made it very clear that once we reached fifty students, I'd get an assistant and they would expand the building to make another classroom. Are we getting another classroom?"

"Uh... How many students do you have now?"

"Forty-six."

"Well, then I guess not."

"What are your subjects?"

I hesitated. It was L'académie Mélangé, how advanced could they be? "I'm comfortable with pretty much anything."

She raised her eyebrows. They were coal dark, like her hair, which was cut to within a quarter inch of her scalp.

"How's your calculometrics?"

Blank. "Good, but I may have learned different methods than you teach here."

"Great. Maybe you can show us a few things." She displayed her green palm. "I'm Claire LaCroix. Everyone calls me LaClaire."

Maybe staying a while wasn't a bad idea afterall. I'd love the opportunity to chat with Aro. Maybe even force a confession out of him.

I raised my fire. "Benoit Molyneux."

Imbécil. Why had I used my mother's maiden name? A hundred thousand families and I picked the second most likely to identify me.

"The help is much appreciated, Benoit. Last week of school is always hectic. I'll probably have you take over the grading so I can get the final ready."

I glanced behind me. Sheri waved.

"Friend of yours?" Claire asked.

"Old girlfriend," I said. "Sad really. Just can't let me go."

It was a little disturbing how quickly I'd picked up this lying thing.

I thumbed through the stack of history essays on my desk. What in the rainbow had I gotten myself into? For the first hour, I considered slipping out of the classroom as soon as Claire's back was turned, but then realized I had no place to go. If I went back to Baptiste's apartment, who knew if anyone would be home? Or what if Baptiste's parents turned me in? There had to be some sort of a reward for my capture. The stairwell was out—someone was bound to see me and call the cops again. I was supposed to stay "outta sight" until Dad returned tomorrow. I definitely didn't want to hole up in the tube slide again. At least here I was out of view of the patrolling pokers and nosy neighbors.

It helped that Claire didn't make a big deal of my arrival. She left me alone with my work, said nothing about removing my shadow glasses, and best of all, didn't try to introduce me to the class, who incidentally, didn't seem at all surprised by her blinding attire. When she called roll, there were only two students absent: Baptiste Wedel and Aro Loup. Baptiste I could understand. His parents were probably keeping him home to recover. But why was Aro missing? So much for extracting a confession out of him.

Jeannette was the only other student I recognized. I was surprised they would let a Red Mélangé go to school with Blue and Green Mélangé. The black-haired Orange looked even smaller next to the other kids. She kept mostly to herself and didn't seem to recognize me with the suit and haircut. Although she did stare plenty, along with the rest of the class. More often than not, they caught me staring back.

I'd never seen so many exotic shades. And the idea of children of different ages all meeting together in a single classroom seemed absurd. How did anyone learn anything? When Claire checked up on me, I couldn't help but voice my curiosity.

"According to the Board of Education," she explained, "a roster of forty-six students doesn't merit two teachers—at least not at the illustrious Academié Mélangé." She patted my hand and continued, "At least they finally gave me a support team." Which made me feel like a royal crépe bag.

After some reading and basic math exercises, Claire announced it was time for recess.

Recess? What was this, daycare?

The break turned out to be a blessing since Claire followed the children outside to supervise. For the first time that morning, I found myself alone. I took a recess of my own and went in search of a telephone. With the risk of being overheard on both ends, I wouldn't be able to give Orie a lot of details, but at least she could let Granny know I hadn't yet been devoured by the Commissaire's dogs.

I searched the hallway, Claire's office, and even a few storage rooms. The only phone in the school sat on the desk of the director. As the bearded man was currently asleep at his desk, I decided against disturbing him. Although I did notice he wore a plain suit and tie in sensible colors. As a fellow faculty member, that at least made me feel less underdressed.

I returned to the classroom to find Jeannette kneeling on a counter behind Claire's desk. At the sound of the door, she slammed a cabinet closed and spun to face me. Without a word, she tucked something into her oversized jacket, hopped down, and ran past me into the hall. It wasn't until the class returned from outside that I found out what she'd stolen.

Claire put her hands on her hips and studied the students. "I'm missing four eggs," she said. "Who's been into my cupboard?"

Out of the corner of my eye, I glanced at Jeannette. She seemed remarkably composed. She was either a very good actor or she wasn't new to the business of thievery.

"Whatever prank you're planning better not involve my trike."

A few students giggled. If it was any other kid, I might have turned her in. But Jeanette had risked everything to find help for Baptiste. And I had risked a lot to bring her out of the police station with me. Getting her into trouble again seemed a bit counterproductive.

For the next hour, students celebrated the vernal equinox by attempting to stand eggs upright on their desks. Definitely not a lesson plan Madame Axelle would've approved, but it kept even the older kids engaged. Claire had me help the younger ones so they wouldn't break their eggs. Their squeals of delight when I got one to balance upright lightened my mood, and after a while, I began to relax. It was hard not to appreciate the riot of color in the room. Lots of Limes and Teals, even a Dark Purple. But they were just kids—and they seemed at least as smart as the Blues I'd grown up with.

For the first time since I'd been painted, I felt like being a freak of nature might not be the absolute end of the world.

Lunch was interesting. Students sat outside on aluminum picnic tables eating food they'd brought from home, or that they'd purchased from the overpriced outdoor vending machine. I had recently discovered a wad of bills in my breast pocket and decided I couldn't miss another meal if I was going to sit cooped up in that tiny school room for another four hours.

The vending machine took only coins, but I realized the lunches from home looked a lot more appetizing anyway. At first I was able to get a cupcake and a half a peanut butter sandwich for five cuivres, but the students quickly got smart and started charging me quadruple what one might pay in the grocery store. I forked over the cash gladly. Where else was I going to spend it? And some of those kids looked like they could use haircuts of their own.

After I'd eaten enough to make up for all the meals I'd missed over the last two days, I felt slightly sick. Naturally, that was the moment a fight broke out at one of the tables. Since Claire had already disappeared inside, I strode over and pulled the kids apart. Or tried to. I got kicked in the shin, and while I was rubbing my leg and shouting at them to act like adults, an errant fist knocked my glasses off.

To my surprise, the punching and kicking stopped abruptly. I recognized one of the brawlers—and from her look of shock, she now recognized me too. Jeannette sat straddling a boy twice her size, who had both hands clamped over a bloody nose.

"Brutus Nazeer?" she said. Had she heard Baptiste call me that at some point? This close I could see the brown freckles covering her face.

I shook my head slightly to let her know now was not the time, then grabbed the glasses, popped one of the dark lenses back in place, and repositioned them on my face.

"My name is Monsieur Molyneux," I said in a gruff voice.

When Jeannette made a skeptical face, I lifted the glasses and winked at her. She seemed mollified, but the boy who was still on his back was looking more confused by the second. I pulled Jeannette up by the arm, then helped the boy sit up.

"Better clean yourself up in the fan."

With a glare at Jeannette, he headed back inside, both hands still clamped over his dripping nose.

"He try to steal your lunch?" I asked.

"I ate mine on the way to school," Jeannette said. "Is Baptiste okay?"

I nodded.

"I knew it was you!" she said. "What did you do to your hair?"

The disgust on her face embarrassed me more than it should have.

"Call me Benoit, okay? At least while we're here."

"Thanks for helping Baptiste," Jeannette said. "Eventually."

"What do you mean by that?"

"I had to follow you around for like an hour, saving your light, before you finally helped him."

I glanced around to make sure no one was listening. "I think you're confused. I saved you, remember?"

Jeannette scoffed. "You don't think I could have gotten away from that sad excuse for a poker? He was like twelve."

"You were unconscious. But it doesn't matter. If you want to think you saved my light, then—"

"How'd you get out of the river?"

"A Green helped me... or a Yellow."

"It was a Green boy kissing a Yellow. And he didn't jump in after you until I got their attention from the other side of the river."

I swallowed. "Oh. In that case, thank you. Did you break the window in the barracks, too?"

"No, my rock broke the window in the barracks." She raised an eyebrow. "And by the way, I didn't punch Wart in the nose."

"What?"

She began walking toward the other students. "He tried to steal the light box when I was already setting it up. So I tripped him. He fell on his face."

"And then you sat on him?"

"Just making sure he was okay."

"How thoughtful."

I followed Jeannette to a nearby table where two girls were playing Firearchy. She sat down. "I play winner."

Since I still had a few questions for her, I sat down as well. "Tell me about Aro."

Jeannette shrugged. "Cause he isn't here to hog the game, everyone and their horse wants a turn." She hesitated, then mumbled, "Thanks for not telling LaClaire about the eggs."

"You going to eat them?" I whispered.

"Already did."

"Raw?"

A teenage, crème-skin plopped down next to me on the bench. "So you're the new aide?" she said. "How come Claire doesn't make you take your shadow glasses off?"

"They're prescription. I lost my others."

"That's so funny. I'm Questa by the way."

I gave her a stiff smile. So much for getting a few more questions answered. I'd have to try to corner Jeannette again before school let out. I still didn't understand her relationship with Aro. She had been waiting for him at the bridge as if they'd been friends. And although she hadn't let Baptiste die, that didn't mean she was trustworthy. I needed to know what part she had played in Aro's blackmail scheme, and whether she would endorse Baptiste's version of events to the authorities. With three witnesses, the Dominateur would have to believe us. Or if not them, at least the public. If we could convince enough Blues of the truth, Whisnant would have no choice but to charge Aro instead.

Questa flipped blue-streaked hair over her shoulder as if to make sure I noticed. "So, what part of Ham-V do you live in?"

Before I could think of a vague enough answer, I noticed her fire. At first glance it looked a bit like mine, but now I could see something was off. For one thing, her serum seemed dark and cloudy—so much that I couldn't see the actual glowing stamen at all. Instead, her entire serum chamber glowed with a greenish-blue light. Sort of like a cloud illuminated from behind by eyelight.

"I've never seen a fire quite like that," I said carefully.

"Neither has anyone else. It's a condition. I'm the only one at the school who's not technically a Mélangé—but Blue Campus wouldn't take me." She grinned, popped a chocolate truffle in her mouth, then promptly spit it out on the table. "Ew, coconut." She picked another truffle and devoured it. She offered one to me.

"You're Blue?" I said as I took one. "Technically they're supposed to let all pure Blues in, regardless of whether their families can pay the tuition."

"Yeah, well—when your uncle buys a black-market 'fire-whitening' serum bag that gives you an incurable light infection, people like to keep you at a distance."

I grimaced. "Sorry about that." I casually lowered the truffle from my mouth.

She shrugged. "It's okay. Draining the pus is actually kind of fun."

I didn't shiver in disgust, but it was a close thing. I was trying to think of a polite way to extricate myself from the conversation, when we were interrupted.

"Are you going to eat that?" Jeannette said, pointing at the coconut blob oozing on the table.

We both stared at her until she shrugged and popped the

partially masticated truffle in her mouth.

"You like chocolate?" I asked, mostly to alleviate the awkwardness.

"Is that what that was?" she said with a look of ecstasy.

I handed her the truffle that had been melting in my hand. Jeannette beamed, and it disappeared quicker than the first.

Questa rolled her eyes and leaned in close to me. "She's such a fake. She just wants you to feel sorry for her because she thinks you're cute. Well, most of the girls in class do, but you don't see them pasting themselves all over you." She seemed to realize how close she was and straightened.

I leaned toward the lightbox, pretending to watch the game.

Jeannette's face had surprised me. That look of pure joy could not have been faked. The idea that she had never had chocolate before put a lump in my throat. If I went more than four hours without a meal I got cranky. But I had never been hungry enough to steal and eat raw eggs. Was life really that desperate for Reds?

"Where do your parents buy food?" I asked her.

"Usually I get it. Since I've got green in my fire I can shop in Hameau Vert. Well I used to be able to. I doubt Aro will be my escort anymore."

"How does Orange have Green in it?"

Jeannette looked at me like I had crêpes for brains. "I reacted with a Green. Red and Green make yellow for some reason. But since it was only one Green, all I got was dark orange."

"If you say so. Don't they sell chocolate in Hameau Vert?"

Questa butted in. "Anything that's not fish is super expensive here. But they give discounts for Blue Mélangé." She raised her fire. "That's how I got the sweets. Still cost me a month's babysitting wages."

"That's insane." Mom was always complaining about the high prices of fruits and vegetables, but Dad said it was to be expected on an island without any space for farming. If Blues felt the pinch, how did Reds survive? They must eat fish all day long.

The more I looked at the girl, the thinner she looked. Was she malnourished? Was it stunting her growth? If only there was a way to give her some of my blue without having to take her orange in return. For her it may be a question of survival.

Well, even if I couldn't give her a permanent discount coupon—I could at least help her fill her pantry for a while.

When the game ended, Jeannette began to set up the box again. "You want to play me?" she asked.

I'd already spent too much time outside, but a few more minutes probably wouldn't hurt. I'd see any pokers coming from a long way off. I slid over and helped Jeannette put the starter marbles into bags.

"You know," I said, "they make light boxes big enough for several players at a time."

Jeannette gave me an I'm-not-stupid look. "Aro doesn't want people ganging up on him. He'd lose all his money."

"Any idea why he's not here today?"

She shook her head.

"What does Aro look like? I couldn't see him very well last night."

"He's sort of normal-looking."

"Normal-looking?"

"Yeah, not really tall or skinny. Sort of brownish hair, I guess."

That was a lot of help. I'd just have to keep an eye out for that crazy turquoise fire of his. "You ready to be crushed like a snail shell?"

"You're going down."

It took Jeannette ten minutes to beat me. I was still saving up my green marbles to trade for a blue when she bought the King's Orb and ended the game.

"Double or nothing?" she asked.

"We didn't bet on the first one."

"Oh, I didn't really know what that meant."

I smiled. "My pride can't survive another beating like that. I've got to get back to grading." Especially if I was going to keep this job for a few more days. As much as I disliked schoolwork, criticizing someone else's was pretty fun.

But first I was going to hide a few cuivre bills in Jeannette's backpack. I had considered giving it to her in the open, but I didn't want to take a chance on her creating a scene or having the rest of the kids begging me for cash.

A Lime Green crême-skin boy slid into place on the table and began organizing the marbles. Jeannette seemed disappointed but poured hers into the sorting tray and picked out the starting reds.

Pus girl waved at me as I left the lunch area.

"See you soon," I said with an uncomfortable smile.

On the way to the classroom, I noticed Claire's office door standing open. Her voice drifted into the hallway.

"We don't have any new students. If you don't mind waiting here, I can get the director."

"We'll wait," came a man's voice.

"Just so I know," Claire said, "what does the boy look like?"

The man cleared his throat. "Sixteen years old, muscular build, long dark hair, blue fire with a tinge of green. Possibly calling himself Jacque Pierrot, but his real name is Bruno Nazaire."

I'm pretty sure I set a record for silent sprinting. Once I was back outside, I saw the brown scooters parked on the street. They must have arrived while I was playing Firearchy with Jeannette. Stupid, stupid, stupid.

Should I run? Where would I go? Maybe I could find a dumpster to hide in. But if I took off now, it would draw attention. Claire and the kids would wonder why I'd disappeared so suddenly. Then so might the pokers. If they suspected I was their man, they'd spread the word that I'd cut my hair and was wearing a suit.

But if I had a valid reason for leaving suddenly...

I would need Jeannette's help. I sat next to her. The Lime Green boy was watching her with a bored expression, waiting for her to decide which orb to recruit. I grabbed his draw bag. "Can I see this?" Then I accidentally-on-purpose dumped his marbles onto the grass. "Oops. Sorry."

Jeannette gave me a dirty look. The boy seemed more embarrassed than anything but dropped to his knees and began collecting his marbles from the ground.

"The pokers are here looking for me," I whispered to Jeannette. "I need an excuse to get out of here. Can you take this wad of money and start running home? That way I can chase after you, shouting."

"No way," Jeannette hissed back. "They'll send me to jail."

"No, they won't. And you can keep the money."

"They'll just make me give it back tomorrow."

The Lime Green kid was back in his seat, watching, but I didn't care at this point. "Please," I whispered. "They'll kill me."

Jeannette gave me a sideways look. "I'll do it if you react with me."

The Lime Green's eyes bulged. My sentiments exactly. The girl was off-the-cliff insane if she thought I was going to become a Red Mélangé. Even with my old future in tatters, even wanting to help her not be hungry anymore, I knew reacting with an Orange would be like asking someone to cut off my arms and legs.

And anyway, I had no idea what my Dad was planning. If I started casually reacting with the locals, I'd probably ruin everything.

"You know I can't do that."

Jeannette shrugged. "Your turn," she said to the Lime Green.

"It would ruin my life."

"Figures," Jeannette said. "Most people would rather die than be Red."

Whether it was her eloquent reminder that my life depended on not getting caught or the fact that I'd just spotted two more pokers scooting down Rue Principale toward us, my resolve buckled.

"Fine, but we should do it in private."

This time it was Jeannette's eyes that went wide. Without a word, she slid open the bulb access door in the wooden game box and inserted her light hand.

The rational part of me screamed to be heard over my panic, but I shoved it down. I would become part Orange. Yes, it was disgusting and stupid and permanent—but it did beat dying by a few hundred miles. And Whisnant would never think to look for me across the river.

I offered a silent apology to my parents, then slid my light hand into the box and clasped Jeannette's fire to my own. For a moment, the battery-powered bulb inside warmed my fingers. Then our fires recognized each other. The exchange of energy was immediate and brutal. The orbs on the playing surface lit up like a multicolored galaxy of stars. Not quite as private as I thought.

The Lime Green fell backward off the bench.

My arm froze, then tingled as if it had fallen asleep. When my hand came free, a wave of nausea swept over me. Jeannette extracted her hand from the box, her expression a mix of wonder and embarrassment.

Come to think of it, I was mortified as well—but I had done the right thing. When my shade changed in a few hours, I'd be unrecognizable to the pokers. I just had to disappear until then.

"How fast can you run?" I said, handing her a wad of bills. "No matter what I scream at you, keep going until you reach the Taudis."

She only had time to take the money before someone grabbed my collar from behind and yanked me to my feet.

"Got you!" he said.

CHAPTER THIRTEEN

AN INNOCENT VICTIM

I jerked my head around to see who had a hold of me.

It was the bearded director.

"I saw everything," he said, a manic glint in his eye. "What in the violet rainbow were you thinking?"

Extreme relief warred with bone-jarring dread. The director didn't know I was Bruno, but he was about to draw a lot of unwanted attention to Benoit Molyneux. "I'm not sure, actually," I said. "Maybe we can pretend you missed it completely?"

He scoffed and pushed me toward the school entrance. "You and I should have a conversational in my office."

Nope, not a noun. At least his defective vocabulary was distracting me from my panic. He suddenly seemed much less menacing to me. I realized I could easily outrun him. The question was whether it was worth the risk. Would the pokers suspect who I was? If I stayed and he revoked my aide position, it would be a great excuse to leave in a hurry.

"Maybe we could just talk about it out here?" I said. "Behind a tree or something?"

He ignored me.

I could outrun him, but not the pokers on scooters. Would he send them after me? If I stayed, I could keep my head down and pretend to be docile. And the second anyone suspected me of being a sixteen-year-old killer, I'd bowl them over and escape across the river.

I fixed the director with my most bored expression. And with forty Mélangé students looking on, he escorted me and Jeannette across the schoolyard, through the door, and straight into Claire.

"Oh, Director!" Claire said. "I've been looking all over for you. We have a couple visitors."

Ah, crêpes.

"Tell them to wait. I won't be ten minutes."

That's right. Put your foot down.

"They're actually from—"

"Irregardless, your new aide has been pushing the parameters since he arrived, and it's time we have a little word."

No. Just, no. That sentence made my teeth hurt.

"Of course, 'sieur." Claire gave me a questioning look.

I shrugged in apology, feeling as if I'd somehow betrayed her. Or maybe she was simply confused by the director's incoherent syntax.

We entered. Halfway down the hallway, Claire's door still stood open. I didn't see the pokers yet, but we'd have to pass the room on the way to the director's office. I had to make sure the Director didn't happen to glance into Claire's office. But it also had to be silent, or it might cause the pokers to stick their heads into the hallway.

I touched Jeannette's shoulder and put a finger to my lips —then lifted her onto my shoulders. She screamed.

The director turned around to look at us. One of the pokers appeared in the doorway.

Black. Blackity. Black.

I hopped down the hallway, making sure to keep the director between myself and the poker. I kept my fire pressed into Jeannette's ankle and facing away from Claire's doorway.

"Put her down immediately."

I ignored the director. Claire, who had followed us inside, squeaked every time Jeannette's head got too close to an artificial light fixture.

I began to chant in Ulfish as I jumped, a rhyme Granny used to sing to me. As I had hoped, my obvious neglect for the safety of one of his students prevented the director from taking his eyes off me. I overtook him as we passed the poker. The brown-clad man even raised his fire, ready to greet the director.

I swung Jeannette forward as if I'd lost my balance. She screamed again, right on cue. I used the forward momentum to recklessly sprint to the director's office.

"What's wrong with you?" the director yelled.

Out of the corner of my eye, I saw the poker lower his light. Claire approached the poker and seemed to be explaining the situation.

Jeannette swayed precariously as I stopped, but I threw open the door and entered, taking care to kick over a chair.

My spectacle was engaging enough, apparently. The director entered immediately behind us and slammed the door. His face resembled a raw tuna steak.

Jeannette laughed as I crouched and slid her to the floor. "Can we do that again later?"

I glanced at the director, then cleared my throat. "We'll talk about it," I said under my breath.

Jeannette found a chair and began swinging her legs.

The director stared at me, mouth moving soundlessly as if he couldn't decide what to say first. Finally he regained a measure of composure and pointed at the chair I'd kicked over. "Sit, Monsieur Molyneux. Don't speak unless you're spoken to. And take those off. Novelty eyewear is not permitting at our school."

Not permitting? Was Téle not his first language? "They're actually prescription. Claire told me—"

"Claire is not the Executive Director of L'académie Mélangé. And I don't care whether you can see me—I want to see you." He'd obviously practiced that title. It rolled off his tongue with lilting fluidity.

I gave Jeannette a subtle thumbs-up, then checked to make sure no one was standing outside the door. I slowly righted the chair, sat down next to Jeannette and removed my disguise.

"Thank you," the director said. "Obviously we're letting you go."

My heart jumped in my chest. "Really? Thank you!"

"As in ending your employment."

"Ah." I pretended to be upset by this.

"Monsieur Molyneux, do you realize you're the only faculty member to break six of the foundational mandates in a single day?"

"Six?"

Jeannette cast a worried glance at me.

"I think you're making that up," I said. "Which six rules did I break?"

The director seemed to take a perverse glee in my challenge.

"Make that seven—insubordination to a Senior Scholastic Mentor. In case you're curious, that's Academic Mandate Sixteen, page seventy-six, paragraph four, subparagraph W."

I let out an appreciative whistle. Now I knew what he'd been studying instead of basic grammar.

His beard twitched a little, as if he'd squelched a smile, and then he continued to list my offenses. I didn't interrupt him. If he could just lecture us for the next three hours or so, the pokers wouldn't recognize me when I walked out.

But after only a few minutes, he finished with, "And I'll be writing a very strongly worded letter to the Education Board."

He turned to Jeannette. "As for you, young lady, I can understand why you might be confused about all this. Who wouldn't want a little blue in their fire after all? But you have to remember—we are who we are. We're born with our shade, and it's our responsibility to make the best of it."

He made a face I'd often seen on my mother. It roughly translated to "You kids make me crazy." At least he didn't seem furious anymore.

"Have you both forgotten the King's Requirement?"

We shook our heads, but he recited it anyway. "If the

throne thou dost desire, temper white thy inner fire. Make the Crystal Scepter shine, then the kingdom will be thine."

I tried to appear interested. That's right—keep reciting nursery rhymes. Maybe the pokers would give up and go home.

"This declaration was given over fifty years ago by the last of the kings only weeks before he died. So far the Haut Commissaire has come closest to achieving a pure white light."

Jeannette stifled a yawn. But for me, the lecture was just getting started. It was time to make this interesting.

"First of all," I said, "the rantings of a senile king is no basis for a system of government—and even if it were, the King's Requirement doesn't state that Almost Whites can play ruler until the real king shows up. The Commissaire is a fraud. And for future reference, a parameter is a variable, not a boundary to be pushed. If you want to talk about perimeters, let's talk about why there is no fence separating your school from the street. And if you ever say irregardless again, I will personally beat you with a dictionary."

For a moment, the director appeared to be choking on his own tongue. Before he could get out much more than, "How dare—" the door opened, and Claire stuck her head in. "Sorry, Director, but the royal soldiers are getting impatient."

The director launched himself from the chair. "Soldiers? Why didn't you tell me?" He disappeared down the hall, leaving the door wide open behind him. Claire cast a worried glance at me and Jeannette, then followed the director down the hallway.

It was now or never. I took off my suit jacket, pushed it to the bottom of the trash bin, and put on my shadow glasses. It wasn't much of a wardrobe change, but at least it would make the run more enjoyable.

"Guess you'll be needing this." Jeannette pulled the wad of bills from her pocket and held it out to me.

"It's yours," I said. "All you have to do is give me a guided tour of Taudis Rouge."

"Chanmé! I'll take you after school."

"How about right now?"

We strolled casually out the back entrance and ran for the woods.

I had no idea what the director would think when he found us missing from his office—but as far as I knew, he had no reason to suspect I was actually a teenager. I really hoped he didn't say anything about me to the pokers.

"Can you get a new job?" Jeannette asked. We'd been running for ten minutes, and despite her short legs, she hadn't slowed me down.

"Even if I can't, I was pretty awful as a teacher's assistant."

She shrugged. "Did more than the Director. He just sits in his office brushing his beard."

"You think you'll get in trouble for running off?"

"Maybe," Jeannette said. "But I don't think he'll disqualify me from the prison prize. That's all I care about."

"Prison what-now?"

"Prison Prize. The scholarship thingy."

"No idea what you're talking about, but it doesn't sound all that great."

Jeannette crossed the street, then waited for me to catch up. "The kids who do the best on the last test get the prison..."

She trailed off as a copper-haired woman approached, pushing a baby carriage. The Green eyed Jeannette's unusual shade, then glanced at me. I lifted my fire slightly, taking care to seem bored. She returned the gesture and began shaking the baby's rattle above the carrier. I wouldn't have thought anything of it except her child was clearly asleep. She passed. I tried not to look behind me, but eventually I caved and snuck a quick glance.

She had stopped the carriage and was staring at us.

Blackened Crêpes. She was probably committing our description to memory so she could turn us in.

"We're okay, right?" I asked, trying to walk faster without looking like I was trying to walk faster. "You can be on this side with an escort?"

"Yeah, as long as I have a good reason. Like school."

I was about to ask whether the authorities considered going to the arcade with Aro a good reason, when I noticed Jeannette had several folded newspapers tucked under her arm. Was that what the woman had been staring at? "Did you take those from someone's paper box?"

She sighed. "If it's full, they're obviously not reading them."

"People go on vacation."

"Yeah, Blues." She patted the papers. "Anyway, I need these."

"What we need is not to be arrested for stealing newspapers."

We ran in silence for a few more blocks, then reached Green Park. I was glad Jeannette seemed to know her way around Hameau Vert better than Baptiste.

"What were we talking about?" Jeannette said. "Oh, the scholarship.

A couple passed, holding hands. The sight was so distracting I nearly collided with a jogger.

While I apologized to the woman, Jeannette continued her one-sided conversation. "Can't believe you haven't heard of the prison prize. The winners get a single shade fireproof mint."

"Fire improvement?"

"Yeah. It's a trade," Jeannette continued. "Blue prisoners get out faster, and the students get some of their blue. It's like community service."

I slowed. "There's no way the Doms would allow that."

Jeannette shrugged. She did that a lot. "I think Aro's grandpa is trying to change it. But LaClaire says it's a really old tradition—like a million years or something."

"It must be a well-maintained prison."

"I've always wanted to be Violet," Jeannette said. "If I win, I'll—" She squealed and pointed at the path ahead. Two brown specks moved toward us with disturbing speed. Scooters. In a few more seconds, the pokers would be close enough to note my large build and brown hair. Not to mention my fire, which was still teal.

"Time for a pit stop." I guided Jeannette toward a heavily graffitied building that could only be the park fanroom. "Stay hidden in there until I call you, okay?"

She obediently wandered into the girls side while I went around to the other, making sure to keep the building between me and the pokers.

I waited just inside the entrance with my back to the wall. If a poker followed me inside, I'd tackle him before he had a chance to set his shock glove. If they both followed me inside, I might have to get creatively violent. The good news was that no one would hear a scuffle. The four-foot ventilation fan in the ceiling predated me by a good ten years and sounded like a train giving birth.

I plugged my ears and waited.

Just when I thought they must be long gone, the door opened.

On sudden impulse, I kicked the door closed. The resultant thud could be heard even over the fan. I slowly opened the door, ready to shove my weight against it at the slightest warning.

A small boy lay unconscious on the dirt. Black ashes. I

was the world's biggest imbécil.

The boy was probably eight or so, and thankfully his green fire still burned. I dropped to my knees and listened for breathing. That's when I saw them. Less than fifty feet away, talking to a policeman with a ruddy complexion, four pokers sat on a pair of scooters.

I repeated my previous expletive with renewed emphasis.

The pokers sat with their backs to the fanroom. Even so, how had they not noticed the boy crumple to the ground? I reached to pick him up but stopped. If he had a spinal injury, moving him could kill him. But I wasn't going to just leave. Maybe I could shout for help and sprint the other way. Knowing how law enforcement worked around here, they'd probably follow me and ignore the boy.

My fire thrummed with energy. I had to make a decision. Every second I delayed put the boy in greater danger. He had a pulse and his breathing seemed fine, but it wasn't worth the risk. Turning a kid into a paraplegic to save myself was not something I could live with.

"Can you hear me?"

I brought my fire to the boy's tiny face. Why did every little boy on the island make me think of Ro? His cheek felt cold.

"I'm so sorry, little mec." I would have to call for the pokers. I'd agree to go with them as long as they first took the boy to the hospital. Would the soldiers try to take Jeannette? Maybe she'd be smart enough to stay hidden until—

In an instant, my light hand felt like I'd plunged it into ice water.

The boy's eyes flew open and he screamed. But it was quickly cut off, as if his air had run out before he'd gotten started. His mouth worked soundlessly as he stared at me, eyes the size of silver coins.

Before I could warn the boy to stay still, I saw the reason for his distress, and I almost screamed myself. The side of his face had gone from milky to bright pink.

What had just happened? Was he allergic to Blue fires or something?

The boy jumped to his feet and tore off down the path, passing within feet of the pokers and policeman. The men watched him run past but didn't appear to notice his face. Hadn't they heard his scream?

I was too shocked to even be grateful for the deafening fan. The mark had almost looked like a burn. But fires didn't get hot enough to burn people. It was probably where the door had hit him. Touching his face had simply woken him.

I needed to get out of sight—but when I tried to stand, my limbs felt like cottage cheese. I barely managed to crawl back to the fanroom and open the door. I slumped against the wall again. This time, in complete exhaustion.

Had reacting with two Mélangé in two days somehow made my fire unstable?

A few minutes later, the fanroom door opened again. I didn't bother to get up. I had no strength to walk, let alone fight.

An elderly Green man entered, jerked slightly when he saw me, then disappeared into one of the stalls.

My breath escaped in a slow wheeze. I thought for sure the man was going to ask if I was the crêpe bag giving little kids head injuries. I hoped the boy had found someone to check him out. His parents would probably call the police at some point.

"Benoit? Benwaaaaaaaaaaaa?"

Jeannette's shrill voice barely carried over the sound of the fan. I knew I'd have to shout even louder for her to hear me, and I had no desire to spook the old man in the stall again —even less to draw the attention of the pokers outside. Jeannette would have to hold on a bit longer.

I shook my head. Some escape this turned out to be. Either I was Port's unluckiest sixteen-year-old, or the Créateur was torturing me.

When I finally emerged, the eye crowned mount Tremper, and the law enforcement officials were nowhere to be seen. Jeannette, however, stood in full view a few feet away, ripping bark from a tree. From the pile at her feet, she'd been at it awhile.

"I almost came in to get you!" Jeannette said when she noticed me.

"You said you were going to wait until I called."

"Don't worry, I hid my light when anyone came by."

I stared at her, my eye twitching slightly.

Then took a breath. At least she hadn't been carted off to the police station. It was a miracle no one noticed her fire, which still hadn't changed shade. Supposedly our reactions would complete at the same time. But had anyone mixed orange with teal before?

"Let's go," Jeannette said. "I'm starving."

"Me too."

Jeannette took off toward her home, alternating between skipping and galloping. I followed at a discreet distance while scanning the park for the little boy I'd assaulted. Green kids swarmed the nearby playground area, and a group of teenagers huddled over a squirrel trap. I didn't see any little boys face-down in the dirt, so hopefully the kid had found some medical attention.

Pont en Pierre gradually grew until it loomed over us. The cobblestone arch stood as empty as if it had been midnight. The river muted all sound. No one waded or fished in the water. It felt like we'd stepped into another world. On the far side, beyond a cluster of sparse trees, lay the tumbled-down dwellings of the Red. Whether they were all nocturnal or accustomed to staying out of sight, I couldn't see a single person about.

I slowed. Blank, was I really going into Taudis Rouge?

Jeannette reached the cobblestones first and pulled herself up onto the wide railing. Then to my horror, she began to run along it.

"What are you doing?" I shouted.

Her giggled response dissolved into the rushing of water.

Did I really have to follow her over? My only other option was to find another hiding place in Hameau Vert. That might work until my red showed up. Then I'd be off-sides without an escort.

And in that moment, the fragile structure of my identity collapsed. It wasn't a slow topple, either. Bruno Nazaire shattered into dust and splinters, leaving an unrecognizable mass with a bad haircut. This new reality took up much less space than the old me. In fact, I was having trouble finding myself in it at all.

One thing was clear. Within a few hours, the one who had been Bruno would belong in the Taudis as much as the reddest Red. To become what? I took a step back from the bridge. What kind of person throws away everything for a life of hunger and stench and disease?

Being popped at a poker graduation suddenly seemed noble and courageous. Isn't that what a good person would do? Pay for his own mistakes? At least it would be quick. I watched Jeannette get smaller as she crested the bridge. She still hadn't turned around. She didn't know I wasn't coming.

It was the shriek of a little boy that pierced my cloud of wretchedness.

"That's him! He burned my face!"

The shouted accusation crippled my newly-formed resolve. I recognized the boy even with half his head in bandages. It looked as if he had brought his entire extended family along to hunt the criminal who had hurt him—twice.

A dark curtain parted in my mind, revealing what I'd always known to be there. The truth about who I was. I couldn't pretend anymore that I was a good person. When everything else had been ripped away, all that remained was a selfish, spineless criminal.

And there was only one thing for a selfish, spineless criminal to do in a situation like this. I ran.

CHAPTER FOURTEEN

INTO THE RED

I reached the top to find Jeannette waiting for me.

"I can't believe you're actually coming," she said.

I smiled. But inside I felt like pitching myself off the bridge.

"I did pay for a tour."

"In case you're worried, a lot of people think it's dangerous on our side, but it's actually not. Well, it can be. But probably not if you're with me. Unless they don't care that you're with me."

I cast a glance at the crowd of Greens gathered around the base of the bridge. From the shouts and fist waving, I figured they weren't in the mood to hear my feeble explanations.

"My middle name is Andre, which is almost an anagram of danger."

Jeannette furrowed her eyebrows.

"Let's hurry," I said. "I'm really excited about meeting your family." And having them hide me until Friday. Or forever, if my parents disowned me.

Before I realized what was going on, Jeannette grabbed my dark hand and started the descent. I nearly pulled away but realized I would soon be part of her world. She understood the rules. The quicker I assimilated to Red life, the less attention I'd draw.

But still—holding hands in public? With someone I barely knew? I'd heard the lower colors weren't as averse to touching as Blues, but this seemed wildly inappropriate. I could feel her fire humming against my dark palm.

Then we stepped onto the pebble-strewn ground and my discomfort doubled. Red Town. Dirt, weeds, and the overwhelming stench of decay. Jeannette paused and glanced at me, as if to ask what I thought.

"I didn't expect it to be so... pungent."

She laughed and pointed her thumb at a dog-sized lump covered with a layer of flies. "That's been there a few weeks."

I pulled my hand from Jeannette's and covered my mouth and nose. "Why do they leave it there?"

"Who's they?"

"Nevermind."

My hand did nothing to block the scent of decomposition. I pulled my shirt over the lower part of my face and followed Jeannette uphill. We walked by several shacks that looked abandoned, and a tree made out of old fishing rods. Was that what passed as art here? After a few minutes, I lowered my shirt. The smell of urine had replaced the smell of death, and it was much easier to ignore.

Jeannette continued along a winding path that led us past a rusted car without wheels. A cat watched us from the hood. Most of its fur was missing. Where were all the people?

We slipped through a gap in a plastic slatted fence, and suddenly they were there. Half-naked kids drinking from a hose, filthy women hanging laundry on rolls of chicken-wire, skeletal figures smoking in an alley. I'd never seen so many Reds in my life.

"You get out of here!"

A toothless old man came at me with half a baseball bat. He wasn't going very fast, but Jeannette grabbed my hand again and led me up a rise and around a corner. Under the circumstances, I didn't find the contact nearly so uncomfortable.

"Maybe you better hide your light until we get to my house."

I nodded and pocketed my fire. I smiled like it wasn't a big deal, like I wasn't petrified at being trapped here. Each step took me deeper into this festering wound of a city. I thought about what Mom would think if she knew where I was and felt the urge to go back and let the old man end my misery.

"Are you feeling okay?" Jeannette asked.

I nodded, this time not able to smile. I knew if I tried to speak it would come out as a scream or a sob.

"Good, cause that's my house at the end of the street."

Finally. I picked up the pace and stopped in front of a cozy, wooden structure covered with bird droppings.

Jeannette laughed. "That's our neighborhood pigeon coop. Our house is there." She pointed, but all I saw was a wide, dark-haired crême-skin sitting on a milk crate. In his red glowing hand he held a knife the size of my forearm and was using it to sharpen a box of pencils. He sat in front of a five-foot pile of old blankets and towels.

"Who's this?" the man asked Jeannette in a barely audible voice.

"The mec I told you about," Jeannette said, "from the bridge."

They'd been talking about me? I glanced back the way we'd come. From the higher vantage point, I could see the river winding its way through town. The bridge seemed miles away.

When I faced forward, Jeannette had vanished and the man with a knife was on his feet.

"Where did Jeannette..." I trailed off.

The man blew the shavings from a pencil, still staring at me as if waiting for something. He was not a tall person but had broad shoulders and impressive dark stubble from ear to ear.

"Nice outfit," he finally said.

I looked down at Dad's blue silk tie. Well, it had been blue at one point. And my white shirt looked like I'd used it to collect river rocks. Was he being facetious? Or was he hinting he'd accept it as a compensatory gift for not sharpening my fingers? I took a slow step backward. "Are you her father?"

He shook his head and glanced behind him where a sheet

had been stretched taut as if to cover an opening. There was no way anybody lived in that misshapen mound of rags. Something wasn't right here. Had Jeannette run off? I tried to remember whose idea it had been to come to the Taudis.

The Red turned, and with his formidable blade, lifted the stained sheet. Behind it lay a circular opening, nearly as tall as I was. Something stirred in the shadowy depths of what I now recognized as a cast-iron drainage pipe. I'd once seen a stack of them next to the street in Ville Bleu—the day they updated the neighborhood sewer system.

Nope. Nope. Nope.

Even if it wasn't currently being used to transport human waste, the idea that anyone would willingly enter such a place was absurd. This was clearly a trap. Inside the lair, I would find some sort of carnivorous animal or a gang with arm-length blades of their own... and more dirty rags to quiet my screams.

I weighed my options. If I ran, the man would catch me in two strides. If I tried to get the knife from him, I'd probably lose an arm. Or a hand. My whole body went numb as I remembered stories of ancient light thieves.

"You don't want my fire," I said. "It's polluted with Green, see."

The large man raised a lip. Was he snarling at me?

In the gloom of the opening, an orange light appeared, illuminating a small face. "Aren't you coming in?" Jeannette asked. "Mama wants to meet you."

I hesitated. I was relieved that Jeannette hadn't left me, but that didn't mean it wasn't all part of the act. Mama could be their pet alligator.

I pointed to the man out front. "Who is this mec?"

"That's my brother, Philippe."

"What's with the knife?"

"Useful things," the Red said, his face suddenly inches from mine. "Ever tried to sharpen a pencil with your teeth?"

Jeannette grinned. "Come on!"

I swallowed, crouched, and stepped under the sheet. The

smell wasn't pleasant, but at least it wasn't the stench of raw sewage. More like leather-that-had-gotten-wet-too-often mixed with decaying wood. In the time it took to remove Drea's glasses and slide them into my shirt pocket, Jeannette was well ahead of me. I followed her bobbing light over a horizontal plank of wood lined with several pairs of shoes, a pile of newspapers, and then around a tattered couch cushion propped up by two stacked wooden pallets. Then her light disappeared.

"Jeannette?" With each step, the curved metal seemed to contract around me. "I can't do this."

Jeannette lifted a moth-eaten blanket, and my panic receded a little. Daylight shone through another sheet at the far end. Thank the Créateur, there was another way out. A red glow illuminated the remaining length of the pipe. Between me and the exit lay another pallet crowned with a filthy mattress—a long-haired figure held a coffee can over a propane stove.

As my blue-green fire lit the tiny living space, the can slowly descended into the fire. "Finally here," said a voice.

Three things happened at once. A sharp hiss made me jump, the smell of week-old fish hit me like a three-hundred-pound forward, and from behind a cardboard wall, a second red light launched itself at me.

My body responded without thought. Before I registered what was happening, I dodged the tackle and slammed the attacker face-first into the ground.

Or rather into the heap of junk at my feet.

The figure at the stove vaulted over the mattress. I braced myself for another attack, but the person ignored me and crouched to help the first attacker to his feet.

Her feet.

The person I had upended was a short, chubby woman. Suddenly Jeannette was there, propping the woman up as if she might fall over again. "Mama? What happened?"

Whoops.

The long-haired figure faced me, and I saw her clearly for the first time. Well, as clearly as I could in the shifting red light. A teenage girl with a sharp, demonic face and murder in her eyes. "Your friend slammed her to the floor."

Jeannette glared at me.

My face felt as hot as my fire. "She jumped at me."

"What is wrong with you?" the older girl said in a voice that suggested she didn't actually want to know. "What kind of black-for-brains, toilet-pouch attacks a woman trying to hug him?"

Toilet pouch? "How was I supposed to know she was—"

"We didn't believe half the stuff Nett told us about you," she continued. "But now I think she underestimated the depth of your turpitude."

Was that even a word? And Jeannette had known me for less than twenty-four hours. How much could she have said about me?

"I didn't—"

"Get out," the girl said. This time her tone of voice made it sound more like, "I hope you die soon."

"Listen, I'm really sor—"

"Get out!"

Gladly. My stumbling passage back through the tube grew more frantic the closer I got to freedom. Finally, with an exultant cry, I threw the front sheet aside and hurtled into the street.

Straight into a large, red-faced police officer.

CHAPTER FIFTEEN

SPILLED MILK

Enormous hands clamped onto my arms. "What's the hurry?"

Before I could respond to the officer, he swore softly and released me. "I didn't expect Philly to be telling the truth."

"First time for everything," came another male voice.

I stepped away from the officer, unsure why he had let me go. Three Green policemen watched me. One had coffee-and-milk skin and a double set of dimples. Another had a forehead so large it looked like his other features had slid down into the bottom half of his face. His long brown hair appeared to be recently blow-dried—Granny would've loved it. The one I'd run into was by far the scariest. With his grizzly-bear shoulders and ruddy complexion, he looked out of place between the two dandies.

I waited, but there were no cries of triumph or shouts of "that's him!" Wasn't the whole island out looking for the killer Mélangé? Even with shorter hair and the suit, surely they'd at least be suspicious. If they hadn't come here looking for me, why else would they risk crossing the river?

Behind me, someone let out a strangled cry of fury. The teenage girl—who was an older version of Jeannette—dropped to her knees next to a body. The scruffy Red pencil sharpener lay on his face in the street, red light still burning in his hand.

"What did you do to him?" the girl shouted. She didn't seem all that scared of the policemen.

"He's lucky he didn't get worse than a tranq dart," Dimples said. "Can't parade around Red Town with dangerous weapons." Philippe's blade hung from the officer's belt.

Jeannette and her mom stepped down from the pipe. Jeannette joined the teenager—her sister?—next to Philippe, but the older woman stood staring at the officers as if afraid they might shoot her next.

"Can I help you, officers?" Jeannette's mother said with a quick glance at Philippe. "My son uses the knife only for preparing fish." She nodded slightly at a woman who'd come out of her house. Several more Reds watched from windows.

Dimples drew the knife and pointed it at the sheet covering the pipe. "Claude and I were just discussing your place of residence and why we didn't see any inspection tags."

The woman ran a hand through her dark hair as if she'd just realized what a mess she was. "We definitely paid this year." In the light she looked less like a rugby forward. I tried not to stare at her pale, unpainted face. The only woman I'd seen without make-up was Granny. My mother wore hers to bed and fixed her face before she came out of the shower.

The officer with the red complexion—apparently named Claude—nodded vacantly, clearly distracted. I thought he was staring at Philippe's unconscious body, but then Jeannette's sister pushed her charcoal hair back from her face.

The sharp features, which had looked demonic in the shifting red light, now seemed delicate and well-proportioned. She was surprisingly attractive for a Red. Not that I'd seen many young, female Reds, but if her fire had been Blue, the mecs on my team would be tripping over themselves to get her parents' phone number.

Claude made no effort to conceal his interest in the girl. So maybe he wouldn't notice if I slipped away. I glanced at the river. It seemed far away, but I was pretty sure I could find the way without getting lost. Or murdered.

"Philly-boy told us the inspector was inside," Big Forehead said with a glance at me. His lip hung in a half-sneer as if deciding whether to buy the story.

"That's right," said the sister. "It's all taken care of. We passed." She cast the briefest glance in my direction before rolling her brother onto his back and brushing the gravel from his face.

This time it was Claude who spoke. "If you mean passed out a horse's back end. Let me see that report, Monsieur Inspector." Six faces turned to me.

I opened my mouth but found I had nothing to say.

"We're not going to the shelter!" It was Jeannette. Her mother quickly hushed her.

Jeannette's declaration surprised me. According to my social studies teacher, the community shelter was state of the art with beds for nearly half the residents of the Taudis. Why pay to live in a pipe when the family could stay for free in a much safer environment? Mom always said Reds were stubborn. They were used to filth and didn't want to deal with the requirements of finding a job and maintaining hygiene.

"Get out of here, grasswipes!" a child called from a window. The face disappeared almost instantly, replaced by a sheet of cardboard—obviously the Taudis' version of shutters.

"Maybe he's not the inspector," Dimples said, with an appraising look at me. "You know anything about a blue-green Mélangé in nice clothes and shadow glasses? Apparently assaulted a five-year-old and escaped over the river."

Automatically, I glanced at my shirt pocket. Miraculously, Drea's glasses weren't there. They must have fallen out inside the pipe.

Claude squinted at me. "Hold on there..."

I stopped breathing. I knew what he was about to say—something about a murder on Blue Campus, and how I looked awfully young to be an inspector.

There was only one possible way out of this. I did my best to scowl. "Of course I'm here to inspect the dwelling. Why else would I subject myself to this filth?" I brushed at the dirt on my sleeves.

Big Forehead absently played with his hair as he examined me. "Where's your materials?"

Where *are* your materials—I silently correct him. Out loud I said, "Why would I sully my things? I knew this place wouldn't pass inspection. I'm only sorry I went inside to confirm it. I'm going to have to bathe in tomato sauce to remove the smell."

Jeannette began to cry, and her sister's eyes went from cold to icy.

Well, what did they expect me to say? There's no way the Greens would've believed I was an inspector if I said a sewage pipe was a safe place to live. If I had, they'd ask for proof, which I didn't have. Helping people out was well and good, but there had to be a line. I couldn't put an entire family in danger because they were too stubborn to move to a community shelter.

"So they didn't pass?" Dimples asked.

"Of course they didn't pass," I said. "If you'll excuse me, I'm headed back to write my report."

I glanced at Jeannette's mom. She at least seemed to understand the impossibility of my situation. Her eyes weren't angry, just sad.

A seed of guilt spouted in the pit of my stomach. Could I have helped them somehow? No. As Granny often said, doing the right thing is usually hard and often unpleasant. It was clear to me that this home was unsafe. They would be much better off in the city-run shelter. Jeannette would thank me later.

And although I wouldn't have tranquilized their brother, it was probably a good idea to get that massive knife off the streets.

"You've got until eyefall," Claude said to the stout woman. "Anything left inside will be dumped in the river."

The teenage girl responded in a less-than-respectful tone, but I was already halfway down the street. A moment later, one of the officers called out that they weren't finished with me, but I was far enough away to pretend not to hear. I forced myself to maintain the same purposeful gait. Not escaping—just anxious for a shower. I expected to hear boots running behind me, or at the least more shouting, but the only noise was someone rattling around in their shack, a nearby goat, and the distant rush of the river.

At my first opportunity I turned a corner and sprinted toward the sound of water. My time in Taudis Rouge hadn't gone anything like I'd planned, but one thing was certain—I wouldn't be back. Not for a hundred thousand cuivres.

Despite my hurry to leave Red soil, I also had no desire to reunite with the extended family of my five-year-old victim. After wrapping the silk tie around my fire, I pocketed it and crawled under the summerlight side of the bridge. Then I sat in the least muddy section and waited for eyefall.

It felt strange to be looking at Hameau Vert from the wrong side. Once I was finally able to relax a bit, I used the quiet time to plan my next move. First priority was to get an update from Orie. A payphone would be too exposed. The one place I might be able to call in privacy was Baptiste's house. Maybe he could even hide me for the night.

Although I still hated to involve him and his family, at least he'd had a day to explain things to his parents. Hopefully they would be the helpful type and not the knife-wielding-lure-you-inside-then-attack-you kind.

Once the park had grown quiet and half-light passed to full darkness, I crossed the bridge. With my light still covered, I moved quickly and kept to the shadows.

It seems the Créateur was done torturing me. I made it to Baptiste's apartment building without seeing a single fire. Had Whisnant actually stopped looking for me? Somehow I doubted it.

I was pretty sure Baptiste's apartment had been on the top floor, the third window going from darkways, lightward. I climbed to the fifth floor and knocked.

A red-haired woman cracked the door. Her eyes went wide. She looked behind her, then at me again. Finally she opened the door slightly wider and said, "Can I help you, 'sieur?"

Had I seen her before? "I'm looking for Baptiste."

She glanced toward my pocketed light hand. "Sorry, don't know of any Baptiste."

"You sure—chubby, blond kid, thirteen but looks ten?"

She tilted her head. "Two doors down."

Before I could thank her, she disappeared.

I knocked on Baptiste's door.

Then again.

Nothing. Maybe I could hide on the roof. I started back toward the stairs before remembering the curfew. It was well past eyefall—that meant everyone had to be home. This time instead of knocking, I cupped my hands to the door and shouted as loudly as I dared. "Anybody in there? Baptiste? It's your big brother."

A faint voice shouted something that sounded like "open".

I tried the knob. The door swung inward, revealing a tidy living room with bookshelves lining three walls. The artificials were on, but besides threadbare furniture, the room was empty. I closed the door behind me. "Baptiste? It's Bruno."

"In here." His voice was clearer now.

I engaged the deadbolt, crossed the front room, and entered a short hallway. "If you're in the fan, I can wait." But the entrance to the fanroom stood open and unlit.

"No, in here."

From the door on my light side came a tapping.

I tried the knob and found it locked. "How do I—"

Wait. Why was the locking mechanism on the outside? I turned the center of the handle and the door opened. Baptiste wore mismatched socks and a pair of much-too-small gym shorts. His shirtless torso rippled like frosting melting off a cake. The room behind him was the size of Mom's walk-in closet. The only open space in the windowless room was a narrow pathway between his desk and bed. Cartoon alligators in top hats covered his comforter and pillowcase.

"The front door was unlocked," I said, trying not to stare at his sagging flesh.

"Greetings, Bruno!" he said, apparently not at all embarrassed by his ensemble. "Or would you prefer I call you Benoit?"

"Were you trapped in here? Where are your parents?"

Baptiste's smile drooped slightly. "It's just me and Papa."

Crêpes. I should have remembered. The bully had used that fact to assassinate Baptiste's remaining self-confidence. "Aro Loup is a blank-head. You know that, right? Don't listen to anything he says."

"Papa went to see the Director of Education about a home-school permit," Baptiste said as if I hadn't spoken. "I always stay in here when I'm home alone. He'll be back soon."

"Are you sure? Because it's already past curfew."

Baptiste tottered to the dining area and pulled the curtains back from the sliding glass door. When he saw the darkness, he started mumbling to himself at high speed.

"Baptiste, did your Dad lock you in that room? What if you had to use the fan?"

"Papa gave me a bottle. I have good aim. Mostly."

A bottle? This "Papa" character sounded deranged. "It's still not safe, buddy. Especially since the front door is unlocked—was unlocked. I took care of it."

Baptiste walked to the fridge. "Can I offer you a beverage? Citrus juice, water, chocolate soy milk?"

Due to our lengthy conversation the night before, I knew Baptiste didn't respond well to pressure. Best thing was to roll with the topic changes and bring up my questions later.

"Citrus, I guess. Thanks."

While Baptiste ambled toward the fridge, I went to take another peek at his room. The knobs had been reversed. Other than that, I didn't see anything weird like chains or manacles. It smelled awful, though. On the desk I noticed an old juice bottle filled with dark yellow liquid.

"Baptiste," I called. "On second thought, I'll have the chocolate milk."

Once we were both seated at the dining table with our drinks, I began to work on the knots in my tie. Baptiste hummed absently and blew bubbles in his milk.

"You think your dad will let me hang out tonight?" I asked. "I kind of reacted with a Red Mélangé earlier, and I probably shouldn't be parading my shade around outside."

Baptiste didn't respond or even change his expression. But I could tell by the intensity with which he now blew bubbles that the question had stressed him out. Would his dad kick me out as soon as he saw the orange in my fire? Or maybe he'd try to lock me up, too.

Maybe sleeping here wasn't such a great idea. But I should probably stick around until Monsieur Wedel got back.

"Does your front door not lock from the outside?"

"We lost the key. Dad doesn't want to pay the hundred cuivre fine so we only lock it when we're both inside."

That made no sense. If he hadn't trapped Baptiste in his room, Monsieur Wedel could have kept the front door locked. But a change of topic was in order. Baptiste was blowing so furiously that a puddle of chocolate milk had formed around his glass.

"How's your fire?" I asked. I had noticed some scabbing

but didn't want to make it obvious I was examining it.

He nodded.

After a moment, I added, "You didn't go to school today."

He shook his head.

That was it? Baptiste didn't wonder how I knew? I'd planned to tell him about my visit to L'académie Mélangé but upon reflection, decided it might be better to keep that little disaster to myself.

"What did your dad say about everything that happened yesterday?"

"I told Papa that Aro stole my books and was belittling me. Papa didn't notice my fire. At least, he didn't say anything about it."

Great. So Monsieur Wedel still knew nothing about me. No wonder Baptiste was hesitant to have me stay over. Looks like I'd have to explain everything from the beginning.

"Want me to use my teeth?" Baptiste asked.

I realized he was talking about the knots. "No thanks. Do you have a knife?"

"No knives in the house, but I have six pairs of safety scissors in my room. Which color?"

"Surprise me."

When he came back, Baptiste held out the scissors but not to hand them to me. He obviously wanted to be the one who used them. I almost objected, but the tips were blunted after all. "Be careful."

I held out my hand. "Also, do you have a phone? I need to see if my Granny Jade left me a message."

"Jade? Is she Green?"

"Blue. I guess her parents just liked the name. Or the color," I added, noticing Baptiste's disappointed expression. "I'm sure she—"

With a final snip, the tie fell away. For a moment, we both stared at my glowing palm.

Then Baptiste absently reached for his glass. "Where did the green go?"

I couldn't respond. I'd been expecting some exotic shade of brownish-teal—but this? It was almost as though the red and green had canceled each other out.

"I reacted with Jeannette."

Baptiste spilled his milk. I barely registered the liquid dripping onto my legs and his mumbled string of apologies as he went to find a rag. All I could think was that it was finally over—my life had been returned to me.

Baptiste sopped up the milk with what looked like a knitted pot-holder. "Jeannette from my school is Orange," he said. "I don't see any orange."

"Maybe it's just the artificials. Can you turn them off?"

Baptiste flipped a switch so only our fires illuminated the room. Compared to mine, his shade seemed almost entirely green. I strode into the fanroom and closed the door. I examined the mirror, the tile, the chrome towel holder. They all reflected pure blue light, but it was a shade I'd never seen before —a washed out, almost icy blue.

Baptiste knocked. "You should turn on the fan. A hundred-and-twenty volt ventilator disperses the Sulfur Dioxide in your flatulence nearly thirty times faster than natural diffusion."

I carefully washed my fire with warm, soapy water. Once again, it had become my most prized possesion.

"Sulfur Dioxide is a by-product of luminogenesis," Baptiste continued through the door. "The esca produces a small amount of waste that is channeled to the small intestine."

I opened the door.

"Sulfur Dioxide is highly toxic and can impair breathing. Prolonged exposure can even be fatal. When combined with water, it becomes sulfurous acid which, although not nearly as strong as sulfuric acid... Why are you smiling?"

I picked Baptiste up by the armpits and launched him upward. "Because I'm Blue!"

"Please don't do that again. I have haphephobia which is the fear of being touched."

"Oh, sorry." I lowered him and grinned. "You have to be the smartest thirteen-year-old I've ever met."

Baptiste straightened his shirt and nodded. "My IQ is between 175 and 180 depending on which test you use." He smiled slightly. "But I have seven other phobias, the worst of which is—"

"*Mon frère*, I'd honestly love to stay and talk all night, but this changes everything. Whisnant won't be looking for—whatever shade this is. I can finally go back to Ville Bleu!"

"What about your face?"

Oh, right.

I'd sort of forgotten that all three heads of law enforcement had gotten a good look at me. Short hair or not, all it would take was a single poker recognizing me. I looked down at my milk-soaked, mud-splattered slacks. "This was supposed to be my disguise."

"You can borrow some of our clothes," Baptiste said. Without waiting for a response, he skipped down the hall.

I debated following him but instead sat at the table and took another long swig of chocolate milk. Maybe the elevator shoes and collared shirt would be good enough to get across the barrier. Once there, I could work out how best to stay hidden until my dad worked his magic with the family fortune.

Baptiste appeared and slid a pair of flannel pajamas onto the table.

"These are nice," I said. "Kind of small for me, though. What about some of your dad's clothes?"

Baptiste placed a chubby hand on the well-worn pajamas. "I believe this is Papa's loosest fitting outfit."

What? Monsieur Wedel must have been closer to Baptiste's size than my own. "Oh. That's okay. I'm getting pretty good at keeping to the dark streets."

"Ville Bleu has over sixteen hundred outdoor artificial lamps," Baptiste said. Then he made a face as if trying to push out a sulfur dioxide cloud. "Alexandrie is tall," he said finally.

Okay.

"Alexandrie?"

"She left most of her clothes in the closet when she left."

"Your mom?"

"Papa said she wouldn't need her blacking clothes in the blacking mental institution."

This time, I was the one who dumped milk everywhere.

CHAPTER SIXTEEN

UNCOMMON SCENTS

I n addition to most of her apparel, Madam Wedel had left boxes of costume jewelry, numerous hair extensions, and a rather disturbing collection of paper dolls. With Baptiste's permission, I requisitioned a pair of white jogging pants and a baggy, hooded sweater with an enormous bejeweled kitten on the front. The sweat pants didn't quite reach my ankles, but with my hood up and extensions flowing out the front, I could almost pass for a thickset female jogger.

My pecs didn't look as large or as feminine as I'd hoped, but I figured if the pokers got close enough to tell the difference, it would already be too late for me. A pair of pink socks and plastic jewel-encrusted sneakers completed the ensemble. And thank the Créateur, Madam Wedel had wide feet.

By the time I was dressed, had eaten most of the food in Baptiste's fridge, and released a good amount of sulfur dioxide —among other things—in his fanroom, Monsieur Wedel still hadn't come home. Baptiste didn't seem worried. Apparently his father had no sense of urgency and had often got caught out after curfew.

"He usually finds an open lobby," Baptiste said. "Once he slept in a phone booth."

I glanced at the door. "Probably best if I stay the night then."

Baptiste's face went slack. He almost looked bored, but I was pretty sure that on him the expression indicated a panic overload.

To give him some time to process, I picked up the phone

and dialed Orie's number. I had called a half hour ago with no answer.

This time, a male voice said, "*Bonsoir.*"

I almost hung up but then realized it wouldn't be so strange for Orie to get a call from a classmate. "*Bonsoir.* Can I speak to Orie, please?"

"Who is this?"

I swallowed. "Benoit from campus, I had a question about some study notes."

"I haven't seen Orie all day. You happen to know where she might be, Benoit?" He gave the name a strange emphasis as if he didn't buy the study notes story.

"Sorry, 'sieur. When she comes home, will you let her know I called and that it's important?" Hopefully she'd get the hint and stick by the phone.

The man said something, but a chorus of barking from outside the building drown him out. It wasn't the yips of a pet defending its territory, more like several wolf-dogs had stumbled into a cat sanctuary.

I hung up the phone and followed Baptiste to the balcony door. He wrenched back the curtain and yelped.

Far below, Capitaine Sébastian and two other suited men strode toward the lobby entrance. Each held a leash attached to his own personal polar bear.

"Holy blank," I said.

Baptiste began a rhythmic tapping against the wall. "All three at once. The guards usually walk the badger hounds one at a time. And they always stay near the riverbank."

"Wait, those are the Commissaire's dogs?" They looked nothing like the newspaper drawings. Their heads were the size of a baby-carriage and their sky-white bodies moved low to the ground. They almost looked like short, elongated ponies with the head of a long-snouted bear. Although they could probably eat a normal-sized dog in a single gulp—the badger hounds were more striking than menacing. "They're enormous."

"They bark like that when they have the scent of whatever they're hunting."

The air in my lungs turned to lead. They couldn't be following my scent. They'd need an item of clothing like a scarf or a shirt.

Black.

This was the second time signing autographs had come back to bite me.

"I led them right to your door," I said in a strangled whisper. Was hiding a fugitive a capital offense? They'd probably started at the school and followed my scent from there. That meant the Director was not as dumb as he seemed.

"You should leave out the window," Baptiste said.

Five stories up? "You have a forty-foot rope lying around?"

"Maybe you can make the shower curtain into a parachute. I read about a—"

"Baptiste, you should go to a neighbor's apartment or something. Sébastien isn't looking for you. I'll tell them I broke in."

The frenetic barking faded for a moment, then took on an echoing quality. They were inside the building—probably coming up the stairwell.

"You have to go now!"

Baptiste resisted my attempts to pull him toward the door and began rocking on his feet as if about to start dancing.

The barking jumped in volume. Baptiste would never make it out the front. Maybe I could lock him back in his room.

Something slammed against the door. Then again. Shouts.

It was over. Baptiste continued to rock, eyes closed. The pounding and barking and screaming on the other side of the door blended together in a disturbing parody of music.

At the very least I could tie him to a chair or destroy the phone like I'd done at the station, make it clear that Baptiste was the victim and had no way to call for help. I took my muddy white shirt from the ground, but when I grabbed Baptiste's hand to tie it behind his back, he dove toward the kitchen sink.

"I'm not going to hurt you!" I closed my eyes and tried to block out the sound of wood cracking. They'd be through the door in moments. The worst part was that I was still dressed like a thirty-year-old woman with questionable taste.

I opened my eyes and found Baptiste inserting my fire into a garbage bag.

"That's not going to fool anyone, little man."

He ignored me, pulled the large, yellow bag up my arm, and tied it at my shoulder. Maybe I should just punch him. If he had a bloody nose, he'd look like a victim more than an accomplice.

A loud crack came from the door. I wasn't sure what they were using to break the door in, but it sounded like another couple hits would do it.

Baptiste grabbed a second garbage bag and motioned for me to step into it.

"Will you at least hide under your bed?" I asked him.

"Please put your foot in, Bruno."

My heart broke. The poor kid was in such a state of panic, he didn't even know what he was doing. He thought he was helping somehow. I tied the bag around my upper thigh while he prepared another—presumably for my other leg.

"The average canine smells at least ten thousand times better than a human," Baptiste said. "That's like us taking an eye exam from four miles away."

I nodded. I didn't trust myself to speak. The panic had faded the moment I knew there was no escape. I still felt on edge, however—as if balancing between laughter and uncontrolled sobbing. Instead of focusing on the splintering door, I kept thinking about what Ro would've looked like at age thirteen. Would he have been as smart as Baptiste?

"They track invisible pieces of your skin that fall off

while you run."

Okay, now he was really losing it.

He bagged my other leg. As he finished tying the bag onto my dark arm, a crunching sound made us both look. Light shone through a jagged gap in the door. I caught sight of sharp white teeth and black gums. The barking grew even more frantic. Another crunch.

Baptiste stood back and examined me. I could only imagine how ridiculous I looked. At least it would distract from my jewel-encrusted jogging suit.

"Okay," he said. "You should probably go down the fire escape now."

"Baptiste, you really... wait, fire escape?"

I opened the back door and stepped outside. Sure enough, rusted to match the color of the bricks, a narrow ladder hugged the side of the building. It stretched from the rooftop to about ten feet from the ground. I'd have to climb onto the railing and stretch. The safety ladder was positioned between Baptiste's balcony and the apartment next door. Each pair of balconies shared its own escape route.

With this glorious discovery came the resurgent panic—for myself, and for the safety of Baptiste. I couldn't leave him to deal with Sébastien on his own. My eyes fell on the jumbo-size jar of mayonnaise Baptiste used to make my cheese sandwich. The image of a dog sniffing every inch of my suit popped into my head.

"Take that raw meat out of the freezer and rub it over my old clothes and everything I touched. Maybe it'll distract Sébastien and confuse the dogs. What about something even stronger, like hot pepper?"

Baptiste's eyes went wide and he ran to the cupboard. "Red pepper may overload the canine's olfactory receptors."

"Baptiste, tell them I threatened you. Can you cry? You should try to cry."

The loudest crunch yet. The door couldn't possibly hold up to anymore abuse. My fire felt like it might melt through the plastic bag. I had to go. Now.

Baptiste seemed to sense this too. "Wait," he said, then threw a tiny metal tin in my general direction. I caught it by instinct.

A hand reached through the hole and unlocked the apartment door. I dove for the balcony.

The next few seconds were a blur. I somehow managed to launch myself over the railing while simultaneously sliding the pepper tin into my front hoodie pocket. Unfortunately I missed the ladder, thanks to the stupid bags around my arms, but my chin caught one of the rungs and slowed me down long enough to find a foothold. For a moment I clung to the ladder, trying to clear my vision. My jaw felt like it had been knocked completely off.

The strange thing was that I didn't feel the pain yet. What I felt instead was hot saliva of a frenzied animal trying to fit its maw through the bars of the railing. I still didn't feel very steady, but I decided I'd rather fall to my death than get my face eaten by a badger hound. I began my descent just as another dog appeared on the balcony, followed by Sébastien.

I only got a quick glimpse of him since climbing a shaky ladder while wearing four plastic bags took most of my concentration. But he looked like he was debating coming down the ladder after me. About that time, the second dog, which must have been slightly less stupid than the first, realized it could go over the railing. It was halfway over when Sébastien grabbed it around the middle and wrestled it back inside the balcony.

Above me, I heard a sound like cracking ice on a lake. Bits of brick and concrete streamed past me. The weight of two horse-sized dogs was too much for the balcony. Would it knock me off the ladder when it fell?

Sébastien must have realized the danger as well, because the next time I glanced up, I saw no heads peeking over, canine or otherwise—probably already running for the stairs.

Only two more floors to go. I sped up.

A deafening bark from below nearly made me lose my grip. One of the guards must have stayed behind to watch the exit. I immediately started climbing upward. I'd have to go to the roof and try to find another way down. Maybe a nearby branch I could—

Out of the corner of my eye, I saw the badger hound charge the wall. What in the rainbow? The moment before it hit, the animal reared up on its hind legs. I wasn't worried—I was still a floor and a half from the ground.

Then it jumped.

I yanked my foot up just in time to avoid losing it. Before I could congratulate myself on my quick reflexes, the dog's teeth caught the garbage bag and pulled me free of the wall.

Crêpes.

The night sky and the dark ground became a blur of shadows. Despite not knowing which way was up, I reached out my hands for something to hold onto. Bad idea, it turned out. A jolt of pain shot up my dark arm—then I landed on something warm and soft. Well, landed isn't quite the right word. The squirming, kicking dog absorbed some of my momentum and sent me careening in another direction. My second, less hairy landing occurred a moment later.

My non-deadness took a moment to sink in. I lay on my back in the grass. I had somehow survived falling nearly two stories. My dark hand didn't feel normal, in fact my whole arm was numb, but I was breathing!

Then a paw the size of a dinner plate put a stop to that.

Apparently the badger hounds had been trained not to eat people's faces off. In fact, once the animal had the full weight of its upper body pinning me to the ground, it seemed positively buoyant.

If I'd been able to expand my lungs, I probably would've thought it was adorable. Horrible breath though. How was it that I couldn't breathe but could still smell the rancid odor of its mouth?

I was growing delirious or brain-dead or something. I

reached up and attempted to push the paw off my chest. The weight increased. I felt the tip of a claw pressing on my collar bone, and the panting puppy instantly became a rabid wolf again. The growl vibrated my entire body.

The guard appeared to be pulling on the leash in an effort to control the dog, but the more it pulled, the more it seemed to sense its prize would be taken away. The animal looked like it was considering taking a small piece of my face while it had the chance.

I became aware of a sharper pain digging into my rib. The tin. Despite my quickly diminishing brain function, an idea began to form—but I needed full use of my hand.

Stupid bags. Why had I let Baptiste—

No. Concentrate. Ignore the pain. I lifted my hand and waved the large bag tantalizingly in front of the dog's nose. My thoughts began to melt away like dirt clods in a stream. One of the last I managed to hold onto was the irony of the yellow plastic making my blue light shine green. I would die a Mélangé after all. That's right puppy, look at the pretty light. Pretty... green...

Next thing I knew, my arm was violently jerking back and forth. And I could breathe... slightly. The dog had the garbage bag in its jaws and was shaking its massive head. This had caused a shift in the dog's weight and allowed me a slight inhale. It was a miracle the dog hadn't caught my hand in its jaws as well.

The bag, which was obviously not designed to protect against sharp-toothed mammals, finally ripped in two. The moment my light hand—still trailing part of the bag—was free, I shoved it into my sweater pocket and pulled out the tin.

The full weight of the animal returned. A short, involuntary whine escaped me. I brought the tin to my mouth, ripped off the entire cap with my teeth and thrust the container toward the dog's face. The momentum of the movement sent a storm of dark-red powder directly into the badger hound's eye.

I felt its shriek as much as heard it. In an instant the dog's weight was gone. Fresh oxygen brought a rush of clarity.

I rolled to the side and sprang to my feet. A sharp pain in my dark hand made me gasp. My eyes and nostrils burned from the pepper. Gold sparks swirled in my vision, but after a couple of drunken steps, I found my footing and ran.

No shouts. Not even a bark. The only sound was the high-pitched yowl of the half-blinded dog. I assumed the guard was busy trying to control the thing, but I wasn't about to turn around and check.

As soon as I was out of sight, I took a sharp turn, then another.

Stupid. What was I doing? It didn't matter how many times I turned, the dogs would follow my scent. Two of my bags were in tatters, and I was pretty sure sweat was dripping off my face onto the sidewalk. I stopped, ripped the bags completely off, and stuffed them in the bushes. At least now I wouldn't sound like a dozen hissing snakes when I moved.

I began speed-walking toward Ville Bleu. I figured I'd hear the dogs well before they got close. Hopefully by then, my body would be ready for another sprint. But I knew the dogs would catch up to me eventually. I should have grabbed that tin and sprinkled the pepper behind me as I ran. Or maybe I'd be easier to find now that I smelled like a spice rack.

As my pulse slowed, the pain in my chin faded, but the throbbing in my dark hand became unbearable. Only then did I look and see my injury. The third finger had bent sideways so that it now covered my middle finger and part of my pointer. Nausea welled up in me, and I had to focus on the path ahead to avoid reacquainting myself with the cheese sandwich.

Broken finger. Big deal—happened all the time on the pitch. We all laughed about it. But it didn't seem quite as humorous with the mutilated finger on the end of my own arm.

The sound of distant barking sent a wave of cold sweat up my back. Time to pick up the pace. As I ran, I pulled up the hood of the sweater. The brightness of my fire nearly blinded me. Had the guard noticed my new shade?

Not that it mattered much. The time for disguises was over. I had to contact my family somehow and tell them to hurry up the bribing process. If Whisnant couldn't be bought, we'd try the Dominateur or the Commissaire. Worst case scenario, we could leave several thousand cuivres with the soldiers guarding one of the city entrances. I was about done with this island anyway.

But where did that leave Baptiste? I should have hit him, bloodied his nose at least. The thought that they might be forcing Baptiste to answer questions almost made me turn around.

Even if I went back, the only thing I could do was turn myself in. And if Sébastien decided to blame Baptiste, my surrender wouldn't do him any good. Créateur protect him. It seemed his life was a tragedy even before he snuck onto Blue Campus.

A howl sounded somewhere behind me—much closer. My jog became a sprint. I tried to keep to the main streets. Although I was now moderately familiar with the disorderly layout of the Hameau, a single dead-end might bring about my own.

When I reached Rue Principale, I nearly tripped over my gem-studded sneakers. Shoppers, dog-walkers, and couples out for a stroll filled the sidewalk on the Blue side.

As far as I could tell, no one was paying attention to me. I lowered my head, straightened the extensions—which had miraculously survived the rabid animal attack—and crossed the street.

Maybe the crowd would work to my advantage. More people meant more smells. If I couldn't lose the mutts, I could at least slow them down. With my eyes on the ground, I navigated the busy sidewalk. I caught a few strange looks, but I couldn't tell if they were due to my unfeminine body-shape, or my ice-blue shade. I brushed as many people as I could manage while not appearing intoxicated. Maybe they would carry my scent for a while, get the dogs to bark up the wrong tree, so to speak. That actually gave me another idea. I needed to make a stop at Blue Garden.

Distant barks made a few people look toward Hameau Vert. Definitely not as distant as I would've liked. Sébastien would probably arrive in the Ville soon. At least with all these night-owls about, I should have plenty of warning. I doubted any of the beau monde had actually laid eyes on the Commissaire's badger hounds—much less encountered three of them hurtling down main street.

After a couple blocks, I began to relax slightly and stopped glancing over my shoulder. I was home. Shouldn't I feel relieved or at least nostalgic?

Yet, as I dodged a group of women comparing wedding rings and teens shouting profanity at a Green nanny pushing a baby carriage, I felt a flutter of sadness. Was I insane? How could I be upset about leaving Hameau Vert? Nearly every moment I spent on the Green side had been full of terror, discomfort, and general misfortune. All the same...

I realized it wasn't the winding streets or the outdated buildings I missed, but the people—some of them—and the feeling of... of what? Misery?

No. My time among the mixed and lower colors seemed somehow more authentic than my entire life. My return to Ville Bleu made the contrast even more obvious. But being with my family again would be worth it. I could put up with another few decades of ostentation and façade.

Someone screamed. It was far enough up the street that I didn't panic, but it was definitely time to get lost. More screams, followed by shouting. I slowed, then turned down a side street. I passed a man who asked what was happening.

I shrugged and continued my slow jog toward the winter-dark side of the city. My fire, I noticed, had grown oddly cool. Since I jumped from Baptiste's balcony it had been supplying me with a near constant stream of energy. When it eventually gave out, the pain and exhaustion would hit all at once. I had to find someplace to hide and call Orie again. I wish I knew where she lived.

I decided to jog the rest of the way to the Garden. When I arrived, I swore. The park was even more packed than Rue Principale. Wasn't it a weekday? It dawned on me that today would've been the last day of finals on Blue Campus. The students and their families were out celebrating. My plan might still work—but it would be risky. I jogged around the perimeter of the park and searched for a secluded spot to hide.

A good-sized crowd congregated around the stone tables, most of the Blues over seventy—probably an impromptu Firearchy tournament. One man waited patiently for his dog to finish his business. I thought several anxious-looking women were staring at me, but as I jogged past, I realized they were watching a small group of middle-school kids near the pond. Countless croquet wickets made the large grassy area looked like a sloppy postoperative staple job.

Ro had loved croquet. He used to pull the wicket out of the ground as soon as his ball went through, as if it were his prize.

I slowed as I approached the forested area next to the pond. Although the park seemed to contain at least half of Ville Bleu's sixteen-hundred outdoor street lamps, there were enough dark patches among the trees for my purposes. The brisk walk became a stroll—directly toward one of those pockets of shadow. Just a beefy female jogger looking for a bit of quiet recoup.

The foliage enveloped me like teammates in a scrummage. Once sure I was completely hidden, I peed on the closest tree. Then I casually wandered to another concealed spot and repeated the process. I managed to mark four trees before I ran out of eau de Bruno.

Now came the hard part. I had been planning to use the lake to both wash off some of my scent and make a break in my trail, but the park was not nearly as vacant as I'd hoped. A person wading through the water in their jogging outfit would certainly be noticed and commented upon. When they saw the guards and dogs, even a four-year-old could figure out what was going on. Was it too much to hope that the badger hounds lost my scent in the crowd? I couldn't count on it.

At the dark edge of the pond, behind a bush—which turned out to be prickly—I stripped to my boxers. With a broken finger, this wasn't as easy as it sounds, or as quick. Next, I rubbed my sweaty clothes against the trunk of a large oak, then tossed the pants, hair extentions and sweatshirt into the air. They kindly clung to the upper branches, all but invisible in the darkness. The socks weren't as willing to help me out, so I buried them in the mud with the shoes. Although my feet were still healing from the night before, I wasn't far from my house. Anyway, if all went as planned, I wouldn't have to run.

The large pond was only three feet deep in the center, but because numerous signs prohibited swimming, the Ville youth did it regularly. Usually, during the hottest part of the day, but furtive night swims were not uncommon. No one, however, swam alone. Apparently breaking rules wasn't as fun if you were the only one doing it.

I waded into the frigid water, which on my still-bandaged feet, actually felt nice. I moved away from the forested area until the water reached my knees, then I made my way around to the group of middle-school kids I'd seen earlier. Four boys sat in a circle around a single girl. It looked like a game of *Vérité ou Conséquence*. One of the mecs noticed me and pointed.

I waved my newly acquired blue. "Anyone want to race across the pond?"

They stared for a moment, whether at my unique shade or my sudden appearance, I couldn't tell.

"We's busy," one of the boys said. I immediately recognized his grating voice from the night before when he'd shouted at Baptiste and me to get back to our side. Little blackhead.

"We are busy," I said. "Not we is. And I can see you're busy being a limp crêpe. What about the rest of your friends? They can't all be as timid as you are."

The other three boys looked at each other. None seemed inclined to accept my offer. This was not going as planned.

Wild barking echoed from one of the side streets. What had Baptiste said? That's the sound the badger hounds made when they caught the scent of their prey?

I prepared to start in on the blackhead's dainty upper arms—which undoubtedly made swimming difficult—when the girl stood, kicked off her sandals, and stepped into the water. She yelped and glared at me, but the boys were already removing their shoes and socks. The mec who looked a little older than the others pulled off his shirt, glanced in my direction, then put it back on.

The pre-teens were helpfully loud as we half-swam, half-crawled our way across the muddy pond. Okay, I pretty much crawled the whole way, but on the plus side I didn't break any more fingers. Since I let the blackhead win the "race", his enthusiasm and volume increased, drawing more attention.

But not so much that they didn't notice the meter-high dog enter the park, leading the Captain of the Royal Guard.

CHAPTER SEVENTEEN

TREE, HOUSE

I t was the screams from the bank that did it. From the Blues' reactions, I could see why the Commissaire kept the dogs hidden—and why Sébastien only dared bring one into Ville Bleu.

I started a breath-holding contest. The kids were too awestruck by the badger hound to participate, but it gave me an excuse to stay underwater for longer periods of time while the dog sniffed its way around the park... along the exact path I had walked.

Reactions to the enormous animal varied. Many parents grabbed their kids and ran. An elderly man shouted about park regulations, and a pair of college-age boys even got close enough to try to touch it. Without exception, every park-goer who hadn't fled was watching the bear-sized dog.

After coming up for air the third time, I saw Sébastien disappear into the wooded area, followed—at a distance—by at least two dozen spectators. I swam to the edge of the pond farthest from where I'd entered and stepped onto the grass. Sudden heat flared in my light hand, but I resisted the urge to sprint. Instead I casually hobbled along the street as if I'd simply forgotten my beach towel—and my swimming trunks. Hopefully the route to Chateau Nazaire would be free of pedestrians.

I knew going home was a horrible idea, but I had literally run out of options. Orie was unreachable. Marin lived on the other side of town, and he was probably staying with Drea anyway. I should have spent more time during the school year memorizing girls' addresses.

At any rate, I wasn't going to be stupid about it. I'd stake out my house from a distance. If I caught sight of a poker or one of the other badger hounds, I would... well, I'd probably run the other direction and get caught, because other than trying to scale the ridiculously high wall topped with razor wire and living as a hermit on the coast, I really was all out of ideas. My parents had to be home by now. Surely they'd have a plan. I thought about finding a phone, but dismissed the idea. It would be faster—and less conspiculous—to check out the house.

"Hey, wait up!" came a feminine shout behind me.

I feigned deafness and kept walking.

"I know you can hear me, Bruno!"

I spun to face the middle-school girl who, like me, dripped a trail of pond water along the pavement. How did she know my name? I walked toward her. Anything to keep her from shouting my identity again.

"Do I know you?" I said, trying to sound pleasantly surprised rather than accusatory.

"You said hi to me on Monday morning."

I stared at her.

"You were walking with the coffee mec on your team."

"Oh. Marin. Yeah. Good to see you again. I should probably go get some clothes on."

"I heard some stuff about you."

I closed my eyes. This was not the time to have a Q&A with a virtual stranger.

"They said you were Mélangé. Did you really kill a poker?"

"What's your name again?" I asked.

"You don't remember? I've met you like four times."

She had to be exaggerating. "Look, I appreciate you not telling everyone who I am."

"I didn't do it for you."

"What?"

"I figured if I outed you, you might hurt one of us."

"Seriously? I'm not going to hurt anyone. I was just trying to... Why did you chase after me? Aren't you worried I'll attack you or something?"

She shrugged, then glanced back toward the pond.

Black. She was trying to delay me. Had she told one of the boys to get Sébastien? Or maybe she was just hoping the dogs would catch my scent.

I ran.

"Bruno Nazaire is here!" the girl screamed. "The soldier killer is getting away!"

At least I had grass to sprint on this time. Her voice gradually faded behind me. Hopefully Sébastien would underestimate her as I had done. He didn't seem the type to drop everything and follow the advice of a soggy little girl.

I took a shortcut through the Cathedral grounds, then continued to run along the strip of grass between the curb and the sidewalk. So far no more upstanding citizens had screamed my name, and I hadn't heard a bark for several minutes.

When I approached my house, from the back this time, I felt almost cheery. Light illuminated every window, a clear indication that Granny was home. Although I didn't see any pokers patrolling or hiding in the yard, I tucked my fire into my armpit and watched from the bushes. I knew I didn't have all night. The dogs would find my scent again as soon as they took another circuit around the lake. But Whisnant would be a fool not to keep a few pokers here just in case.

Yet the house seemed quiet. After a few minutes, I spotted Granny's blue light on the first floor. By backing up, I could see her through the window above the kitchen sink—washing dishes, apparently. I took a chance and extracted my light hand from under my arm.

"Come on," I whispered. "I'm right in front of you."

I waved my fire, but Granny seemed awfully interested in those dishes. I left the safety of the undergrowth and crept toward the kitchen window, waving my light above my head. Man, that woman was distracted. I was almost to the point where I was too close to see her when her eyes met mine and doubled in size. In that same instant, a large figure in a brown uniform appeared behind her.

I dove sideways. As soon as I landed, I once again tucked my fire under my arm. Had the poker seen me? From my angle, I hadn't seen his face, so maybe I'd been quick enough. I waited, listening for the sound of the back door opening. Instead I heard Granny singing.

Singing? Maybe she was trying to tell me I hadn't been spotted? Home was obviously not safe at the moment. I'd have to go hunting for Drea's house. I remember her saying they moved close to the Cathedral since her sister was always going back and forth. I had taken two steps toward the back bushes when I realized Granny was singing in Ulfish—a lullaby both Ro and I had fallen asleep to countless times. Was she telling me to go to my bed? Or to come back when everyone was asleep?

But the lyrics weren't right. She was repeating two words over and over.

Nafdin Boonvifen. On the tree tops. But she was even singing that wrong. Sounded like she was repeating "*Boonhast.*" What was hast? She knew I didn't understand Ulfish!

Hast. Hast. That word did sound familiar. I was pretty sure Granny said it every time we arrived home from vacation. *Endeir zel Hast.* Finally back? No... finally home.

On the tree home? The tree house! Maybe she had left me supplies or a note up there.

With my fire still mostly-covered in my armpit, I crawled to the red oak nearest the back porch and attempted to climb the ladder. This proved impossible with one hand under my armpit and a broken finger, so I used both hands and tried to keep my torso between my fire and the window.

At the top I found nothing. No notes, and most disturbingly, no food. Baptiste's cheese sandwich felt like hours ago.

The tree house had seen better days. A thick layer of dead leaves and twigs covered the floor and sap dripped down the walls. The sap, at least, gave me an idea. I dabbed sap on a leaf and stuck it to my fire. I repeated the process until my light was almost completely hidden.

I could no longer hear Granny singing. I really hoped this was what she meant. If I had misinterpreted her message, I'd be trapping myself in a tree for no reason.

I peeked toward the window and felt a smile spread across my face. From the higher angle, all I could see was the dishes in the sink—and Granny's fire as she signed a rapid message in firespeak. Whether it was because I'd had some practice a few days ago or was just more used to Granny's signs, I didn't have any trouble keeping up.

—EN UNABLE TO HELP.
THEY ARE TRACKING YOU WITH DOGS.

Yeah, I'd noticed.

WHEN I SHOUT YOU JUMP ON ROOF.
WE MEET AT YOUR BEDROOM WINDOW.
STAY OUT OF SIGHT.
MAKE NO SOUND.

What? I must have translated that wrong. The roof was too far away to jump from the tree house. I squinted into the darkness. I mean, there was a branch that got sort of close. Maybe if I was a hundred pounds lighter I might be able to—

Granny's scream turned my blood to ice. Through the window I caught a flash of bright red before her hand disappeared from the sink. She continued to scream in pain. Had she cut herself on purpose to drown out the sound of my feet hitting the roof?

Son of a Violet, blackheaded crêpe bag.

Without allowing myself time to think, I climbed out

onto the large branch extending toward my bedroom. I started crawling, but that proved exceptionally awkward. I pulled myself to my feet and walked along the branch while using higher branches to balance. The sound of Granny's screams propelled me forward. If I didn't make it to the roof before she stopped, I'd be blacked and she would've cut herself for nothing.

Nearly there.

The house fell silent. No no no.

Another prolonged wail erupted from inside, and without stopping to ponder how stupid it was, I took two running steps and launched myself toward the roof.

I landed hard, cried out in pain as my broken finger met the shingles, and slid to the edge of the roof. Just before I toppled off, my heel caught on the rain gutter. The metal bent with a screech, but it absorbed my momentum. I pressed my back into the shingles and willed my center of gravity to stay put.

I heard distant barking but no screams. Had I jumped in time? Did it really matter? I had no idea how sturdy the gutter was. As soon as it gave way, I would plummet two stories onto the rear walkway. My survival instincts were screaming for me to adjust my weight and pull myself higher, but the image of a poker staring at the ceiling, waiting for another sound, kept me plastered in place. The gutter creaked. My limbs began to shake.

Finally I decided it was either make some noise or shatter most of my vertebrae on the bricks below. I slowly pushed against the gutter. Somewhere along the length of the roof, a metal band snapped, sending me two more inches farther over the edge.

For a terrifying second, I wondered why I hadn't fallen. My body felt like it weighed six hundred pounds and someone was tipping the roof, trying to dislodge a tenacious spider. Yet somehow I wasn't moving.

I stayed in that impossible position somewhere between

ten minutes and four hours. Then a window scraped.

"Bruno, what are you doing?" came Granny's whisper.

"Oh, you know. Trying to keep the bones inside my body."

After a pause, something brushed my dark arm. I craned my neck and saw Granny, halfway out the window holding one end of her apron.

"No offense, Granny, but you'd better tie it to something."

"Grab it. We only have a pair of minutes. I sent Balthis looking for medical supplies in the basement. He can't stand the sight of blood."

Balthis? Sergent Whisnant himself had been here waiting for me?

I took a breath and went over the motion in my head. Light hand across to grab the apron string. I'd just have to be fast.

One, two, three....

I jerked, but nothing happened. My fire was literally stuck to the roof. What the? When I saw the crinkled leaves I remembered the sap. It had probably been the only thing keeping me from sliding off the roof. I'd have to use the hand with the ugly finger.

I grabbed the apron, then pulled my light hand straight up to unstick it. Granny braced herself against the window pane and dragged me upward.

"Where are your clothes?" Granny asked when I reached the window.

"Distracting the dogs, hopefully." I lifted my leg to climb inside, but Granny stopped me. "Better if you stay out. You need to be ready to make dust if Balthis barges in."

Make dust. Crêpes, I missed Granny's awkward Figgy euphemisms. She retreated into the room and opened a few drawers. In the artificial light, I finally got a good look at her. "What happened to you?" I whispered.

She brought me an armful of my clothes and shrugged. "It hasn't been the best week, but I'm fine."

"Fine?"

She wore a stained and tattered bathrobe. She smelled like she'd been drinking. Her silver hair lay limp and tangled against her face, and her eyes seemed to have sunk several inches into her skull.

"You have to stop stressing out," I said. "You're going to kill yourself."

Granny glared at me. "Get dressed."

I held up my broken finger. Without warning, she grabbed my wrist and finger, and tugged. I opened my mouth to scream, but the jolt of pain had been surprisingly brief. I examined my hand. My finger was once again facing the right direction.

"Where did you learn how to set a broken finger?"

"No bruise or swelling. It was dislocated."

"Ah."

There were definite benefits to having an iatrophobe in the family.

Granny steadied me as I began to dress. "You going to explain your shade, or are we pretending I didn't see the green in your fire yesterday?"

Somehow I buttoned my jeans without getting sap all over them. "I don't know what's happening to me." My voice cracked on the last word. After a couple sharp breaths, I was able to blink away the burning in my eyes and continue dressing.

Granny watched me for a moment, then changed the subject. "Do you know why your father spends hundreds of cuivres on electricity every year?"

"Dad said... that started after Grandpa died."

"It started with the phone calls."

Why was she bringing this up now? "What phone calls?"

"I don't know how the man got our number. He seems to prefer me since he moans and garbles only when I answer. Your father finally started turning off the ringer every night."

"Can't they call the operator or something?"

"We dropped our enquiry after they traced it to the Royal

Barracks."

"What? Are you saying one of the royal guards has been harassing us for years?"

"Your father believes we have an enemy that might not be entirely sane."

"Blank." Granny's extravagant electricity use suddenly seemed perfectly rational. Why hadn't anyone told me?

"That's why I think you were targeted—and why no amount of money is going to protect you."

"Why would a royal guard have something against our family?"

A sound of static and garbled shouting drifted up the stairs. Whisnant's radio? The interruption seemed to jolt us both back to reality.

Granny handed me a pair of sneakers. "You have to get outside the wall."

"What? No. I need to wait for Mom and Dad." I pulled the shoes on and sighed. I'd almost forgotten what shoes felt like when they fit. It was glorious to be back in my own clothes.

"Your parents have been stuck outside the winterdark checkpoint since yesterday."

"Stuck?"

"Whisnant won't let them in until they give you up. He's sure we know where you are. He's kept me on house arrest these last few days, hoping you'll come home."

I couldn't keep this up. Now Granny and my parents were paying for my stupidity.

"Don't get any ideas," Granny said. "I recognize that look."

"What look?"

"Same one you had before you killed Duveteux."

For a moment I couldn't breathe. "I—how did you..."

"She was smart. I knew she wouldn't just disappear."

I slowly zipped up my jacket. "I left her in the woods."

"You loved that cat. And so did I. You had no right to—"

"She killed Ro!"

Granny pressed her light to my mouth. The gesture startled me, but then the warm hum of her light on my face deflated my anger, leaving only the pain and guilt.

Granny slowly lowered her fire. "Sacrificing your best friend to avenge your brother is a noble sentiment, but I'm afraid you've always leaned toward the melodramatic. Kittens scratch things. It's what they do. If anyone is to blame it was your father. He's the only one of us that would've recognized the swelling as a serious infection."

"So because Dad's job takes him away for weeks at a time it—"

"I'm saying think about how your noble sacrifice would affect your parents. Turning yourself in won't help Andres and Cristelle, or me for that matter."

"How can you say that? Mom must be dying out there. Are they sleeping in the car? And if you haven't left the house in almost a week, what are you eating?"

"I've got plenty of wine and strawberry preserves to last a month. But if you take away my hope, you might as well abandon me in the woods like your cat."

"Your hope—they're going to catch me either way. The only question is how much damage they can inflict on my family until I give in."

"The only damage that matters to me or your parents is losing you—and that's a dipped-in-black guarantee."

I blinked. That was the first time I'd heard Granny swear in Téle.

"You'd still have each other. You honestly think my parents would rather be dead than let Whisnant have me?"

"You'll understand when you're a parent," Granny said. "Now you need to go. No more questions. Get as close to the gate as you can before coming out in the open. You should be able to jump the bar. They may try to tranq you, but—" Her mouth went slack even as the wrinkles around her eyes stretched taut.

I followed her gaze to the base of the oak tree. There, sniffing the bark, was a white dog the size of a pony. Sébastien appeared and skidded to a stop next to the animal. No leash. That was bad.

Granny waved for me to climb inside. As quietly as I could, I slowly pulled myself through the window.

"Balthis!" Sébastien shouted. "He's on the roof!"

I launched myself into the room.

"Out the front!" Granny said. "You've got to make it to the checkpoint."

I flew down the stairs, through the living room, and past Whisnant who held Granny's box of medical supplies.

"Hey!" he yelled as I sprinted past him.

I reached the front door, unlocked it, and flung myself back into the night. Then I took off down the street toward the winterdark checkpoint. In my own clothes with shoes that fit, I felt almost superhuman.

Then I heard the barking behind me, and I suddenly felt as if I were running through tar.

Faster. I wasn't going to make it. Heat continued to pour into my body from my fire, but no matter how quickly I pumped my arms and legs, the sounds of the dog grew steadily closer. My heart sank as I realized I would have to turn darkward to get to the checkpoint a full block away. The dog would only have to leap a couple short fences and he'd cut me off. I'd never make it.

Créateur help me. What was I supposed to do? How was I supposed to—

Above the tops of the trees directly in front of me stretched the spires of the Crystal Cathedral. It was closer than the checkpoint. I wouldn't have to make any turns. Would they let me in? Legally, they'd have to. The property belonged to the church.

When I reached the intersection, instead of turning toward the city exit, I dove through the hedge surrounding the cathedral grounds. This hurt a lot more than I'd expected. At least the barrier might slow down the enormous dog.

I fell easily into rugby mode as I dodged trees and hurdled

bushes. Behind me, shouts had joined the barking. Sébastien and the dog had made it through the hedge.

I reached the front steps of the cathedral took them three at a time. The badger hound reached the base of the steps just as I reached the large double doors. Locked.

No.

I raised my fist to pound on the frosted glass door when it opened. An elderly Green with a portable vacuum strapped to his back shuffled out. I slipped past him through the open door.

"Hey, you can't—"

"Harborage!" I shouted into the cavernous darkness of the main hall. "By the twenty-ninth dictum, I invoke the right of harborage!"

A cry of pain sounded behind me. I turned in time to see the door fly open and shatter against the wall. Sergent Whisnant strode into the cathedral, his triumphant smile made eerie by the green light of his fire. How had he kept up with the dog? Had he stashed a scooter in the bushes?

I spun back toward the darkness and collided with something cold and hard. For a moment, I lay on my back, trying to figure out which part of my face was bleeding. Then the green light descended on me.

"How in the black rainbow did you get your blue back?" He picked me up by the hair and dragged me across the rough stone floor. "Not that it matters. When the dogs are done with you—"

Light flooded the cathedral.

"How dare you!"

CHAPTER EIGHTEEN

THE PROPOSAL

I t took me a moment to realize who was shouting. Not Whisnant or even Sébastien, but a dark-haired woman in a silk nightgown. "You have no right to step foot in this sacred edifice!" she continued.

"Apologies, Priestess," Whisnant said. "We were just leaving."

"And the door!" she shrieked.

Whisnant lifted me under the arms and quickened his pace toward the entrance. "Of course we will have it fixed immediately."

"Harborage," I croaked. "By the twenty—"

Whisnant wrapped his arm around my face, cutting off my air.

"Who is that boy?"

"Common criminal, Priestess. Terribly sorry to disturb you."

Although it was still half-concealed by dead leaves, I raised my fire toward the woman.

"Leave him," she called.

Whisnant ignored her and stepped through the doorway.

"Heretic!" she screamed. "If you remove that child from this property, you will be arrested and tried as an infidel."

Whisnant stopped.

"Think carefully, Sergent," the woman said. "Is your government prepared for hostile engagement with the Ecclesia Neocatholica?"

Whisnant dropped me at the threshold. "I'll be back with

the required paperwork," he said. "Until then, my troops will be outside."

"If your soldiers set one foot on church property before the writ is in my hand, there will be consequences."

The next few minutes passed in a haze of pain and delirium. Eventually I ended up in a bed with cool sheets and a silk pillow. Someone was cleaning the sap off my fire when my exhaustion overcame the pain in my head, and I collapsed into a dreamless sleep.

What felt like thirty seconds later, someone shook me awake. "Got to get up, Bru-baby."

"Marin? Leave me alone." I rolled onto my side and pulled the blanket up over my head. Something felt wrong. I ran a hand over my scalp. "What happened to my hair?"

"Casualty of war, *mon frère*. Now get up."

My eyes focused on Marin. "What are you doing here?" I examined the rough stone walls and the oil lamp in the corner.

"You are in the vaults under the cathedral, and at this moment, most of the royal army is above us searching for you."

"The dogs?"

Marin shook his head. "Like they're going to let those monsters into a church."

I sat up. Other than a slight throbbing, my head felt pretty good. In fact, I couldn't remember the last time I'd felt this rested. "How did they get the writ so quickly?"

"Quickly? Bruno, you've been out for over twenty-four hours. I thought for sure the fumes would wake you up."

"What fumes?"

"We bleached your hair and cut it. Now get your lazy derriere out of bed. I'll tell you the plan on the way."

"Where are we going?"

Marin slid both arms under the mattress and flipped me over.

"Mallory has been hiding me and my mom for a couple days now," Marin said, his fire trained on the path ahead. The narrow tunnel felt otherworldly.

"Mallory is the priestess?"

"High Priestess. And Drea's sister. Watch your head."

"Wait, why is your family in hiding?"

"Dad tried to make a formal complaint about my treatment—but instead of relaying the message to the Commissaire, Dom Gravois had him arrested for treason. He's been in a holding cell at the police station for the last two days."

"What? Why didn't he go straight to the Commissaire?"

Marin didn't answer. After what happened to him at the station, it couldn't be easy to have his dad there. When several minutes had passed, I had decided to offer my condolences when he stopped abruptly. "Hear that?"

It sounded like a distant, rushing wind. Then an icy drop of water landed on my shoulder.

He pointed upward. "The river."

The tunnel seemed to narrow even as stood there. I took a few steps back the way we had come. "I'm not going into the Taudis."

"Sorry, mec—don't have a choice. Orie needs you to pay someone at the community shelter."

"What does Orie have to do with any of this?"

"I'll explain everything, but first you've got to tell me how you got rid of your green. And why it's so bright all of a sudden."

I glanced at my fire and reluctantly followed him deeper into the tunnel. "I reacted with an Orange girl."

Marin shot me a skeptical look, then brushed something off his shoulder.

A white cricket the size of my hand hopped past me and vanished into the darkness.

I shivered and did a quick check of my own person. "Maybe it was a delayed reaction to the artificial serum. Why does this tunnel even exist?"

"Tunnels. Ancient priestesses used them to smuggle or rescue babies or something. Apparently they're a couple-hundred years old."

I glanced at the ceiling and quickened my pace. "Tell me again why it is so crucial that we get to the Red shelter."

"That's where the forger lives."

"Could we start from the beginning?"

"Orie stopped by while you were comatose. When she saw you were Blue again, she came up with a plan to get both our families off the island."

"Wait, we're all running away?"

"More like a tactical retreat. Once we're on the mainland, Mom's going to file a lawsuit against the Télesphorian government to get Dad freed."

"Do my parents know about this?"

"Orie said she'd get a message to them. Turns out her dad's got connections with a mec across the river who forges documents—enough false passports and travel visas for all three of our families. We're supposed to meet back underneath the cathedral by midnight tomorrow. He's going to fit us into two full-sized sedans and sneak us through the checkpoint. Chanmé, right?"

"You really think her dad's going to agree to this?"

"She seemed pretty confident. I think she's used to getting her way."

"But I've never even met Monsieur Talbot. Why would he stick his neck out for me?"

Marin grinned. "Because by that point, you'll be family. Mallory has agreed to marry you and Orie before we make our escape."

I tripped and landed on my stomach.

"Careful," Marin said. "Rocks are slippery here." He tried to pull me to my feet, but I shrugged him off.

"This is a joke, right?"

"I know it's a bit young, but a sixteen-year-old ceremony is not unheard of. Anyway, marriage does have certain privileges." He wiggled his eyebrows.

"Whether it's tomorrow or ten years from now, I can't marry Orie."

"Why not? She's cute, rich and obsessed with you. What's not to love?"

I sat on the damp ground. "If I would've known this was your master plan, I would've taken my chances back at the cathedral with the royal soldiers."

Marin's smile disappeared. "Are you serious right now? You're going to throw away the one chance to protect our families because Orie isn't your type?"

A dozen biting retorts sprang to mind, but then I remembered Granny in that stained housecoat with her limp hair and bloodshot eyes. If by some miracle Monsieur Talbot gave in to his daughter's mad scheme, it probably would be our only chance. But to be married tomorrow night? "Why can't we just sign the paperwork? Is my word not good enough?"

"You can't blame her. People nullify betrothals all the time. And there was also something about having increased leverage to get you out if you're already paired to her."

I nodded. It all seemed like an elaborate delusion, but Marin was right. If Orie was going to put her family in danger to save mine, I couldn't deny her. It was the only way.

"Do we just hang out down here until it's time to get the documents?"

"You could, I guess. But I'm not really sure how much oxygen is down here. Plus it's cold. Oh, and you're the one who's got to get the documents." He pulled a wad of bills from his pocket and handed it to me. "Instructions are inside. And before you surface, you need to rub this all over your body." From his other pocket, he pulled out what looked like a tube of toothpaste. "Drea bought it in Tjarda last summer. It dyes your skin to make it look like you've spent too much time outdoors."

"Weird."

"You owe me, by the way. Drea wanted to apply it before you woke up, but I convinced her to wait."

I tried not to think too hard on that. "Aren't you coming with me?"

"To the Taudis, are you insane?"

I glared at him.

He grinned. "I'm taking one of the other tunnels that leads to Drea's basement until the search is finished. My mom is there waiting for me."

Why did one of the tunnels lead to Drea's house? And it seemed a bit strange for Marin to hang out in his girlfriend's basement, while I—the one wanted for murder—made shady transactions with Red thugs.

Marin seemed to read my thoughts. "I did offer to get the documents," he said. "But Drea wouldn't hear of it. Guess she does like me after all."

"It's fine. I was in the Taudis yesterday. I at least know what to expect. And I won't have to worry about the dogs. But am I supposed to keep my blue fire pocketed the entire time?"

"The skin-dye should make you look like some sort of muddy-Mélangé."

"You want me to dye my fire?"

"It's not permanent." He slowed as we reached a split in the tunnel. "Ah, crêpes, I forgot which way she said to go."

"*Chanmé.*"

"Don't get excited. I know one of these leads to Red High, and the other to the tin mines."

"Then we go dark," I said. "If we're facing summerlight toward the Taudis, it means the light side goes eyerise to the mines."

"Unless we got turned around somehow." Then without warning, he screamed.

I hit my head on a low hanging rock and swore.

"Sorry," he said. "Rat—I think." He cleared his throat. "I should probably get going. My mom's probably chewing rocks by now. See you tomorrow night, I guess." He raised his fire.

I returned the gesture. Although I'd done it all my life, the motion seemed ridiculously formal. And cold. Maybe the Greens were onto something with those handclasp-things. I decided now wasn't the time to educate Marin on Green culture, but I did give his shoulder a brief squeeze with my dark hand.

He furrowed his eyebrows, then grinned. "You are one weird pigeon."

CHAPTER NINETEEN

HUMANITARIANS

T he skin dye turned my fire a sickly mustard green. As
soon as the cream dried on my body, I got dressed again
and set off down the darkways passage. This tunnel
seemed much rougher than the earlier one, as if the excava-
tors had begun to lose steam. As it moved steadily upward, it
grew increasingly narrow until I had to crouch—then crawl. I
alternated between singing Granny's Ulfish lullaby and chanting swearwords.

Just as I was getting ready to turn around, the tunnel ended. And not the yay-this-horrible-ordeal-is-over kind
of ending, but rather the holy-blackened-crêpes-I'm-going-to-
die kind of ending.

I may have screamed for help several times before I felt
the breeze on my ankle. I scrambled backward and found a
narrow hole recessed into the corner of the tunnel. I trained
my light into the hole. My puke-shade fire reflected what
looked like standing water—maybe ten feet down.

I really hoped this wasn't the entrance to the mines because there was no way I was going all the way back to the fork
only to do this all over again. The hole looked wide enough for
me to fit down, but I didn't relish the idea of being stuck until
someone came looking for me.

Eventually my impatience overcame my anxiety. I
dropped through the opening and splashed down into something that was definitely not water. At first I thought I'd
landed in a backed-up sewage pipe, but it had a sharper smell
of decay. The cold sludge was the perfect height to seep in-

side my shoes and soak my socks. Even with my dark hand over my mouth and nose, I couldn't keep from gagging. When I finally managed to pass my fire over my immediate surroundings, I found I was in a concrete drainage pipe, not unlike the one Jeannette's family lived in. Directly adjacent to where I'd fallen, lay the source of the stench. It may have been a large mammal at one time—possibly a deer or a cow which, after weeks of decomposing in a stagnant pool, had created a colorful—and lively—soup. It took a good deal of effort to keep the contents of my stomach in place.

It wasn't until I pocketed my fire that I was able to tell which direction was out. In the darkness, a patch of slightly lighter dark betrayed the exit end of the tube. Unfortunately, the mound-o-maggots was between me and clean air. My shoes were already as soaked as they could get. I should have carefully stepped over the carcass and continued on my way. But I had just seen what looked like an eel or a long leech swim by my foot, so I wasn't thinking all that clearly. I took a running leap over the obstacle. I made the jump but botched the landing. My foot slipped in the muck and I fell backward onto the carrion. Or rather, into the carrion, as it had—for three unholy seconds—completely enveloped me.

When my sanity resurfaced, I found myself outside the pipe, rolling in the dirt. Somehow I resisted the urge to rip every stitch of clothing off and bury myself in the clean soil. If I'd learned anything this week, it was to not take clothes and shoes for granted—even if they smelled like garbage on fire.

The patch of clean dirt turned out to be the high school parking lot. At least I think it was. Hard to tell with only two bent bicycles and a rusted out scooter for reference. Red High was bigger than I'd expected and much more terrifying—unfinished cinder block with burlap curtains in place of glass panes. It did have electricity; at least the outdoor stairwell and front entrance were lit. Since I didn't see any other lights on, I crawled through a window in search of a shower. I didn't find one—not even a sink—but there were toilets. And anything was preferable to my current state. I removed the lid from one of the toilet tanks and used it as a wash basin.

I felt bad about the mess, but what did they expect with no glass in the windows? Wild animals probably snuck in and made messes all the time.

I didn't recognize myself in the mirror—not even up close. Although it was hard to tell whether the skin discoloration was from the dye or the mud. I realized there was no fan. Instead, most of the walls and ceiling were open to the air. That didn't seem very safe. What if there was no breeze to carry away the sulfur dioxide?

Nope. I had to stop trying to solve everyone's problem. I was here to get some travel documents then—I slapped both hands to my pockets. They were empty. The wad of money and the instructions!

I scoured the parking lot and found two or three bills but no instructions. I even held my breath long enough to peek inside the drainage pipe again. A quick examination of the putrefaction ecosystem didn't yield any results. And despite knowing that my life and those of my family might depend on it, I couldn't bring myself to fish around in the sludge for the instructions.

How hard could it be really? There couldn't be an overabundance of forgers living in the shelter. And the fake names didn't matter. We could pick names at random, and the moronic pokers at the checkpoint wouldn't have a clue. Marin already told me the important stuff. And even sixty cuivres had to be a small fortune to the people on this side. Surely that would be plenty.

And maybe I'd come back after eyerise and take another look.

Now to find the shelter. I didn't bother wrapping my fire. There was really no point in sneaking around the Taudis. After taking on the evil cow in the culvert, the idea of a mec with a knife didn't scare me. I'd just step close enough to them to give them a whiff—maybe ask for a hug.

No one was going to bother me.

The Taudis at night was a circus—but instead of dancing bears, acrobatic boys jumped from rooftop to rooftop. Burly men tossed watermelon-sized stones back and forth—either a game or a workout routine. Strangest of all, hundreds of spectators sat outside their shacks and hovels as if waiting for a parade to begin. Garbage covered most surfaces like pungent, oversized mold. There was an obscene amount of touching going on, and more laughter than I expect to hear on this side of the river.

Most people stared as I passed. A few nodded in greeting. One teenage girl even invited me into what—from twenty feet away—smelled like a public outhouse. I politely declined. Although several Reds covered their noses as I passed, most didn't even seem to notice my stench. Maybe they were used to exotics smells. I didn't understand why the locals seemed more accepting of me than on my last visit, unless it was that my shade was disgusting and I looked like I crawled out of a dumpster. In other words, I couldn't have looked more at home.

I didn't expect to feel this relaxed. Maybe it was because in all my time in the Taudis, I hadn't seen a single poker. By comparison, Ville Bleu was full of them. Even before they were hunting a murderer, it wasn't unusual to see pokers patrolling the streets, supervising outdoor Naissance parties, or flanking entrances to stores. I was starting to think their presence was less about keeping the Blues safe and more about keeping them in check. No one cared if the Reds got a little rowdy. But if the people with vast resources at their disposal decided to cause a stir, that could be very inconvenient for the Dominateur.

There was no need to ask for directions. Hunting for the shelter was a bit like locating a skyscraper in a trailer-park. At four stories tall with attractive plastic siding and glass windows, the community shelter looked completely out of place among the primitive dwellings. And given that it was the only well-lit structure in five square miles, it was impossible to miss.

Why in the blank rainbow would anyone rather live in a sewage pipe?

Strangely, the mood grew more somber the closer I got to the shelter. When I arrived, I found several hundred people lounging about the property. I'd never seen so many Reds in one place. What were they all waiting around for?

Ten feet from the door, a muscular figure with a green fire stepped forward and kicked me in the thigh. I fell sideways with a yelp of surprise.

"Go dunk yourself in the river," he said. "No way you're coming in here like that."

Where had I heard that voice before? I shielded my eyes

from the bright artificials. It was the double-dimpled, coffee and milk officer I'd seen on my last visit to the Taudis. After biting back several choice words, I picked myself up. "I'm here to meet someone."

He narrowed his eyes. "Have I seen you before?"

I made a face of revulsion, then scratched under my arm in a very non-home-inspector sort of way.

Dimples jerked forward as if coming in for another kick. I fell for it. Metaphorically and literally. I picked myself up again and spread my arms wide "Want a hug?"

Dimples drew his tranq gun and leveled it at me. "You've got three seconds to get off this property."

"Put your piece away, *flic*," someone shouted.

Most of the loitering Reds had paused their conversations to glance our way. Dimples scanned the crowd as if trying to single out the loudmouth.

"I mean, look at the poor mec," a girl's voice called. "Probably his first night in Toi. And he looks hurt."

Toi? Is that what they called the shelter?

"Ern't it time to turn in for the night, anyway?" another man shouted.

Several seconded that motion. Reds moved toward Dimples, followed by others. What seemed like a thousand Reds converged on the entrance.

Dimples seemed to forget all about me. He backed up to the entrance and shouted to keep things orderly, but he kept glancing to the side as if planning his escape should things get ugly.

An old man patted me on the shoulder as I passed. When I glanced back, he was smelling his hand, a troubled look on his face.

"Wow," said a middle-aged mec on my dark. "That's quite an aroma. Do you need someone to look at that?" He gestured to my shirt, which I realized was stained with blood as well as dirt. "The in-house medic is a toilet-pouch, but I've got a nurse friend."

I rubbed at the red stain. "Oh, uh... no thanks. It isn't mine."

He raised his eyebrows as if impressed. Before he could respond, a girl of about six handed me a twenty-cuivre bill, indicating that she'd found it back where I'd fallen.

"Thank you very much."

The kid smiled. What teeth she had looked like miniature oyster shells. I swear I felt a physical pain in my heart.

I pointed to the shelter. "Do you live here?"

She held up her dark palm. Hmm. Maybe she didn't speak Téle. "Do you have DEN-TISTS over here?" I tapped my teeth.

Her smile faltered, and she covered her mouth with her fingers.

Yup. Pretty sure that's the first time I felt guilty for having teeth. I handed her back the twenty. I wanted to say something helpful about buying a toothbrush but figured that would come across as snobbish. "Keep it out of sight."

She ran off. Forty cuivres should be plenty to hire a forger. Hopefully.

Because I didn't know what else to do, I shuffled along with the crowd until it formed—at Dimples' insistence—some semblance of a line. The woman behind me blinked a few times when she got close, then decided to give me some personal space. If anyone else noticed my stench, they didn't comment, which I found both unnerving and comforting.

The line moved faster than I expected. When I got near the front, I saw that in addition to Dimples—who was still waving his dart gun about—two teenage boys stood on either side of the entrance, green fires extended. They seemed to be examining the Reds' dark palms as they passed.

When it was my turn, I faced my dark palm up at the boy closest to me and smiled slightly. He pulled his t-shirt collar up over his nose.

"First time?" the boy said through his shirt. "Got one for enrollment!" he shouted so abruptly, I almost took off running.

"I'm not staying," I said. "Just looking for someone."

"No one gets in without a tattoo."

A tattoo?!

A third Green boy appeared with a clipboard and what looked like a battery-powered inker.

"Hold up," I said.

The boy coughed, then took a large step back and motioned for me to step out of line, which I reluctantly did. "Just need to ask a few questions." His sticker name tag read JP. His wispy blond mustache hairs were so long and fine, they looked like a cat's whiskers.

"Can't I just pop in, look for my friend, then leave?"

JP took another step back and coughed again.

"It's that Chartreuse kid," came Dimples' booming voice.

"Yeah, well, I tried."

No need to feel embarrassed. It's not like I messed my pants or something. I fell into a rotting carcass and came out kicking. I should be proud.

"If you're looking for someone," JP said pleasantly, as if he wasn't standing several feet away covering his nose, "you could always wait until morning. Everyone has to vacate the building at five am for surface cleaning."

"Okay, maybe I'll do that."

"Got a place to sleep?"

I stared at my fire.

"You sure you don't want to enroll? Just a little ink and you'll have dinner, shower, and a warm bed. Only hurts for a minute."

If I stayed I could also get a head start on finding the document fixer. "You convinced me."

"Great," JP said. "What's your last name?"

I went through a mental list of all the names I'd used so far. I didn't want any repeats. Before I could decide on one, someone answered for me.

"Loup," she said. "His name is Aro Loup."

Jeannette pushed past Dimples and showed her dark

palm to the teenage door guard. In the light of the awning artificials, I could see a small round mark.

"Hi, Aro." She waved her light and I nearly choked on my
spit. Her fire was jellyfish pink. How in the rainbow had that
happened?

"Hello..." I wasn't sure if I was supposed to say her name
or not. "Nettie." I searched her face for signs of anger or alarm,
but she seemed genuinely friendly—especially considering I
abandoned her family to the police yesterday. She probably
realized I did them a favor.

"Hurry and get inked," she said, "so I can show you around
this dump."

The place was nicer than most of the buildings in Hameau
Vert. Leagues ahead of Baptiste's apartment. Jeannette said
the pink was the result of her reaction with me. Despite only
arriving the night before, she seemed to know most of the
other residents. She was anxious to hear how I'd gotten my
new puke shade and why I was covered with blood and mud
and smelled like "rhino crack" as she put it. I explained with as
little detail as possible. Although I was glad she didn't hold a
grudge about me getting them kicked out of their pipe, I didn't
fully trust her. Little kids were notoriously bad at keeping
secrets.

Her siblings, however, were not nearly so gracious. I encountered Philippe in the shower. His hair was different. He

looked as if he'd tried to cut it while jogging. The healing cut along his temple seemed to support that theory. At first he didn't seem to recognize me, but I think because I was staring at him for signs of recognition, he scrutinized me as well—whereupon his memory seemed to clear up.

We got reacquainted as he held me by the throat and gave very specific details about what he'd do when he got his hunting knife back. If he noticed my smell, he didn't mention it. For my part, I did a lot of nodding, apologizing, and wiggling so the scalding water would burn my back evenly.

Eventually some random Reds came to my aid and talked Philippe out of melting any more skin off my back. After my personal space bubble was restored, the shower was quite nice. I used half the soap in the dispenser. Once dressed in simple clothes provided by the shelter, I braced myself and sniffed at the skin of my arm. I got a whiff of dead rodent. A vast improvement over corpse-strewn battlefield.

On my way to the cafeteria, I noticed a lot of mecs with wet hair and fresh clothes. The women, strangely, seemed content to stay dirty. The line for food took forty minutes, by which time I was ready to start picking things out of the trash. A university-age Yellow Mélangé served the fish stew. She had coffee skin and hundreds of neat black braids. She smiled at me, but by the time I saw and returned it, she had moved on to the girl behind me.

I took my tray to the table I'd see Jeannette eating. Her sister—who I since learned was called Véronique—stood the moment I sat down. I thought she was going to hurl accusations at me, but she only glared and then found another table. It took me a moment to recover. If the look she'd given me had been a dentist's drill, my teeth would all be powder.

Reds. I'd never understand them. And that light. Garish, hideous crimson. How could they tell when their hand was bleeding?

It was a pity the rest of her was so attractive.

Not that I was attracted to Véronique—but I could see

how others might be. If they were really desperate. Or hadn't seen a girl in several decades.

"What's wrong with your skin?" Jeannette asked.

"I told you, I used outdoor browning—"

"That's not brown."

I examined my forearm. It had a pale yellow hue. I'd noticed it after the shower but thought it had been the artificial light. Clearly the dye hadn't set properly—most likely because I went for a bloody swim shortly after applying it.

"I like your yellow hair though. And your fire is different too."

That had been impossible to miss. The soap had lightened the dye such that instead of booger yellow, my shade appeared pale greenish-blue.

"Do the girls not have showers?" I asked, anxious to change the subject.

"Yeah, but no one uses them."

"Why not?"

Jeannette shrugged. "Mama says I can't either. Last night we used wet wipes from the nursery."

"Where is your mom?"

"You should call her Mama DeGrave. Everyone does. She's sick in bed."

Probably from living in a sewage pipe for so long.

Well, I suppose that wasn't really fair. "Hope she feels better soon."

Time to deal with the whale in the bathtub. "I'm sorry about yesterday. I panicked. Didn't mean to... I didn't hurt your mom, did I?"

Jeannette ran her finger around the inside of the apple juice cup then licked her finger. "She's fine," she said. "They thought you actually were Aro. He's the only Blue-Green they knew about. That's why I told the guard that. Figured it was better than knowing your real name."

"In that case, I completely understand your family's reaction. Aro is a toilet pouch."

Jeannette's eyes went wide. Maybe I should run some of these words by an adult before I started picking up red slang.

I tried to scratch my forearm, but the movement stretched my shirt across my burned back. After a few quick breaths, I was able to resume eating. "At least the food's good," I said, which was as close as I could get to I-told-you-so without sounding like a toilet bag myself.

Jeannette didn't respond. She'd emptied her bowl so she must have liked it a little bit. I offered her my peanut butter cookie and was profoundly relieved when she declined.

"Jeannette, have you heard of anyone around her that... is good at making government forms or copying someone's handwriting—that sort of thing?"

"In Toi?"

"Where?"

"Oh, yeah. I forget you people call it the Taudis. You can ask Philippe. He's got a lot of friends that do stuff."

"Do stuff?"

"Mama calls it nefarolous dealings."

That sounded promising. "Nefarious," I said automatically. "Maybe you can ask him for me?"

She pointed at the line. "You can ask him. He'll be here in a minute."

Of course Philippe chose that moment to look at our table. In that half-second of eye contact, he conveyed a startling amount of contempt.

I swallowed and opened a ketchup packet. He wouldn't try to kill me in front of his sister, would he? "Did he try to cut his own hair?" I asked.

"The *flic* did it. After you left."

"Flic?"

"Yeah. The fire-faced milky one took Philippe's knife and cut his hair while he was knocked out. Neek tried to stop him. That's how Philippe got that cut on his cheek... and Neek ruined her only shirt." Jeannette took the ketchup packet I'd opened and squeezed it into her mouth.

"Good thing they give clothes out for free here."

"It's not free."

I held out my dark palm. "Okay, for the price of a few drops of ink." I kind of liked my tattoo. It was a bright red circle about as big as my littlest finger. The friendly green had told me—through his shirt—that the O stood for *opportunité*. A new life. "How did your family survive before you came here?" I asked. "Did Philippe sharpen your neighbors' pencils?"

"He was a trash man."

"Oh, he got to drive the garbage truck?"

"No, he dug through people's trash to find stuff he could repair and sell."

"Attention," came a loud male voice. I looked to see one of the teen volunteers standing on a chair. The only one I hadn't yet spoken with. "It's nine-thirty. Use the next half hour to get cleaned up and take a shower before bed."

Complaints erupted from the back of the food line. The Green ignored them.

"All lights will shut off automatically at ten. See that you're in your room. Anyone found outside the halls after lockdown will spent the next night in the recess room."

That didn't sound so bad. I looked at Jeannette, but she didn't seem excited. "I know I've seen that kid before," I said, "but I don't know from where. It's not like I know a bunch of..."

Crêpes.

It was the Police Chief's son.

CHAPTER TWENTY

DIRTY

G abe Collins looked much younger without the brown soldier uniform. Had he figured out who I really was? Did he know his father was looking for me? My fire had already begun to tingle. Soon, it would grow unbearably warm in expectation of a major energy expenditure. "I've got to get out of here."

"Tell me about it. I'm so sick of—"

I spun in my seat. "When is it going to be enough?" I said with unintentional ferocity. "This place is paradise. I did all of you a favor and, as thanks, I get dirty looks and first-degree burns."

Jeannette wrinkled her nose. "The beds aren't comfortable."

I clamped my jaw shut so I wouldn't say something I'd regret. She was a little kid—a product of her environment. Mom was certainly right about Reds, though. It didn't matter how much you gave them, they kept wanting more and didn't want to do anything to earn it.

JP, the cat-whiskered Green who gave me the tattoo, entered. My eyes followed him automatically because he was walking too quickly to be casual. He went straight to Chief Collins' son and said something close to his ear. Gabe scanned the room.

I leaned over as if picking up dropped silverware. When I chanced a look up, Gabe and the other volunteer were striding toward the exit.

"Are you going to finish your cookie? I only said I didn't

want it because Mama said it's polite to decline."

"Yeah, sure." I waited until the boys disappeared out the door, then jumped from my seat and took off after them.

"Where are you going?" Jeannette called.

"Mind dumping my tray?" I was too far away to hear her response. I stepped into a narrow hallway. Empty.

As I got farther away from the loud cafeteria, I heard laughter coming from down the hall. I ran in that direction, turned the corner, and screeched to a stop. An old Red man pointed toward the stairwell. He looked familiar. I was pretty sure the last time I'd seen him, he was threatening me with half a baseball bat.

"Thanks." I was glad he overcame his pride and found the shelter. But why was this place run by kids? Where were all the adults?

When I opened the stairwell door, I heard another slam. All was quiet. There were only four floors. I knew whatever the boys were doing probably had nothing to do with me, but in the off chance that someone had recognized me and Gabe was going to inform his father... well, it's not like I'd be able to do much. But maybe I could reach him before he said too much over the phone—pull the cord out of the wall or something. Then what?

Maybe I should just leave the shelter while I had the chance.

No, I hadn't found the forger yet. The fate of three entire families hinged on that. I had to be certain my identity was compromised before I tried to escape. I knew the second floor was mostly fan rooms and storage. The third floor held the sleeping and cleaning quarters, mecs to the eyerise, women to the eyefall, with an infirmary in between.

Fourth floor was administration. That's where they'd be headed if they intended to turn me in.

My bare feet padded silently up the linoleum coated stairs. By the time I reached the top, my entire hand felt like it was ablaze. I tried the door marked STAFF ONLY and found it locked. A buzzer button protruded from the wall at shoulder level.

I chewed on my lip and waved my fire too cool it down. Could I ring the bell and pretend I had a question? Or would I be offering myself up in a crystal goblet?

Below me, a door creaked open, then clicked shut. I waited but heard nothing. Had someone peeked their head in? Or were they standing in the stairwell without making a sound...

"Hello?" I said just loud enough to carry to the bottom floor. "I'm kind of lost."

Another door slammed open.

"—only a disgusting fat lady."

"I know, did you see all those rolls?"

I leaned over the railing and saw the tops of three heads headed back down the stairs.

"I'm gonna talk to my dad. They need to make showers mandatory."

"And make the staff do twice as many facility inspections!"

"Yeah, it's important to keep those showers in working order. And how are we supposed to know if they're working unless someone is using it?"

It sounded like the boys made a habit of spying on the girls' showers—and tonight had been disappointed to find only a "disgusting fat lady." I realized I was clutching the handrail so tightly, the metal had grown warm.

"The problem will be Adisa. Of course, my dad ignores her reports, but still."

I felt my throat jerk. Several assertive words fought to get out while my mind desperately rammed them back down. This wasn't any of my business. I needed to find the forger and get out. I could not afford to draw attention to myself.

But my mouth is apparently attached to my heart, not my brain.

"Filthy toilet bags," I said in a loud voice.

The stairwell went quiet. In the space between the railings three faces appeared.

"Stay out of the women's showers."

A dull metallic clang echoed from below, as if one of the boys had taken off his belt and hit the railing with it. About the time I heard several sets of feet running up the stairs, I remembered that all three of the boys were older than me and JP outweighed me by a good fifty pounds. I was about to get my crêpes handed to me.

I rang the buzzer. My hand ached with the heat of my fire. It felt like my skin would melt off any second. What was going on? This couldn't be normal.

The pounding feet grew louder.

I knocked. Through the frosted glass, I saw a big, dark nothing.

Then they reached my level. I faced my attackers head on and... they ran right past me to the door.

And there were only two of them. Had JP stayed at the bottom to guard the exit?

Gabe pressed the buzzer repeatedly, then knocked. "She's definitely the girl from the boat."

"She's off-the-cliff is what she is," the other boy said. "You sure someone's in there?"

"I don't know!" Gabe screamed. He slammed his weight against the door.

That's when I heard the other footsteps. Quiet, almost silent. But then a scraping sound began, like metal on metal.

I looked down the winding stairs and saw some sort of enormous kitchen utensil. I was pretty sure it was the ladle the Yellow girl had been using to dish soup. Whoever was climbing the stairs was scraping the ladle along the railing. And even from two floors up, I could see the large dent in the scoop.

Pretty sure that was new.

I was starting to feel scared, and I hadn't even been the one spying in the showers.

Gabe seemed to realize no one was going to open the door, and he ran down the steps past me, followed by the other Green. They were obviously trying to beat soup girl to the third floor.

They didn't make it. Over the railing I saw thrashing limbs as cries of agony filled the stairwell. I hurried down the stairs—whether to help Adisa or the boys, I wasn't sure.

When I reached them, the floor seemed to fall out from under me. One boy huddled on the landing, whimpering and rubbing his head. On the lower landing, JP lay unconscious. And directly in front of the door to the third level, Gabe lay curled in a ball pleading for mercy as the ladle came down repeatedly on his arms and legs.

But it wasn't Adisa.

Tears streamed down Véronique's face as her arms pumped up and down. Was she punishing the boys for spying in the showers—on her mother? From the savagery of her swings, she wasn't planning to slow down anytime soon.

"Véronique, no!" I knew before I shouted that she wouldn't hear me. Her back heaved so wildly, she seemed to be convulsing.

I rushed forward, my fire outstretched. "Véronique you have to—"

Véronique screamed and arched her back. The ladle clattered down the stairs and landed next to JP.

Gabe launched himself down the stairs after the ladle. I thought to retrieve it and fight back, but he crawled past JP and continued down the stairs.

He hadn't touched the utensil, which was now bent so badly it looked like a paperclip. The door slammed shut.

When I looked back at Véronique, she was twisted in an effort to look at her back. I felt the heat drain from my face.

An oozing, blistering wound the size of my palm glared at me through the charred edges of her shirt. Just like the boy in the park.

No. I hadn't touched her. I know I hadn't touched her.

Had I?

"Véronique..."

"What did you do to me?"

The ground level door creaked open again and heavy footsteps thundered toward us.

"I'm sorry," I said lamely. "I didn't mean to."

Once again, Véronique's dark eyes pierced me. It wasn't hatred I saw in them but something else—an almost hungry look.

Philippe appeared and stared down at JP's inert form. He glanced at his sister, then ran his hand along JP's spine.

"I had to," Véronique whispered.

Philippe turned JP onto his back, listened for breathing, then began mouth to nose resuscitation.

The gravity of our situation hit me all at once. Not only had I ruined my chance to protect my family and my friends, but for the second time this week, I was about to get arrested for murder.

"Get off me," JP mumbled.

The whimpering boy in the corner seemed to think more violence was forthcoming and scrambled up the steps to the upper landing. Distant shouts rang up from the first floor.

Gabe moaned and called Véronique something that evaporated any pity I might have felt for him. Philippe took a single step up the stairs, his expression black.

The third floor door opened. Jeannette's mother stepped out in a towel. Her eyes were red and swollen as if she'd been crying. Her face went pale when she saw Véronique kneeling over the Green. She looked to Philippe, who grabbed the mutilated ladle and climbed the stairs.

Gabe squeaked and rolled into a tighter ball. Véronique, her mother, and I all cried out for Philippe to stop. He ignored us and tapped the bottom of Gabe's shoe with the ladle. Then he slung a surprised Gabe over his shoulder, ran down the stairs, and out onto the first floor.

Mama DeGrave crouched to embrace Véronique who

gasped with pain.

"What happened to your back?"

I looked at my shoes.

Véronique shook her head as if she couldn't yet talk about it.

"What in the rainbow is your brother doing? Why did he tap that boy on the foot?" Mama DeGrave asked.

Véronique shrugged.

I cleared my throat and tried not to look at the discharge dripping down Véronique's back. "I think it was so Philippe could truthfully say he was the one who hit him."

"It doesn't matter," Véronique said over her mother's shoulder. "The grass-wipes will tell everyone what really happened."

I shook my head. "I doubt it. I doubt they'd want the entire shelter to know they got beaten bloody by a girl."

Véronique let out a little squeak, then sprinted past me down the stairs. Mama DeGrave called after her, but she kept running. Before she reached the bottom, the room went dark.

A door rattled.

"No!" Véronique screamed. "Philippe, you stupid idiot!"

And that's how I came to spend my second night in a stairwell.

"Yeah..." I said. "That can't be right."

"I'm telling you, the first night we were here, a two-year-old got stuck in the fanroom. Everyone could hear her crying all night. They literally can't open any doors after lockdown."

Véronique sat cross-legged near the first level door. I lay on my stomach on the first landing. It had been several hours since the lights went out. The remaining Green boy had begun sobbing the moment he realized he was trapped. He cried for a good twenty minutes before Mama DeGrave started up a halting conversation with him. They had talked off and on for a while, but they'd recently grown quiet. Well, one of them was quiet. The other was snoring softly.

"I can't believe there's not an override or something," I said. "What if there was a fire?"

"Adisa said they have a state-of-the-art sprinkler system."

"How did you end up with her ladle by the way?" I asked carefully.

Véronique hadn't been nearly as upset about her blistering back as I'd expected. In fact she hadn't even mentioned it.

Conversation was slow at first. But I persisted since I was going stir-crazy, and Véronique was the only one also awake. The fact that she was easy on the eyes had nothing to do with it. In the end, it didn't matter how cute, or brave, or interesting she was—she was Redborn. I'd sooner marry the Widow Meuglé. Anyway I had committed to pairing with Orie.

"I asked and she gave it to me."

It took me a minute to realize we were still talking about the ladle.

"I think she knew what I was going to do with it. It's something she and probably every other person in here wanted to do to them."

"You were spectacular by the way." Stop, Bruno. Stop before this gets weird.

"A spectacular psycho."

Immediately following the incident I would've wholeheartedly agreed with her, but after three plus hours of secretly watching her profile by the light of my fire, I decided it wasn't my place to judge. Véronique had pocketed her fire moments after the lights went out. I thought it was to avoid being seen through the window, but as the night wore on and she continued to hide her light, I began to suspect it was something else.

"Did you knock JP out with a single swing?"

She didn't respond.

"So, that's weird about Jeannette, right? I mean, have you ever heard of someone going from Orange back to Red? Well, dark pink."

"Why did you react with her?"

That was one question I was not prepared for. I realized I couldn't say "to help her out" because that would sound arrogant and condescending. I also couldn't tell her the truth because then Véronique would know how selfish and manipulative I was.

"Seemed like a good idea at the time," I finally said. I waited for a follow up question, but instead she laughed.

Definitely did not get goosebumps. Or immediately start thinking of funny things I could say to draw out another. I knew I wasn't in the Taudis to bond with the locals. I needed to ask Véronique about the forger. But first, it might be good to clear the air. Especially since I'd learned the shelter wasn't the candy kingdom I'd first thought.

"Look, I'm really sorry about yesterday. I think—"

"Can we just not talk about it?"

Well, that was unsatisfying. "Your mom seems nice."

"Yeah, she likes people even after they smash her face into the ground."

"I thought you didn't want to talk about it."

"Just shut up about my mom, okay?"

How did this conversation get so perilous all of a sudden?

Véronique raised her dark hand to her eyes. "Can you also not shine your fire in my face? That thing is like a hundred watt bulb."

"Sorry." I folded my arms underneath me and tried to figure out if that had been a compliment.

Stop. It doesn't matter if it was or not. Just ask her the question.

"So, Jeannette may have told you, I'm kind of not Sergent Whisnant's favorite person right now."

"Who's Sergent Whisnant?"

"A toilet bag."

"You are such an idiot. It's toilet pouch."

"He's one of those too."

I thought I heard her snicker. Or she might have been choking. I pressed forward. "Basically I'm trying to sneak out of the city and start a new life on the mainland. The only thing we're missing is the falsified travel documents."

I paused, but she didn't comment.

"You don't happen to know of anyone—maybe around the shelter—who's good at forging government papers?"

"Cause Reds are all criminals?"

I didn't take the bait. "My friend Orie sent me with instructions on how to find this mec and—"

"Don't say mec."

"Um... any particular reason?"

"It's demeaning to women."

Don't ask. Don't ask. "How?"

"Mec is short for *méchanicien* which was the last classification to assign female apprentices. Since girls apparently didn't have the *je ne sais quoi* to work with machines, it became synonymous with manliness. So, of course boys started using it to refer to each other. Even after women finally got to be mechanics, men refused to address them as mec. Instead it was greased heifer or the like."

"Heifer?"

"Did that bleach seep into your brain? A heifer is a cow."

"I'll try not to use the 'm' word anymore. As I said, I'm supposed to find this male human who Orie says is the best at what he does. Any ideas?"

"Sorry. Guess I'm not up to date with the criminal activities of my neighbors. Give me another twenty-four hours, and

I'll have everyone's occupation memorized."

"Simple 'no' works too."

"The only one who might know is my brother. But he's in jail for trying to protect me."

And most likely being prepped for execution. Assaulting a royal soldier, even if not in uniform, had to drain Whisnant's serum. "I'll ask around, then."

Véronique adjusted her position and let out a tiny gasp.

I wanted to say something like, sorry about your back, I don't know how that happened, but even in my head it sounded patronizing. Besides, my back hurt too. And it was her brother's fault. So we were even. Sort of.

If he happened to survive the week and I happened to escape with my family, we could try to liberate Philippe along with Marin's dad.

"So..." I said after a few minutes of silence. "You into any sports?"

"I'm not a weak little girl, if that's what you're getting at."

"Actually, it was a set up to tell you I'm a pretty accomplished athlete."

"Weightlifting is not a real sport."

For once I was glad it was dark. She didn't see the grin break out on my face. Automatically, scenarios where I might need to remove my shirt in a gallant gesture began forming. I could use my shirt as a mini-hammock for her legs... or a Bruno-scented pillow? I sniffed my collar. Perhaps as a bandage for her back...

Nope. Stop. She was a different species. Even if I could live with the shame of pairing with someone from the slums, I could never sentence my children to a life of squalor.

"I do track," she said.

A runner. That explained why her calves were so nicely shaped.

Black. I had to get out of here.

I stood and stretched, careful to keep my light out of her eyes. "I think I'm gonna go up a couple levels and try to sleep."

"I thought you'd never shut up."

Excuse me? "You really are nothing like your sister."

"Because she can stand you?"

"Because I can have a conversation with her and not feel guilty for being born."

"Join the party."

Did she mean she liked her sister too? Or that she also felt guilty for being born? I'd meant it as a preposterous joke.

"I thought you were leaving."

Was I? Oh yes, because I kept staying stupid stuff around her. I'd already asked her about the forger. There was no other reason to stay down here.

So why was I still staring at her?

"Well," she said, "as long as you're standing there like a brain trauma patient, you can help me with something." She reached behind her head and grimaced. "I think my hair is caught on my back."

"You know you could take your fire out of your pocket."

"Fine, I'll do it myself."

"No, I'll help. My fault anyway." That was a close as I'd come to admitting I'd somehow given her second degree burns with my bare hand.

She stood, rolled to her knees and leaned forward, back to me. I raised my fire and felt as if all my ribs had been smashed inward to stab my internal organs. Through the charred hole in her shirt, the inflamed wound on her back made my shower burn look like a bug bite.

I knelt over her and carefully gathered her hair. As she said, several strands seemed to be caught in the partially formed scabs. If I ripped them free that would probably start her oozing again, or maybe even bleeding.

As much as I would've loved to give her my shirt to wear, I knew it would only infect her wound. Maybe if I pulled the strands out one at a time.

"You smell awful," she said.

"Well, I was running up and down these stairs, trying to

keep out of your way. You should have seen their faces after you beaned JP."

"They do make deodorant—to keep people from knowing you've been running up and down stairs."

"They don't make deodorant that can compete with my manliness."

I thought I saw her cheek twitch.

"Can you hold this? I need both hands."

She took the majority of her hair. My dark hand felt strangely empty without it. I brought my fire closer to the wound and with my dark, slid the hair out strand by strand.

"What's taking so long?" Véronique asked. "Just find the hair that's stuck and pull it out by the roots."

The back of her neck was kind of mesmerizing. Three of her beauty spots made an equilateral triangle. "Don't want you to have a bald patch." I slid another strand of hair out of her wound.

Véronique fidgeted. I needed to engage her in conversation not sit here and count her moles.

"What was Gabe talking about when he said you were the girl from the boat?"

Véronique stiffened. "I have no idea."

Right.

As I pulled the last hair from her raw back, I felt a deep pang of disappointment. I had no excuse to stay.

But it was for the best since no kind of relationship could exist between us.

Well, that wasn't true. Why did every girl I meet have to be a potential mate? I didn't see any reason why we couldn't be friends—after she got to know the real me. But I'd have to let her know up front, so she didn't get the wrong idea.

"Véronique?"

"Yes, Bruno, what is it?" she said in an exasperated tone.

A thrill passed through me at her use of my name. I blame that rush of endorphins for what I said next. I was obviously not thinking clearly.

"We can only ever be friends."

Véronique stood and turned to glare down at me. "Did you think I was flirting with you?"

I was so horrified by the way that came out, all I could do was stare at her.

"Well, let me make my feelings for you a bit clearer."

A few minutes later, I managed to fall asleep on my stomach, three landings up, with a split lip.

CHAPTER TWENTY-ONE

REVANCHE

When I was first learning rugby, I often felt I was the only one on the team who had no idea what was happening. Waking up in the community shelter was kind of like that—except much worse.

I awoke to people running up and down the stairwell. A loud speaker announced breakfast was canceled and residents had to be out in thirty minutes. I wasn't able to find Véronique or her mother in the stairwell. Surely, I would've heard if the police had dragged them away.

I made my way downstairs amid half-dressed, bleary-eyed Reds. Did they normally wake everyone up at this time? From the conversations around me, I gathered that the lockdown had started twenty minutes earlier than usual—due to an assault on a couple volunteers—and residents and staff had gotten trapped all over the facility. Nearly a hundred spent the night in the cafeteria. Others slept as best they could in the fanrooms, the other three stairwells, and even in the front foyer. The attacker had been caught and taken away. No one seemed to know if the attacker was a man or a woman.

I really hoped Véronique didn't do anything stupid—like run off and confess the moment the doors opened. I should have stayed awake with her.

It wasn't until I got outside that I spotted someone I recognized—the Yellow whose ladle had been mangled beyond repair. She was listening to a sobbing Red woman.

"Excuse me, Adisa?"

"One moment. Yes, I understand, Marie. I'll have a word

with the Chief, but I—"

"I'm sorry to interrupt," I said. "But what the black is going on here?"

The old woman glared at me.

I ignored her. "Did they take Philippe?"

Adisa nodded.

"Did anyone tell them what those boys were doing?"

The old woman began to sob again. Adisa kissed the top of the woman's head, then took me by the arm, and walked me briskly toward the front entrance.

"You're the new resident. Aro, was it?"

"Have you seen Véronique? They didn't—"

"She's on the bus."

"What bus? What is going on here?"

Adisa squeezed my arm, then came in close. "I know everything you're going to say and I feel the same. But we can't talk about it here. If I were you, I'd get on the bus and pretend you didn't see anything unusual last night."

"I'm not getting on any bus."

"Are you going to pay for last night's meal and lodging?"

"Of course not."

"Then you have to spend the day collecting snails."

What in the blackened rainbow? "Who's in charge? I need to talk—"

"Listen," she hissed into my ear. "The Chief's son spent last night trapped in the cafeteria with a crowd of angry residents."

"Did they kill him?"

"It might have been better if they had. When his father—look, we can talk about this tonight. I've got to get everyone out before Officer Terry tranquilizes them."

"He shoots people who aren't out fast enough?"

But she was already gone.

I followed the flow of Reds out the front and found two lines. A short one led through a pair of officers. Jeannette and her mother stood in a longer line which led to a two-level bus the color of dried blood.

"Madame DeGrave!"

She turned at my approach. "Please, call me Mama. Thank you for protecting my daughter last night."

"Is she okay?"

She pointed toward the back of the bus. Véronique stared blankly out a lower window.

"Where are you going?"

"Mama did it yesterday," Jeannette said in an eager voice. "We're going upstream where it's shallow to collect crayfish and water insects and what else Mama?"

"Sludge worms, snails and larvae." Mama DeGrave curled her fingers into a fist but not before I saw the crisscrossing cuts covering most of her dark hand.

"Are they paying you for this? It's Friday. Doesn't Jeannette have school?"

"I got expelled for stealing," Jeannette said. "I'd rather collect sludge worms, anyway."

Expelled? I gestured at the other line. "What about those people?"

"If you pay your balance you can wait outside the facility."

Jeannette gave me a told-you-so look. The food and clothes really weren't free.

I glanced again at Véronique.

"How much do you owe?" I asked Mama DeGrave. "All of you together?"

"Well, a night including clothing is ten cuivres a person, meals five. Since I worked ten hours yesterday, it's about forty-five cuivres without adding Philippe's. But I don't mind working. I just wish I could send Véronique to school. She has her last final today."

Why had I given that little gingivitis girl twenty cuivres? I could have brought her a whole bag full of toothpaste and brushes later.

"Okay, Officer Terry," came Adisa's voice. "That's everyone."

"We'll see," Claude said with a grin. He left his long-haired partner to take care of the line and strode into the building.

I ran directly to the officer at the front of the payment line. I knew I needed the money to pay the forger, but there was a whole wad of bills outside that drainage pipe near Red High. Anyway, I was the reason Jeannette's family was dealing with all this. I couldn't just leave them.

"Back of the line," the large-foreheaded officer said.

"I need to pay for someone before the bus leaves," I said with an apologetic glance at the woman next in line. "Jeannette and Véronique DeGrave and their mother."

"It's fine," the woman said to the officer. "He can go first."

The officer squinted at me as if trying to figure out where he'd seen me before, then over his shoulder. "DeGrave, three females."

For the first time, I noticed a desk, mostly hidden by the line of people.

"You're Aro Loup, right?" said the Green seated behind the officer. I recognized him at once as the volunteer who'd spent the night in my stairwell. His name tag read Josué.

I nodded but prepared myself to make a quick escape if Josué decided he wanted me in jail with Philippe.

He looked at me, then the list. "Four, without breakfast... sixty cuivres."

I pulled the two bills out and set them on the desk. "I can bring the rest tonight."

"It's all here," Josué said.

To my astonishment, he held three twenty-cuivre bills. Two wrinkled, and one crisp and folded as if it had just come out of Josué's own pocket.

He handed me four white plastic wristbands. "Collect your old clothes from the green bin. Laundry usually costs another three cuivres, so if anyone asks, you paid. Doors reopen at eight tonight."

"Got another one!" Jeannette called.

Only ten minutes after eyerise and we'd already found four of the twenty-cuivre bills. So far, no sheet of instructions on how to find the document forger.

Josué had been a bigger help than I first thought. Apparently white wristbands were only for students and Hameau Vert day-workers. All other residents had to stay on the shelter property.

Véronique sat on a bench outside the school, studying for her final. Mama DeGrave, despite our admonitions that it wasn't a good idea, was headed to the police station to try to get Philippe out. I had offered to go with her, but she assured me the white wristband gave her immunity to the normal escort laws, and she didn't want to get me caught too. Whether she was able to get Philippe out or not, she promised to ask him about a Red forger.

Eyelight was beating down on my back when I finally called off the search. Eighty cuivres would have to be enough. Véronique was inside taking her exams. Mama DeGrave hadn't yet returned, and Jeannette was starting to worry.

"Shall we go check on her?" she asked.

"I can, but are you sure Madame LaCroix won't let you take the final? Maybe you should go see."

"The Director said if I come back, he'll have me arrested."

"Sorry," I said. "I didn't tell anybody about the eggs."

"Oh, that's not why I was expelled. Yesterday, Aro gave me this big apology and said he wanted to be friends. Then he gave me his watch. Except at the end of the day, he told the Director that someone stole it. No one believed what really happened."

"I'm not surprised—the mec is a blankhead."

"They expelled Baptiste too."

"What?"

"LaClaire found a switchblade in Baptiste's backpack. He swears he's never seen it before."

"How did she know to look?"

Jeannette shrugged. "Director said Ecol Vert won't even take him since he has that on his record. He'll have to be home-schooled."

"So, basically, Aro is running the Académie." I spend a single day sleeping and everything goes to black. I shoved the eighty cuivres into my pocket. "I think we should make use of these white bracelets and pay a visit to our mutual friend."

"Won't he tell everyone who you are?"

"He's never actually met me or seen me up close." Then, switching into Granny's guttural accent, I said, "And I'm Rolf Zimmerman who just moved from Ulfig."

Jeannette blinked. "You are?"

Since Véronique had borrowed Jeannette's shoes to take her final, I lifted Jeannette onto my shoulders for the walk to

L'académie Mélangé.

The weather was glorious, and it almost distracted me from the fact that I was no closer to procuring travel documents—and that hundreds of people were still hunting me. Still, it didn't require a lot of concentration to sneak. After three days as a fugitive, I automatically walked close to buildings, kept to the shade as much as possible, and constantly scanned the streets for Greens in uniform.

"I forgot to tell you last night," I said. "I may have told some people you were a spy for Capitaine Sébastien. Just in case someone asks."

"I like the way your hair feels," Jeannette said, apparently indifferent to my confession . "And the color. But Véronique thinks you looked better with dark hair."

I slowed. "She was talking about me?"

"That's pretty much all she talks about."

I stopped completely. "What does she say about me?"

"That you're an idiot and a snob, and she can't stand you."

"But she liked my hair before I cut it?"

"She told Mama this morning it's a shame good looks are wasted on someone like you."

I began walking again but felt a little warm and fuzzy under the ribs. "I guess I didn't make a very good first impression."

"I don't think she hates you as much as she did."

"Why do you say that?"

"Cause she doesn't swear as much when she talks about you."

Jeannette went rigid as I climbed Pont en Pierre, so I lowered her and let her walk.

"Your sister seems... complicated."

"She's not. She's just a brat sometimes."

"Yeah, why is that? Last night, I was trying to be super polite, but she somehow managed to get angry again."

We reached the top of the bridge. My gaze followed the river's zigzagging descent down the mountain. Farther down, the trees gave way to shrubs, then the vegetation disappeared entirely. It was hard to believe that the vast majority of Télesphore Island was covered by uninhabitable desert. Except for the coastal fishermen, the entire population lived in the fertile raised valley at the center of the country. I'd spent so much time thinking of the city as Télesphore that I sometimes forgot how much more of it there was.

"Véronique doesn't like me to give away all her secrets," Jeannette said. "She says she's not going to tell me any more stuff if I can't keep my mouth shut."

"Secrets?"

Jeannette shrugged. "You should ask her."

"I already did. What if I was to make it worth your while?" I pulled out the wad of bills and removed a twenty. The twisted feeling in my gut was telling me to put the money back in my pocket—that it didn't matter what Véronique thought of me or why she seemed so hostile. All that mattered was getting out of Télesphore with my family.

But what if I never found the forger? What if I got caught, and Whisnant confiscated all the money? It wouldn't do anyone any good. But if I gave just a little to Jeannette's family, no matter what happened, they'd have an easier time at the detention camp—as I'd begun to think of it. Twenty cuivres to them would probably be a month's wages.

"Cash for info?" I asked.

Jeannette held out her hand, and I placed the bill in it. Then she started down the Green side.

"Well?" I said. "Why is Véronique so angry all the time?"

"Depends on who you ask. Neek says she's not angry. I think she's grumpy because I get to go to the Académie while she's stuck at Red High. Mama has a different theory."

"Which is?"

We reached the bottom of the bridge and I lifted her back onto my shoulders.

"That'll cost you another twenty."

What? The little grifter. I was about to protest but then

noticed her dirty, little feet. They were so scratched and ragged, I was tempted to take my shoes off right there and give them to her. Not that they would have fit.

Twenty more cuivres would leave me with forty. If that didn't end up being enough for documents, I could ask Jeannette for a loan. I pulled out another bill. It disappeared from my hand.

"Mom says it's because of La-la."

"La-la?"

"He's my other brother. Véronique feels guilty—like it's her fault he's gone."

"Where did he go?"

"Last Octobre, Véronique got herself stranded out in a boat. La-la jumped in to save her, but he couldn't swim."

Jeannette held out her hand again, but it suddenly felt wrong to be forcing these family secrets out of her.

"I'm sorry."

"There's more to the story." She wiggled her fingers.

"That's okay. Don't want Neek to get mad at you."

We passed a few Greens in the park. Although most looked at us, it seemed to be out of curiosity rather than desire to enforce the border laws. Jeannette shifted her weight and I winced.

"Can you move your money to your front pocket—it's digging into my shoulder."

Jeannette pulled the folded paper out. "Oh, it's a few pages I ripped out of one of the books at school. I was going to use them to study for the final. Mama said if I got the color improvement scholarship, I could get groceries for us in HV. Maybe even chocolate."

Some distance down the street, I spotted a large coffee-and-crême officer that might have been Dimples. I backtracked and detoured down a side street.

"You should study," I said. "After I'm done talking to Claire, I'm pretty sure she's going to let you take the final."

Once again I asked myself what I was doing. How was this

trip back into Hameau Vert going to help me and my family escape? It wasn't. And if the Commissaire's dogs stopped staking out the cathedral, they might even catch my scent.

But Jeannette and Baptiste were my friends—and Aro needed to pay for his lies.

After a few seconds of crinkling, Jeannette said, "Which four parts make up the esca?"

"Are you asking me?"

"I don't even know what an esca is."

"That's the scientific name for the fire organ. Can you name the elements... without looking at the paper?"

Jeannette sighed. "Cartilage, epidermis, combustion stamen, and... dome?"

"The dome is part of the epidermis. Serum is the fourth part. That's the clear liquid that combines with the oxygen in your blood to initiate the exothermic process."

"Huh?"

"The stamen mixes air and fuel to make heat and light."

"Yeah, but what's the point?"

"Of the fire?" I jumped over a mud puddle. "It's the body's way of making energy. Our bodies extract nutrients from food which are used to produce serum. It's like a pouch of liquid energy waiting to be tapped. That's why you die if you pop it. No more energy means your organs shut down."

"Like Baptiste."

"Which reminds me, I still owe Aro a complimentary tooth loosening."

"He'll just cry to his grampy," Jeannette said with surprising bitterness. "That's another thing that I don't get. If his grandpa is so high up in the government, why is he a Mélangé? Did his dad marry a Green or something?"

"Have you not had this conversation with your mom yet? Babies are always born Red, Green, or Blue."

"I think I knew that," she said. "But what about Adisa?"

"She would have started out as a Green then reacted with a dozen or so Reds—I'd like to hear that story myself." Had she gotten gang-painted?

"What about Baptiste?" Jeannette asked. "He says he was born a Blue-Green."

"He's confused." I thought about asking Jeannette how she'd become a Mélangé but figured I'd done enough prying into her history. What if it was a traumatic experience, and I triggered some sort of freak out?

Jeannette adjusted her weight on my shoulders. "So... what would happen if a Blue and a Green had a baby?"

I hesitated. How had we gotten into this? Hopefully Mama DeGrave wouldn't be upset with me for educating her ten-year-old daughter in genetic reproduction. "Intershade marriage is against the law—because any children would follow the inferior parent."

Blank, that sounded a lot less rude in my head.

"What I mean to say is: Green is dominant, and Red even more so. I guess the Dominateur is worried about Blue disappearing altogether."

"But who cares what the Dominateur think? Aren't they a bunch of fat, old men?"

"Well, they kind of make the laws, too. They could probably send pokers to give you the zappy-finger."

Jeannette sighed and leaned forward so her stomach rested on the top of my head. "Then what's the point of the Commissaire?"

"I guess he's the head geezer until the new king shows up."

"My brother says white fire is a myth," Jeannette said, her head rocking back and forth above me. It was starting to make me nauseous.

"He's probably right."

"The director is dumb if he believes that King's Request Thingy."

I laughed but couldn't help feeling a little guilty. Before Grandpa Zacharie died, he used to talk about white fire all the time, like it was his quest to discover the secret. Of course, he also believed the Commissaire's staff had magical powers. But even if Grandpa had been slightly crazy, I would've liked to ask his advice on how to un-screw up my life.

Jeannette folded the pages and shoved them into her pocket. "You sure you don't want to hear any more of my sister's secrets?"

"I can't afford it. I still have to pay for travel documents."

"Okay, how about this," Jeannette said. "I tell you the secret, and if you think it's good enough, you can owe me."

I smirked. This girl was either a natural entrepreneur or a trained scam artist.

"I promise you won't regret it…"

"Fine. Give me this big, amazing secret."

"Well, last night before dinner, Véronique helped out in the basement with the laundry."

"You think that's worth twenty-cuivres?"

"When your clothes came out of the washer, they still stunk, so Véronique scrubbed them by hand."

A powerful emotion sprang up inside me. Strangely, I couldn't tell if it was mortification or glee. "Okay, that's a little better."

"Adisa said when she tried to help scrub, Véronique snatched your clothes out of her hand."

Definitely glee. "Okay. I'll make a note that I owe you twenty more cuivres."

"You want to know what it was that she snatched away from Adisa?" Jeannette asked.

"A sock?"

"Your boxer shorts."

I gave Jeannette forty cuivres.

When we arrived at the school, I lifted Jeannette up to peer through the window.

"LaClaire is sitting at her desk," she said. "I don't see the Director."

"You think you can get her attention without any of the kids seeing you?"

Jeannette abruptly twisted, and I nearly lost my hold on her.

"What are you doing?"

"Trying to hide. Ivy Soigné saw me and shouted for La-Claire to look."

The back door clanged. A moment later, Claire appeared around the corner and pressed a hand to the base of her throat. "I thought the soldiers had come back."

Claire wore a red satin hoop dress with tiny purple bows tied into her short black hair. "Jeannette, if the Director catches you here, he's not going to be happy." She looked at me. "Is that..." she narrowed her eyes. "Benoit?"

I had not expected her to recognize me so quickly. But seeing as how I'd been with Jeannette when I left, and there couldn't be that many new stocky Mélangé in the area, I suppose she would've had to be pretty dense not to figure it out. Hopefully, it wouldn't be so easy for the pokers.

She stepped closer. "What's wrong with your skin? Are you sick?"

"I'm here because of Aro. You know that he framed Jeannette and Baptiste as revenge for helping me, right?"

Claire put her light to her forehead and closed her eyes. "Yes."

"And you still let them be expelled?"

"It's complicated."

"Is it true Baptiste can't even attend Ecol Vert now?"

"I need to get back inside," Claire said. "I'm sorry."

I cut off her retreat. "His grandfather is paying you, isn't he?"

Her panicked look was all the confirmation I needed.

"And I actually thought you were a decent teacher."

"'Selle LaClaire?" A Blue-Green boy peeked around the corner.

"Back inside, Matthieu. Have everyone go over their notes for the exam. I'll be in shortly."

The boy left and Claire leaned toward me. "I hate that it has to be this way. I want to drop-kick that little crêpe-bag several times an hour."

Jeannette laughed, but Claire didn't crack a smile. "But the school can't survive without his grandfather's support."

I shook my head in disgust. "And that support will only continue as long as Aro gets everything he wants."

"And makes straight Z's."

"Well, Jeannette," I said. "Guess your education is less important than the rest of your classmates."

Claire stuck a finger in my face. "I begged Vernon to let them stay, but Aro threatened to have me fired, so don't try and—"

"How much is his grandpa donating every year?"

"Between five and seven thousand cuivres depending on how many awards Aro receives."

I cocked my head. "Really? That's all?"

Claire's eyes bulged, but before she could say whatever was on her mind, I grabbed the red pen hanging from her neck on a lanyard.

"Can I borrow this?"

She uncapped it, and I tore off a corner of Jeannette's textbook pages.

"Where did you get—"

"Focus," I said. "I'm writing down my account number and PIN. Give this to a Blue you trust. It's La Banque d'Espargne, not the Blue Credit Union. Take it all out at once. It's close to thirty thousand cuivres."

Claire's mouth grew steadily larger. "But I can't—"

"Not to sound snobby," I said, "but it's really nothing. I haven't been saving like I should."

Claire put her fingers to her mouth and began blinking rapidly. I thought she might be having a seizure, but then she spoke and her voice was thick with emotion. "What do I tell Vernon?"

"Let me take care of Aro and the Director," I said. "Retribution will be swift and brutal."

CHAPTER TWENTY-TWO

FIREARCHY

"**H**ello," I said in an Ulfish accent. "I'm Rolf Zimmerman. My family just moved here." I tried not to make eye contact with the kids. They had seen me just two days ago and were probably still talking about my reaction with Jeannette.

"I know it's the last day of school," Claire said, "but Rolf needed another exam-level score to graduate. I hope you'll make him feel welcome."

A Lime Green girl raised her hand. Claire looked at me as if unsure what to do.

"Did you have a question?" she said finally.

"Why is his skin yellow?"

"Rosalind, that's not a—"

"It's okay," I said, struggling a bit to keep the accent sounding authentic. It always took me a few minutes to find my groove. "I have a weak liver. My parents brought me for treatment at Bl—the Green Medical Center." Crêpes, I almost said Blue Hospital, which would've seemed strange since with my dyed skin, my fire still appeared blue-greenish.

Another, older girl raised her hand. "Are those real blood stains on your clothes, or is that like, a strange Figgy fashion?" She smirked a little, and I realized I'd spoken to her a couple of days ago. She was the girl with pus in her fire. I was pretty sure she recognized me.

A few of the bigger kids had already been whispering and grinning, as if they were in on the joke. But so far, none of them screamed out, "Hey, that's the mec that pretended to be your assistant, then ran off with Jeannette."

It was probably a good thing that I'd asked Jeannette to hide out in the girl's fanroom for now. But in the end, it didn't matter if they suspected. It only mattered that Aro believe me.

I glanced down at my stained shirt and grimaced. "On our trip over here, a crate of fish guts leaked into my suitcase. We were able to wash the smell out, but as you can see, I'm going to need some new ones."

A few students laughed. One or two of them looked like they were trying to work out why anyone would keep a crate of fish guts and how my suitcase ended up near it.

"Enough questions for now," Claire said. "Rolf, why don't you have a seat in the back row. We'll be silently reviewing for the test for another few minutes, then after lunch, we'll start the final." She handed me a thick book entitled *Comprehensive Juvenile Education - Simplified for Students of Mixed Shade and Cognitive Deficiency.*

I walked to the back of the classroom, trying to seem like a slouchy teen as opposed to an older somewhat-inexperienced teacher's aide. A few of the teenage girls tried to catch my eye, but most stared at my blueberry-booger shade.

I recognized Aro's turquoise light at once. It was twice as bright as any of the other students'. As I passed his desk, he stretched out a dark hand to me. "Aro Loup," he said. "Welcome to Freak School."

I could see why Jeannette had trouble describing the kid. He had a plain face, sort of brownish hair, and was utterly forgettable. Apart from his unique fire, he didn't have a single defining characteristic. He seemed older than Baptiste, but it was impossible to tell by how much.

"Sorry," I said as I passed. "My doctor says I can't touch anyone who looks young enough to pick their nose."

I expected laughter, but the room went deathly silent.

Aro whispered something under his breath that made my

fire flare hot, but I chose to ignore it. The confrontation would come soon enough.

I sat, opened my book to a random section, and began to read.

> The Dismemberment Decade—the period between 1041 and 1049 when the practice of snuffing became popular. Snuffing is the act of cutting off another's light hand for personal use.

The pus girl—Questa, if I remembered correctly—reached into her open backpack, grabbed something, then popped it into her mouth. When was the last time I'd eaten? Last night?

> Typically, within two minutes of being detached from the body, the stolen fire would go out. Snuffers went to great lengths in their attempts to keep it burning. Methods included: cauterizing the wrist to keep the blood inside, freezing it, immersing it in water, vinegar or alcohol. Many ate the severed hand or ground up the esca and smeared it all over their body, hoping to affect a more dramatic reaction with their own fire.

A plastic crinkle drew my attention back to Questa, who had just popped another something into her mouth. Maybe I could get her attention and make horse-eyes at her. No, the fewer people I interacted with the better. I'd eat as soon as I got back across the river.

> A few snuffers even cut off their own light hands to attach the stolen one, but without exception, both thief and victim died. In 1049 the Fire Protection Law was enacted. Anyone trying to steal another's fire—including a Red's—would be put to death.

In the side margin someone had written,

Ha! Who would want to steal a Red's fire?

Movement caught my eye. Aro had leaned forward to whisper something in Questa's ear. She shook her head. Aro sat back, sulked a little, then took his pencil and slowly pressed the tip into the girl's back. She turned and hissed something at him. He laughed.

As soon as she faced forward, he jammed his pencil hard into her back.

Questa cried out.

I very nearly stood up and brought my knuckles down on Aro's head.

"Questa?" Claire said, now standing. "Are you okay?"

She looked down at her open backpack, seemed to consider, then said, "Bit my tongue. Sorry."

When Claire sat back down, Questa silently placed a candy on Aro's desk, then at a few more whispered words from Aro, she slid her backpack behind her. Aro pulled out the entire bag of candy and stuffed it into his pocket.

That little son of a Violet.

The moment Claire dismissed us for lunch, I grabbed the light box from the recreation shelf and brought it outside. I'd just finished setting up the starting marble groups when Aro strode up to the table.

"Sorry to tell you," he said in a tone that helped me understand Claire's drop-kick inclination, "but we have a certain order of things here. Today it's my turn for the box."

"So, sit down," I said. "I'm assuming twenty cuivres is high enough stakes."

Aro glanced around as if looking for someone, then sat. "Let's make it forty," he said. "Unless you don't have it."

I shrugged. "Loser pays forty. Cheaters pay double."

Aro froze with his hand in his sphere bag. "So if I win,

you're going to say I cheated?"

"Only if you cheated." I shook my draw bag.

Aro double checked his starting marbles.

"Youngest player starts," I said.

"I'm not an idiot," Aro said. He drew five red marbles and bought a green from the auction line. He hesitated, then dropped them all into his side of the box.

"A minimalist?" I said with a grin. "I expected a little more sophistication." I drew my marbles, ignored the auction line and spent everything in the shop. Then I poured my handful of marbles into the box.

A ring of students had formed around the picnic table. A couple of kids were brave enough to actually sit down, but most began to eat their lunches while standing. The Lime Green girl who'd asked about my sallow complexion sat on Aro's light side. Rosalind, was it? She was about eight or nine. Strange that she would dare to sit so close to Aro, especially since she was pointedly not watching the game.

Looks like I had found his new accomplice.

As play progressed, I began to grow uneasy. This entire plan hinged on Aro trying to cheat. Maybe he was still nervous about my threat.

"My great uncle is the one who taught me how to play Firearchy," I said as I pulled out the discard drawer and emptied it into my bag. "We're actually staying at his house."

Aro was next to draw. I saw a flash of red in his hand, but when he presented his five marbles, there were four greens and a blue. Wow, he was good at this. I hadn't even seen him drop it onto the grass.

"You've probably heard of him. He's on your Dominateur Council as Dom of Athletics and Recreation or something."

For the first time, Aro looked interested. "I'm sure he knows my grandfather then."

I feigned surprise. "Oh, does he cook for their luncheons or something?"

Aro's poisonous glare was so distracting, I almost missed

the second red marble fall. How had he gotten that out of his bag? It wasn't even his turn. Little blackhead.

"No, my grandfather is also on the Council, and he deals with things much more important than sports and games or whatever Dom Zimmerman is in charge of."

"Really?" I said as I took my turn. "What's his name?"

"My grandfather doesn't like me to say."

"Makes sense," I said. "I'd be embarrassed of you, too."

Aro casually bumped Rosalind's pear with his elbow. It wobbled off the edge and dropped onto the grass.

Rosalind leaned sideways, but I was already diving under the table. "I'll get it."

"No, wait!" Aro said.

"Hey, Aro," I said much louder than strictly necessary. "I found all the Red marbles you've been missing."

"What?" he said. "Those aren't mine. They're probably extras. Or yours. You probably dumped them."

I emerged from under the table and held the three red marbles out for everyone to see. "Well, that's easy enough to check." I spotted Questa and waved her over. "Come open our bags and see which one is missing reds."

Aro swallowed. "They're not mine. At least, I didn't drop them intentionally. I mean, they might have fallen, but—"

Questa poured my marbles into her dark hand and counted my five starting reds. "Not Rolf's," she said. When she emptied Aro's, she found none.

"They're in my drawer."

She pulled out the drawer and displayed the single red marble to the spectators. "This court finds Aro Loup guilty of jettisoning undesirable playing pieces."

"No, I'm pretty sure I bought a purge sphere and—"

I slammed my dark hand onto the table so hard, several marbles jumped off the top of the light box. "You've been caught. You're a cheater, Aro. You owe me eighty cuivres."

"No I don't," Aro said. "We didn't shake on it. Since you didn't put the money on the table, I assumed—"

"So, you're a liar as well," I said, growing louder with each syllable. "You don't have a grandfather on the Council, do you? That was just another lie in your pathetic attempt to impress your classmates."

"That's not a lie!" Aro screamed. "And he doesn't want me to tell anyone his name because people might try to manipulate me to get favors from him."

I stared at Aro a moment. "Prove it then. Go into the Director's office right now and call him. Oh wait, your grandpa probably didn't give you his phone number because he doesn't want anyone to try and manipulate you for it."

"I have his number—but he's very busy. I'm not going to bother him."

Questa scoffed.

"It will only take five seconds," I said. "Call him up and ask him what my uncle's first name is. If he's on the Council like you say, he'll be able to tell you."

Aro stood. "Okay, fine. If the Director says I can use the phone, I'll call."

I lifted my arms and looked around the picnic area. "Who's not afraid of heights?"

Several kids raised their hands. I picked the smallest one, which happened to be Rosalind. She followed me to the nearest tree, and I lifted her up into the branches.

"Nice," I said. "Can you get any higher? Be careful. Perfect. Now show me your best frightened face. Chanmé! Now I'm going to go get the Director. No matter what he says, just keep looking scared and don't move, okay?"

Rosalind grinned and nodded.

A handful of students took that as their cue to run inside screaming, "Director, Ros is stuck in a tree! Rosalind can't get down. Come save her, Director!"

It took a little longer than I expected to get him out, but when he emerged, he marched over to the tree and began shouting at the little girl.

I escorted Aro inside but told Questa to keep everyone

else out so it didn't look suspicious. Claire approached as we neared the Director's office, but I gave a quick shake of my head and motioned for her to disappear. She gave an awkward, "Hello, boys," then retreated back into the classroom.

Aro grabbed the doorknob of the Director's office. "Locked."

I pushed him aside and opened the door. "Hurry up. If he gets back before you learn my uncle's name, you fail."

"I'll call, but you have to shut the door."

The kid looked genuinely scared. He was really going to do it.

I stepped back into the hall and closed the door.

"What's going on?" Claire whispered. I could see the hem of her hoop skirt peeking around the corner.

"So far so good," I whispered back.

I didn't catch very much through the door—but I did hear Aro say, "Can you tell him I just have a quick question?"

After a minute, he hung up and opened the door.

I glanced at my fire and pretended not to be eavesdropping.

"I told you he was busy," Aro said with a sullen expression. "I'll see him tonight at classifications. I'll ask him then."

"You're graduating? I thought you said you weren't even fifteen yet."

"I'm not going to be classified," Aro said. "But I happen to know they're having a special presentation afterward."

I narrowed my eyes at him. He returned it with a smug smile.

"Didn't your uncle tell you?" he said with false surprise. "Well, if he doesn't trust you, I'd better not say. But I will tell you this—they aren't letting any children watch—even siblings of graduates. Must be something... unwholesome." He took a piece of candy from his pocket and put it in his mouth. "You want one?"

I knew his offer was another move in his game. Instead of taking the bait, I grabbed him by the shirt and lifted him above my head. He kicked my thigh, narrowly missing his intended target. I lowered him to the ground and pinned his arms and legs to his sides.

"Weak liver, huh?" Aro said with a sneer. "Who are you?"

"Wouldn't you like to know," I said, this time without a hint of an accent. "Let's just say your granddaddy hired me to keep an eye on you."

Aro's sneer melted into an expression of terror.

I put two fingers into his mouth and popped the candy onto the floor. "That didn't belong to you," I said, my face practically touching his. "Why don't you return that bag to its rightful owner."

I waited until Aro nodded, then pulled him to his feet by the shirt and let go. He stumbled forward, tripped and landed on his face.

For a moment, I almost felt sorry for the kid. Then I remembered his snakelike voice as he urged a mentally-challenged boy to drown himself.

"Baptiste Wedel and Jeannette DeGrave are coming back. If you as much as look at them funny, you'll be the one stuck up in a tree. Or maybe several trees at once."

He shot me a confused look, then my meaning seemed to dawn on him.

After he left, Claire joined me in the hallway. "You make it look so easy," she said. "I can't say I approve of your methods, though."

"Not done yet," I said. "See if you can keep everyone outside for another ten minutes."

"We're already late starting the exam."

The doors at the end of the hallway burst open and the sound of two dozen over-excited kids filled the building.

I slipped inside the Director's office. "Five minutes," I said through the crack. "Try to keep him away from the office."

Claire made a squealing noise but didn't stop me from closing the door.

I turned the lock, then realized Vernon would have the

key. With my back against the wall, I pushed the desk with my feet until it hit the door. Then I picked up the phone and pushed redial.

"Black for brains," came a gruff voice. "I said to call back in a few hours. Not minutes."

"This is Vernon..." I glanced at an envelope on the desk. "Vernon Arsenault Paresseux, Head Director of L'académie Mélangé." Good blank, no wonder everyone called him Director. "I need to speak with the grandfather of Aro Loup, immediately."

"I'm afraid that's not possible, but if you want to leave a message, I can—"

"This is an emergency," I said. "It involves his grandson's future at our school, and I guarantee he's going to want to hear what I have to say."

"One moment."

My pulse beat wildly against the plastic handset. Multicolored lights passed the frosted glass window as the students filed back into the classroom.

"What can I do for you, Director?" came a new voice on the line.

The door rattled. "'Selle LaCroix, why is my office locked?"

"Am I speaking with the grandfather of Aro Loup?" I asked in as deep a voice as I could manage without sounding ridiculous.

"Yes. Where did you get this number? My secretary takes care of donations to the school. I'm not sure if that LaCroix woman told you, but we have something of a—"

"Claire LaCroix has nothing to do with this," I said. "In fact, she begged me to let your grandson stay. But I will not overlook his delinquent behavior another day."

"How dare—"

"I have documented his illegal activities, and they include orchestrating the cutting of a barrier fence and painting of a Blue which resulted in the death of a royal soldier."

The lock turned and the door rattled again. "Who's in there? Open this door immediately."

"Do you have evidence to support this claim?" The voice sounded vaguely familiar, but it was hard to tell over the phone. I'd heard several of the Doms speak at events.

"We have several eye-witnesses," I said. I covered the mouthpiece with my hand when I wasn't speaking. The Director was getting louder and throwing his weight against the door. "In addition, Aro has been caught cheating, manipulating students, he even assaulted one girl to steal her bag of sweets. And most disturbing, he convinced one of my students to attempt firecide, which resulted in the boy's hospitalization."

"Where did you hear such a thing?"

"I witnessed it with my own eyes. Your grandson is a sociopathic criminal. The only way he will continue at my school is if you remove me and appoint Claire Director. For some unfathomable reason, she's taken a liking to the little toilet bag."

Something slammed against the door. The desk moved a few inches. I replaced the handset onto the receiver and pulled the desk back from the door.

A red-faced Director tumbled into the room. "You have no right to be in here."

"I just donated thirty thousand cuivres to your school," I said. "If you don't believe me, ask Claire. Meanwhile, I need a student phone list."

The Director examined my discolored clothes. "Where would you get thirty thousand cuivres?"

The phone rang. The Director reached for it, but I pulled the cord out of the phone. It fell silent. "Before you say anything stupid, like get out of my office, go have a private word with Claire. When you return, I'll expect that contact list."

The Director looked to me, then the phone. "Don't touch anything."

As soon as he left, I plugged the phone back in and dialed

Orie's house. Claudette answered and said neither Orie nor her father was home. I hung up and the phone immediately started ringing again. I picked up the handset.

"Please don't call here again," I said, then hit the switch hook. This time I dialed my house.

"Hello?"

"Mom!"

"Bruno! Thank the Créateur you're safe."

"What about you and Dad? Granny said you were stuck outside the checkpoint."

"Your father is here with me. We're not sure why they let us in—something about a bloody shoe found in a rugby bag in Ulfig. Seems to have thrown everything into confusion. Where are you, Bruno?"

"I'm still trying to get us travel documents."

"Travel documents? Why?"

"Didn't Granny tell you?"

"The house was empty when we got here. The front door was wide open."

Black. If Whisnant did something to Granny I'd—

"Bruno, you need to come home right now, do you hear me?"

The door opened and the Director handed me a paper. He started to say something, but I shooed him out and close the door.

"Bad idea," I said. "In fact, you two should probably get out of there too. Pack—"

"Tell me what's going on."

"Listen to me. Pack a single suitcase. We're leaving tonight. One of my friends has arranged everything. We're meeting tonight at the Cathedral. Try not to be seen, and if anybody in uniform stops you, play dumb."

"Your father wants to talk to you."

"Bruno?"

"Hi, Dad."

"You sure you know what you're doing? I can go to the

Commissaire right now and try to work this all out. I'll tell him we've been targeted by someone in the Green Barracks."

"I think it's too late for that. They don't care about justice anymore—or who started this. It's all about stringing me up as an example. I'll meet you at the Cathedral tonight at midnight. High Priestess DeLaney will let you in. Tell Granny if you see her."

If she's still alive.

"Got to go. I'm hiding out at L'académie Mélangé for a little while longer, then I'll probably head back over the river."

"Over the river?!" Dad shouted.

"No time to explain. Love you, Dad." I hung up, found Baptiste's number on the roster and dialed.

"Yes?" said a high pitched voice. It wasn't Baptiste.

"Is this Monsieur Wedel?"

"Yes, and you are?"

"One of Baptiste's friends from school. Is he available to talk?"

"He's being punished."

"Okay, well this won't take long. I just have a really important message from his teacher. Can you please put him on?"

A few seconds later, Baptiste answered.

"It's Bruno," I said. "I wanted to make sure you're okay. Did the mec with the dog interrogate you or anything?"

"I can't really talk right now."

"Is someone there? Are they listening right now?"

"Papa."

"Is your Papa the only one in the house with you?"

"Yes."

Why would he care if his dad was listening? "How fast can you get to school? I fixed everything with Claire, and she'll let you take the final."

"Can't today. Papa needs me here."

"Baptiste, did you hear me? This is your chance to win the fire improvement scholarship. Tell your dad you're not expelled anymore and get down here."

"Thank you for the message. Maybe another day."

What in the rainbow?

The line went dead.

I hung up the phone, yanked the cord out of the wall and more or less replaced the desk. When I returned to the classroom, I found Jeannette taking the final with the rest of the kids. Both the Director and Claire stood when I entered. I approached Claire.

"Thank you for getting Jeannette set up," I said. "Did Aro say anything to her?"

"Hasn't said a word since he came inside," Claire said.

"Baptiste isn't going to make it, which is a shame because..." A thought occurred to me. "I can't take it for him, can I? As a proxy?"

"Sorry," Claire said with a hint of a smile.

"Technically," the Director said, "you are still on record as an enrolled student—which means you could take the test for yourself... er, Rolf. If you won the scholarship you could give it to whoever you want."

"Whomever."

"Exactly."

"Okay, I'll take the test. If only to keep Aro from winning. Director, can you please keep watch at the window and let me know if anyone approaches the school?"

The Director glanced at Claire as if she were the one to assign menial tasks to but then seemed to remember thirty-thousand reasons to suck it up and do what I asked.

CHAPTER TWENTY-THREE

AMOUR ROUGE

J eannette grinned at me as I took my seat. I waved my fire at her. I had to admit, my light did seem a lot brighter than it had a week ago. Could that be from all the reacting I'd been doing? But surely someone would've documented a correlation between fire age and luminosity. Maybe it came from reacting across the color barrier. Although the brilliance of my fire would make me easier to be spotted in a crowd, it was certainly nice to be able to see my test clearly. I flipped the exam over and read the first question.

```
According to ancient folkloric texts, the Crys
tal Scepter was used:
     z) As a club to beat wouldbe assassins
     y) As a gavel during council meetings
     x) To see the future
     w) To harness the light of the King's fire
```

I tried to think. Didn't the King's Requirement say something about the Scepter? Make the something, something... shine? I circled 'w'.

To my extreme delight, the test questions seemed to get progressively easier. That is until I reached the very last question. It was longer than the others and worth ten points.

```
List these Télesphorian Kings in order of their
reign.
          z) Jacque the Cerulean
```

y) Xavier the Gold
x) Johannes the Scarlet
w) Jean Pierre the Blue
v) Grégoire the Teal.

Great. The only thing I remembered about Télesphorian kings was that the last one had died fifty years ago. I'd just have to work it out.

The Blues had to be more recent—I knew something like the last five were Blue. I was pretty sure Jean Pierre was the one who gave the King's Requirement. Before that would probably be Jacque, then the Mélangé Grégoire. But Johannes the Scarlet? I didn't even know we'd had a Red king. Had Axelle even taught us that? The name didn't sound Télesphorian, so I assumed he was the same Johannes who discovered the island. That left the Gold for the number two spot.

No sooner had I filled in the numbers, than the light switched on. The class moaned. We dropped our pencils to the carpet and passed our tests to the front.

Afterward Claire sent us all outside for a brief recess. Most of the students sat in a circle in the grass and discussed the final. This was the first time I realized there had been three different tests to compensate for the age differences between students. That also meant there would be three winners of the shade improvement scholarship. A smaller group of kids gathered around Jeanette, asking about how she'd ended up Pink. I couldn't hear what she was saying, but at least no one looked in my direction.

I kept a close eye on the roads but didn't see any pokers or giant white mutts. I thought about taking off back to the shelter to see what Mama DeGrave found out about the forger —but if I waited another half hour, school would be out and I might not draw as much attention. Anyway, I didn't want to leave Jeannette to walk home alone, white bracelet or not.

While we waited for Claire and Vernon to finish grading the exams, I found a miniature rugby ball in the toy box and organized a two-hand-touch match with some of the other students. We were having so much fun that several groaned when Claire called us in for the awards presentation.

Once we were all back in our seats, however, thoughts of rugby fled and the room filled with an anxious silence. The Director stood and cleared his throat. "You all did very good."

"Well," I corrected automatically, then grimaced.

"Well," he said with a stiff smile. "But as you know, there will only be three students chosen to represent our school and receive the shade improvement scholarship. The highest score for the six-to-nine-year-olds is Antoinette LeSueur."

The class applauded and a cute little Blue-Green girl went up to receive her certificate. I clapped too, until I remembered Jeannette was nine. I glanced over at her, and she gave me a sad smile. I suddenly wished I'd spent less time pressing her for secrets and more helping her study.

"The winner of the ten-to-thirteen-year-old division is Aro Loup."

What? The kid had to have cheated. Or maybe the school was due for some new lunch tables.

Only a couple people clapped as Aro shook the director's hand.

"The highest score for the fourteen-to-sixteen-year-olds and winner of the third scholarship is Rolf Zimmerman."

I was surprised by the applause when I walked up to receive my certificate.

"I'm giving this to Baptiste," I said quietly to Claire. "When and where will he get the improvement?"

"We're meeting on the street in front of Harlequin Municipal Penitentiary. Visiting hours are at seven o'clock tonight."

"Aren't classifications at eight-thirty?"

"Were you planning to attend?" Claire asked. "I was under the impression you wanted to avoid government officials."

Why had I asked? Was it because Véronique would be there? Did I somehow think I'd be able to slip in, watch the most important moment of her adolescence, then sneak away to my midnight rendezvous?

"Just wondering how long will it take. Baptiste's dad seems like a control freak."

"As long as it takes to shake hands."

The moment I stepped outside the Académie, a royal blue utility vehicle with tinted windows rolled toward me.

"Rolf!" Jeannette shrieked.

"I see it," I said. "Get ready to run."

The vehicle picked up speed. Then it clipped a street sign, launched over the curb, and struck a bike rack which stopped it's momentum with a deafening screech.

I released Jeannette's hand. "It's okay. It's just Granny."

The window lowered and a wrinkled hand gestured to the back door.

"Come on," I said. "I'll see if she can drop us near the bridge."

The back door was locked.

"It's the small button below the wiper knob," I said.

The cab light came on. Then the back window lowered.

"No, on the... never mind." I reached inside and unlocked the door.

Jeannette hopped inside and I followed her.

"What are you doing here, Granny?" I asked once the door was closed and we were rolling onto the street.

"Who's this adorable little thing?" she asked. Her hair and clothing didn't look any better than it had two nights ago, but she certainly seemed in higher spirits.

"This is Jeannette. Does Dad know you took the car?"

"Of course he does."

"And he let you go?"

"He chased after me a few blocks—but honestly, I'm a grown woman."

I glanced at Jeannette and mouthed, "seatbelt." She seemed to have no idea what I was talking about, so I fastened it for her. "Well, thanks for picking us up. I was worried when Dad said you'd disappeared."

"Your little Talbot friend stopped by and somehow convinced le sergent to finally get out of my hair."

"Orie?" I noticed a water bottle under my foot and drank half in one go.

"A nice girl but slightly anxious. She brought me to the Cathedral and had the high priestess explain everything."

"Oh, good." I offered Jeannette water, but she shook her head.

Granny looked at me through the rear view mirror. "Not good. It's a horrible plan."

"Granny, watch the—"

The bicyclist swerved out of our path.

"You've never mentioned this Orie character before—and now you suddenly want to sign her paperwork?"

"Well, if you have another option, I'd love to hear it."

"We'll discuss it with your parents over dinner."

Jeannette and I shared a look.

"I can't go home, Granny. I still need to get the travel documents. And you can't bring a Red Mélangé into Ville Bleu! No offense, Jeannette."

"Well, your parents didn't seem too thrilled with the idea of you crossing the river."

"Trust me, Gran. It's the safest place for me right now." I emptied the bottle and slid it into the seat-back pocket.

"We don't have to go across the bridge, either," Jeannette added. "Higher up the mountain, the river is shallow enough to wade across."

"I've been there twice before and nothing happened to me." Well, nothing I was going to tell my over-protective grandma about.

"How would we get a hold of you?"

Granny pulled a map out of the glove compartment and tried to flap it open with one hand. I reached over the seat and grabbed the map.

"I'll call you from Baptiste's house later tonight. Then we can decide whether to go with Orie's plan or try something else. Did she tell you how I was supposed to find the forger? Also, I may need some more money."

After half a mile on a dirt road, Granny pulled over and we got out. While Jeannette examined the sapling sprouting from the front bumper, Granny pulled me aside.

"What's the story with the girl?"

"I know her from school. Her family helped me out last night."

Granny sighed. "Okay, but I'm coming with you to see that you get across safely." She grabbed my fire and examined it. "So, what shade are you nowadays?"

"Same as the last time I saw you—this is just skin dye." I began walking summerlight through the trees, the others followed. Granny seemed surprised when Jeannette grabbed her hand, but she didn't pull away.

"I wish your grandfather were alive," Granny said. "He might have been able to explain what's going on with your fire."

"Was he a doctor?" Jeannette asked.

"Luminogenetic research scientist," I said.

Granny helped Jeannette over a tangle of rusty wire fence. "My husband wasn't a patient man, and he tended to overeat. But there wasn't a soul on Port who knew more about fires."

Although it had been nearly six years since his accident, Granny still talked about him every day. I slowed and set my fire on Granny's shoulder as we walked. A week ago, I wouldn't have dreamed of touching her like that, but after all the touching I'd been doing with Greens and Reds, I'd decided I felt good.

"Did Grandpa ever say anything about someone's esca getting hot enough to burn someone?"

Granny shot me a look. "No... but the esca is the least understood part of the human body. We know it aids the body in storing and distributing energy, and it may cleanse impurities from our blood, but we can't pinpoint exactly why our body shuts down without it."

Jeannette crunched a pine cone under her foot, then stooped to pick up another.

I pressed a finger into my glowing palm. The slight pressure caused an unpleasant sensation halfway between an ache and an itch. "Grandpa always said my soul was in there."

I expected Granny to laugh, but she was examining Jeannette's pine cone and pretending to be amazed. After a few more yards, she said softly, "He certainly had some unorthodox theories. After your parents signed papers, he used to corner Andre and explain his latest research. He claimed the esca was capable of far more than we could imagine."

Once I might have scoffed at such a comment—but the light at the end of my arm was starting to feel like a power tool with no instructions.

"You mean like magic?" Jeannette said.

"Who knows what he meant," Granny said. "But it inspired Andre to change his area of emphasis. Maybe one day, he'll carry on my husband's research."

This was highly unlikely since Grandpa's journals had burned up in the lab combustion, but I wasn't insensitive enough to say so.

"Why did Dad become a surgeon instead of a scientist?"

"Esca research is nearly impossible to fund," Granny said. "Noo one wants to volunteer for a research study that might land them in the Red Slums. No offense, dear."

We reached the river and found Jeannette had been right about the wide shallow water. Jeannette crossed easily. Before I could, Granny placed her fire on my cheek, something I remember her doing only twice before—after Ro died, and a few weeks later when I'd woken from a nightmare and wouldn't stop screaming.

"Don't fetter yourself to someone you don't love," Granny said. "Even if it seems the only way. This Télesphorian custom of teenage betrothal paperwork is dispassionate and absurd."

I smiled. "How do the Figs do it?"

"We fall desperately in love, then sacrifice everything to make it work."

Personally that sounded like the more absurd of the customs, but I nodded. "Drive carefully."

"Don't be ridiculous."

We were about a hundred yards from the community shelter grounds when a spear came hurtling out of the trees and stuck in the soil in front of us.

"Watch it!" Jeannette shouted. "We're walking here."

I pulled her closed and clamped a hand over her mouth. "It's probably the Feu Noir. You realize I have over two hundred cuivres on my person."

Jeannette squirmed out of my grasp. "It's not the Feu Noir, blankhead."

I was getting ready to tackle her and retreat to the trees when Véronique stepped out of the underbrush. A torn, discolored sheet circled her torso and held several more spears to her back. "You like your eyes?" she asked.

Jeannette and I glanced at each other.

"They're okay, I guess." Was she trying to say I had beautiful eyes? She wouldn't be the first girl to notice them.

She strode to the stick in front of me and pulled it from the ground. "Then don't wander into range when someone's practicing their javelin throw."

"Pretty good arm," I said.

"What would you know about it?"

"I play rugby for TC."

She tossed the javelin between her hands. I could now see it was a roughly carved wooden rod with a blunt point on both ends. "Really?" she said. "Catch this then."

I snatched the stick out of the air before I even realized she'd thrown it.

"Holy fish eggs," Jeannette said.

Véronique blinked, her mouth open slightly.

I tossed the stick back to her. "As I said, I like my eyes. So maybe don't throw pointy objects at my face?" The remark came out with a little more hostility than I'd meant. She hadn't thrown it very hard, after all. And it hadn't been at my face. I don't even think it would've hit me.

"You're not as clumsy as you look," Véronique said.

"Is that a compliment?"

"I don't know. Is your head going to explode?"

Jeannette stepped between us, wearing the expression of a long-suffering parent. "I met Bruno's grandma. She has a pulchritubinal fire."

"The word is pulchritudinous," Véronique said.

That couldn't be a real word.

Véronique took a hair tie out of her pocket and tied Jeannette's hair back. "Your fire is pretty too, you know."

Jeannette scoffed. "Is Mama back?"

Véronique nodded. "They let Philippe go. Chief Collins told him he'd get a free night stay at the shelter for the misunderstanding."

I bunched my eyebrows. "That doesn't sound like him."

"Yeah, something's definitely slippery."

"Where's your mom?" I asked.

"Philippe didn't know anything about the forger," Véronique said. "I didn't think he would."

I cocked my head. Wasn't she the one who insisted her brother would know?

"What time is it?" Jeannette asked. "I need to go number two."

"Little after four-thirty, I think," Véronique said. "You still have three and a half hours before the shelter opens."

"I'm not going in the woods!" Jeannette said.

"Go down to the river," Véronique said. "It's not like

you'll be able to get to a stall right at eight anyway. There's always a rush for the toilets as soon as they open. That first night, I waited thirty minutes." She seemed to realize she'd given more detail than strictly necessary and cast a quick glance in my direction.

I winked at her.

Why did I do that? That was a completely involuntary eye twitch.

Véronique seemed just as confused as I was by the gesture —disgusted even.

Time for a distraction.

"Véronique," I said, "can you and Philippe ask around to see if anyone knows where we can get those documents?"

"Where are you going to be?"

I pulled some pine needles off a branch and smelled them. "I've got to call my parents. I should be back before the shelter opens."

"I need to use a phone," Véronique said. "I'll come with you."

Jeannette and I both looked at her.

"Is that okay?" Véronique said. The last time I'd seen her vulnerable was just before I got them kicked out of their house. What a blankhead I was.

Suddenly her prickliness seemed understandable, war-ranted even. And I had to admit, without a smirk or a scowl, her face was much easier to look at. She even had a smattering of freckles I hadn't—

Stop. That.

"Sure," I said in my most aloof voice. "If you think you can keep up."

She loaded Jeannette down with her sticks, then began a brisk jog in the direction of Pont en Pierre. Apparently she was taking me seriously.

I grinned and took off after her.

"Mama's not going to be happy!" Jeannette called out after us.

My grin faded as I realized the distance between Véronique and me was still increasing. I paused briefly to tighten my laces. Then I blew on my fire and shifted into Champion Athlete mode.

When I arrived at the stone bridge, Véronique approached me with a worried look. "Did I slow you down? You really don't have to wait for me."

After my breathing slowed enough for me to speak, I said, "Did you… take a… shortcut?"

"Is that a compliment?" she asked.

I smiled. "Would it mean a lot coming from a semi-professional athlete like myself?"

"It would mean the world to me," she said, clasping her hands under her chin. "Could you please autograph my fire, Bruno?"

An intense flash of—something—caught me by surprise. I couldn't tell if it was the thought of touching her fire or the way she'd said my name, but for a moment, I couldn't seem to keep my teeth covered.

"Are we going cross or what?" she said. "At some point I'm going to need to be back to change my clothes."

"Huh?"

"Aren't you being classified too?" she asked as she started up the bridge.

I followed at a distance so she wouldn't smell me. "Sup-

295

posed to—but probably not worth getting executed."

"You'd get to be a med student for a few minutes at least."

"Very funny." They'd swarm me the moment they realized I was—

Wait, did she say med student? How did she know about my career aspirations? Had I mentioned it to Jeannette?

"So…" I said after a pause. "What are you hoping to get?"

She turned her all-too-familiar glare in my direction. "Seriously? Are you really that dense?"

Apparently.

"The process is not the same for Reds," she said. "Haven't you ever been to a classification ceremony?"

"Only child."

She stopped and turned to face me. "Reds don't even have evaluations. The Education Board automatically sorts us as Tongues—which is ironic considering we're the only group without a say in the government."

"Tongues? What form of energy does that represent?"

"Kinetic. Movement. Manual labor in other words. Some become sewer workers or street pavers, but most end up in the tin mine."

My cheeks burned like she'd slapped me. I'd been so caught up in my own problems, I hadn't really stopped to think what everyday life was like for Reds. Even if they were dirty and lazy, working in the tin mines didn't seem like something I'd be able to endure for a single day, let alone my entire life.

Yet another reason to cut off my perverse infatuation with the river trash.

I ignored the stab of guilt at that thought and forced myself to continue up the bridge. It was for the best. If Granny thought saving lives wasn't a good enough reason to marry, I could imagine what she'd think of picking someone because she was pretty.

Not that I'd even consider marrying a Red. The thought repulsed me.

Or at least it should have.

I realized I could no longer hear Véronique's footsteps behind me. When I looked, I saw her walking back down the bridge toward the Taudis.

Had I offended her somehow? Maybe the Créateur could see my confusion and was making my decision easier.

But she'd seemed determined to make that call...

I caught up with her. "I promise I'll shut up."

"It's not that," she said. "It's this bridge. I thought I could handle it."

"You don't like the bridge?"

Véronique wiped a tear off her cheek. I nearly fell over backward. 'Selle Porcupine crying?

"For one thing I'm not great with heights. But that may just be because I have some not-so-good memories of this place."

"You want to talk about it?"

She shook her head. "I'm gonna head back. Guess I did slow you down after all."

"Neek," I said. "I don't know what happened to you here, but if you want to try to face it, I'll help you."

What was I doing? Let her go.

I extended my fire.

Bruno, you blackhead.

I had finally convinced myself to withdraw my hand when Véronique put her fingers in mine.

Holy mother of pearl.

We crossed the bridge with her dark hand in my light. It was the single most uncomfortable five minutes of my life.

And I didn't want it to end.

I was so distracted by the prolonged contact that I didn't noticed the pokers waiting for us on the other side.

CHAPTER TWENTY-FOUR

SHATTERED

"'Sieur, what business do you have with that Red?"

Fear exploded outward from my chest until I was drowning in it. But before I could sprint back up the bridge, Véronique tightened her grip on my hand. That slight change of pressure transformed me from Rolf the timid foreigner who hid from pokers, to Bruno Nazaire the Blue steamroller.

"I'm dying of cancer," I said with all the disdain I could muster. "And I'm going to enjoy the time I have left. You don't like it, you can puncture yourselves."

The pokers looked at each other. "I'm sorry, but the Haut Commissaire has ordered a tightening of security before to-night's events. Our orders are to—"

I doubled over, stuck my fingers down my throat, and vomited all over his boots.

"I'm so sorry," I said. "You should head back, mon amour. I'm sure these royal soldiers will help me home and get me cleaned up."

The pokers stepped aside. "Be quick," one said, while the other wiped his boots on the grass. "If you're caught, you crossed at the shallows upstream, understand?"

After the bridge, Véronique latched onto my upper arm. Why did that thrill me so much? Was it really her pretty face that was clouding my judgement? If she were hideous, would I shake her off my arm?

I tried to picture Véronique as an unattractive person, but my brain rebelled against the thought. I managed to summon the face of the old, toothless man at the shelter, minus the facial hair and placed it on her body.

That wouldn't work—the rest of her was too attractive. And I had to do something about that silky black hair. I imagined the entire old man with a few less years and female everything else.

Frightful to say the least.

If I'd been stuck in a stairwell with old and gross Véronique, would I have even gone down to speak with her? Maybe only to ask about the forger. And to congratulate her on kicking the serum out of those perverts. I might have stayed to hear a little about her life in the Taudis simply out of curiosity. But I certainly wouldn't have flirted as I had—especially since I was technically spoken for.

The realization that I would rather speak with old-man Véronique than Orie brought me up short. Maybe if I talked to her and got it out of my system, I'd be able to do what was best for myself and my family.

I tried several times to start up a conversation, but Véronique seemed to have lost her ability to use multisyllable words. Strange to think that for her, this was the dangerous side of the river.

We walked the rest of the way to Baptiste's apartment in silence.

A short man with a sharp nose and blue eyes answered his door. He wore two oven mitts. Véronique moved to hide her fire behind her back, but I grabbed her hand and held it instead. She scowled at me but didn't pull away. Amazing how quickly one could get used to these strange Red customs.

"Monsieur Wedel?" I said, unable to wipe the stupid grin from my face. "We're friends of Baptiste."

The man furrowed his blond eyebrows. "Now is not a good time," he said with a hint of a Verlish accent. He tried to close the door, but I held it open.

"It will only take a minute, 'sieur, but it's important that I speak with your son."

"And use your phone," Véronique said. "If that's okay?" Then she arranged her cheeks and lips into such a radiant formation that I nearly reached out to touch her teeth. Blackened crêpes. How did she do that?

"I suppose that's fine," Monsieur Wedel said. His eyes followed her as we entered. I decided I didn't like him.

He strode into the hallway and tried to be subtle about unlocking Baptiste's door, but I was watching for it. At least the man knew enough to be ashamed. In a way that made his abusive parenting worse.

Baptiste emerged wearing pajamas that were made to look like a poker's uniform. It even had a large plastic watch and an attached brown glove.

"Hey," I said. "You didn't have any trouble the other night, did you? After I left?"

Baptiste glanced at his dad, who was pulling a tray of potatoes out of the oven. "They yelled at me a little, but when I didn't say anything, they left."

I also looked at Monsieur Wedel. How much did he know?

"'Sieur, I apologize for involving you and your son in all this. Once we make a call, we'll be out of your beard."

Véronique—who had finally managed to free her hand—shot me a strange look. Clearly she wasn't familiar with the Blue idiom and was confused by the man's clean shaven face.

"Would you like to call first?" I asked her.

She shook her head, so I grabbed the phone and dialed my house.

Dad answered. It was great to hear his voice. Granny had returned with only cosmetic damage to the utility vehicle, and everything had been packed for the trip. He wasn't bothered that I still hadn't gotten the documents, since he had bought a pair of forty-foot ladders and rope to tie them together to reach the top of the wall. He had also purchased a commercial size floor mat that he planned to lay over the razor wire.

"The cargo barge leaves tonight at eleven," Dad said. "They've got room enough for up to thirty people, but it will probably take a couple hours to climb down the mountain on foot."

"But we're supposed to meet Talbots and Faringoules at midnight in the cathedral."

Monsieur Wedel looked over at me with a startled expression.

"You'll have to get ahold of them earlier," Dad said. "Isn't Orie getting classified? I'll see if I can find her family and tell them the new plan."

Assuming they went along with it. "I think she's going to want to get classified first."

"Well, I suppose they can catch up."

"Is Marin's dad still being held at the police station?"

"Haven't heard anything," Dad said. "Come home right now. We're going to head up to the campsite and set up the ladders. There should be enough trees on the other side to get down. If not, we can use the rope to repel."

"Okay," I said. "I'll be there in thirty minutes at the latest."

This time, it was Véronique who looked startled. Ah blank, I'd forgotten about escorting her back across. Maybe she could hang out at Baptiste's and go straight to classifications. Except she needed to change. Black.

"Créateur's light guide you," Dad said. He wasn't usually religious. He must be really nervous.

"Likewise," I said and hung up.

While Véronique made her call, I washed my hands and took over grating the cheese since Baptiste kept cutting his fingers.

"Dad's not happy," Baptiste whispered, "because I got expelled and he has to be my teacher next year."

"Crêpes, I totally forgot," I said. "I told the Director Aro planted that knife. He said you can come back next year. In fact, you need to meet 'Selle LaCroix in front of the penitentiary at seven tonight."

"That's out of the question," Monsieur Wedel said.

"The Director said I can transfer my shade improvement scholarship to your son," I said. "You can go with him, of course. The extra blue might make a difference for his future."

Monsieur Wedel finished transferring the potatoes to a serving dish, then pulled off his oven mitts.

Wow. His cyan fire was nearly the same shade as Baptiste's. I hadn't seen many adult Mélangé, and it was difficult not to stare.

"By the way," I said, "thank you for letting me use your wife's old clothes. They probably saved my life." Actually, the red pepper was much more useful, but I didn't want them to think their sacrifice was for nothing.

"What clothes?" Monsieur Wedel asked.

I briefly explained how Baptiste had helped me escape the dogs and assured him that the hunting party was due to a big misunderstanding. I wasn't actually a dangerous criminal.

The longer I spoke, the darker his expression grew. When I finished, he looked ready to murder someone, and Baptiste had gone as white as the sky.

"Is there a problem?" I asked.

"Baptiste knows Alexandrie's closet is off limits," Monsieur Wedel said. "His punishment will be severe." He walked to the door and held it open. "It's time for you both to leave."

Véronique cast a panicked glance my way. Apparently she wasn't done with her phone call. Luckily there was plenty I had to say to 'Sieur Wedel.

"Baptiste has been through enough," I said. "You have an hour and a half before he needs to be at the prison. It's important that he be there."

Monsieur mumbled something in another language, then said, "Out. Before I call the police to escort you out."

I doubted he would actually call. I knew the relationship Hameau Vert had with law enforcement. And I certainly didn't want to leave Baptiste alone with his Dad after I had somehow drained his serum.

I stepped toward the little man, allowing him to appreciate my height and build. "You can't lock kids in their room for hours at a time—especially if you leave the house. What if there were an emergency? I don't know how they raise kids in Verl, but in Télesphore City, we protect our children from crêpebags. Whether that be school bullies or their own parents."

Someone touched my shoulder and I jumped, ruining the effect I was trying to create. "It's fine," Véronique said quietly. "I'm finished. We should go."

I raised my hand and trained my light on Monsieur Wedel. It was incredibly rude, but I needed him to know I was serious. "If I find out you've been mistreating my friend, I'll lock you in that room and see how you like peeing in a juice bottle."

Véronique dragged me into the hall by the elbow. The door slammed behind us.

"Sorry," Véronique said, "he looked like he was ready to empty your dome."

"Something's not right with that mec—male person," I

hastily amended.

We'd only taken a few steps toward the stairwell when Baptiste cried out. Véronique put a hand on my arm.

A crash echoed through the corridor, followed by another cry. I met Véronique's eyes, then we both ran back and pounded on the wood.

"What's going on in there?" I shouted.

Baptiste was repeating something that sounded like "Please."

"Open up!" I slammed my full weight into the door but only bruised my shoulder.

Two doors down, someone peeked out into the hall. I sprinted to the door and grabbed the knob before the orange-mustached man could close it. "Can we use your phone to call the police?"

The Green hesitated, then nodded. He looked vaguely familiar, but I couldn't think where I would've seen him. He led us into his cluttered house. A milk-skinned woman and several light-haired children stared at us from the dinner table.

The man handed me the phone. "He's always getting on that boy, but it's never been this bad."

Now that I held the handset, I realized how useless it would be to call the police. Even if they managed to get here before Baptiste was seriously injured, most of the Green officers were incompetent.

In fact, Officer Juenes basically told me to take matters into my own hands. "If you care so much about the blond boy, why didn't you help him when it mattered?"

I'd abandoned Baptiste once and he nearly died. This time, I was going to enforce the law myself. I strode to the sliding glass door that led to the patio balcony. The door wouldn't budge.

"Could somebody help me here?"

One of the little Green boys jumped up from the table and pulled a long wooden rod out of the sliding track.

Before I could try it again, I noticed a framed portrait

drawing on the wall and froze.

"Bruno?"

Véronique's voice brought me back to the present. I'd deal with the portrait later. I shoved the image from my mind and stepped into the cool evening air. The eye had recently closed behind the mountain, but there was still enough light to see the brick-colored rungs. I hopped the railing, clattered onto the escape ladder, then dove for the next balcony. Although I demolished a flower planter, I was pretty pleased with myself.

Until I realized there was no ladder between the second patio and Baptiste's. I'd have to jump six feet at least. I pulled myself up onto the railing. My hands were slick with sweat.

I've never considered myself a coward, but having to jump between two balconies five stories up was definitely the scariest thing I'd ever had to do. Catching the opposite railing with my dark had would be relatively simple. It was the light hand that would prove tricky. Come down with too much pressure on my palm and I'd pop. But if I aimed more toward the fingers and slipped, I'd be just as dead.

I'd just have to jump higher and avoid the railing altogether. After two practice bounces, I extended my knees and leaped.

I didn't quite make it.

My foot clipped Baptiste's railing on the way down, and I landed hard on my face. Luckily he had a moldy strip of carpet as a doormat, so I just knocked my brains loose rather than spreading them across the balcony.

It took a moment for my head to realize it was still mostly intact. I took two long breaths, grabbed the sliding door handle, and pulled myself up. On the other side of the glass, the curtains were drawn, but I could still hear Baptiste inside, begging.

What was I waiting for? I stepped against the railing, leaned back, and kicked with both feet at the sliding door. The glass shattered and the curtain went flying.

The cries fell silent. I peered inside. Baptiste and his father stared at me with identical expressions of surprise. Crêpes. Baptiste wasn't huddled in a corner with a black eye—he was standing in the middle of the room, looking as healthy as ever. His dad sat on the floor with a book in his hand, surrounded by piles of torn pages. Other than that, the only thing out of place was a broken lamp

"Everything alright in here?" I asked as if I hadn't just destroyed their patio door.

"Are you insane?" Monsieur Wedel said.

Baptiste rubbed at his face. "He's ripping my books."

"You chose this." Monsieur Wedel tossed the book across the room where it collided with the disembodied lampshade. "If you don't value your mother's belongings, then you don't value your own."

Someone pounded on the door. "Bruno!" came Véronique's voice. "You okay?"

I opened the door.

"Oh good, you're alive," she said.

I stepped aside so she could enter. "We may have slightly misjudged the situation."

Monsieur Wedel got to his feet, his face almost as bright as Véronique's fire. "I let you into my home, allow you to use my phone—and this is how you thank me?"

I looked at the cherub. He was a sniffling, tear-soaked mess. Did he really care so much about his books? From his screams, you would've thought he was being dismembered.

"Obviously I'm not a parent," I said, "but I can't help but think you're doing an excrementary job."

Monsieur Wedel eyebrows knitted. "Get out," he said. "I'm teaching my boy a lesson, and it has nothing to do with either of you."

I hesitated. Véronique seemed ready to leave, but Baptiste was watching me with a desperate expression, like I had the power to save his precious encyclopedias.

"I'll pay for your door," I said, "and your wife's clothes.

But you're wrong about it not being any of my business. Baptiste is obviously trying to be a good son. Destroying his books seems a little childish if you ask—"

The short man launched himself at me. Before I could think, my rugby instincts took over and I spun out of his way. Even as I felt him brush past me, I realized he was going too fast.

With a sickening clunk, the man's head hit the heavy wooden door and his body went limp.

ATONEMENT

I was blacked.

I had literally kicked my way into a man's house, goaded him into attacking me, and broken his neck.

"Is he dead?" Baptiste asked, his hands on top of his head.

Véronique knelt by the motionless figure. "He's breathing."

Monsieur Wedel made a strange choking sound. I crouched, ready to check his airway, and realized he was crying.

"Maybe we should go," Véronique said.

"Five minutes," Baptiste said and pushed me out of the way. "Wait until I ask Papa."

Ask him what? "Baptiste," I said, "he could be seriously—"

"You said I was born Mélangé," Baptiste said to his father. "Was that true or just another lie?"

Monsieur Wedel continued to heave in silent sobs. It was horrible watching a grown man cry into the carpet—especially since it was my fault he was down there.

"Why won't you tell me anything about Mama?" Baptiste continued. "Because she has a mental disability like me?"

Monsieur Wedel rolled onto his side and put his hand into his pocket.

"Be careful, 'sieur," I said. "Your spine might be injured."

He ignored me and pulled out his keys. Was he delirious? Why did he need his keys? Then I noticed he was opening the blade of a tiny pocket knife attached to the key ring.

I shot to my feet and pulled Véronique back. "We're leaving. You can put that away." But instead of pointing at us with the knife, he readjusted the blade in his dark hand and brought it down on his Cyan fire.

"No!" I landed on him and pinned his wrists to the floor. I checked his light hand and didn't see any leakage. Thank the Créateur I'd caught him before he'd punctured it.

Monsieur Wedel didn't seem pleased with the interruption. His back was apparently fine, because he was able to kick at me with both legs. As his struggles grew more desperate, I had to put my full weight on him.

After several more erratic attempts to free himself, the man relaxed, breathing hard. I was feeling a little tuckered out myself. I tried to take the knife from his hand, but he wouldn't release his grip.

"You've got at least one good reason to live," I said. "Your son needs you."

Monsieur Wedel clutched the knife so tightly, his hand shook.

"Besides, you've got steady work, a nice apartment," I said, hoping he didn't glance at his patio area, "and you're a Blue Mélangé. Focus on the good things."

"I lied to her," Monsieur Wedel said, his eyes still full of tears. "I knew she would find out eventually, but I hoped after we had a child, she would forgive me."

I took some of my weight off him. "Everyone makes mistakes."

"I knew exactly what I was doing. I came from Oland as a Mélangé."

He was Olish? Guess I wasn't as great with accents as I thought. I glanced at Baptiste. "Does he get like this a lot? You think it would help to—"

"I told her I was Blueborn," Monsieur Wedel continued. "I let her get pregnant, knowing the baby would be Green."

Baptiste was too engrossed in his father's confession to pay me any attention. "So Mom was a..."

"Her name was Alexandrie Ereaut, and she was the most

beautiful Blue in Télesphore."

Baptiste looked at the carpet. "No wonder she left."

"She was excited to have you—and determined to force an intrauterine reaction."

"A what?" Baptiste asked.

I couldn't believe we'd finally found something the boy genius didn't know.

Véronique crouched next to Baptiste. "It's when the mother reacts with the baby through the belly. My mom tried to do it with Jeannette, but it's really hard."

"Why would they want to do that? Isn't it easier to wait?"

Véronique smiled. "Normally you can only react with a person once, right? But if you react with a baby early enough while its fire is still developing, your fire won't recognize it after its born. So your mother loved you so much she wanted to react with you twice."

"Alexandrie succeeded," Monsieur Wedel said. "As soon as her hand turned green, she knew I'd lied to her." Monsieur Wedel let out a shuddering sigh and dropped the knife.

I kicked the keys out of reach and helped him sit up. "Really am sorry about the door," I said. "And your neck."

"Alexandrie wanted to terminate the pregnancy, but I wouldn't let her."

Baptiste's face crumpled. "Aro was right. She didn't want me."

Véronique dropped to her knees and pulled Baptiste into an embrace. "She made a mistake. If she knew the boy you've become, she'd cross the Ocheanum to find you."

Blank, Véronique was really good at this.

Monsieur Wedel began to cry again. "After she gave birth, I thought she would be able to overlook his shade. I had a two-week business trip—but after the first week, I got a call from the Welfare Board. Alexandrie had…"

Baptiste's pulled away from Véronique. "You have to tell me, Papa. I'm not a baby anymore."

Monsieur Wedel nodded, but it was a moment before he

could talk. When he did, he spoke to me, as if it would somehow lessen the blow. "When I got home, I found Alex in jail and Teest in foster care."

No one said anything. Véronique looked at me, and I know we were thinking the same thing. Should Baptiste be listening to this? Regardless, the kid had been kept in the dark all his life, and he wasn't going to be satisfied until he knew everything.

"They had already cleaned up everything, but I read the police report. She'd filled a hamster bottle with milk and attached it to his crib. Then she shut the door and didn't go into his room for four days."

Véronique's face was wet with tears.

I don't think any of us wanted him to go on, but he did. "They found him in the same diaper I'd left him in. He had sores. Ants had gathered to the sour milk. It was the smell that saved his life. The neighbors complained to the landlord and when Alex didn't answer, the police came."

I felt sick. Monsieur Wedel had been right to keep this from Baptiste.

Monsieur Wedel covered his eyes. "The doctor said he'd never seen a case of otomyiasis that young."

"What's that?" Baptiste said.

"My brother Philippe had that a couple years ago," Véronique said. "It's a sort of ear infection caused by bugs." An ear infection caused by bugs? I had a feeling Véronique was sparing us the details.

"Intrauterine reactions are more powerful with the baby still developing," Monsieur Wedel said in a surprisingly gentle voice. "Which is why you came out a nearly even mix of green and blue. That was your mother's parting gift. She was grateful I'd arranged for her to be sent to a nice mental health facility in Deatherage instead of serving her time in prison."

I stood up and looked around. "Well, I think I'll see if your shower curtain will cover that opening. Have any duct tape?"

We'd just said goodbye to Baptiste when the orange-mustached man's family came into the hall to make sure everything was all right. All four kids gathered around to ask if I were an acrobat and whether I could teach them to jump from the balcony. After the warning glare from their mother, I quickly shut that down.

As we passed their door, I asked the woman, "Do you have an older son?"

Tears sprang to her eyes, and she led me inside to the drawing I'd seen earlier. Pinned next to it was a funeral program. Both showed a similar sketch of an unsmiling young man with a goatee, dressed in the uniform of a royal soldier.

The woman laid her hand on the glass of the frame. "This was our son, Arnaud. He was murdered five days ago on Blue Campus."

My heart fell into my stomach. "I am so sorry."

And I was. As much as I'd imagined Baptiste's grieving family, I'd never thought about the poker's. Sure, their son had tried to kill me, but they didn't know that. It wouldn't have made the loss any easier for them.

The younger ones gave me a hug, but I couldn't look any of them in the eye. They wouldn't want anything to do with me if they knew I was responsible for their brother's death. What I wanted to do was tell them the whole story and ask their forgiveness—but I knew that was a bad idea. How can you ask someone's forgiveness for killing their son? They'd call Whisnant for sure and that would be the end of my exodus to the mainland.

There had to be something I could do, though. Something I could give them.

Money? That felt so impersonal and tacky. A thought occurred to me. "Madame LeFebvre, how do your kids feel about Ecol Vert?"

"I home school them," she said. "Several were being bullied and all of them were falling behind in their studies."

"I'm friends with the teacher at L'académie Mélangé," I said. "I happen to know she's very good. All of your children would be in the same class, so they could help each other and prevent any bullying. Although I don't think the Académie will be having any problems with that in the near future."

Monsieur LeFebvre sat down next to his wife. "Don't you have to be Mélangé to attend the Académie?"

I raised my fire. "If it's okay with you and their mother, I'd like to react with them."

The parents looked at each other, then the orange-mustached man—who looked so much like his dead son—shook his head. "I'm sorry, we don't really know you. It wouldn't be appropriate."

The woman hesitated, then nodded.

Véronique stepped in from the hall. "You ready to go?"

I needed to leave. I had my Blue back. I'd even tried to make amends and they'd rejected my offer. But I knew that at this point my shade didn't matter much. My future had been set when I hit Arnaud with that shovel. Whether I was Blue, Mélangé, or rainbow-colored, I was still wanted for murder and if I wasn't executed, I'd likely spend the rest of my life in hiding.

But if I did manage to get out of the city tonight, I knew the guilt of what I had done to this family would follow me forever. I had to try to make this right.

"It would actually be a great personal favor to me," I said.

"With only a few more students, the class size would be large enough to get 'Selle LaCroix some help and even expand the school. I really care about those kids. I know you care about yours. Please allow me to share my blue with them."

The woman looked at her husband. "I could go back to nursing."

Véronique and I took the elevator since we had bad memories of stairwells.

"Can bugs really cause an ear infection?" I asked as the doors closed.

Véronique stared at the buttons.

"L stands for Lobby," I said.

Véronique pushed the L. "A parasitic flesh fly laid its eggs in Philippe's ear. That's what otomyiasis is."

I shuddered. Could Baptiste's subconscious remember that far back? Was that why he was so frightened of flying bugs?

"I think Philippe needs to find another line of work."

"Tell me about it. When he comes back from trash digging, he smells almost as bad as you."

Ouch. "By the way, I really am sorry about getting you kicked out of your home. I didn't realize the shelter was so..."

"Toilet pouchy?"

"I was going to say governing."

"I wasn't a huge fan of the pipe anyway," she said with a

shrug. "Why did you react with those Greens?"

The doors opened and we stepped into the empty lobby. The windows were mostly dark. Half-light—soon it would be dark.

"My shade used to be my identity," I said. "But I think I'm over it."

"Over it?"

I leaned against the wall. "I realized my fire is a tool—not a status symbol."

Véronique pulled herself up to sit on a low window ledge. "That doesn't explain why you reacted with four random kids."

I knew we shouldn't be loitering. My parents were probably already starting to worry, and I still had to drop Véronique off at the bridge. But I couldn't bring myself to leave the building. The dingy, cigarette-strewn lobby felt safe.

"I'm the one who killed their brother."

"That makes more sense," she said. "But Jeannette said you were defending some kid."

"Baptiste." I briefly recounted Aro's sports bet and how it resulted in the destruction of my dreams followed by my downward spiral into delinquency.

"So, it hasn't been the best week for you."

"It hasn't been all bad." And I realized it was true. Although I still wasn't sure how this all would end, the last few days had stretched, terrified, and forced me to find out who I really was. Despite everything, I felt happier than I ever remembered feeling. What did that mean? Why did the thought of saying goodbye to Véronique fill me with dread? Why could I still feel her fire against my dark palm?

I realized she was watching me.

"What are you thinking about?" she asked.

"You, mostly."

Her face registered surprise and embarrassment, but before she turned to look out the window, I thought I saw the corners of her mouth turn up.

Something happened inside me right then. A sort of realization mixed with a warm tingling in my belly. Whether this was love, hormones, or a childish infatuation, it filled my entire being with light.

Would I find that with Orie at some point? Would she ever make me feel like I'd finally woken from a sixteen-year sleep?

It was getting to where it was physically painful for me to look away from her.

Maybe I was more Fig than Télesphorian. Granny said the Ulfish fall desperately in love, then sacrifice everything to make it work. Even if it wasn't actual love, I knew that I had to help Véronique and her family. I wanted her to be safe. And I wanted to be the one keeping her that way.

"I'm going to ask you something, but don't want you to say anything until I finish, okay?"

Véronique raised her eyebrows as if to say, "Spit it out already."

I knew this was abrupt, but I was out of time. Classifications were in a few hours, and I wouldn't be back to the Taudis. If I didn't at least give her the opportunity to come with us, I knew I'd regret it forever.

"I'm leaving Télesphore tonight. I want you and your family to come with me."

Véronique stared at me.

I swallowed. "We're going to climb over the wall and catch a boat to the mainland. I'm sure he can help Philippe find work. It might not be the life of your dreams, but it has to be better than Taudis Rouge."

"Can I talk now?"

I nodded.

"I appreciate the offer, but what makes you think it will be any better somewhere else? At least we have friends here. I'm sure the mainlanders feel the same way about Reds. We'll probably be arrested as soon as we step off the boat."

"No, I won't let that happen. If I need to, I'll react with all of you so you'll have Blue in your fire. Whatever it takes."

"That doesn't make any sense."

"What?"

"Why would you do that? Why would a Blue stick his neck out for a bunch of Reds?"

Could I tell her? Véronique, I know we only met three days ago, but all I want is to make you happy.

Even in my head, it sounded crazy.

"Have you even thought this through?" Véronique said. "There is a reason they only have guards at the entrances. That fence is sixty feet tall." She hopped down from the window ledge and looked toward the double doors.

"Are you sure it's that high?" Whenever we'd driven through the checkpoint, it hadn't seemed that imposing.

"If it was easy to get over, someone would have done it by now."

I sat down on the floor. I'd always thought the fence had been to keep the native Red fishermen from overrunning the city, but it was obvious now the razor wire was to keep us in. "My dad is going to tie two ladders together."

Véronique sat down next to me and pulled up her socks. "I'm just saying that if we make even one mistake, if we overlook some detail, we'll most likely fall to our deaths or get caught and be executed in front of thousands of people"

I didn't have a response to that. My gaze fell to the cracked tile. Maybe she was right. Maybe I should accept Orie's offer.

I suddenly felt like I wanted to cry.

Véronique leaned over and peered up at me. She was smiling. "It would be an exciting way to go, though." She held my gaze for a moment, and I saw something in those dark eyes I hadn't seen before—a deep reservoir of compassion. This was the real Véronique. I'd finally found her. And she was definitely worth getting executed for.

My excitement abruptly returned. "I trust my dad. He'll get us off the island. Then you can go anywhere you want, your whole family."

Véronique shook her head. "If we came with you, it wouldn't be the whole family."

"You mean your dad?"

"My brother."

"Oh. Jeannette told me about La-la. I'm sorry."

Véronique looked sadder than I'd ever seen her. "Yeah. Me too."

Every moment I spent here with Véronique was putting my family in greater danger. They were probably all in the vehicle waiting for me—maybe even driving around trying to find me. Staying was selfish and irrational, but this was my last conversation with Véronique and I wasn't ready to end it.

"Is La-la a family name?"

"His name is Nicolas," Véronique said softly. "When I was little, I called him La-la. He liked it, so it stuck." She kicked a cigarette butt across the room. "I miss him."

"It's not your fault," I said. "It could have happened to anybody."

"You don't know anything about it." Her voice had turned cold.

"Jeannette told me—"

"We didn't tell Jeannette what really happened."

"Oh." I opened my mouth to change the subject, but she cut me off.

"A few Green boys asked me to go for a ride in their boat. I'd never been across the river, so of course when they asked me, I was excited. Only it turned out they wanted to do more than just show me the river."

A sudden rage sprang up inside me. No wonder Nicolas had jumped in to save her. "Who were they? What were their names?"

"You met them at the shelter, remember? The benevolent volunteers."

"But were you okay? I mean, did they..."

"I was fine. La-la overreacted." She gave me a sad smile.

"That seems to happen a lot in my family."

The impulse to help her nearly overwhelmed me. Nothing else mattered. I took her light hand. To my surprise, she didn't pull back. I brushed her fire with my fingertips and then without even asking permission, pressed my light blue palm into hers.

Véronique ripped her hand from mine. "Are you insane?!"

"It's okay. I want to. Even if you decide not to come with me, at least you'll get a better job."

"Forget it," Véronique said. "I'm not ruining your fire just so I don't have to work in the sewers."

"Ruin my fire?"

She sighed and almost grinned. "It's not as ugly as the rest of you."

Granny had said, "Don't fetter yourself to someone you don't love." By now I was sure I would never join the Talbot family. Whether Véronique learned to like me or not, I'd never be happy with Orie. At the same time, I now understood why she had taken Drea on in a wrestling match, threatened Claudette, and risked her own safety to help me. I understood because that's exactly what I would do for Véronique. Somewhere between the fifth floor and the lobby, my entire life had rearranged itself into a circle with Véronique at the center. And the strangest thing was that in three days, her Red fire had gone from repulsive to positively pulchritudinous.

I stood and extended my light hand, as if to help her up.

She narrowed her eyes, then accepted the help with her dark hand. "Nice try."

"I think I'd look good as a Violet," I said. "My fire is already age nine. Might as well make it an even ten." Wow. Was my fire age almost in the double digits? I'd never even heard of anyone over five.

She brushed off the back of her jeans. "Why do you want to react with me so badly?"

That was a good question. I was about to give her a good answer but noticed a police officer standing just outside the front entrance.

"I, uh…"

It was the old lady, Officer Juenes. I doubted she'd recognize me—the last time I'd seen her I'd had long brown hair and pale skin. Still, it would be better not to give her the chance. If she saw Véronique's fire, she'd probably call us over and ask her what her business was on the Green side.

"There's a police officer outside," I said.

"Took them long enough." Véronique said. "Madame LeFebvre called them after you hopped the railing."

"Why is she standing by the entrance?"

Véronique shrugged. "Waiting for backup? Just walk past her. It's not like we done anything wrong."

"Did anything," I automatically corrected. "Or we've done…"

"That's what I said."

"Can you actually hide your fire for a minute?"

Véronique's eyes grew cold. "Excuse me? Is that your answer?"

"I didn't mean… answer to what?"

"Why do you want to react with me?"

There had to be another exit somewhere. I scanned the lobby.

"Can we talk about this later?"

"It's fine. Don't worry about it."

I looked at Véronique. Her cheeks had colored. I couldn't tell if she was angry or embarrassed. Whatever the case, I couldn't afford to have her disappear into her shell again. She had just started opening up. I forced a grin. "Maybe red's my favorite color. Now if you could…" I pantomimed shoving her light into her pocket.

I thought she'd laugh or at least roll her eyes. Instead she took a shuddering breath. "Goodbye, Bruno." Then she strode to the front entrance and disappeared outside.

I expected Officer Juenes to stop her, but the old woman had crouched to lock her bike to the handrail and didn't seem to notice Véronique pass.

Of course, as soon as I stepped through the door, Officer Juenes straightened and made eye contact. "Any idea what's going on in there? We got a call from this address but didn't get a room number."

"Sorry, I don't know anything."

I scanned the dark street for a single red light, but Véronique had disappeared. She was smart enough to hide her fire until she got across the river.

I'd have to beat her there. I guess this was my chance to prove I was the better athlete. Then I could apologize for being an insensitive blackhead and convince her to reconsider my offer.

Before I could decide which route to the bridge would be fastest, a scream split the air.

Véronique.

I looked in the direction of the sound. A hundred yards away, set against the dark backdrop of Green Park, a flailing red light appeared, surrounded by three green.

Was it Gabe's posse? I could probably take two at once but not three.

Véronique screamed again.

Without stopping to think of the consequences, I reached for Officer Juenes's tranq gun.

It wouldn't come loose.

Officer Juenes grabbed my arm. "What in the white rainbow do you think you're doing?"

I checked the holster. No straps. Why wouldn't it come out? I pulled harder but only managed to lift the woman off her feet.

Something cold and hard hit my wrist. I thought she was trying to fight me off. Then I heard the clicking sound.

She had handcuffed me to the railing.

"Thought you'd steal a helpless old woman's dart gun, eh? Lousy hoodlum. That safety holster was worth every cuivre."

"I was going to return the gun. Don't you hear that girl

screaming? She needs help!"

Officer Juenes squinted into the darkness. "I'll go take a look. You stay put until my fellow officers get here."

"Please take these off. I can help you."

She ignored me and crouched to unlock her bike.

"There's no time for that. You have to help Véronique."

A few feet away, something fell onto the concrete with a tinny jingle. I peered up at the apartment building. Baptiste waved at me and pointed at the ground. He'd dropped the his dad's keys. The pocketknife was already open. I waved back at him, grateful for his awful aim.

While Officer Juenes unlocked her bike, I inched the keys closer with my foot. As soon as they were within grabbing distance, I stood, pulled Officer Juenes to me by her collar, and pressed the dull side of the knife against her throat.

"I saw how fast you put those cuffs on me, so I know you can take them off just as quickly."

She opened her mouth, but I pressed harder with the knife.

"I'm sorry to do this, but you once told me if something needed to be done, I should take matters into my own hands."

I felt her swallow against the knife.

"You have ten seconds to free me from this railing and put your gun in my hand."

It only took her six. But whether it was her nerves or the

fact that she was older than the Tjarden Petrified Forests, she unlocked the cuffs from the railing first. I didn't wait for her to unlock the cuff on my wrist. As soon as I had the gun, I pocketed my fire so they wouldn't see me coming and took off toward the green lights.

I didn't have to go far before I heard them. They were headed straight toward me.

"I told you I saw a Red come out of that building."

As my eyes adjusted to the dark, I saw a wide figure leading Véronique along by her hair. He looked too big to be a teenager.

"Isn't that a stroke of luck, Claude? The Law Enforcement Board was just saying how they needed one more execution for soldier graduation tonight."

Claude. The officers must have been headed to answer Madame LeFebvre's call and seen Véronique without an escort.

"Let go of my hair, flic."

The slapping sound that followed filled me with white-hot rage. I pointed the tranq gun and fired. There was a short burst of compressed air, then nothing.

"Now shut your face, girly, or we'll save the poker the trouble of popping you."

I'd missed. Although I hadn't ever fired a gun before, I was light-handed with everything else. Should I risk pulling out my fire? How many darts did these things hold?

I stepped back from the path and let them get closer. This time when I fired, there was a cry and the officer holding Véronique fell to the ground. I pointed at the next green light and fired.

Another cry of surprise. Two green lights thrashed about, slowed, then lay unmoving on the ground. The red light shot off toward the park and disappeared.

Good. With her fire hidden, Véronique should make it home. If the pokers were still guarding the bridge, she could take the wet route.

I searched for the third light, but the last one must have been smarter than the others and hidden his fire. I waited and listened.

Bushes rustled next to me, much closer than I'd expected. I didn't have time to raise the gun before something large crashed into my legs. I fell backward and the gun flew from my hand. While the policeman was off balance, I rolled and kicked my legs free. I managed to stand, but before I took a single step, he grabbed my shirt. I kicked into the darkness and connected with something soft. His grip on my shirt didn't loosen. I kicked again and pushed off him. The fabric ripped free. I sprinted toward the Ville Bleu.

I'd gotten away. And thanks to the complete darkness, the officer wouldn't be able to identify me.

That's when I felt a prick on my shoulder blade and my limbs turned to lead. Vertigo engulfed me and I fell forward onto my stomach. Just before the tranquilizer overtook me, I heard the officer speak. It was Dimples.

"Well, well. Aro Loup. Your army of river trash isn't here to save you this time."

CHAPTER TWENTY-SIX

THE PRICE OF FREEDOM

I awoke in a cell. My head throbbed and the light hurt my eyes. Covering my face didn't help. Officer Juenes's handcuffs still dangled from my light wrist. Apparently Dimples hadn't bothered to take them off.

I realized the light wasn't coming from the ceiling but from my turquoise palm. Why was it so bright? The only other fire I'd seen like it belonged to—

"Monsieur Loup, the home inspector," Claude said from the other side of the bars. "Thought a haircut would fool me, did ya?"

"Good morning, Officer." My jaw hurt when I spoke and I tasted blood. Funny, I didn't remember getting punched in the face. "I'll be informing my grandfather you like to beat unconscious children."

Claude smiled. "Your grandfather's on his way down here. In fact that's the only reason I'm still here. Been calling for the last half hour—he finally just answered."

I got shakily to my feet. The entire lower half of my shirt had been ripped away, revealing my sickly yellow stomach. Despite my ridiculous appearance and rubbery legs, I managed to cross the cell in three semi-confident strides.

"Let me go and I'll make sure you're promoted."

"Nice try. You shot two police officers and assaulted another. Not even Gramps can save you now." He knocked once on the bars as if to make sure they would hold, and then disappeared through a door.

At least he didn't have me hanging upside down in the closet. I turned to face my bed and almost cried out. A coffee Blue lay watching me from the top bunk.

"Aro Loup, huh?" he said with a grin.

"Monsieur Faringoule!"

He sat up. "Have you seen Marin lately?"

"I saw your son yesterday morning," I said. "Did you know they're planning a mass exodus to—"

The door opened. I spun, ready to fall into my Rolf voice and deny ever pretending to be Aro.

My muscles relaxed as Officer Sheri DuPont entered. When she'd chased me down to return my shirt, her stringy brown hair had partially hidden her pockmarked face. But today she had it pulled back in a tight bun. She walked straight to our cell.

"Foyle said he saw you at the community shelter across the river?"

I nodded. "Is he the one with the dimples?"

"Can you get back in there?" she asked as she unhooked the keys from her belt.

I showed her the tattoo on my dark palm. "This will get me in. Why?"

"I will let you out, but only if you go straight there and warn them."

"Yes, of course. Warn them of what?"

Sheri unlocked the cell door. Monsieur Faringoule dropped from the top bunk.

Claude entered just in time to see Sheri opened the cell.

"Dogface DuPont?" he said. "What the black is going on?"

Sheri unholstered her tranq gun and shot him.

Claude pulled the dart out of his cheek, grinned, then fell to his knees.

"You ugly trull," he said. "You're finished here." He toppled onto his side and lay still.

"You should have let me do that," I said.

"There's no time," Sheri said, blinking away tears. "I overheard Chief Collins talking with his son this morning. Gabriel is going to trap the Reds inside. He said a bunch of people would die, and the Chief said, 'Be careful not to be seen. And make sure it looks like an accident.'"

"You think he'll start a combustion?" I asked.

Sheri nodded. "I think so. He said something about cutting the power." She handed me a wad of bills. "Foyle took this from your pocket."

"Who is he supposed to warn?" Monsieur Faringoule asked. "The Reds? Won't the little crêpe-bag deny everything and do it tomorrow instead?"

"What time is it?" I asked.

"Just after seven."

How was that possible? My fire had already changed colors, yet I reacted with the LeFebvre kids less than two hours ago. Had the reaction completed faster because I'd done four at once? Or maybe my fire was getting used to all these reactions and growing more efficient at it.

"They don't open the doors until eight," I said. "Once lockdown is initiated, it's supposedly impossible to override."

"That can't be right," Monsieur Feringoule said. "That would be an enormous legal liability. Someone has to have the power to open the doors."

I walked to Claude's prone form. "I agree. Trouble is, I think Chief Collins might be the only one with the ability to override the lockdown." I detached Claude's keys from his belt and pocketed them. "Just in case one of these works to get in the administration office," I said in response to Sheri's look. I also slid Claude's tranq gun into the waistband of my jeans.

"There is one other person who should have full access to the system," Sheri said. "He's in charge of all the law enforcement facilities in the city. In fact he is Chief Collin's direct superior."

"Perfect," I said. "Where can I find this person?"

"He's Head Warden at Harlequin."

Well, that was a lot closer than the shelter. But how stupid would it be for the city's most notorious fugitive to walk right into the prison and ask to see the boss?

"So… this Head Warden guy—does he work very closely with the other law enforcement agencies? I mean, what's his job description?"

Monsieur Faringoule and Sheri shared a look.

"Do you think he's up to date on, say, recent fugitive— never mind." It didn't matter. Hundreds of Reds were going to die. Giving my life to stop it was not even heroic. It was common sense. "'Sieur Faringoule, you should go straight to the Cathedral. Ask for Mallory. She's hiding Marin in the underground vaults."

I felt a hand on my arm.

When I looked, Sheri's gaze was locked on my face. "That was you sleeping under the stairs in your suit, wasn't it?"

Blank. I looked toward the door as if I hadn't heard. How much longer did we have before Grandpa Loup showed up?

"And running around HV," she said, her eyes sad.

"You were pretty fast on that bike," I said. All the disguises had been necessary, but I still felt as if I'd betrayed her. "My real name is Bruno, by the way. And since I'll probably be dead tomorrow and you'll be out of a job, take some of my blue."

Monsieur Faringoule looked as though I'd asked her to be my wife.

Sheri shook her head.

I held out my light hand. "I insist. You sacrificed your career to help me and a bunch of Reds you've never met. At least let me make sure your next job is better than this one."

"You mean when I get out of prison?"

"I'll have a word with the head warden," I said. "I'm sure him and I will be bosom buddies before the night is over."

Sheri gave me a melancholy smile, shook her head, then

grabbed cell door. "If you aren't out of here in ten seconds, I'm going to put you back in your cage."

I ran down the dark street in a sort of surreal delirium. The sleeves of Monsieur Faringoule's suit coat hung well past my hands. He'd lent it to me to hide the handcuffs which Sheri had been unable to remove due to Juenes using a fifty-year-old pair of restraints that had a different key. In my dark hand I held Claude's stolen set of keys, and I was vaguely worried that the dart gun in my pants would go off and shoot me in the backside. I was hungry and thirsty, and I'd had to go to the bathroom since I'd woken up in jail. I had no idea if my new favorite person in the world had made it home safely, or if she was going to be burned to death in an hour. My parents were most likely driving around Ville Bleu by now, probably Hameau Vert as well, looking for their son whom they probably presumed dead. Would they delay setting up the ladders until it was too late? On top of that, my best friend, his future wife, and Orie were all counting on me to get those travel documents. At least I'd held on to the money this time.

I felt like I was living someone else's life. I was tired of being Benoit, Rolf, and Jacque or whoever the black else. The only happy thought was that for better or worse it would all be over tonight. Either I'd be free or I'd be caught and slated for execution.

Either way, at least I wouldn't have to pee.

"I thought Baptiste was coming," Claire said.

I was surprised that she and the other two students were still standing on the sidewalk in front of the prison. "He's not here?" Had his dad changed his mind again?

"Well, it's nearly a quarter past seven." Aro said. "Are we going to stand here all night?"

Claire and I pretended he hadn't spoken.

"You look like day-old fish," Claire said. "Everything okay?"

"Let's just say it's been an eventful afternoon."

Claire guided Antoinette toward the guard checkpoint. "That might explain your fire. I could see you coming from two blocks away."

Aro followed, apparently trying to keep as much space as possible between us. I wondered if his grandpa had given him an earful yet.

As we entered, I told the door guard to keep an eye out for a chubby blond Blue-Green and to let him in. Another guard escorted us inside the penitentiary. It felt a little counter-intuitive since I'd spent the last week avoiding law enforcement.

The three Blue prisoners were already cuffed to their tables and waiting for us when we came into the cafeteria area of the facility. A guard directed us each to pick a donor. Aro went straight to a Dark Blue woman with blond dreadlocks.

"Actually, I needed to speak with the head warden."

The guard chuckled.

"I'm serious."

Antoinette hesitated, then sat in front of a toothless man with half a nose. That left Baptiste with the tattooed Blue sporting the two-foot goatee. Hopefully he showed up soon.

"The head warden is a very busy man."

"It's important. Please let him know I need to speak with him as soon as possible."

The guard glanced at Claire, who shrugged, then unclipped a radio from his belt. "Flannery, will you see if the warden can come down to the visitor area? We have a Blue Mélangé with an important message."

"Copy that," the radio crackled.

"Meanwhile," the guard said, "shade-mix with your donor." He wandered to the other end of the room, sat down, and began filling out paperwork.

This didn't feel right. Even if the inmates were handcuffed to the table, there should have been someone supervising us more closely. These were criminals, after all.

I sat down, feeling vaguely hypocritical. "How's it going?"

The prisoner picked at his long, yellow fingernails. "Fabulous."

The man was seriously creepy, maybe it's a good thing Baptiste hadn't shown up. His dad probably would've taken a look at the man and bolted. But I guess I didn't mind getting stuck with him. In fact, after my week of infamy it was almost like we shared a sort of connection. MAA - Mecs Against Authority.

"Hey. My name's Rolf."

"Hi, Rolfie," he said in a fake high voice. "My name's Beau. Did you come over to play?"

Suddenly I was feeling much less fraternal.

He tore off a fingernail and flicked it at me. "What'd you do to your fire? Looks like you've been playing with plutonium."

I looked him in the eyes, determined to regain control of the conversation. "So, you're a big bad miscreant. You in for tax evasion or what?"

"Conned some Blues out of their life savings."

"You sell them imaginary real estate or something?"

"Better than that. The poor fools expected to wake up from surgery with a white fire and take the throne."

I put a hand to my head. "You're Dr. Piette."

"You hear that, Gums? I'm famous!"

The toothless man in front of Antoinette rolled his eyes.

I shuddered at the thought of Beau operating on people. "My dad said you put your patients out, then tampered with their eyes to make them less receptive to color."

Beau smiled at his own brilliance. "And because no one wanted to admit to requesting the procedure, I made and spent several fortunes before someone finally went public."

"Impressive. Well, thanks to me, you now have six months less than you did."

"Oh, thank you. And a special thanks for letting me live the rest of my life as a Green Mélangé."

I stared at him. "They're making you do this?"

Beau spit on the table. "You think I'd be sitting here talking to a prepubescent freak because I wanted to serve the community?"

I thought about showing him how prepubescent my fist was, but I knew he was just trying to get under my skin. Plus he was a lot bigger than me.

"Hurry it up, Rolf," Claire said.

Aro and Antoinette had already finished, and their donors were being uncuffed from the tables. The toothless man lifted his chin at Beau. "You're supposed to react with them, not antagonize them."

Beau laughed. "Are you kidding me? This kid's as cocky as La-la without any of the charm."

A chill ran through me. "Did you say La-la?"

"Nobody was talking to you."

"Is he Red?"

Beau narrowed his eyes. "You know him?"

"He's still alive?"

"As far as I know. Hey Gums? Did La-la get shanked yet?"

"You kidding me?" Gums said. "Someone shank him, they be a riot. He the only one cozy with the cons and the guards."

I was so distracted by the news that Véronique's brother was not dead that I didn't even correct the man's heinous syntax. La-la was in prison. No wonder Véronique didn't want to leave the country.

"Rolf, we've got to go," Claire said from behind me. "What's the problem?"

I stood up. "This is not the prisoner I want to react with."

CHAPTER TWENTY-SEVEN

A LITTLE EXERCISE

Being an only child, I'd gotten pretty good at manipulating my parents. As an adolescent, I discovered the technique worked on teachers, coaches, and the majority of females between twelve and fifty-five. All I had to do was adopt a wounded expression and explain how much it would mean to me to have something particular happen.

But for some reason, it wasn't working on Claire. No matter how I pleaded, she refused to back me up about picking another prisoner.

"This isn't a buffet," she said. "It's a penitentiary. Now react so we can leave. I thought you were in a hurry?"

Beau seemed to be enjoying the debate. "If it makes any difference, I haven't washed my hands once since I got here. I'd hate for the poor little tike to catch a disease."

The prison guard finally noticed something going on and sauntered over. "There a problem?"

"Yes," I said. "I was told as the winner of this scholarship, I'd be able to choose my color-donor."

"Those three were the deepest Blues we had," the guard said. "You won't find anybody better."

"I don't like this one's attitude. Frankly, I think he deserves the extra six months."

Claire rolled her eyes.

The guard scratched his head. "Did you want me to find another couple—"

"I want you to bring me Nicolas DeGrave. And I still need to speak with the warden." The clock on the wall said seven thirty-five. Whether I had spoken to the warden or not, in about ten minutes I'd need to leave in order to make it to the shelter before eight. If I'd been thinking, I would've asked Marin's dad to find and warn the warden while I went straight to the shelter.

The guard removed a clipboard from the wall and flipped through several pages. "No Nicolas."

"Try La-la."

He looked, and then shook his head.

"You sure? He's a Red. How many Reds can you have?"

The guard's face twisted into a suspicious glare. "We've got more Reds than all the other shades combined. I'm afraid you'll have to pick someone else, or just react with this pond scum." His expression made it clear he didn't buy my story about wanting to react with a Red. Who would, really?

Why did it have to be so crêpe-burning difficult to give my Blue away? I walked back over to the pond scum, who was now braiding his goatee. "Why can't he find him?" I asked.

"Suppose he isn't looking hard enough," Beau said. "But I'll tell ya how you can find him yourself."

Why would he do that? So he didn't have to be the one to react with me? I brought my head as close as I dared. "How?"

"Tell the guard you need to go to the fan. He'll take you into a long hallway with a red door at the end. The guards go in and out of there all the time. Just walk toward the fanroom, and then at the last second, slip in behind someone. Take a left and the last cell on your right is La-la's."

"Couldn't I just tell the guard where to find him?"

"I suppose you could, if you trusted him to take you there. Awful funny about him not being able to find the name, though."

Beau was probably right. I didn't have time to play games with the prison workers—and I wouldn't even be lying about needing to use the fan.

I returned to the guard. "On second thought, I will react with this prisoner. Only thing is, I've really got to pee first."

Claire looked like she wanted to grab me by the ear. The guard, however, strode to a nearby door, unlocked it, and pointed down the hallway. I thanked him and walked like I was close to wetting myself.

I saw the red door immediately. I had planned to empty my bladder, then come out and follow someone through, but a janitor was already headed toward the red door. There was no guarantee I'd have another chance like this.

I followed the man, but halfway to the door, he stopped and lit a cigarette. Black. He had seen me but didn't appear to notice I was out of place. All I could do was continue in that direction.

I straightened my posture and, once again, channeled Bruno the steamroller. I'd nearly reached the red door when it opened, and a pair of guards emerged. I kept my eyes directly ahead and strode past them. To my amazement they kept walking. I dashed the remaining ten feet and caught the door.

"What's that mec doing?"

"Hey, buddy, that's restricted."

But they were too late—I'd already slipped through the door into a cell-lined corridor. I turned left and sprinted to the end, praying I didn't run into more guards. The handcuffs fell out of my sleeve and jangled as I ran. I doubted I could have looked any more suspicious to the inmates watching me from behind the white painted bars. Something about them bothered me, but I couldn't put my finger on it.

I skidded to a stop in front of the last cell on the right. That's when I realized what had seemed strange about the other prisoners—they were all shades of Blue. Beau had said they kept the Reds in a different area.

The pond scum had led me to his own empty cell.

Leaving the secured area was not nearly as much fun as getting in. Even though I was standing perfectly still with my hands out, the guards still felt the need to tackle me. They ignored my renewed demands to see the warden and dragged me back to the cafeteria area. Claire's face was so red she could barely speak. Aro and Antoinette both stared at me as if I'd lost my mind. The only one smiling was Beau.

"I guess I should have mentioned they don't have a high tolerance for rule-breaking around here. Guess you won't be reacting with anybody today."

The guard readjusted his grip on my collar and dragged me toward the exit.

"I was going to react with Nicolas," I called to Beau.

"Liar. I'm La-la's only Blue friend. He told me so."

"I'm dating his sister, Véronique." Or at least I wanted to be. "I'm sure she'll be happy to find out you 'protected' La-la from reacting with me."

Beau's smile dissolved into uncertainty.

Outside, Claire told me I was a fool for throwing away an opportunity any Mélangé would have killed for. Then she told me how lucky I was the prison didn't press charges, and that they hadn't called the police, which really would've put me in an awkward position—and then finished up with a lecture about embarrassing myself and the school.

"At least I'm not extorting money from the government," I mumbled under my breath. "If you'll excuse me, I need to—"

"Don't get self-righteous with me, Monsieur," Claire said. "Aro passed his classes and the school got new equipment. It was a win-win."

I glanced around, but Aro had already taken off. Antoinette was slumped on a nearby bench, looking as if she'd rather be in bed.

Without warning, Claire shoved me into the bushes lining the prison front entrance. "Pocket it!" she hissed.

I pressed my light into the soil and rolled over top of it. It was the most awkward position I'd been in since exiting the secret tunnel, but when I saw the brown boots clomp up the stairs, the pain in my wrist and shoulder seemed to vanish.

"Are you Mademoiselle LaCroix?" a gruff voice asked.

Through the lower branches, I saw Antoinette watching me with wide eyes.

"Yes," she said. "What brings royal soldiers into Hameau Vert?"

"Looking for a blond boy, short hair—goes by the name of Aro Loup. We were told he's one of your students."

"Aro doesn't have blond hair," Antoinette said.

"What she means," Claire said, "is that it's bleached. Aro is one of my students, and you actually just missed him. If I was back at the school, I could give you his address."

"We have it, thank you," a female voice said. "I'm sorry, we aren't allowed to say why we're looking for him."

Claire sat on the bench next to Antoinette. "I've had Monsieur Loup in my class for several years now. Frankly, I'm surprised you haven't arrested him sooner." She spoke animatedly to Antoinette until the boots returned the way they'd come and crickets drown out the sound of their heavy footfalls.

Claire stood. "Did you find the coin?"

I painfully extracted myself from the bush. "Yes. Thank you for noticing it."

Antoinette didn't seem fooled in the least, but at least she didn't ask any questions. She yawned and looked at her pink novelty watch.

"Could I ask the time?" I said.

Antoinette looked startled but then whispered, "Seven forty-five."

Fifteen minutes to reach the shelter. Shouldn't be a problem.

Claire scouted ahead to make sure the pokers were out of sight, then motioned me forward. I'd just come around the side of the prison to get back on the main walkway when someone called my name. A slender young man with thick eyebrows stared at me from behind a fence. He was Red. "Beau said you know my sister?"

"Yes."

Claire zipped up her polka-dotted parka. "Rolf, you are the most distractible boy I know. What happened to your big hurry?"

"I'll only be a second."

I approached the fence. The man stood in a large recreational area with a track and a grass field. Two chain-link fences separated us with a path in between. No way our hands would reach. A few hundred yards down the fence, a guard patrolled the path with a miniature snow lizard. Wicked coils of razor wire topped everything. It hurt just looking at them.

I glanced behind me to make sure the pokers hadn't reappeared, then raised my fire. "Are you La-la?"

He nodded. His eyes were a little darker than Véronique's, but he had the same high cheekbones and slender nose. He looked to be in his early twenties.

"They said they didn't have a Nicolas DeGrave."

"Nicolas is my middle name. I'm listed under Nicéphore."

Nicéphore? No wonder he went by La-la.

"I thought you were dead," I mumbled, for lack of a better topic.

"Is that what Véronique told you?"

"No. I guess I just kind of assumed." We really didn't have time for chit chat. "Listen, your sister is in danger—and the rest of your family too."

"I just spoke to her on the phone," La-la said. "Didn't seem happy about moving to the shelter, but sounds like she's not letting anyone push her around."

"Gabe Collins is planning to burn down the shelter tonight," I said. "The chief knows and isn't going to stop him. The only person who might be able to override lockdown and evacuate everyone is the head prison warden."

"Does my family know?" La-la said. "You've got to warn them."

Claire grabbed my shoulder. "Rolf! You're only drawing attention to yourself. I thought you were trying to keep a low profile. Not to mention, you're going to get me fired."

"Claire, if the head warden doesn't stop Gabe, Jeannette and hundreds of Reds are going to die. So back off."

"The warden's name is Yanic Channon," La-la said. "If that helps. And he's usually here on Fridays."

"What do you mean Jeannette's going to die?" Claire asked.

I quickly explained the mission given to me by Officer DuPont, and Claire grew paler with each word.

"Why didn't you tell me?" Claire said. "I would've insisted we see the warden. But now we're back out here. What excuse could I possibly give after you—"

"Hey, get away from that fence!"

I took a step backward. "We could complain about how I was treated. Got lost looking for the bathroom and I got assaulted by two sadistic guards?"

Claire put a hand to her forehead as if considering whether she wanted to get involved at all.

"Lady, get back to the street!" the guard shouted. His leashed lizard jumped onto the fence and began climbing sideways toward us while its master jogged to keep up.

"My name's not Lady," Claire said. "It's Mademoiselle LaCroix. I'm the Assistant Director of L'académie Mélangé, and I'm afraid we have a problem."

Assistant Director? That was a nice touch.

"Well, 'Selle LaWhatever," shouted the guard while the lizard tugged at its leash, trying to get over the fence, "there's gonna be a bigger problem if you don't get your children away from that fence."

"Tell them to bring Nicéphore, too," I said. "Say he's an important witness."

Claire pointed at La-la and screamed, "I demand to speak to Warden Channon immediately! This prisoner shouted vile things to me as I passed."

Or that.

CHAPTER TWENTY-EIGHT

RAIN OF FIRE

L a-la entered, a welt on his cheek that seemed to change color as I watched.

"He's here now," said the warden. "So out with it." The man's dark coffee skin had a lustrous sheen to it, as if he'd just swam a vat of vegetable oil.

Claire glanced at me.

"I apologize, Warden," I said, dropping the Ulfish accent. "We had to see you immediately, and this was the fastest way Mademoiselle LaCroix could think of."

Claire suddenly found her fingernails fascinating.

I continued before the warden could offer his thoughts on the matter. "I have an urgent message from Officer Sheri DuPont."

The warden's shoulders lowered slightly and he sat back in his chair. "A capable woman," he said. "Wanted her for a guard, but Louis snatched her up. What's the message?"

The clock said seven fifty-eight. No time for superfluous details.

"The Chief's son plans to burn down the shelter tonight with Reds in it."

The warden made a face. "Gabe Collins, the royal soldier? That's ridiculous."

I could tell from his expression that no amount of reasoning or explanation would convince him. I'd have to come at this from a different angle, one that was easier for him to believe.

I shook my head as if trying to wake up. "Sorry, I meant

the chief's son is the one who told DuPont about the scheme. It's one of the Feu Noir that's trying to burn it down—probably some Red getting back at another for insulting his light. All I know is that the shelter will be destroyed, and hundreds are going to die if we don't do something."

This time the warden picked up the phone. He dialed, waited, then furrowed his eyebrows. "Strange. It's not connecting."

"The shelter?" Son of a Violet. Had the phone lines been cut? I'd have to sprint. I was halfway to the door when the warden said, "No, the police station."

I spun. "Oh, their phone recently had an accident. Can you please call the shelter? Ask for Adisa." Anyone besides the Green officers and Gabe's hoodlum friends.

He ran his finger down a list of numbers taped to his desk, then dialed.

"Channtelle, have you opened the doors yet? Hold off for a few minutes... I understand, but... Don't talk to me like that... I received a tip that the Feu Noir is planning to start a combustion on the property... Yes, that's why I said to keep the residents outside until the systems can all be checked out... Thank you... Don't let any Green's in there. The last thing we need is the death of... So have Adisa gather some residents she trusts and tell her to be careful... Yes, the sprinklers and the pipes going into... Okay, okay... Please call when you —"

He glared at the handset then hung up. "Sorry," he said to no one in particular. "My ex-wife."

For the first time since I left the police station, my body relaxed. My legs took on the density of rubber, and I realized how cool my fire had grown. I barely made it to the chair before collapsing.

"Thank you, Monsieur Channon." Claire laid her green light on the warden's arm. The heavy-set man looked as surprised as I was at the intimate gesture. I couldn't tell if Claire was inordinately grateful, or if she was just sleep deprived.

"I… uh, should be thanking you."

Claire used the warden's phone to apologize to Antoinette's parents and assure them their daughter was not being held for ransom. La-la—who was handcuffed and bruised—crouched by my chair. "My sister told me about you."

My fire tingled. "She say how much she was in love with me?"

"She said you were a toilet pouch."

I smiled as if it were a joke, but inside my heart was suffocating.

"The sweetest toilet pouch she's ever met."

The pressure in my chest eased a little, but then I remembered La-la had spoken to her before I'd somehow drained her fluid.

"I'm sure she feels differently now," I said. "After you spoke with Véronique, I'm pretty sure I mortally offended her."

"That's not too hard with Neek. What did you do?"

"Asked her to come with me to the mainland."

"That's it?"

I shrugged. "And told her red was my favorite color."

La-la grimaced. "Smooth. That was the line the Green kid used to get her into his boat."

I closed my eyes. Her abrupt departure made more sense at least. "It's hard to read her. Sometimes she seems almost happy, then the next moment she treats me like a stray dog that peed on her sleeping bag."

"She doesn't trust easily. Some pretty blacked-up things have happened to her."

Shame burned my neck and cheeks. "I know. But the problem is she's too hard on herself. She acts as if she were responsible for your death—well, imprisonment."

La-la rolled his eyes. "That girl thrives off guilt. Remind her that it's my own crêpe-licking fault for punching the flic. And anyway, I'm over halfway through my sentence. In twenty-five weeks I'll get my janitorial job back and everything will be better."

It took me an embarrassingly long moment to do the math in my head. "They gave you a year just for punching a policeman?"

"Thirteen months. Didn't Véronique tell you what happened?"

"She just said you jumped into save her from the boys, but you couldn't swim."

"Well, first I ran across the bridge and pushed the emergency beacon. When the flic finally arrived, he tried to arrest me for being on the Green side without an escort. I told him what was going on and he just laughed and said maybe my sister would get a few cuivres for her time."

"I would've done more than punch him." My fists, I noticed, were already tightly clenched. "Which officer was it?"

La-la stood and sneered as if rekindling his hatred of the man. "Don't know. But he had a ruddy complexion, like he drank too much."

Since I didn't want to have to crane my neck to look at him, I stood as well. "Claude Terry. Still, thirteen months sounds like a lot for—"

"He also had to save me. Since I jumped in and obviously couldn't swim, they charged me with attempted suicide. They probably would've donated me to the poker graduation, but they already had enough executions lined up."

The phone rang. It was the warden's ex-wife again, giving her report. No evidence of intended arson had been found, and the sprinklers and water pipes were all in working order. With the Commissaire's permission, they had brought in several royal guards to patrol the perimeter. So far no sign of any suspicious characters. While the warden argued with Channtelle about whether to let the residents inside, I continued my quiet conversation with La-la.

"Trying to kill yourself isn't a punishable offense," I said, fairly certain of myself.

"It is if you repeatedly try to drown the person rescuing

you."

I smiled. "You must have been some kind of angry."

"We're a passionate family," La-la said without any sign of humor.

Two weeks ago, I would've been surprised by his story, but lately I'd come to realize how things were done in Télesphore. Most officials in the city were either incompetent or glaringly corrupt.

La-la sighed. "They make it illegal for us to use the Blue and Green pools and then wonder why none of us can swim."

The warden slammed the phone down. "Despite my advisory, she insists on reopening the shelter." He glanced up and seemed surprised to see La-la still there. "You can take the prisoner back to his building," the warden told the pair of guards flanking the door.

"Wait," I said. La-la had been a huge help and it didn't seem right that he should have to go back to his cell while the rest of us clapped each other on the back. "I choose him as my shade donor."

The warden chuckled, but Claire gave him a he's-not-kidding look. The warden's smile faltered. "I'd lose my job if I let a Blue Mélangé react with river trash."

I took a step toward the desk. "You're not going to lose your job. There's no way it's against the rules because no one would ever consider the possibility."

"You're not helping your case," the warden said. But then he sighed and, for the first time, spoke to La-la. "I am grateful for your help in keeping my daughter safe. Adisa is the only good thing to come from my marriage."

Wait, the warden was Adisa's father?

"If that's true then show it," I said. "Cross out Beau's name on the form and write Nicéphore DeGrave's. I'm sure Claire doesn't care. I guarantee my parents won't say anything about it."

The truth was they'd be horrified, but there was no question in my mind that this was the right thing to do. Not only because making La-la a Violet would help him feed his family, but if he had less than six months left on his sentence, there was a slight possibility the warden would let him out tonight. From what I could see, the form was also a legally binding contract that guaranteed a half year decrease in the donor's sentence. And if La-la was freed tonight, maybe Véronique would consider bringing her family with me to the mainland.

The warden put his hand on Claire's arm. It wasn't his light hand, but coming from Monsieur Business, it seemed like a marriage proposal. "You will witness that this was voluntary?"

She nodded and gave the warden a smile I hadn't seen since I'd given her my account number and PIN.

One of the guards left and returned with the scholarship form, which was amended with La-la's official name. As soon as La-la signed the paper, I clasped his light hand with mine. Because he was still handcuffed, my light hand was sandwiched between both of his.

Terror, excitement, and joy welled up inside me at the feel of his fire on mine. The fact that I was milliseconds away from mixing shade with a pure Red felt completely surreal. Not to mention stupid. But I couldn't bring myself to regret it. Whether Véronique came with me or not, I knew things would be a little easier for them from now on. And this reaction would ensure that I would never get caught up in my own importance again. I didn't want to forget what I'd learned this week—that shade was just another way for blackheads to treat others badly. For sixteen years, my identity had been founded on belonging to the beau monde—the beautiful world. Now I finally realized what that phrase actually meant. Every person, every shade, every life was pulchritudinous.

The muscles of my arm spasmed, for a moment my hand and wrist bones felt melted together as if they'd been carved from a single white stone. With a barely audible fizzing sound, our fires flared white. My joints seemed to return and I pulled back my shaking hand.

The guards' eyes were wide. Apparently they hadn't thought I'd go through with it. My fire had just turned ten, I realized. That had to be a national record or something. I didn't know whether to be proud or embarrassed.

The warden turned La-la toward the door. "We'd better get moving. I've got to get down to the stadium. My son is graduating from the Royal Military Academy tonight."

"Congratulations," Claire said a little too enthusiastically. "Wait… the stadium? Isn't that where they're having classifications?"

"They're combining it with the soldier graduation," the warden said. "First time ever—Sergent Whisnant's idea."

Claire touched the hair at the nape of her neck. "Well, that should be interesting."

"You're welcome to join me at the ceremony," the warden said. "You might have to sit next to Channtelle, but she's not all bad."

He certainly referenced his ex-wife a lot. It was safe to say he was single and looking.

"We'll see," Claire said.

I shook dark hands with the warden and thanked him for his help. He tried to move past me, but I wasn't finished.

"Monsieur DeGrave will get the standard sentence adjustment, right?"

The warden smiled. "Nice try."

I grabbed the paper from the desk. "This form you signed says because he participated, he gets twenty-four weeks knocked off whatever is left. Didn't you read the fine print?"

The warden tilted his head like he was about to tell me not to be silly but then glanced at Claire and seemed to reconsider. "I suppose that would be fair."

"Great. Since he has less than six months left in his sentence, you can let him go tonight."

The warden scowled. "Now, let's not get ahead of ourselves. There's paperwork involved. It'll probably take at least a couple days to organize a—"

"What's to organize? You open the door and let him go. Are you in charge here or not?"

"Rolf," Claire said. "Yannic has been more than accommodating, already."

No. It had to be now. Unless they released him tonight, he'd miss the boat and probably be stuck in the Taudis for good.

I used my wounded look. "You're right. You've done so much for us already. Thank you." I stepped toward the door and made an exaggerated sigh. "Sorry, Nicolas. I know you're anxious to see your family. Claire and I were hoping we could take you now, but the warden is a very busy man. We'll tell you all about your sister's classification."

The warden gave an uncomfortable laugh and glanced at Claire. "I'll... see if I can't expedite the process a little." He opened a filing cabinet and pulled out a scarlet folder.

While he thumbed through the papers, I picked up the phone. "May I?"

He nodded and continued to examine La-la's file.

I scanned the number list on the warden's desk, but he didn't have the cathedral phone listed. I'd have to stop by on my way back home and tell Marin and Drea the new plan. I dialed my home number.

"Mom?"

"Blackened bones, Bruno," she said. "You said you'd be home hours ago. Your father is driving all over the city looking for you."

"I'm sorry," I said, careful not to speak too loudly. "Have Dad set everything up. I have to do something, but then I'll meet you at... that place."

"You need to come home right now."

"I'll be at the vacation spot soon, I promise. And hopefully I'll have some people with me."

"What people?"

"Sorry, Mom, I have to go. Don't wait for me at home."

I hung up and realized La-la stood much closer to me than

strictly necessary.

"I'll talk to Neek for you," he said. Then he hugged me.

I squirmed. Random displays of affection were still new to me, especially when administered by other mecs. After a second, I pulled away. "I'm actually going to accompany you to the shelter. I want to make sure everyone is okay and... talk about future plans."

The warden slid the folder back into the cabinet. "It says you don't have any belongings, so if you'll sign here, I'll show you to the door myself."

"You are a sweet man," Claire said.

The warden dismissed the comment with a wave, but he seemed to be surpressing a grin. "We can take care of the paperwork tomorrow."

La-la signed the document. Then he kissed Claire on both cheeks, shook the warden's hand, and gave me another hug. Were all Reds this touchy or was it just Véronique's family? I almost would've preferred a slap on the backside. At least those were short.

The phone rang. It was a guard telling us Antoinette's parents were waiting outside and not patiently.

"Well, Claire, I'm going to escort La-la home so he doesn't get reported." I couldn't wait to see Véronique's face when I walked in with her brother. She'd be so happy. Hopefully happy enough to trust me with the lives of everyone she loved.

"I've never met anyone quite like you, Rolf," Claire said, then held out her dark hand to me.

I grabbed it and pumped it up and down. "Call me Bruno."

Such a strange custom. But it was starting to grow on me.

When we arrived at the shelter, I was ready to burst a lung. What had started out as a friendly jog turned into a friendly competition, which morphed quickly into an assertion of our manhood.

In the end La-la could barely walk from the exertion. I alternated between suppressing my gag reflex and trying not to wet my pants. I should have taken a couple of minutes to use the prison fan.

Although I did see a Green in a dark suit—one of Sébastien's guards?—walking around the building, no one seemed to be monitoring the entrances. Maybe that was why I didn't see any Reds waiting outside.

We found Philippe in the nearly empty cafeteria. He shot to his feet and started kissing all over La-la's head. So weird.

And yet... I couldn't help wondering what if would feel like to have Véronique greet me like that.

After I finally caught my breath and my lunch stopped trying to exit the wrong way, I looked around. "Where is everybody?"

"Done eating," Philippe said. "The Chief showed up and announced free food and bed—tonight only."

Free? Once again, that didn't sound like Chief Collins. Maybe he was embarrassed about the failed arson plot and was trying to distract everyone with the gesture.

La-la took a fry from Philippe's plate. "I think he means

our family… one of them in particular."

Philippe narrowed his eyes. "Mama is probably shower-ing. Véronique took Jeannette to the fan."

The fan. If I didn't use it soon, I really would wet myself. It felt like I was in labor with a urine baby.

"Stay here," I said. "When I come back, I want to talk to both of you about something important."

The brothers shared a look.

"Is this about the document forger?" Philippe asked.

Before I could answer, La-la said, "What do you want with AC?"

My fire flared with sudden excitement. "You know him? I need him to make documents for me, my family, and some other people."

"It's a she," La-la said. "And she does good work. Do you have money? The supplies alone cost a quart of serum."

"What? I'm not going to give her—"

"It's an expression," Philippe said with a grin.

"Oh. I have money. I need the travel papers in a few hours." Maybe Orie's plan would work after all. Scaling the wall and jumping onto a tree never sounded very realistic to me any-way.

La-la raised his eyebrows. "I'll look for her. She's around."

I took the wad of cash out of my pocket, thrust it at La-la, then ran—or rather waddled—to the fan.

The overpowering scent of lit matches hit me the moment I entered the fanroom. If it hadn't been for the fumes—and the deafening sound of the exhaust fans—I would've as-sumed I was on the wrong floor. The fanroom was so full of people, I could barely see the stalls. I nearly broke into sobs when I realized they were all in line to use the toilets. Al-though there were over thirty stalls in the large room, the waiting line snaked around the sinks and past the… urinals! Only a few were in use. The Reds standing in line didn't seem particularly impatient. Apparently the huge wave of toilet use after dinner was a regular occurrence.

I walked slowly toward the urinal while looking back at the line with a questioning expression: this is okay, right, none of you just have to pee?

No one shouted at me to get back in line, so I continued to the nearest urinal and made use of it.

Relief and exhaustion replaced my bladder anxiety. In fact, once I gave birth to my half-litre of pee, I began to have trouble keeping my eyes open.

Then several things happened in quick succession. The artificials blinked out, leaving only the deep red of the hundred or so fires. Several younger boys cried out in surprise. The sound of the enormous ventilation fans lowered in pitch and volume, then stopped. The room grew eerily silent.

I was suddenly wide awake.

"Check the door," someone said. One man pulled on the door, but it didn't open.

The majority of Reds seemed more irritated than worried. Maybe they thought someone had initiated lockdown earlier, and they'd have to spend the night on the bathroom floor.

But I knew this was more than just an early lockdown. The giant system of ventilation fans wasn't supposed to turn off—ever.

This had to be Gabe. I sniffed the air for smoke, but all I could smell were the sulfur dioxide fumes of human waste. My fire had grown warm. A few Reds gathered around the vents and spoke in anxious voices, but most of the men and boys continued to file into the stalls to relieve themselves.

It was okay. Channtelle and Adisa knew about the threat. They'd find a way to get the doors open. And if there was a combustion, the sprinkler system would take care of it. I looked up and saw several delicate looking metal structures, like inverted flowers sprouting from the ceiling. They would work without power. They had to. Dad had once told me that heat broke the glass filament, released the water pressure, and triggered the sprayers system wide. Everything would be fine.

It wasn't until I heard the first cough that I realized how wrong I was.

"Everyone stop using the toilets!" I shouted. "Without the fans, the Sulfur Dioxide will build up and..." Do what? It wouldn't kill anyone, would it? I'd always known ventilation fans were for safety reasons, but how bad could it actually be?

A few of the men laughed. Others glared as if they didn't appreciate being instructed in their bowel functions. Most ignored me completely and continued to enter the stalls as soon as one became available.

I moved to the door and tried the knob myself. What kind of stupid system locked all the doors when the power went out. This really was designed as a prison more than a rescue shelter.

After about ten minutes, the coughing grew more regular. One boy sat down on the floor and held his head. A young man sloshed water from the sink onto his nose, grimaced, and looked around as if to gauge how everyone else was feeling.

After twenty minutes my own throat started to hurt. My breathing was quicker than usual, and I felt like I'd just ran ten laps around the pitch. This was getting serious. Baptiste had been chattering on about sulfur dioxide—what had he said?

Something about it being toxic and unbreathable? Had he said it could be fatal? "Listen to me!" I shouted again. "Don't you feel it? The sulfur dioxide concentration is too high. It's making it hard to breathe."

The boy on the floor now had both hands pressed to his chest and was gasping.

"He's right," an older man said. He stepped in front of another Red who was about to enter a stall. "Until the fans come back on, we need stop using the toilets." A few other men chimed in, and those in the line reluctantly dispersed. The stalls emptied. "Hold your flatulence!" another man shouted. A few of the younger boys laughed, but that turned into coughing and soon, the panic began to set it.

A tall, shirtless Red with a hairy back picked up a garbage

can and repeatedly struck the door, then one of the frosted glass windows. This couldn't have been easy since the windows were covered with iron bars. But he positioned the edge of the can just right and was able to make contact with the window. Although the glass eventually splintered into a thousand pieces, there seemed to be some kind of thick plastic coating and wire mesh that kept the pieces together. Another man ripped a door off a stall and managed to shatter another window. But no matter how many times they hit the broken glass, the barriers remained intact—no fresh air was getting in.

"Calm down!" shouted the old man who'd spoken earlier. "The more you breathe the faster it will affect you. "Breath through your shirt."

Immediately all faces disappeared behind gray and tan fabric.

The coughing was non-stop now. My nose felt as if someone had tried to pierce it with an electric drill. My throat hadn't hurt this badly since I had strep. Several men had gathered around the boy on the floor who was now on his back, his little chest rising and falling like the beat of a bird's wing. He was dying.

Did Channtelle realize what was going on? Where were the royal guards that were supposed to be preventing this disaster? I moved back to the now dented door and pounded with my fists. "Channtelle? Adisa? We can't breathe in here!"

One man in his twenties lay down on the floor and began sobbing. Now all the sinks were being used to rinse noses and sooth throats.

Several people were crying now. One boy kept calling for his mom.

That's when I realized there would be hundreds of women and girls trapped in the other fanroom. Jeannette and Véronique!

My fire ached like it was trying to heat up but couldn't get enough oxygen. My head had begun to swim. For what seemed like several hours—but was probably only a few minutes—the fanroom echoed with coughs, shouts, and sobs.

This had to be the worst possible way to die. Mass suffocation.

I noticed one man on his knees, his hands clasped near his face. How had I not thought to pray?

Créateur, save us. Don't let these people die like this. Please.

Wash.

The thought was so random, I figured I must be losing my mind from lack of oxygen. I curled into a ball on the floor.

Créateur. Do you not care that we are dying?

The room grew quieter. Although the coughing continued, the shouting and sobbing fell silent. The room flashed white. I looked up, expecting to see that the artificials had turned on, but two men stood in the center of the room, their light palms raised and pressed together.

Had they just reacted?

They dropped their hands, hugged each other, then extended their fires to others, who came forward. Twice more, the room flashed. Soon, most everyone in the fanroom seemed to be either hugging or reacting. The coughing was getting worse, the old man had even spit blood onto the floor. But despite the expressions of pain and the shallow breathing, I saw peace in the eyes of many as they pressed their palms together and mixed their shades.

Rather than growing self-centered in their last moments, they had looked outward. Some of these people had to be complete strangers, but there didn't seem to be any discrimination.

A young boy with his collar up over his nose even approached me, his red fire raised to the level of my shoulder. A week ago, I would've panicked and run—in fact I had done just that when the Blue from the Ulfig Prep raised his fire to me.

But today, the gesture brought an overwhelming feeling of belonging and brotherhood.

I pressed my light hand to his, our fingers straight up. The searing pain in my throat seemed to lessen slightly as my muscles tensed and our fires flared. The boy's smile was radiant. And it wasn't because I'd just given him some of my Blue—we'd both be dead before our colors changed—but because two complete strangers had trusted each other, without words. An understanding passed between us that surpassed language and even shade. We saw each other as men. And realized we were the same.

I reacted with two more Reds before my coughing got so bad that I couldn't remain upright.

Thank you, Créateur. For letting me see. For letting me know them as you do.

Wash.

I coughed up blood.

Wash.

Fine. I'll wash. The sinks were all in use, but I didn't think I could pull myself up anyway. I crawled toward one of the stalls. The toilet bowl was clean, but I flushed it again just in case. Then cupped my hands, scooped up water and brought it to my face.

My face tingled. I washed again, and the tingling grew stronger. I splashed more water on my face and the tingling became a burn. I realized suddenly that it wasn't a pleasant burn. It hurt.

What was happening? It was almost as if the water had turned acidic.

Hadn't Baptiste mentioned something about an acid? It wasn't as strong as sulfuric acid—but it was made when sulfur dioxide combined with water.

The gas was water soluble. It dissolved in water.

The sprinklers!

I crawled out of the stall. "Does... anyone... have... a lighter?" I shouted between coughs.

Several people shook their heads. "Confiscated," one man said.

I needed heat. I might be able to break one sprinkler and make it spray, but the entire system wouldn't deploy unless only the filament burst because the chemical inside grew hot. Where could I get heat?

As if in answer, a sharp pain stabbed my fire and traveled up my arm.

My fire was suffocating—but it still felt warm in flashes. I had burned that boy's face and blistered Véronique's back. If I could only figure out how to do that again.

"Help me... up!" I shouted. "Lift... me to the sprinkler."

For a moment everyone stared at me, then four or five coughing men with swollen lips and noses, pulled me up by the arms, then got underneath my legs. I extended my light above my head.

Still too far.

But whether or not they realized how it would help, the men seemed to understand what I was trying to do. They called others, who joined them, pushing me higher, inch my inch. Finally I stopped moving upward. My fire was still nearly two feet from the sprinkler head, but I knew it was as close as they could get me.

I closed my eyes. My fire had grown cold. The limbs holding me up shook as violent coughing racked their bodies.

Help.

Although my fire and other appendages felt cold and clammy, I sensed a warmth gathering at my torso. My body was conserving my remaining energy, trying to keep my organs functioning.

I had to let go of that heat. I had to send it down my arm and into the world.

I willed the heat to move into my arm, but nothing happened.

The coughing below me grew more violent. I realized I could no longer breathe. Below me, someone collapsed. Then another. The remaining arms finally gave out and I fell to the floor.

Panic flooded my limbs, washing the cold away like a furnace. Searing heat ripped up my arm and exploded from between my fingers. I tried to cry out, but my throat was swollen shut. Cold, wet darkness wrapped itself around my face.

Before the icy black swallowed me completely, I felt the burning rain.

CHAPTER TWENTY-NINE

CLASSIFICATIONS

Someone slapped me awake.

Everything hurt. What was covering my face? I was suffocating again. I clawed at whatever was pressing against my nose and mouth, but a pair of strong hands held my wrists. I felt something cold and oily drip down my arm, and I realized my light hand was in a serum pouch.

"Relax, muscle head," Philippe said. "You're going to need to wear the oxygen mask for the next few hours. You're on the hospital floor with about two hundred others."

I stopped struggling and he released my wrists. The windows were still dark. How long had I been out?

"Is everyone okay?" I asked through the plastic mask. "Véronique?"

Philippe looked over his shoulder. "She and Jeannette are fine. Luckily they'd just left the fanroom when the power went out. Although the fumes from the fanroom had begun to circulate through the entire building. Good thinking with the sprinklers. It burned everyone, but the acid went down the drains. The water cleaned enough sulfur dioxide out of the air that people could breathe again."

"How did they get the doors open?" I croaked. My arms were bright red and felt like I'd spent too much time outdoors.

"One of the royal guards had to bite through several yards of duct tape to get the breaker box open. He got the power back on about ten minutes after the sprinklers went off. They're blaming a group of Reds for the attack."

"That's probably my fault. I blamed the Feu Noir because

the warden didn't believe the chief's son would do such a thing."

I expected Philippe to grab me by the throat, but he only nodded. He looked sad. Oh, no.

"How many..." The word "died" turned sideways on the way out and lodged in my throat.

"Just one," Philippe said. "A boy with asthma."

I covered my eyes with my dark hand and tried not to think about that boy's little chest heaving. "You know his name?"

"Guillaume Frazier."

I wiped at my eyes and tried to sit up, but Philippe pushed me back down. "I'm sorry about slapping you awake, but La-la will be back any minute with AC. She agreed to do the documents but wasn't excited about the short notice. You're going to need to give her a list of names, approximate ages, and general descriptions."

"What time is it?"

"Almost nine."

I'd only been out for about fifteen minutes. I coughed and it felt like my throat had been twisted into a knot and barbecued. "Why is my hand it a pouch?"

"Precaution," Philippe said. "Acid is not so great for thin membranes. A lot of the people trapped in there sprang leaks."

I twisted the old-fashioned cuff around my wrist. I'd have to steal the old woman's keys before we made our escape. There was no way I was going weeks on a boat with a rusty, incriminating bracelet.

"They're saying you shot flames from your hand," Philippe said.

I lifted the oxygen mask slightly so I could be understood. "Listen to me, Philippe. This is important."

"I'm listening."

"I want you and your family to come with me to the mainland."

Philippe shrugged. "Sounds good to me."

That was easy.

"How did you plan to get us there? You going to kill the rest of the royal soldiers?" He smirked.

How did he know about that? "No, we're going to—"

La-la appeared and pushed another chair next to my bed. Then Adisa sat down and pulled out a notepad.

"I'm assuming you want the basic L-12 travel permissions?" she said. "Those are only good for two months, but they're cheaper and less regulated."

Adisa Channon. AC.

"Aren't you friends with Véronique?" I asked loudly. "How could she not have known you were the—"

La-la clamped a hand over my mouth, and Adisa glanced around at the other beds. La-la slowly removed his hand then whispered, "The names of our members and their functions are shared only on a need-to-know basis. The Feu Noir has only survived this long because we know how to keep secrets."

What? La-La and Adisa were members of the most violent gang in the Taudis? "I had heard the leader of the Noir was a female," I said, "but I figured she was Red, too."

"She's actually Blue," Adisa said. "Obviously not me."

"That's ridiculous. A Blue Feu Noir?"

"Tell him," La-la said. "He already knows about the tunnels."

Adisa leaned in close. "High Priestess Mallory DeLaney is our leader. As was her grandmother before her."

Okay, so that kind of made sense. I looked at Philippe. "You in the... group too?"

La-la answered. "He's helped us out a few times, mostly opening the dog pens to create a distraction."

"They don't think I'm stealthy enough," Philippe said with a sneer. "And I didn't know Adisa did forgeries until ten minutes ago."

This was a lot to take in. Did I really want to bring a family full of criminals with me? "Have any of you... killed anyone?"

Adisa scowled. "We don't kill people. We dress in black and use the underground tunnels to steal food for starving families."

La-la grinned at me. "I heard Mallory forgot to warn you about our gatekeeper."

I bunched my eyebrows.

"My idea," he continued. "Too many Reds were trying to sleep in the culvert and discovering the tunnel entrance."

"Yes, congratulations," Adisa said. "You're the father of the rotting deer carcass legacy." She turned to me. "Now let's get these documents started before my boyfriend comes back and hears us."

"Your boyfriend?"

"He's the handsome guard who broke into the breaker box and saved your life."

A Yellow with a Green boyfriend?

"You didn't happen to pull anybody out of the river recently, did you?"

"I thought that might have been you," Adisa said with a wink. "Looks like my man saved your life twice."

I managed an awkward smile. "Does he like rugby? Maybe I can autograph a shirt for him."

When Philippe dropped me on the tile of the cathedral basement, I thought Mallory was coming to help me up. Instead she stepped over me and started kissing Philippe.

"Philly," I said in a monotone. "Allow me to introduce you to the High Priestess." Apparently to him, celibate meant single.

When they broke apart, Mallory gave me a hug. Clearly, she'd been spending a lot of time with Reds. "You're early," she said. "Drea and Orie just left for classifications."

"Where is Marin?" I said through the mask.

"Packing the car with his parents," she said. "What happened to you?"

"Acid rain," Philippe answered for me.

Mallory grimaced. "I guess that explains why he looks like a boiled lobster."

"At least his skin isn't yellow anymore," Philippe said. "Who's idea was the skin dye?"

Mallory gave an embarrassed chuckle. "Guess I should have went with the expensive stuff."

"Should have gone," I said. "Sorry, ignore me. I have a neurological disorder—makes me blurt out unsolicited grammatical advice."

"You poor thing," Mallory said as she roughly tightened my oxygen mask.

"I'll be back in an hour," Philippe said, planting a kiss on her forehead. "Need to help La-la get our stuff together."

"Stuff?" Mallory said. "Wait, your brother's out of prison?"

"Long story. Monsieur Nazaire has invited the whole family to cross the Ocheanum with him. The travel documents are being forged as we speak."

Mallory's face fell. "And what am I supposed to do?"

"Come with us," Philippe said.

"And leave our little band of rebels to dissolve? Your people need you, Philippe. Are you really going to abandon them so easily?"

Philippe cleared his throat. "We'll talk about it," he said. "At the very least I need to get my mother out of here. You can't deny that things are getting worse." He hopped into the hole and vanished. Mallory replaced the large flat stone, then pulled the back over it.

"So, you've convinced my boyfriend to take the selfish road, huh?"

Since when was surviving selfish? But her accusation still planted a seed of doubt in me. And guilt. As if I hadn't destroyed enough lives this week. Was I about to cripple the only organization that administered actual relief to the people?

She rubbed a hand over my short hair. "Just teasing you. I'm the selfish one, wanting to keep my Philippe within kissing distance."

I made a face to express my distaste for the topic.

"It's actually a good thing you showed up early," Mallory said. "Turns out the last ship leaves the island at eleven tonight. Which means we'll need to leave right after Drea and Orie get back from the stadium."

Eleven? There was no way anyone could scale the wall and hike down to the coast that quickly. Good thing the travel documents were on their way.

I used the cathedral phone to call home, but for once my parents had listened to me and weren't waiting there. I'd have to go find them at the wall and tell them the new plan.

I really hoped this worked out. What would the royal soldiers think when vehicles containing Reds, Blues, and Miscellaneous tried to pass through. Papers or not, they'd have to be suspicious.

"Does the Dominateur attend the Classification Ceremony?" I asked.

Mallory shook her head and adjusted the robe on the ironing board. "Not usually. But from what I've been hearing, even the Commissaire is planning to attend this one. Maybe they're making some sort of announcement."

"The warden at Harlequin said they're combining it with a poker graduation."

Mallory stopped ironing. "They can't. There will be children watching."

"Apparently they aren't admitting kids," I said. "But if it's a poker graduation, Whisnant will have to be there, right? And probably a bunch of pokers too."

Mallory nodded, then quickly picked up the smoking iron.

"If the Commissaire is there," I said, "he'll have his Guard. That means Sébastien. And I know the Chief of Police always comes to classifications to welcome the Greens sorted as Eyes."

Mallory met my gaze. "So, if there's an incident at the checkpoint..."

"It will be hard to contact them, let alone get them there in time to help. We could drive right through the gate if we needed to."

Mallory swore. "You'll need to leave as soon as possible. I should have thought of that. Now I'll have to go hunt Drea and Orie down and—"

"No," I said. "Everyone knows who you are. You're practically a celebrity. If you started interacting with the graduates, every Dom in the stadium would be watching to see what you are up to."

"I can wear a disguise," Mallory said.

"No offense, but you don't look anywhere near sixteen. Let me go. I can blend in with the graduates. I'll find Orie and Drea and tell them to sneak away. I'll need to find La-la's sister, too. She had already left for the stadium when we made our plans, so she doesn't even know her family is leaving with us."

"Well, you certainly don't look anything like Bruno Nazaire, the rugby star," Mallory said. "But I do have a few items that might make you even less recognizable. For starters, we should tuck those cuffs into the serum pouch."

"Fine," I said. "But as soon as anyone else gets here, please send them up to the eyefall campground. My parents will be the ones trying to climb over the wall."

I left out the front door of the cathedral wearing a pair of costume glasses and Marin's tuxedo which he'd brought earlier from home. Apparently they had debated whether it was safe for Marin to attend, but in the end his parents didn't want to take the chance.

The night was sticky and humid. I kept an eye out for dogs and pokers, but all I saw was the occasional Blue family half-jogging toward the stadium. Mallory had told me not to worry about speed. With my red skin and oxygen mask—connected to an oxygen tank on a small wire cart—I looked authentically sickly, which would lessen suspicion about the serum pouch. So I walked slowly. The serum pouch was a little cramped with the cuffs, but it was nice to have it covered. I had no idea what my shade would be once all those reactions completed. It had to be some nasty shade of brown. Mom had named me Bruno because of my hair, but maybe it was prophetic.

I made it to the stadium without being stopped. Cars lined Rue Principale, and an empty white bus sat at the edge of the parking lot. I had no trouble slipping into the stream of tardy Blues and Greens headed for the entrance. It struck me as funny that after going through so much to escape the stadium, I was now sneaking back in.

The music of a children's choir echoed through the entrance tunnel as I entered the stadium. At once the smell of grass and noise of aluminum bleachers filled me with a longing that almost brought me to my knees. My old life seemed so far away now. Only two weeks ago, rugby had defined me. Now I didn't know what I was. A freak? A criminal?

What if I'd just followed Drea to class instead of going to find Baptiste? I would be graduating with the Blues. I would be making my parents proud.

But then I would never have met Véronique. If I could just rescue her from the Taudis, maybe losing my old life would be worth it.

The Bluebirds—TC's world famous prepubescent vocalists—stood on a raised platform in the middle of the pitch. They finished their song and didn't wait for the applause to die down before they began the Hymn to Télesphore. As one, the spectators stood and extended their hands, light up.

Several rows of empty folding chairs faced the stage. Where were all the graduates?

"Is it usually this crowded?" I asked a Blue woman walking next to me.

She glanced at my serum pouch before shrugging.

"Where are the graduates supposed to go?" I asked.

The woman turned to her friend on the other side. "Another reason we should have a separate ceremony. Not all of us enjoyed being pawed by the riffraff."

Wow. No wonder nobody liked Blues. "I've got an incurable disease," I called after her, stretching my vowels like the older Reds did sometimes. "But I'd take that over whatever it is y'all got. You need help pulling that crystal spire outta your —"

A Blue man smacked the back of my head, nearly knocking me over. No explanation. Apparently I wasn't worth speaking to. So much for my tux lending me an air of sophistication. I realized Greens could rent one—as could a Red, if he saved long enough.

I asked directions from a Green man, and he was much more helpful.

"Are you a soldier or student?"

"I'm getting classified."

He nodded. "I think the crowd is so large because of the soldier graduation. Usually those are kept private."

I smiled in agreement, but just then spotted a pair of children wearing alloy gloves. I realized no one had bothered to man the doors. I spotted another little girl even younger than the first pair, and I began to feel nauseous. This wasn't right. Didn't these parents understand what was about to happen?

The man directed me to the eyerise entrance tunnel. I found the graduates standing in lines, organized by name and shade. Madame Blanc from the Education Board stood on a step-stool, shouting instructions.

I lowered my head and walked passed the Blues in their spotless formal wear, the Greens and Mélangé in their somewhat shabbier versions, all the way to where the Reds stood, adjusting their third-hand button-up shirts and trying to blend in.

I saw Véronique at once. She was practically swimming in a black dress that obviously belonged to her mother, yet somehow she still managed to command the focus of everyone in the area. Red boys waved to get her attention. Greens and Blues craned their necks trying to get a get another look at her.

I pushed into line next to her, earning a glare from the Red boy that had been trying to carry on a conversation.

"I'm a toilet pouch," I said.

I guess I'd been hoping for a smile or even a nod of agreement, but she just shook her head. "What are you doing here? I thought you were leaving?"

"Not without you," I said in a low voice.

She gestured to my head and mask. "Is this another disguise?"

"Sure," I said. "Listen, La-la's out of prison."

Véronique's gaze jerked toward the pitch. "What? He's not one of the executions!"

"No, he's safe. He and Philippe are gathering up your stuff.

But we need to leave right now."

Someone grabbed me by the arm and swung me around. Before I could even put my hands up to defend myself, the mask was ripped away and I was being kissed full on the mouth.

I pulled back and replaced the mask. It really had been harder to breath without it. "Hello, Orie. Nice to see you, too."

Orie gave me a weak smile and brushed imaginary lint off her sleeve. She wore a form-fitting sequin dress. I couldn't help but wonder if the turquoise was in my honor.

"See?" she said. "Drea's not the only one who can be spontaneous."

"Mallory said to come back to the cathedral immediately," I said, feeling Véronique's eyes on me. "If we leave now, most of the law enforcement will be—"

"Daddy won't agree to that," Orie said, then her voice grew softer. "You like my fainting act on your doorstep? Daddy says I'm probably the only person in Port that can turn their fire off for a few seconds. I don't even know how I..." She trailed off when she noticed Véronique. "Who's this?" She pointed as if Véronique were a portrait drawing.

How could I express what Véronique meant to me? She's the girl I want to spend the rest of my life with? That would probably get me slapped from both sides. "This is a friend."

I decided I didn't want to have a repeat of Madame Axelle's classroom. Better to let Orie think she had won, then spring the nullification form on her. I took Orie by the shoulders. "You need to get Drea and leave," I said. "The travel documents will be here, but if there is any trouble at the—"

Orie pressed her fire to my cheek. Véronique and the nearby Reds quickly looked away. "Bruno," she whispered, her eyes full of laughter. "It's over. You don't have to run anymore. We're not going anywhere."

"Um, Orie. Maybe you shouldn't be using my name—Whisnant is here somewhere."

"Balthis is not looking for you anymore," she said with a

disdainful glance at Véronique's dress. "I told you I'd take care of it and I did. I found your report in Claudette's car and took it directly to the Commissaire. Said I'd go to the paper with it if they didn't leave you alone."

"You did?" That was gutsy. "But what about Marin? And..." She wouldn't care about the DeGraves.

"Young lady!" called Madame Blanc. "Get back in line with the Blues. And you with the serum pouch, where do you belong?"

"Right here, Madame."

"Fine, but take off that ridiculous oxygen mask."

I was about to protest, but a pair of fighting Greens caught the woman's attention and she waddled off.

Orie gave me a funny look. "Aren't you sitting with the beau monde? Mallory told me you got your blue back somehow."

"I'm staying here," I said, barely resisting the urge to grab Véronique's hand. "I reacted with five Reds tonight. I'm sure your dad wouldn't want me as a son-in-law now."

Out of the corner of my eye, I saw Véronique's expression of surprise. Blank, this must look awful—especially since I'd been out-of-control flirting with her at Baptiste's.

"My dad can pop himself," Orie said. "I don't care if your fire is black. I just want to be with you."

I cleared my throat and tried not to look in Véronique's direction. "Why aren't they looking for me anymore?"

"Young lady! With your shade group. Don't make me come over there." Apparently the fight had been dealt with.

Orie ignored the woman. "I told the pokers exactly what I saw out the window. How that Blue-Green boy came through the fence—how he reacted with you—how he killed the poker and you got blamed for it. Of course, I changed your report to reflect that as well. I can't believe you were so honest. It was almost like you wanted to get executed."

Blue-Green boy? My heart fell into my stomach.

Baptiste.

I grabbed Orie by the shoulders. Well, one of her shoulders. The serum pouch leaked against the other. "Why did you do that?"

She pulled away from me and tried to brush the artificial serum from her dress. "This gown cost six thousand cuivres!"

"Orie, I know you lied to protect me, but I was the one who—"

"You should be grateful. They caught the kid. They're going to execute him tonight in front of everybody. You're free."

Suddenly the joint ceremony made sense. Over the past week, I'd made a joke out of Télesphorian law enforcement. At this point they didn't care about justice, or whom was actually to blame. They cared about recovering their credibility and reasserting their authority. Whisnant and the Dominateur were going to show the citizens what happened to people—even children—who defied them.

"Find me afterward, love," Orie said. She blew me a kiss, then went to join the Blues.

"Baptiste," Véronique whispered.

I swore softly.

A pair of huge iron doors opened, and Madame Blanc directed the students to take their places on the pitch. The children's choir burst into a triumphant graduation chorus.

"We're not going anywhere tonight," I said.

Véronique took my hand.

"I know."

CHAPTER THIRTY

EXECUTION

T hree tiers of spectators cheered as we marched out and took our seats. Half of Télesphore must have come out to watch the first-ever public soldier graduation. On the raised platform, important-looking Blue men milled about in robes, conversing in low tones and writing last minute notes in binders. Five pokers stood to the side of the platform in rigid formation. They were young—probably just classified the year before. The warden's son was the only coffee-skin. Which one of the soldiers was supposed to execute Baptiste?

Was I really going to let them kill me instead?

I racked my brain to come up with a scenario where everybody stayed alive, but I knew it was impossible. The Dominateur needed someone to take the fall. Someone was going to die tonight, and I would not let it be Baptiste. I couldn't fail him like I failed Ro.

The choir finished, and the stadium erupted in cheers once again.

I thought I would feel peace or at least resignation at knowing what I had to do, but I kept seeing the faces of my parents, of Granny. The scariest thing wasn't knowing that I deserved to die. It was not knowing whether I'd have the courage to stand up when the time came. Especially with Véronique holding my hand. Every few seconds, she'd look over at me with a pained expression, as if she knew what I planned to do but wanted to change my mind.

Please, Véronique. Please convince me that the safety of

three families is worth the death of one lonely boy.

Madame Blanc approached a carved ivory podium, and the crowd grew quiet.

"Bonsoir, to the beau monde, and welcome all, to Madeleine Livius Memorial Stadium. We acknowledge the presence of our beloved Dominateur Council and thank them for their years of faithful service."

There was a polite smattering of applause.

"You may have heard that in addition to classifying this year's graduates into their future fields, we will be honored to witness the final test of five brave soldiers."

This time the applause was genuine.

"That, however, is not the only surprise we have for you tonight. For the first time, come to give his personal congratulations to the graduates..." She thrust her fire toward the summerlight gate. A familiar glass sedan rolled through the entrance surrounded by a dozen Green men in suits and flanked by two of the enormous white badger hounds. "The Haut Commissaire of Télesphore."

The stadium buzzed with excited chatter. Smart move on Sébastien's part, bringing the mutts. Talk of the enormous beasts terrorizing families in Blue Garden was probably all over town. As I watched, the dogs dragged their feet behind the car and the guards had to pull them up by the leashes more than once. Sébastien had probably drugged the animals to make them seem docile and harmless. The car came to a stop a few yards from the platform. The badger hounds immediately settled onto the grass and fell asleep. The driver of the glass vehicle hopped out to open the back door.

As one, the audience stood. Véronique helped me to my feet. I made sure to keep hold of her hand. The white-haired leader of Télesphore stepped out of the car. He wore a blue velvet robe and, in his light hand, he held the Crystal Scepter.

It felt like a year ago that I'd spoken with the Commissaire in Blue Garden. I'd forgotten how impressive he was. He waved a dark hand at the graduates, then raised his staff in greeting to the spectators.

The audience didn't seem to know whether to clap or not. A few did. Some whistled. Most stood in silence until the Commissaire took his place next to the Dominateur. Madame Blanc introduced Dom Marcoux, Head of the Board of Education and President of the Classification Committee.

"Greetings, Télesphorians." Marcoux was a dark-haired, coffee and creme with a bushy salt and pepper mustache. "For over a thousand years, the smallest nation on Port has also been its richest."

Cheers. Marcoux was a man who knew his people. The Blues at least.

"The name of our humble island has become synonymous with tradition, prestige, and beauty. Our cultural significance is not due to our genetic superiority but to our ability to face the future as one."

Véronique shot me a look. I knew what she was thinking. Separating shades into mandatory subdivisions was a funny way to show unity.

"Each of us has a part to play," Marcoux continued. "Like a child experiencing the world for the first time, we have learned to organize our efforts, appreciate, and utilize the strengths of our limbs, our senses, and especially our minds."

Was he going somewhere with this? When were they going to bring out the condemned? I debated standing up and getting it over with but didn't trust them to let Baptiste go. I had to make this as public as possible. The audience had to see Baptiste, know what he was accused of. Then when I claimed responsibility, they would demand that he be released.

"We have grown into the most powerful nation on Port, and today, we will all be witness to the classification process which has earned us our place in history."

More cheers. This time the people began stomping their feet as if were a rugby match. Blank, I missed that.

"Just as there are different forms of energy with different purposes, each part of the human body has its specific function which contributes to the health of the whole."

I noticed Sergent Whisnant sitting on the stand behind the row of Doms. Next to him sat Chief Collins who looked ready to fall asleep.

"Before we look to the future, we pay homage to those in our past. Ladies and gentlemen, please, can I have all the Minds stand where you are."

Several hundred people in the audience stood. As a surgeon, Dad was a Mind. That's probably what I would've been classified as. As the Elder Minds continued to stand, Dom Marcoux called the names of the students the Classification Committee believed fit the ideals of intelligence, knowledge, and anatomical expertise.

Drea, Benoit, and several other of my classmates were called up to the stand and be inducted into the Order of the Mind. A few Greens were also invited to the stand. Those not trained as nurses would probably become teachers, librarians, or research assistants. No Reds were classified as Minds.

Once the final name had been called, the sound of rumbling thunder came over the loud speaker to illustrate how the Minds represented energy in the form of electricity. The stands erupted into applause. Then everyone sat, and we started the process all over again with the Eyes, which represented energy in the form of light. The Blue Eyes would become future political leaders and CEO's of major industries. The Green Eyes would become tomorrow's soldiers, or if they washed out of the royal academy, police officers. No Reds were called as Eyes. Once all the inductees stood on the platform, the lights dimmed, then grew bright again—a symbolic gesture meant to celebrate the bright future leaders.

Next came the Noses, who for some strange reason represented heat and served the community. The majority of these were Greens who'd go on to become waiters, cashiers, and secretaries. The sound of crackling flames accompanied the applause for the future customer service reps.

Orie was classified as an Ear which represented energy

as sound. I hadn't even known she was artistic. Either way she was probably giving up a glamorous life as a professional creator of beauty to pair herself with a Mélangé. The Blues would go on to become celebrity performers, professional athletes, and painters of portraits. The many Greens inducted as Ears might go into advertising, music education, landscape architecture, cosmetology, or the publishing industry. The Bluebirds, which had been seated behind the government officials, abruptly stood and belted out a triumphant aria to congratulate their fellow artists.

Finally, the Tongues were recognized. Since the Reds had all been classified into manual labor, and there were many more Reds than any other shade in attendance, the Red initiates simply stood where they were while the few Greens destined for plumbing, welding, and food preparation represented them on the stand. The sound of gusting wind played over the loud speakers as the Tongues took their seats. The half-hearted applause only lasted a few seconds this time. The audience was growing bored.

The only Mélangé graduate—a Lime Green boy I hadn't met—had become a Nose. No one had called Marin's name. He probably would've been an Eye like his attorney father. I wondered if the Faringoules had returned to the cathedral. Mallory was probably wondering why I hadn't returned with the girls. I tried not to think about where my parents were and how they would find out about my death.

"We'd like to thank all the students for their dedicated work," Dom Marcoux said. "We remind you to work hard in your field. Each job is important in its own way."

"They missed touch," Véronique said.

"What?" I said through the mask.

"The categories are based on the six senses aren't they? Thought, sight, taste, smell, and hearing. But what about Touch?"

"Let me go ask." I leaned forward as if I was about to stand, and she pulled me back down by the elbow. The feel of her fire on my arm beat at my fragile resolve to do the right thing. If I abandoned her now, what would become of her family? Would she end up washing her neighbor's laundry at the river like her mother?

"Stay," Véronique whispered.

Don't tempt me. Black, why did I have to make this decision? There had to be some other way. Créateur, don't make me do this. Please.

After admonishing the future generations to strive for professional excellence, Marcoux turned the time over to our beloved leader who had also prepared some words of wisdom for the graduates.

The Commissaire approached the podium. I hadn't remembered him being so thin. But it wasn't frailty. The man actually seemed fit. Although his white hair hung down to his belt, he still seemed to have many more years in him. Too bad. According to Dad, he was the worst thing that ever happened to our country.

"Greetings Télesphorians. Tonight I'd like to address the Mélangé in particular—both the male graduate, and also those older Mélangé in the audience. Many of you did not choose this fate. Others, however, may have thought inter-shade reaction would bring added benefits or status."

He paused and gave a sad smile.

"I can understand this. Who among us has not wanted to be better, more attractive, more talented? It's human nature to be dissatisfied with ourselves."

A Red kid in front of us pretended to gag.

"May I ask something of you brothers and sisters of Télesphore? May I ask you to be happy with yourselves? If each one of us accepted our place and made the most of it, can you imagine how peaceful and productive our lives would be? Embrace who you are. You were born the way you are for a reason, and purity is the only true success."

He raised his withered palm. His fire was a soft pale blue. "Look at my light. This has come from a lifetime of self-discipline and solitude. I am a zero."

Zero? I'd never heard of anyone lower than a two.

"My parents died shortly after my birth, and the parental bonding laws don't apply to non-relative caretakers. Even my wife and I were always careful never to join our light hands, in order to temper our fires as pure as you see now."

No wonder he got picked to be the Commissaire. If his fire had been any lighter, he would've fulfilled the King's Requirement. Is that what it took to become White? Keeping your hands to yourself until you're seventy? What a stupid way to pick a king.

"Thank you for your continued hard work and dedication in making Télesphore great. I now offer the podium to Dom Gravois, the Senior Dominateur in charge of Law Enforcement. May the Créateur smile on our island home."

The audience applauded but quickly fell silent. They knew what was coming.

An older man with a bad hairpiece approached the podium. He spoke of the extensive training the royal soldiers go through and how, despite their green palms, they are crucial to the safety of all Télesphorians. Just when it seemed like he was going to end his speech and sit down, he produced a portrait drawing in a frame. From the back row, I couldn't see it clearly, but I didn't need to. I knew it was the same portrait I'd seen on the wall of the Green family.

"This soldier's name was Arnaud Lefebvre. He was twenty-two years old when he was killed in the line of duty." Dom Gravois paused as if fighting his emotions. "Four days ago he was murdered on Blue Campus. Murdered!" He hit the podium with his fist and the mic gave a burst of feedback. "As a courtesy to the family, we kept this incident out of the papers."

Courtesy to the family. Right.

I glanced at Véronique. Her desperate expression reminded me of Orie's that day in class. Was she worried about Baptiste? Or did she suspect what I had to do? The realization that she might actually care what happened to me was wonderful and horrible. For the first time in my life, I caught a glimpse of what true happiness might be like. Could I really give that up?

I wanted to say no. I wanted to convince myself that nothing else mattered, but I couldn't get Baptiste's face out of my mind. I couldn't forget how he'd given me the little food in his fridge, disguised me in the clothes of his derelict mother, and then made it possible for me to save Véronique.

"Of course we still employed all our resources to find the murderer. Thanks to our dedicated law enforcement team and a brave young eyewitness, we have captured the Blue Campus Killer and you will witness his execution this very night!"

Brave young eyewitness?

About half the audience clapped. Some were obviously excited for the spectacle, but many others seemed surprised by the announcement. More than one person with children moved toward the exit. Gravois smiled and nodded as if he'd been personally responsible for the arrest. "I've asked our Blue heroine to say a few words. Ladies and gentlemen, I give you Orie Talbot."

This time the audience whistled and cheered enthusiastically. Dr. Émile Talbot was a prominent plastic surgeon, so most of the beau monde had hired him at some point.

"This is not good," I whispered to Véronique.

Orie walked slowly to the podium, her face the color of Jeannette's fire.

"I, uh, just wanted to say thank you to the royal soldiers and police officers that helped track down the Mélangé who did this. I'm sorry I didn't come forward earlier. I was scared."

Gravois whispered something to her.

Orie nodded. "The boy is young, but don't let him fool you. He's a sociopathic killer. Through the window of my classroom, I watched him paint my betrothed, Bruno, and then kill the soldier who came to his aid."

I appreciated her trying to protect me, but she needed to

sit down before she dug herself any deeper. I'd never be able to save Baptiste without exposing her.

Orie's voice grew louder as if she were getting into it. "I also wanted to thank the Dominateur for taking care of this so quickly. Parents will feel much safer when this threat is finally eliminated."

Most of the spectators applauded and many even cheered. They didn't have to dig very deep to find their blood-lust. Gravois knew exactly what he was doing by making Orie into another victim. He'd probably given her that scripted speech too.

Orie wiped a non-existent tear from her face, then stepped to the side. Definitely scripted.

Gravois stepped to the podium. "Thank you, Mademoiselle Talbot. You've earned the gratitude of the Lefebvre family and all of Télesphore City."

Orie gave a slight bow and returned to her seat. At least she had the decency not to seem pleased with herself.

"Will the five soldier graduates step forward? Tonight you complete your training by helping clean up our streets." Gravois raised his hand toward the eyerise entrance. "Bring out the condemned."

A cluster of green and red fires emerged from the darkened tunnel. When they entered the stadium, a few people began to boo, and the rest of the crowd took it up eagerly. They knew this would be easier to watch if everyone agreed what a villain that mentally-challenged thirteen-year-old was. The group walked down the pitch toward the platform. I made out four Reds and one Blue-Green Mélangé, each escorted by a poker.

Véronique put a hand on my arm. "Are you sure you want to do this?"

I couldn't answer. I couldn't even breathe. All I could do was stare at that Blue-Green fire and grin.

I knew that fire—and it didn't belong to Baptiste.

"Bruno?" Véronique whispered. "There has to be some

other way for you to..." She trailed off and squinted at the pitch. "Wait, who is that?"

"Aro Loup."

Véronique's head snapped back to me. Her smile was so radiant, I nearly kissed her right there.

Instead I took her hand. It wasn't too late. My happily-ever-after suddenly reappeared in glorious detail.

"Grandfather!"

Aro's voice jerked me from my reverie.

"You know it wasn't me!" he sobbed. "It was Bruno Nazaire! Don't do this!"

Gravois covered the mic. "Stop it, Aro. You've been an embarrassment to your family long enough."

My smile faded. His own grandpa wouldn't even fight for him? Did he truly believe his grandson had committed the crime or was he simply sacrificing Aro to save his own reputation?

Véronique grinned at me, but I couldn't return her gaze. I let go of her hand.

"What's wrong?"

I brought my mouth close to her ear. "I told his grandpa what Aro had been doing, but I thought it would get him grounded or something. I didn't expect them to actually arrest him."

"No, Orie did this. Not you."

"But he's innocent."

"Bruno, it's his fault the poker's dead."

"I know," I said. "And he was a blackheaded toilet pouch to Baptiste."

"And everyone else. He's a criminal that deserves to pay for his crimes."

"But he wasn't even there. He didn't kill that poker."

Véronique pressed her face to my cheek, so her hair fell onto my collarbone. "I'll come with you. We'll all come. But you have to let this go. You can't save everyone."

She pulled back and looked me in the eyes. "Save me."

Before I could nod, before I could tell her what she meant to me, a scream pierced the air behind us.

"He's a child!"

A Blue woman ran across the pitch. She wore a business suit with no shoes, her dark blond hair half up in curlers. Two pokers grabbed her by the arms before she could get near the podium, but still she struggled and screamed at the Commissaire.

"Lord Livius! I'll do anything."

Gravois adjusted his toupee and looked behind him.

The Commissaire stroked the scepter as if deep in thought. "The boy is young." For a moment, I thought he would save Aro, but then he raised his dark hand. "Put it to the vote of the Dominateur," he said. "I am but a placeholder until the rightful heir to the throne returns to reclaim his station."

Gravois scratched under his hairpiece and then cleared his throat into the mic.

"All, uh... in favor of pardoning this young man because of his minor status?"

Three Doms raised their fire, including Marcoux.

"All in favor of continuing with the execution."

At least ten fires rose.

Gravois glanced back at the Commissaire, who nodded. "The Dominateur has spoken," Gravois said.

Aro's mother wore no make-up, and on her shiny pink face, I could see the exact moment hope left her—the moment she realized she had lost her son. She collapsed into the pokers and howled like an animal.

The pain in that sound instantly brought back a string of endless nights, staring at Ro's empty bed and wanting to die. The memories sprang up out of some dark place I'd long forgotten. A pain and guilt so crippling, I had to pretend it was a dream—that I would wake up soon.

Gravois seemed completely unmoved. The man was either heartless or good at hiding his emotions. Madame Loup kicked and fought against the pokers, trying to tear through them to get to her son.

What had Granny said that night on the roof? "The only damage that matters to me or your parents is losing you." As they dragged Madame Loup away, I saw it in her face. She would rather die than watch Aro be executed. I'd seen that same haunted look in Madame Lefebvre's face when she told me of her son's murder.

The murder I had been responsible for.

I couldn't save my brother. I couldn't save the boy suffocating on the floor.

But I could save one woman's child. I could take away Madame Loup's grief as easily as standing up.

And just like that, I made my decision. I knew Granny wouldn't approve, but at the same time, I knew it was right. I removed the oxygen mask and took a few experimental breaths. I wouldn't be running a marathon anytime soon, but I didn't think I would pass out.

"Soldiers, turn your gloves to full power," Gravois said.

"I lied earlier," I said to Véronique. "I don't have a favorite color."

She narrowed her eyes, as if waiting for the punch line.

"Tell your family I'm sorry."

"Restraining soldiers, don your protective gloves."

Véronique picked up the oxygen mask and tried to put it back on me. "No. You're not doing this, Bruno. Don't be stupid."

I took her hand and held it instead.

"Soldiers, take your place in front of the condemned."

The five graduates faced their victims, while the double-gloved pokers held them still. One of the victims struggled, but the poker behind him—who I abruptly realized was Gabe —pulled the Red into a headlock. The other three Reds didn't put up a fight. Aro just cried.

I stood up.

Véronique made a grab for my wrist, but I pulled away.

"Arms extended," Gravois said. The restraining officers

grabbed the victims' dark wrists and thrust them forward with the palm upward. Gabe was grinning. Aro began screaming for his mother.

I made my way down the aisle. I stepped on several shoes and had to knock a few people out of the way. The graduates noticed and started moving on their own.

"Ready," Gravois said, clearly engrossed in the macabre play he was directing.

I made it to the center aisle and strode toward the podium. Crêpes, it was hard to breathe. A murmur passed through the crowd, growing louder with each step. A few of the Doms noticed me. Any second they would call the pokers.

I had to make it to the podium before that happened. I broke into a jog. Stabbing pain radiated down my throat and into my chest. My lungs had to be bleeding—or dissolving into ash. I stopped breathing. It was easier that way.

"Aim." Gravois was still oblivious.

The graduating pokers extended their gloved index fingers and pointed them down at the victims' dark palms.

One of the Reds began praying out loud. Aro had fallen silent and now stared straight ahead as if he were sleepwalking.

I sprinted the rest of the way, jumped onto the platform, and knocked Dom Gravois backward into the other old men.

"The boy is innocent," I said into the microphone. "I am Bruno Nazaire and I killed Arnaud Lefebvre."

It was as if a bomb had gone off. The stands roared to life and everyone on the platform shot to their feet.

"No!" Orie screamed from the front row.

Another cry echoed from somewhere in the stadium and I recognized it instantly.

Mom. What was she doing here? She stood on the pitch near the winterdark entrance. My father and Granny stood beside her. They must have called Mallory when I didn't meet them at the wall. The look of betrayal on Granny's face shook me to the core. What had I just done? My legs went soft and I grabbed the podium to keep from falling over.

Now Granny was screaming. Telling me to run.

She was right. Now that I had cleared Aro's name, why couldn't I jump off the podium and run for the exit? If only I could breathe.

Gloved hands latched onto me and pulled me from the microphone. The pokers surrounded me on all sides. Still the stadium roared in excitement and confusion. The only person that didn't seem to be shouting was a barefoot woman in a business suit with her hair half up in curlers. She stood at the far end of the pitch next to a man with a black goatee. Both of them smiled at me, their expressions a mixture of uncertainty and profound gratitude.

"SILENCE!"

The Commissaire stood at the podium with the Crystal Scepter raised.

To my amazement, the audience obeyed.

"Be seated. We will deal with this in an orderly manner."

The pokers pushed me into a chair.

The Commissaire looked down at the front row of Blue graduates. "Mademoiselle Talbot, is this Bruno Nazaire?"

Orie glanced at me and shook her head.

"Why don't you come up here a minute?" he said.

Orie's face had gone pale. She climbed onto the platform and took the mic. "This boy's name is Rolf Zimmerman."

"Give it up, Orie," I said. "It's over."

"He's a family friend, but he takes medication for multiple personality disorder."

"This is ridiculous. Anyone on the front row can tell you who I am." I elbowed a poker and dove out of my chair.

"Drea!" I said. "Tell these people Orie is lying."

Drea glanced at Orie, then said, "Rolf, you need to get down from there. This isn't funny."

Orie grabbed my arm before the pokers could restrain me again. "He just needs his medication."

The Mélangé graduate called out, "Just kill Aro!"

Several Doms seemed to agree with this notion.

Véronique stood up. "Orie is telling the truth! His name is Rolf Zimmerman. Just let him go home."

The pokers seemed unsure what to do. They looked back at the Commissaire.

This was my chance. I pulled away from Orie and grabbed the microphone. "My father is Andre Nazaire," I shouted and pointed toward where he was standing. "My mother is Christelle Molyneux Nazaire and I live at three sixteen Rue Chêne. Police Chief Collins, Le Capitaine Canard, and Le Sergent Whisnant can all identify me. The badger hounds know my scent. Not only did I kill Arnaud Lefebvre, but last night, I assaulted two police officers and escaped from my jail cell. The proof is still hanging from my wrist."

I pulled off the serum pouch and thrust the handcuffs into the air.

Only I couldn't see them. No one could.

The white fireball at the end of my arm was too bright.

The stadium itself seemed to take a mighty, shuddering breath. It was the sound of ten thousand people crying out in unison. Orie fell back and shielded her face. My eyes watered, but I couldn't tear away my gaze. I never knew such a brilliant white could exist—not even a hint of any other color. How was so much light coming from my little hand? It didn't make sense.

The stadium collapsed into chaos. I couldn't tell whether the people were yelling or crying or cheering. Most of the officials on the platform cowered as if expecting a bolt of lightning.

The only one not cowering was the Commissaire. His wide eyes were locked on my fire. His dark hand gripped the edge of the podium while his light held the Crystal Scepter. The transparent walking stick was four feet tall and topped with what appeared to be a diamond the size of a walnut. Apart from Véronique, it was the most pulchritudinous thing I'd ever seen. A soft, bluish glow emanated along the clear staff a few inches on either side of the Commissaire's grip.

The man spoke softly, yet somehow I heard him perfectly over the noise. "*L'oeil.*" The eye. Then his gaze traveled down my arm to my face, and he said, "*Au pays des aveugles.*" It was the start of a phrase I'd heard Grandpa Molyneux say countless times. In the land of the blind...

"*Le borgne est roi,*" I finished. The one-eyed man is king. I lowered my fire and turned to face the Commissaire. Fear flitted across the old man's face, and he seemed to age several decades. He took a step back and the Crystal Scepter slipped from his hand.

No!

As if watching myself from a great distance, my fiery hand shot out and caught the rod.

The effect was instantaneous. Blinding white light filled the scepter and shot out the diamond, sending a trillion colors in every direction. I, also, nearly dropped the staff. The countless pinpricks of light created a living, breathing tapestry of multicolored stars which illuminated my clothing and danced across the Commissaire's pale face.

A perfect silence filled the stadium.

Among the sea of graduates, a single girl in an oversized black dress stood on her chair and held aloft a crimson fire.

"Long live the king."

CHAPTER THIRTY-ONE

THE SECRET

T he next person to kneel was Madame Blanc followed by the dark-haired Dom with gray streaks in his mustache. "Long live the king," Marcoux repeated.

So... did this mean I they weren't going to kill me?

One of the young vocalists began to sing the Hymn to Télesphore, and the other Bluebirds joined in. Even without their mics turned on, their voices swelled and seemed to fill the stadium. A few feet away, still on the platform, Orie began to sing as well. She did have a nice voice—and it carried to the podium microphone. That seemed to be the cue for the stands to join in. Several hundred fires rose, then a thousand—then ten.

Now what? If the government was trying to kill me before, what would they think of me taking over? I held the scepter out to the Commissaire. Instead of taking it, he glanced at the crowd, bowed his head and slowly knelt before me. The rest of the Dominateur followed suit. In a few moments, everyone on the pitch had dropped to their knees and inclined their head, including Aro and the pokers.

It felt like a strange dream that my brain kept trying to wake up from—one of those really awkward dreams where you're in public but have forgotten to get dressed. I would've almost rather been naked, then at least I'd know why they were staring. But this? People kneeling? Spontaneously bursting into song? Did they no longer care that I'd killed a royal soldier? What in the rainbow was going to happen when they all stood back up?

The song ended. I waited for everyone to get off their knees, but they just stayed there as if they'd forgotten they used to be taller. I transferred the scepter to my dark hand—the dancing lights were giving me a headache—and stepped to the podium. As long as I had their attention, I might as well get a few things off my chest. Then, if they decided to execute me anyway, at least I'd die with a clear conscience.

"Hi. Um... I just wanted to apologize to the Lefebvre family. His death was an accident, but I know that doesn't make it any easier. I'm also sorry to Officer Juenes for... stealing her cuffs."

"Your Grace?" the Commissaire said.

It took a second for me to realize he wasn't being sarcastic. "What? I mean, yes?"

"We rise only when you command it. But in your own time, of course."

"Oh, sorry," I said into the mic. "You can stand up now."

Slowly the people around me got to their feet. The stadium seating rumbled, so apparently some of the spectators had been kneeling as well.

Did this really mean they wanted me to be their king—because of a stupid poem we all learned in middle school? I didn't know the first thing about ruling a country. Passing a political science final and running a city of twenty-thousand were slightly different.

Out of the corner of my eye, I saw movement. A poker had tackled one of the condemned Reds.

"Hey," I said. "Hold up."

"He attempted to escape, Your Majesty," Gabe said.

Little toilet pouch.

"I see."

The Commissaire gave a slight bow. "Your Grace, shall we proceed with the executions? Not the boy, of course."

I glanced back at Dom Gravois. "What did those men do?"

Gravois gesticulated as if the answer were obvious. "They're criminals."

"You will address His Royal Highness with the proper respect," the Commissaire said.

"Of course." Gravois bowed toward me. "Forgive me, Your Grace."

I cleared my throat. "Did they come across without an escort or what?"

Gravois bowed a second time. "If you please, Your Eminence, they're members of the Feu Noir."

I opened my mouth to tell them what the Red gang actually did, then realized no one would believe me. A week ago, I never would've believed it. Instead I nodded as if that were indeed a serious offense. "Were any of them guilty of violent acts?"

Gravois bowed again. This was getting tiresome. "They fought arrest, Your Grace."

Of course they did.

A murmur had gone up from the crowd. I couldn't tell if they were following our conversation or simply getting restless. I caught several dirty looks from the Doms, but they melted into benign smiles when I looked directly. I needed to resolve this situation quickly and decisively. These people expected me to act like a king. And they had come to see a spectacle. I'd have to give them something to tell their grandkids about.

I handed the Scepter to the Commissaire, then adjusted the mic. "Police Chief Collins, please join me at the podium."

The large man hesitantly approached and gave me a hopeful smile. Did he think he was about to get promoted? I lowered my fire under the podium so I could stop squinting.

"As you know, Chief Collins, tonight someone intentionally shut off the power to the exhaust fans in the Taudis Community Shelter."

The Chief didn't say anything, but I could tell from his wild eyes that knew where this was going.

I held up my dark hand and displayed the shiny raw skin of my arm. "I nearly suffocated in that fanroom. One little boy did. Hundreds of others would have been killed if one of the Royal Guards had not heroically restored the power." A few hundred people clapped. I thought I saw Sébastien smile slightly. Now even the Commissaire seemed interested in what I was saying.

"Chief Collins, would you like to tell everyone who it was that attempted to kill hundreds of men, women, and children?"

"I'm sorry, I don't know."

"You do know," I said. "And you knew hours before it happened. Because the boy came to you today at the police station and told you what he planned to do. And do you remember what you told him?"

"He never—"

"You said, 'Be careful not to be seen, Gabriel. And make sure it looks like an accident.'"

The stadium once again fell into commotion. At first I thought it was in reaction to my accusation, but then Sergent Whisnant pushed passed me and sprinted toward Gabe, who had taken off and was already halfway to the exit.

But despite Sergent Whisnant's size, he moved like a gazelle. He tackled Gabe, wrestled the poker's watch out from under him, then forced Gabe to touch his own face. The boy went limp. Whisnant stood and flung the brown uniformed boy over his shoulder. He returned to the podium and dropped him at his father's feet.

"Dominateur Gravois," he shouted loud enough for at least the first tier of spectators to hear. "I trust you will look into this accusation. And I don't expect to see either of these men return to their position."

Gravois seemed thoroughly terrified, but he nodded and directed the pokers to march the Chief—and carry Gabe—to a cell in the police station.

This left the four condemned Reds and Aro with only a single poker, a graduate who looked like he was preparing to wet his pants—if he hadn't already.

"Aro, you're free," I said into the microphone. "Try to stay out of trouble."

Aro bolted for his parents. They ran to meet him, and there was a melodramatic slow-motion reunion. Sentimental and maudlin. But it still managed to make the back of my eyes burn.

"In light of the atrocity committed against our summer-light neighbors, I absolve the four remaining condemned and humbly ask forgiveness for the death of Guillaume Frazier."

That got the Dominateur's attention. The dirty looks turned to expressions of outrage. "Now wait just a minute, you can't—"

"I said they are free to go." And before any of the octogenarians could make a scene, I turned back to face the audience.

"Télesphorians."

I had no idea what came after that. Once again I had the undivided attention of ten thousand people. How did Dad do it? When he addressed his fellow surgeons at medical conferences, he always made it seem so easy. Maybe it was a matter of confidence. Dr. Nazaire was one of the best surgeons on Port and he knew it.

I once had that kind of confidence—before I met Baptiste. Before I realized it was people that mattered, not rugby and high-paying professions. Now I had a different type of confidence. Although I had no idea how to run a country, I knew there were things that needed to change. That's where my assurance came from. From knowing I'd finally figured out what was right. And coincidentally, I now had a chance to do something about it.

"It's been a weird week," I said. "Thanks to those of you who helped me out. And to those that repeatedly tried to kill me, no hard feelings, I hope. I'm not entirely sure what I... sorry, not great at giving speeches."

I noticed Véronique grinning at me. She looked awfully pleased considering our great escape had been canceled.

"Um, one good thing did come out of all this unpleasantness. I found the girl of my dreams this week."

Orie stepped close and beamed up at me.

"Sit down," I whispered to Orie.

She ignored me and smiled out at the audience. I tried not to look in Véronique's direction.

"Neek, I'm sorry we won't be going on vacation tonight—but I promise we'll go soon. You're the most amazing person I've ever met."

Orie and several of the graduates on the front row looked confused.

I threw my hands up at the spectators. "If you're sure you want me to be King, I'll give it my best shot. Maybe I'll make a suggestion box or something, and everyone can put in their vote. I'm thinking another couple holidays and twice as many rugby matches."

To my great relief, laughter and applause broke out. Then a lone figure stepped onto the field and raised his Blue fire to me. I removed my hand from under the podium and returned the gesture to Marin. Another cry of astonishment went up from the crowd as if they'd forgotten just how bright it was.

Marin held his fire aloft and began to chant something. Then the front row of spectators near him took it up. It began to catch on. As more joined in, I heard what they were saying. More stood and joined the cry until the entire stadium rang with, "Long live the King." When the chanting reached a fever pitch, the spectators spilled from the stands and stormed the platform.

"Guards!" the Commissaire yelled. "Protect the king!"

Seemingly from nowhere, the suited bodyguards appeared. While most of them held back my enthusiastic fans, two rushed me to the glass sedan. Another brought the Commissaire and, within seconds, we were in the car with people banging on the windows. What had gotten into these people?

I pocketed my fire, still a bit self conscious about the handcuffs. Hopefully we'd be able to get Juenes' keys before I went to sleep tonight.

The Commissaire raised his eyebrows at me. "Seems the citizens are warming up to you, Your Grace."

It was really wild to be in a see-through vehicle. Although a glass car probably wasn't the safest ride on the market, the view was incredible. I realized that many of the Blues and Greens pressing their faces to the glass were teenage girls.

The Commissaire seemed to be waiting for a response.

"I'm just glad they decided not to execute me," I said with a sheepish grimace.

The Commissaire laughed. "Executing the king for treason? What next?"

Was that really it? The Dominateur were just going to drop the murder charges? Not that I was complaining. "I would like to visit the Lefebvre family at some point." Wasn't particularly looking forward to that, but I knew it was something I needed to do.

The bushy chauffeur started the engine. I was pretty sure it was the same gaunt old Blue that had driven the Commissaire to the Garden to confront the Figs. So far, the Commissaire hadn't given any indication that he recognized me from that encounter, and I certainly wasn't going to bring it up.

The guards herded the people away from the car. I recognized one as Malette. Just then he grinned at me. "The shirt's gonna be worth millions," he shouted over the enthusiastic screams of, "King Bruno, we love you," and "Can you sign my fire?"

It was only after Sébastien pulled his weapon and began shouting that the crowd reluctantly fell back. When they did, I saw Véronique some distance away, embracing La-la. I was tempted to jump out of the car and get one of those for myself—but there would be time for that later. I'd make the trip across the river very soon. Channtelle and I were going to have a little chat about how the shelter was run.

I looked out onto the painted lines of the pitch searching for my parents. I didn't find them, but I did see a chubby blond boy that made me think of Baptiste. "Thank you, little cherub," I said under my breath. "You saved my life. And maybe you saved Télesphore as well."

The first visit I made tomorrow would be to Baptiste's apartment to make sure Monsieur Wedel's parenting methods had drastically improved.

A familiar face at the glass, startling me.

"Dad!" I rolled down the window. "Get in."

"No son, we'll catch up with you later. Your grandmother wanted me to give you her love." His dark hand opened in an awkward way and he glanced down at it.

I almost didn't notice the writing at first. It said—

keep white secret

Did he mean I wasn't supposed to tell how I got my white fire? That was easy enough since I wasn't entirely sure myself. Did it have to do with the shades I reacted with? Or the frequency? Or maybe it was some sort of chemical reaction between the acid residue and the metal cuffs? Or maybe it was connected with my strange new ability to toss heat around.

The car picked up speed and Dad stepped back.

"Got it! Tell Granny thanks! I'll call you as soon as I get to... wherever it is we're going."

"Yes, call when you can." Then he disappeared into the crowd.

The car broke free of the people and pulled onto Rue Principale.

"Aren't the guards getting in? A few of them would fit. Well, not the dogs, obviously."

The Commissaire smiled. "The Royal Estate is only a few blocks from here. They prefer the exercise." And sure enough, as we pulled away, the suited guards set off jogging behind the car led by Le Capitaine.

The Commissaire pulled his long white hair into a ponytail. "So, my brilliant king, what's your secret?"

"Secret?" Had he seen Dad's message?

He gestured to my pocket.

I extracted my fire and squinted. "I'm not exactly sure what happened, 'sieur."

The Commissaire pulled a blue silk scarf from his robe and handed it to me. "Why don't you use this until we can get you a nice pair of gloves?"

I wrapped the scarf around my light hand.

"And there's no need to call me 'sieur. My first name is Gaspard."

I nodded, not sure I'd ever be comfortable using it. Why did he seem so happy about me taking his job? Was he genuinely excited that the Legendary White King had been discovered? Or was this all an act? Would his attitude shift when I started making changes and stepping on very old toes?

"It really is quite remarkable," the Commissaire said. "Could I ask your fire age?"

"Thirteen, I think." Only after I answered did I realize I might be telling him more than I meant to.

The Commissaire's eyes widened. "It must have been some magical combination. Who were these thirteen people you reacted with?"

I leaned against the door but drew back immediately. That glass was freezing.

"You didn't react with any Reds, did you?" The Commissaire asked.

He seemed perfectly genuine—like he really was just curious. I'd spent the last week picturing him as a horrible dictator that sent his dogs out to hunt people, but it seemed Aro's grandpa had been responsible for most of that. I'd need to re-evaluate Gravois' positing in the Dominateur as well.

But as far as I could tell, the Commissaire—or Gaspard—was a kind old man who seemed even more excited than I was about all this. Would it really hurt to tell him who I'd reacted with? Maybe he could help me understand how it happened.

Before I could respond, the car jolted and a horrible scraping sound startled me into silence.

"Avoid the potholes, Zacharie."

The chauffeur nodded. He had small, creepy eyes and a gray beard so voluminous, he resembled a tree in winter. I hadn't seen him at the ceremony. He must have been waiting in the car.

"So, how does this work?" I said. "Do my parents move into the Estate with me?"

"If you like."

"That would be nice."

"The decorators will need a few weeks to get things ready. You can move them in after your formal coronation."

Coronation. Holy blank, this was starting to feel real.

"You're not going anywhere, just yet, right?" I asked.

Gaspard winked. "I'll be here as long as you need me. As will Sébastien. He is the Captain of your Guard and the best I've had in years."

"Yes. He seems... competent." And slightly unhinged.

The car slowed to a stop in front of the Estate. It looked more like an enormous sculpture than a mansion. The stone-worked towers were masterfully shaped—and lit—like torches jutting up into the sky. The layered tiles that made up the many roofs seemed to flow like water in some places and rise like flames in others. The house that was eternally burning.

Gaspard fixed his ice blue eyes on me. "Welcome home, Your Majesty."

"Please, just call me Bruno. I mean, if we're going to be on a first name basis."

"Certainly, Bruno."

I grinned. It felt good to be me again.

"It's been kind of a long day," I said. "Would you be upset if I wanted to go straight to my bed and collapse?"

Gaspard assured me that being king meant I could make my own bedtime. He wished me good night, then sent me with a man—who I think was my butler—to find my bed.

It wasn't until I was alone in my lavish room that I registered that there had been something strange about the way Gaspard had wished me good night. He'd said it in Ulfish, which I figured was just him being cosmopolitan. But near the end with a smile, he'd said something I hadn't bothered to catch.

Mere moments before falling asleep, my mind sluggishly stumbled upon the answer. The last two words hadn't been Ulfish at all. Gaspard had called me by the name I'd given him the first day we met. Karl Brandt.

Apparently the former Haut Commissaire of Télesphore was much more clever than he pretended. And he knew I was a liar.

END OF BOOK ONE

The story continues in

The White Serpent (Colorblind #2)

Available now, on Amazon!

Made in the USA
San Bernardino, CA
26 March 2020